Praise

The
Daughters of
Ironbridge

'A Journey. Compelling. Addictive'
VAL WOOD

'The attention to period detail and beautiful writing
drew me right in'
LYNNE FRANCIS

'*The Daughters of Ironbridge* has that compulsive
page-turning quality, irresistible characters the reader
gets hugely invested in, and Walton has created a
brilliantly alive, vivid and breathing world'
LOUISA TREGER

'Feisty female characters, an atmospheric setting and a
spell-binding storyline make this a phenomenal read'
CATHY BRAMLEY

'Evocative, dramatic and hugely compelling . . .
The Daughters of Ironbridge has all the hallmarks
of a classic saga. I loved it'
MIRANDA DICKINSON

The Secrets of Ironbridge

MOLLIE WALTON

ZAFFRE

First published in Great Britain in 2020 by
ZAFFRE
80–81 Wimpole St, London W1G 9RE

Copyright © Mollie Walton, 2020

A CIP catalogue record for this book is
available from the British Library.

ISBN: 978–1–83877–068–6

Also available as an ebook

1 3 5 7 9 10 8 6 4 2

Typeset by IDSUK (Data Connection) Ltd
Printed and bound in Great Britain by Clays Ltd, Elcograf S.p.A.

Zaffre is an imprint of Bonnier Books UK
www.bonnierbooks.co.uk

To my dear friend Lynn Downing, who always listens and is in all ways lovely.

Prologue

Queenie wondered where she was buried. A pauper's grave, no doubt. But which sorrowful patch of ground? Queenie pictured her now, a pitiful pile of bones in a crowded pit. She imagined the girl's spirit rising from its haphazard burial place, delighted to be free of its chaotic tumble of earth and human remains. Where would it go? Perhaps it would revisit the scenes and sights of its childhood: some sort of poor man's hovel where it was born, maybe a patch of ground where it used to play with other urchins. But once it was done with those, inevitably, it would come to the King house, to Southover. After all, the spirit was only a young girl when she had come there as a maid-of-all-work. And what if the spirit of this servant – this Betsy Blaize – were to come to Queenie's house now? What would she see? Even as she wondered this Queenie questioned why she had conjured the memory of Blaize's spirit after all these years of thinking of it rarely. Out of sight, out of mind. It must be because the house was draped in worry, waiting as it was for the death of her son.

She shivered and glanced at the closed curtains in her bedroom. In her mind's eye, she saw the spirit rise from its scrappy piece of earth across the river, floating up, up into the night sky. Over the tops of trees and industry it would go, seeing the fires of the furnaces emblazon the darkness with their hellish colours. It would skim fleetly over factories and forges, lime kilns and waggonways, pumping engines and brickworks. It might circle the pitheads and the men labouring below them in the bowels of the earth. They would never see the spirit that passed over them, buried as they were like her body, or what was left of it. Onwards, to the river itself, the mighty Severn that scoured out the Gorge and rushed through it, relentless and temperamental. The spirit would travel its length to reach the iron bridge – it would have to visit the site of its creation, after all, the place where Betsy Blaize the girl had carried her newborn child, handed it to a passing Quaker and died. Across the iron bridge it would fly, up over the houses and shops and streets, all good folk sleeping peacefully in their beds, their mattresses soft or hard depending on their gentility. Up the hill to the great house that stood above the town, frowning down upon it. Southover, the house of the hated Kings.

Queenie envisaged the spirit approaching the house from the gravel drive, making no sound as it skimmed the stones, lifting up to the window of Mr Ralph King Junior, Queenie's son, master of the house and figurehead of the King businesses, struck down in his early sixties by sickness. If it glanced through the crack in the curtains, it would see the deathly pale face of Ralph sleeping fitfully in his bed, groaning in pain all the night through. But of course Ralph wouldn't be her final destination. It wasn't him who had wronged her. The spirit would float on, coming around the eastern corner of the house, slowing now, closer and closer, to arrive at its destination: Queenie's own window.

Queenie felt a chill down her spine again and the lamp on her desk guttered like a spent candle. She adjusted her favourite cashmere shawl closer about her shoulders. She had lost some weight in recent years and felt the cold more keenly. Her devoted lady's maid, Jenkins, kept trying to feed her up, complaining that Queenie would soon look like a skeleton if she didn't fatten up a bit. She stood up and walked to the window, then hesitated. A sudden, sharp fear came of what might appear behind it. She scolded herself for her silliness and yanked the curtain open. She saw only the night look back at her, blank and black. The vague shapes of trees moved mysteriously at the edge of the lawns. She did not look at the family graveyard, instead turning briskly and returning to her desk. Today, the doctor had advised Queenie to 'gather your family around you'. The others were here – her grandson Cyril and Ralph's wife Benjamina – neither caring much whether Ralph made it through the night or not. Indeed, Queenie suspected they positively hoped he wouldn't, so they could move on to the next stages of their lives. But there was family not present that ought to be.

Thus, she had sat down to pen this letter to the one person who was absent, who was over the sea, in a foreign city for nigh on twenty years now, her granddaughter Margaret. She pictured her now, her youth having left her, approaching middle age. Had the years been kind to her, Queenie wondered, or would she have aged badly? Margaret's relative poverty, as a teacher of English and pianoforte, would not afford her the King lifestyle, that was certain. Perhaps it would be a blessing to her to return home again, at last, after all these years. Perhaps she would welcome it, after all she had struggled through, as a widow and a lone mother to a daughter. Or perhaps she still considered her loss of riches a small price to pay to be free of the King family. Then, Queenie's thoughts coalesced around another, the girl, her great-granddaughter, Beatrice. Queenie had never met her. Would the girl favour her pale, yellow-haired mother or her dark, gypsy-eyed father? Queenie would soon find out if the answer to this letter were in the affirmative. She set to finish it, dipping her pen in the black ink and looping it out across the page in her neat hand.

As she wrote the words 'your father is close to death', she felt that chill again and hurriedly glanced back at the strip of window open to the dark night. There was a flicker of something there. Or was there? Just a spatter of rain. She stood once more and marched to the window, jerking the curtain over to shut out the night. But as she did it, she knew that it was never that simple to shut out memories – or guilt.

Queenie imagined the spirit she had conjured gliding down from her window and taking its customary place beside Queenie's long-dead husband's grave, standing beside it, looking up at the house. Watching and waiting in the coal-dark night, scored by the rain that fell across the King lawns and into the wild woodland beyond.

Chapter 1

The coach trundled on, the horses struggling up a steep incline, their hooves slipping. Beatrice grasped her mother's hand again and squeezed. Her mother was still snoozing and stirred at her touch, then fell back into her stupor. *Maman always looks tired these days*, thought Beatrice. It was good that they were returning to her mother's family, after all these years. Good that her mother would get some rest, be waited on in the big house and pampered a little. If they were welcomed, that was.

Beatrice glanced at the other passengers opposite them in the coach, two women and a man, all in various states of restless slumber, jogged by the coach's swaying rhythm. But she could not sleep. She had never travelled far from home in Montmartre and never met her English family, so this journey was filled with excitement and tinged with fear. The coach to the port, the ship across the Channel. The sea voyage made her so sick, she told her mother she was dying. But they got through it and then came the long ride north-west. Nights were spent in coaching inns, fending off the lascivious looks and comments of Englishmen. She was eighteen years of age and she was lovely to look upon, or so Maman told her daily.

'We shall need to buy you a whole new wardrobe, Bea,' Maman said, awake now. 'Shropshire society won't be able to cope with your Paris fashion.'

'But how will we afford that?' she asked.

All her life, lack of money had been their constant, tedious companion. She knew how little they had left. The journey had cost them a pretty penny. To hear her mother talk of splashing out on new clothes was shocking.

'All will be different,' her mother replied. 'You do not know your great-grandmother yet, but she'd never stand for a King to be presented in society as anything but the height of sophistication.'

The coach was on the flat now, the horses fleeter. Beatrice leant forward and looked out of the window. The dark, tree-rooved roads they'd come through for miles were thinning out into more open country. She saw the Shropshire countryside broaden into beauty: rolling hills, deeply wooded areas, patches of water, cottages and a church nestled in a valley. Having lived all her life in the dense, populated world of a city, the landscape here was intoxicating to her. She loved her life in Montmartre and its busy, noisy character. She had imagined the town of Ironbridge to be simply a smaller version of

7

what she was used to. But nothing had prepared for the splendour of the landscape here. The coachman called something to the horses and they slowed, then turned onto another road, the sign she'd spied at the junction: Broseley and Ironbridge. Not far now, she hoped.

They gathered pace along the Broseley road. Before long, the greenery faded into brown and a new sight took her interest, the signs of industry. There were brick buildings and a tall chimney, and behind it she could make out great mounds of grey earth. To one side was some kind of structure with a wheel and ropes, and to the other a stretch of grey ground, an open working of some sort, peopled by a blur of many workers and horses going to and fro. Some words painted in broad white lettering on the side of a building caught her eye: KING BRICK AND TILE WORKS. King was her mother's name – her maiden name, that was.

Beatrice grasped the window ledge and leant out further, so she could see the people, the first large group of locals she'd seen for miles. The coach was slowing down, as one of the female passengers, now awake and readying herself, was to alight here. Beatrice watched as the woman clambered out of the other door and was handed her bag from the roof. Beatrice looked through the window at the workers. She could see them clearly. They were digging great lumps of material from the open ground, placing it on handcarts or carrying it by hand. She saw now that some of the workers were children bowed down

8

by the weight of their load. Some of them were so small, her heart went out to them. Surely they were too young for such backbreaking work? Everyone was covered in grey dust, making them seem as if they were people of the clay, arisen from the ground. Beatrice stared at them, until one came from an open-sided building, turned and looked in her direction. She could see his eyes fix upon her. She stared back for a moment, then looked away, abashed. She felt ashamed, to be gawking at this young man working so hard, while she lounged in a coach. She withdrew her head and sat back down beside her mother.

'We are on the road to Broseley and Ironbridge,' Beatrice told her.

'Ah, then we are almost home,' said Maman.

'Look at this place,' she told her mother who leant forward and peered out of the window. 'It has your name on it.'

'It does indeed belong to the Kings. Queenie told me in a letter that the Kings now own this site, as well as having interests in iron and mining.'

Beatrice looked outside again to see the workers labour on, the smoke rising from the chimney, the young man who had looked upon her lost now in the dust and the muck. She struggled to imagine her family owning so much.

Her mother began talking to her of her family, reminding her of each member, telling her of the town of Ironbridge they were now approaching. France, Paris,

Montmartre, their little terraced house on the corner opposite the *boulangerie*, the smell of fresh baking accompanying their every waking morning – all seemed very far away.

As the coach drew closer to their destination, Beatrice called up the sights and sounds of her home: the comings and goings of Maman's pupils; the tinkling sounds of piano pieces and the drumming monotony of scales practice; the halting tones of children learning English, while Beatrice assisted her mother with preparing learning materials, marking work and domestic duties. Sometimes, Beatrice would give lessons to the younger ones herself. She spoke English with her mother at home and spoke French outside of home. She had been raised perfectly bilingual, her English spoken without a French accent, so her mother said, yet with a tinge of French phrasing from time to time. Her fellow Parisians would say she spoke French similarly, with a perfect accent, yet a hint of Englishness in her turn of phrase. Her mother told her every day how proud she was of her, what a good girl she was, how clever and kind. Eighteen years they had been together, every day Beatrice had spent on this earth; they were the best of friends, the greatest team Beatrice could imagine. Their world had been that little house, the streets nearby, the stray yet sociable cats she fed on their front porch, the musical and artistic friends that would bring food and laughter and gossip of an evening. They had a life confined by poverty yet expanded by ideas, conversation and reading; a shabby-genteel existence. A happy one.

But then there came news that Ralph King was ill. It was her grandfather, her mother's father, a man Beatrice had never met. Her mother did not speak of her past often, but as Beatrice had grown older she had asked more and more. She knew that she had been born out of love, a great romance with her father, the artist Jake Ashford. That her parents had run away together from Ironbridge to Paris. Tragically her father had died of a fever before she was even born, leaving her mother a young widow, struggling to bring Beatrice up alone.

She'd never met anyone in her family. The word 'family' only meant Mother, or as she called her, in the French way, Maman. Her whole family was Maman. But now they were going to the house where Maman had grown up, where her grandfather Ralph lived with her step-grandmother Benjamina and her Uncle Cyril, and where her great-grandmother, who they all called Queenie, ruled the roost.

The day was waning and Beatrice suddenly felt very weary, worn out by her worry of what this mysterious family would make of her and Maman. The coach was tipping forwards as they descended another hill and again she grasped her mother's hand.

'Look!' said Maman, and Beatrice saw through the window a broad, roiling mass of water surging forwards and beyond it, spanning the River Severn grandly from bank to bank, the great iron bridge, its backbone covered in jostling traffic and people.

'Ironbridge,' said Beatrice.

'Home,' said Maman.

∞

Curious how small it looked to Margaret, her family home, Southover. As a child it had seemed like a mansion of endless rooms, with the tallest ceilings and longest corridors. But now, having alighted from the coach and standing before it, it was still impressive – far grander than their little house in Montmartre – but somewhat smaller than she remembered. *Strange how memories play tricks on the mind*, she thought. She realised that the house loomed large in her thoughts mostly because of its power over her childhood. It was still much larger than the majority of houses around these parts, and to Beatrice, she thought, as she glanced at her beautiful daughter gazing up at it, it must seem like the Palace of Versailles compared to the simple narrow house she'd grown up in. She felt a pang of guilt that her daughter had never had the finery she'd had growing up, then recalled that finery was no use if you were imprisoned in it. And that is how she saw her childhood, one long stretch of incarceration before she opened the cage door and she flew. And now she was back, nearly twenty years older, wiser and yet exhausted. Despite missing her beloved Paris, the thought of good food, hot water and servants to tend one's every need seemed like heaven to her now. Strangely, she was glad to be here, though a little nervous of their reception. She had left under a storm cloud all those years ago, after all.

Margaret watched as the butler and other staff came out to greet the coach and handle the luggage. Brunt, her family butler of many years' standing, was gone, replaced by a younger man only a few years older than herself by the looks of it. But that was all she had time to notice before she saw that they all wore black armbands and then she felt a shiver up her spine as she realised her father, Ralph King, must already be dead.

Her grandmother had written to her weeks before, to inform her that her father was dying. Margaret had read the letter and sat staring at the walls of her little house for a long time, mulling over the news. To see her father and the rest of her family again, after all these years of self-imposed exile. To bring Beatrice and introduce her to the family Margaret had so longed to escape. It was fraught with worrying possibilities. She had never liked her father. He was a selfish, pompous man, who spent her childhood years dishing up disapproval and disappointment to his only daughter. She knew it was because her mother had died giving birth to her. The thought of seeing him again and having to submit to his rules in any way brought back the old fears of her youth. But she was no longer the young woman who'd run from the King house all those years ago. Though she'd hated her family – their coldness, their cruelty – they were still her family. To ignore a deathbed request . . .

And then there was Bea, who had never known any other family. Margaret was thirty-five years old now. Her health had declined in these recent years, with mysterious pains here and there, as well as piercing headaches and dizzy spells from time to time. Independence was fine when she was well, terrifying when she was not. Her ill health had lost her some pupils and it was increasingly hard to make ends meet. What would happen to Bea if something truly horrible were to befall her? What was more, Beatrice was coming of age and Margaret feared for her daughter's future. In the world of the Kings, a girl of Bea's age would be launched upon the social scene, ready to find a suitable husband. With their meagre lifestyle in Montmartre, such a thing was impossible. It had seemed romantic and worthy once, to live this life of fierce self-reliance, and Margaret was still proud of what she had achieved alone. But she was tired, and she wanted so much more for Beatrice. Maybe her family had changed. So they had come, but it seemed they were too late.

There she was, her grandmother Queenie, standing in the doorway, dressed head to toe in black.

'Margaret, my dear,' she said, in a strong voice. Her hair was pure white now, different from the bright stripes through deep brown and gunmetal grey she'd had when Margaret last saw her. She walked in a confident, upright

14

stride towards them across the driveway, yet smiled wanly.

'Are we too late, Grandmother? Is Father . . . gone?'

Queenie arrived in front of her and took her hands, her grandmother's skin dry and papery yet her hands warm and firm.

'I am sorry to say you are too late. He passed away two days hence, but there was no way to alert you.'

It struck Margaret that she felt absolutely nothing at all. It was akin to being told the *boulangerie* opposite their house had run out of bread, annoying that she'd missed her chance, yet hardly more than an inconvenience. *Am I really so cold?* she thought.

'I'm grieved to hear it and so sorry for our family's loss,' she heard herself saying to Queenie, who cocked her head and smiled a strange little smile.

'Really, my dear? I didn't think you cared for your father one jot! But, of course, you are saying the right things and acting with perfect decorum.'

Queenie hadn't changed, then. She'd always said what she thought. Then, Queenie's face altered suddenly as her gaze shifted aside and fell upon Margaret's daughter, waiting patiently beside her.

'And this is Beatrice,' said Queenie with a kind of breathy wonder. Queenie's eyes were wide open and she swiftly removed her hands from Margaret's. It had been good to feel her grandmother's touch again, the only King who ever really cared about her. Indeed, her

15

brother Cyril and stepmother Benjamina had not even come out to greet their arrival. Typical and, truth be told, something of a relief.

'Why, my dear, you are a stunning creature!' said Queenie and took the girl's hands. Beatrice glanced nervously sideways at her mother who nodded. 'You are the very picture of your father, with those dark eyes. I do not recall much about the artist Ashford, but one could not forget those eyes. And I see you have your mother's fine features. You will do very nicely, my dear. Will you not greet me as your great-grandmother, child? You speak English, I assume?'

'Indeed, I do, Great-grandmother,' Beatrice said, smiling. Yet another glance at her mother showed how nervous and eager to do the right thing she was. 'I would like to offer my condolences on your loss. I am so very sorry I did not meet my grandfather.'

Margaret watched her grandmother place her palms on her daughter's cheeks, who stood rigidly, trying to appear natural. 'You are kind to say so, but you may be the better for it. He was my son, but he wasn't the man I wished him to be. No doubt that appears wickedly unkind to you, but you will learn that your great-grandmother is honest as the day is long and will not brook any flim-flam. Come now, you must be fatigued from your travels. Come inside.'

Queenie led the way. Beatrice took her mother's hand and squeezed it, her face a sweet picture of concern, her eyes seeming to ask if her mother was well, after the bad news.

'I am fine,' Margaret said quietly to her as she squeezed Beatrice's hand back and they walked together into the hallway of Southover, tiled in colourful, geometric patterns, shiny and hard beneath their feet. A new floor in the hall then, using the local tiles, no doubt. Margaret began to feel a little shaken that so much had changed. She felt as if she were in a dream, where a place was familiar yet foreign. The new butler and maids took their cloaks and bonnets as Queenie looked on, never once taking her eyes off Beatrice, whose every nuance seemed to delight her. Margaret was proud of her daughter's beauty, sweet temperament and strength of character, yet there was something in the pit of her belly that made her feel uncomfortable at her grandmother's attentions.

'I believe that Cyril and Benjamina are in the drawing room,' said Queenie, adding, 'And Beatrice, I'm glad to hear that you speak our native tongue beautifully with no trace of an accent! A French accent around these parts would not go down very well. Many of us are old enough to recall the wars with France and we do not forgive easily.'

The butler opened the drawing room door for Queenie, who had waited imperiously for him to do so as if she could not do it herself, which of course she could. Margaret noticed all of these little touches. After nearly two decades away from such a life, it would take her a while to settle back into it. How strange it was to act as if one had lost the use of one's hands to simply open a door. But she decided at that moment that she would not let the maids dress her or wash her or anything like it. She had forged her own dignity in Paris at great cost, an independence hard fought for and won.

The story she had told Beatrice about her father was a lie. Beatrice's father was dead, that was true. But it did not happen when Margaret carried her child, but five years later. And it was not from a tragic fever, but something far more distasteful. Margaret had told her daughter these untruths to protect her from the squalid reality.

After a foolish affair and a runaway marriage, she had left her husband in the early months of pregnancy and walked off into the streets of Paris alone. In the weeks before she'd left, she would lie on the hard cot in the tiny apartment with one window she shared with Jake and daydream about a place she could escape to, a place to call her own, away from his drinking, his womanising, his blaming her for all of his failings.

Their great romance had soured the moment Jake realised she wouldn't beg her family for money. She could hardly believe it when she first took possession of her little house, months later, the birth not long away. It was in a street full of shops and businesses. It had before then been a seamstress's home and she would find scraps of material or the odd pin from time to time. It was basic but it was clean. And it took the last of the family money she'd taken the night she left Ironbridge. The main room had four windows and let in plenty of light. She put an advertisement in the front window for English lessons and soon had her first pupils. She wore the black clothes of a widow, although it would be some years before that became a fact. When the baby came, a neighbourly midwife helped her and the birth went smoothly.

Once she was up and about and the baby sleeping better, she began advertising as a piano teacher and left Beatrice with a friend who was a clockmaker's wife, who was childless and adored babies. Every day, she bought a small bouquet of flowers and placed them in the window. In time, she was able to purchase her own pianoforte, her friends helping her manoeuvre it into the house. She learnt how to tune and maintain it herself. When Beatrice was three, she started teaching her to play. Pupils came daily and their living improved, with enough money to buy some pretty things for her daughter and some decent wine for herself. They had friends, they had freedom, they had each other. There had been suitors from time to time – Margaret had always been a pretty woman – and though she enjoyed flirting with them, she never succumbed. She wanted no more husbands. Her whole life until that little house had been lived in thrall to others, particularly men, directing her destiny and limiting her choices. She'd vowed she would never do that again.

Margaret followed Queenie into the drawing room and she immediately noticed that the picture in her mind's eye was different from the room she now stood in. It had been fully redecorated since she left, with bright flock wallpaper in red and pale pink, quite gaudy, she thought. Benjamina's influence, no doubt. She looked about the room for her fashionable stepmother, wondering how the years would have treated her, so obsessed with her appearance she'd always been. She was only a few years older than Margaret herself – the 'child bride', as she'd always thought of her secretly. But Benjamina was not here and neither was Margaret's brother, Cyril. A wave of relief swept over her. He was the one she dreaded seeing most of all. And suddenly she felt icy cold and a phrase leapt to her mind: *We should never have come.*

Chapter 2

Owen Malone stretched his arms out, hearing his bones crack. His back ached. He shook his head to wake himself up. Since he'd seen the girl in the coach he had been in a daydream and had found it difficult to concentrate on this last hour of his working day. He yawned noisily, prompting his father to glance at him and say, 'Nearly time to go.'

'I'm not done with you yet,' snapped another voice. It was his father's cousin, Adam. They were arguing again.

His father looked more exhausted than anything when he replied, 'We shall go all round the houses and nowt will be settled, mon. We must agree to disagree. Come, Owen. Your mother will be setting the table.'

But Adam stepped forward and grasped his cousin's arm. 'We must be united or we shall fail. Is that what you want, Peter?' Owen did not like the look of this. He admired Adam, always had. He idolised him, if truth be told – his passion for what was right and wrong, for how the working man and woman must be treated. Owen's father knew right from wrong: there was no better man alive. Yet he did not have Adam's fire for change and this disappointed Owen at times.

Peter Malone slowly looked upon his cousin's grasp around his arm and then he smiled. 'After thirteen hours in this place, all what I want is my supper. And I shall have it, cousin. If you dunna mind.'

Adam released his grip, grumbling to himself as he returned to his moulding table. A boy staggered up to the bench and unloaded onto Adam's table a lump of clay from his head that must have been nearly forty pounds in weight. The boy turned wearily to trek back the thirty yards or so to the clay heaps to collect the next lump. He could not have been more than eight years of age, but his face appeared grey and lined, weathered and ancient. Owen grimaced at the sight, grateful that at seventeen years old, he was now an experienced brick-burner trained by his father, working alongside him in the kilns and not a child bearing the clay any longer.

The other workers were arriving to take over from them, as Owen and his father finished their shift. The two of them walked across the brickyard, nodding at their colleagues as they passed them, too tired to talk to anyone, focused only on putting one foot afore the other to make the journey home to their little house, to food and comfort. They left by the main gate, past the stacks of bricks and tiles in symmetrical piles, the finished wares displayed for customers to see from the road. They walked along it in easy companionship, passing by the woods on one side, the river on the other, the marks of industry everywhere about them. Here was a smithy, there the lime kilns, and further along a corn-mill and another brickworks. Men and women were returning home, falling into step behind or before them, coloured by the dust and muck of their trade, whether grey, reddish-brown or black, all dressed in grime-stiffened clothes, heads down, pushing their legs forward.

'Father,' Owen said.

'Arr?'

'If a master were to look upon us, all of us, us working men, trudging home as we are. What do you think he'd see?'

Peter strode forward, quiet, considering.

'He'd see money.'

'Yes, but what would they think of us?'

'I doubt they think on us at all. But if they do, they would see only money, as I say. Their means to make money. That's our role to play on this earth. The working man.'

'You're right,' said Owen, warming to his theme. 'He'd see only a working man, walking along. He'd see only our clothes and our dirty appearance and he'd likely think to himself, what empty-headed clots they be. But every man a-walking along here has thoughts, of plans he makes and ideas for things. He might be thinking on regrets or memories of loved ones. Or he might be dreaming up inventions that could change the world. But a rich man – or woman, for that matter – looking upon us from great heights, from the King house on the hill or . . . from the comfort of a coach, maybe. They would see only our shapes and our filth and if they thought on us at all, they would think we only be like creatures. Or machines, even. With nothing inside but blood and bones, or even that brick-dust filled our heads.'

'Arr, that be true,' said his father. ''Twas always thus and always thus shall be.'

Owen wanted to ask his father another thing, but he kept it to himself. He wasn't ready to share this with anyone yet. The moment he'd come out from the drying shed and spotted that coach pulled over by the brickyard entrance, he'd seen her eyes. The girl in the coach with the bonnet and the hair – what colour was it? It was a shining kind of brown, like a new conker hazed with dew. He was pleased with that description in his mind's eye. His mother always said his father was a poet and that Owen had inherited it, had inherited her cleverness too and her deep thoughts. But he had no deep thoughts about the girl he'd seen staring at him from the coach, only feelings. A spark of something that coursed through him the moment their eyes latched on. What was she looking at, he wondered? What would she think of him? He'd always been proud of his work at the brickyard, toiling alongside his family gang of cousins and uncles and aunts, learning his way up the trade to be a skilled brickburner like his father. But now he'd felt a pinch of shame when that girl looked upon him from the coach, the gloves she wore, that beauty, those eyes . . .

'Son,' his father said, startling him from his reverie.

'Arr?'

'Dunna be giving your mother werrit about all that talk at the yard, all the chunnering about brickmakers' unions and strikes and so forth. You know she'll only fuss.'

'And you know full well she'll be firing questions at us about that very subject.'

His father breathed out heavily. 'I do. But there be no need to encourage her.'

Owen thought for a few steps, as to his next words, which he chose carefully. 'I do think as she thinks though, on this subject, leastways. And I am a man now, entitled to my own views on matters of work and pay and suchlike.'

Another father might have laughed at that, scorned him, his boy. But not Peter Malone.

'I know it. And I am proud of you. You are everything a father could want in a son: upright, hard-working, good-hearted. And you know I worship your mother and she always was a person far cleverer than me. She was going places, Anny Woodvine. Until the sad times overcame her family. She was never the same after that. And I was lucky to have her even glance at me, let alone take me for a husband. But cleverness and anger can be a bitter brew. Think on it. That is all I ask.'

They walked on, Peter frowning, Owen thoughtful. They were passing down the steps beside the bridge now, along the riverside to the cluster of cottages where his home was, where his mother and father had grown up together as neighbours, where he himself was born. His grandparents had passed on some time ago, but before that they'd lived their whole lives here. The door stood open to the springtime evening, the smells of supper wafting over them as they stepped inside, the heat from the hearth filling the small space. And there was his mother, bent over the pot in which she boiled a sheep's head for their supper, her cheeks flushed from the steam. She raised her head and saw them, her dear face weary and careworn as ever, but at the sight of her beloveds, a smile lit up her face and turned it ten years younger.

∽

After supper, Anny Malone liked to sit by the range and knit or sew, chatting with her husband Peter as he puffed on his clay pipe. She kissed him goodbye each morning and kissed him welcome home every evening. After eighteen years of marriage, she marvelled at how little they argued, how fond they still were, while all around them they heard couples rowing day in, day out, threatening all sorts of dreadful outcomes if she didna shut her trap or he didna move his backside, and so forth. But Anny and Peter had always been easy together. Of course, they had disagreements when the squalls of life knocked them about. Everyone did that. But there was a deep and abiding sense of calm between them, bonded by physical closeness. They had always hugged a lot and kissed a lot and embarrassed their only son with it in his younger years, who would cry, 'Leave off, you two!'

Anny smiled upon Owen now, watching him sitting beside them, carving chess figures from bits of wood he found lying about by the river. They already had one chess set that they used on winter evenings and now he was carving another. He'd always been good with his hands, Owen. A good mind too, sometimes beating her at chess, but not often. He'd learnt it a few years back from the master at school and borrowed a set from him to bring home. She'd kept her son in school as long as she possibly could, but he was needed at the brickyard in the warm months and once he'd had that taste of work, he grew tired of the schoolroom. She wouldn't allow their son to be a clay carrier for long. She'd seen the damage it had done to other children, their backs bent, their legs swollen. She did not want him to work at the brickyard at all, truth be known. But he wanted to be with his father. He adored him, followed him every-where, every chance he got. So she agreed to it, as long as he still went to school in the winter till he was twelve and he learnt to read and write properly and to do his numbers. She'd revelled in watching him learn and worked at the table with him each evening when he was younger. She had even learnt chess from him and took to it quickly, a reminder that her brain had once been used for a higher purpose than the washing and sewing she took in at home. She had also started up a small business of making fidget pies, from her mother's timeworn recipe, in small individual portions that she sold to laundry customers for a good amount and to friends and neighbours cheap. It made a good few pennies and it comforted her, as it was her departed father's favourite and she thought on him every time she shaped the pastry. In summer, she made Mucky Mouth Pies from wimberries too, when the delicious blue fruits were ready to pick from the wild or buy from the market. Those were Owen's favourite, ever since he was little.

Dragging herself from her musings she turned to Peter and Owen and asked the question she knew they'd both been waiting for her to ask.

'What's the talk at work, then?'

Peter took a long draw on his pipe. She could see Owen wanted to answer, but deferred to his father.

'More nonsense from Adam.'

'They argued all day, on and off,' added Owen.

'Ruined my day,' muttered Peter.

'I don't know why you let him get to you,' said Anny. 'He's not even your blood. He was your cousin's husband and she died, poor soul. And now he's married again, within a few months.' Anny thought about Adam's new wife, Martha. People did marry after they'd been widowed – of course they did. But when Peter's lovely cousin, Judith, died young, nobody had predicted that her widower would marry again so soon. And Anny's mother had told her a rumour once, that Martha was found by her Quaker parents as a baby left on the iron bridge, but it had remained a rumour and never been proven. She seemed a nice woman, Martha, but Peter's family weren't too happy with Adam's choice and the speed of it. It left a bad taste in the mouth. 'You don't owe him anything. Why let him talk rubbish at you and get under your skin?'

'We are family,' said Peter. 'Cousins by marriage are still cousins. Just because we bicker dunna mean we inna family.'

Anny smiled to herself. Her ploy had worked. She winked at Owen who winked back. Both of them were trying to get Peter to come round to Adam's point of view. Anny knew well that if she criticised Peter's family, he would defend them. He always did.

'So, it wasn't all nonsense, what Adam had to say?'

Peter fell silent again, taking another thoughtful puff. Her son answered this time.

'Adam is talking of a strike!' said Owen, a kind of whispered awe in his voice betraying his excitement at the thought.

The word 'strike' fell into the room with a thud. Anny knew that it appealed to the young and impressionable ones, like her son. But to the old hands, the prospect of a strike was a huge worry. No pay for days, weeks, months even? It could mean the workhouse for some, even starvation for others if it went on too long. But if it worked? If they could twist the Kings into changing their unfair practices quickly, surely it would be worth the risk.

'Conditions of work at the brickyard have been awful for many a year,' said Anny. 'The long hours, the accidents. But what's starting this talk of a strike now? What's changed?'

Now Peter spoke. 'There is a rumour that the Kings are going to drop the pay per thousand bricks by thruppence. That's the talk hereabouts.'

The anger bloomed now in Anny. Her hatred of the King family of nearly two decades rose like bile in her throat and she was in no mood to swallow it. 'They seek to reduce pay when the price of everything else is shooting up?'

'Yes!' cried Owen. She could see he was glad she had spoken. He wanted to voice his opinions, despite his father's ominous silence. 'And I'd wager the selling price of their wares will stay the same, or even rise.'

'Well said, son,' replied Anny. 'And all the while you work longer hours than ever and risk more injury through exhaustion. Will those Kings never stop? I said this would happen when they took over the brickyard. I said you should leave and take up work elsewhere. Those Kings will never change. They let my poor father die, drove my mother to illness and ruin, and put me in prison for naught. How can you go on working for them?'

A pause followed while wife and son both looked at Peter, awaiting his response. But he said nothing, still puffing thoughtfully away. This was the only thing on which Anny could never agree with her husband: the King family. Then, Peter looked at her, his eyes serious and his mouth set in an annoyed grimace.

'I've told you a hundred times, woman, that nothing would change if I moved. All the brickmasters have made an agreement. They fix the prices and blacklist troublemakers. If we moved yards, we'd have yet further to walk to and from work each day. We'd be newer and lower in the pecking order. Any trouble and it'd be last in, first out. We'd have to put up with those outsiders who come from off, who've taken over the local brickyards hereabouts and set up their communes on the riverside, drinking and womanising till all hours. You know all this! At least at our yard there are decent, local families working there and have done for generations. So what if the Kings own it now? Our last master got himself bankrupt and nearly shut the whole yard down. Would you rather poverty and the workhouse, than us work for Kings?'

'Yes!' spat Anny. 'I would rather die than work for them myself.' And with that, she threw down her knitting and stomped outside.

She regretted raising her voice to her husband, she always did. Though since it was so rare, it felt like a small crime to lose her temper with him. But she was proud

31

and did not want to go back in and apologise, not yet at any rate. And besides, she did not regret her words or their sentiment, as she felt it keenly.

It was a warm March evening, still light and busy around the houses, with neighbours feeding their animals and chatting. The smell of boiling sheep's head drifted on the air, as a few of them had bought it this week, a rare deal going cheap. Most of the men she saw wore the same caps as her husband and puffed on the same kind of pipes, made up the river from the local clay. The same pipes, the same clothes, the same food. The same lives. She had wanted more once. She had worked in the King office as a clerical assistant and had been tipped for greater things, maybe even an office worker in Shrewsbury one day. But the Kings had ruined it – the cruel and lecherous young son of the house had tried to woo her, had been rejected by her and had framed her for theft. She could not even bear to think of his name, let alone say it aloud, but yes, Cyril King had sent her to prison with his treacherous lies. It was disproven eventually, but while she was gone, her father had died at the King furnace explosion, an accident that was no accident, that could have been avoided if Ralph King had spent more money on taking care of his ironworks. Her mother never fully recovered and died a few years on.

And what of Anny Woodvine, as she was then, she thought? Had she ever fully recovered? She fell in love with her husband Peter, when he and his mother nursed her back to health after her desperate prison days. She still missed Peter's mother.

She had her beloved and only child, Owen. She'd learnt to put aside the ambition of her youth and see the value in a simple life. The only vestige of the Anny she used to be was that she'd taught herself back then to speak without the rhythms of the local dialect, forcing her speech to echo that of her masters. She still had that touch of the other girl about her, but that was all. That other Anny was gone, long ago. She was proud of their home, which she kept spick and span, just as her mother had taught her. Anny was proud of the work she did and the customers who valued her neat and tidy laundry and mending, always perfectly done, perfectly folded and doing so well she now was able to hire local girls and boys to help with deliveries. She was proud too of the delicious pies she made and the money they brought in. Her father – God rest his soul, taken from this earth too soon – would have been proud to see her do so well and have married such a good man. They loved each other. They had secure jobs. They had a beautiful boy, growing into a fine young man. They were complete. They were happy. But the poison of the Kings and what they had done to her family still crept in her veins. There was no escape from it. She would hate them with all of her heart until her dying day, beyond if truth be known. *When I die*, she thought, *I shall come back and haunt them, the forsaken bastards.*

Chapter 3

Queenie watched the procession of mourners follow the hearse up the road towards the church on the hill. It was a paltry gathering. Cyril had insisted that all the King workers be forced to attend, but Queenie had refused to allow this. First of all, they would lose a day's work and earnings if all their workers were off. Secondly, she knew none of them cared for Ralph King and it would be a spectacle of falsehood. And she couldn't abide false things, lies and mendacity of any sort. Her son was disliked and that was the truth. Nobody would weep for him or even honour him.

She'd loved her son once, but even she had trouble mourning the man he'd become. By the time her husband had passed on more than two decades before, she had grown completely cold towards him. And now for her son, she felt the same. Sadly, Ralph King Junior was a small-minded, self-centred and cruel man, with little natural intelligence. Left to him the King fortunes and name would dwindle to nothing. The best thing that could be said about him was that he lacked the appetites of the flesh that his father had been so prone to. He made a hash of everything he involved himself in, even this, his death, dying before her. The doctor had said it wasn't the gout that killed him as such, but that his overindulgence in food and wine had put such pressure on his liver and other organs, that the unwholesome mixture had poisoned his blood and caused his body to give up the ghost.

Yet there was a small part of her buried deep that had looked upon her dying son in his sickbed and had mourned the baby she had once doted upon. He was a fat, jolly infant and she had adored him so, especially after losing her twin baby daughters to consumption before him.

She was glad he had died before Margaret and Beatrice arrived. Queenie would not want them to have to see him as he was in his last days. That was no way for a man to be remembered. Especially for Beatrice. *Ah, Beatrice!* she thought, and sighed contentedly as the procession reached the churchyard. The pall-bearers, including Cyril, were gathering to carry the coffin inside. But Queenie's eyes were seeking out her great-grand-daughter and there she was, standing demurely beside her mother, watching the proceedings with interest. *I wonder what she makes of us?* thought Queenie. As the thought entered her mind, she was surprised at it. She never gave a damn what anybody thought of her person-ally. It was the King reputation that was crucial and must be protected at all costs. But suddenly, at this late point in her life, this pretty little half-French thing had entered stage left and Queenie could think of little else. Beatrice was in her house and in her life now and Queenie could not be more delighted with her. She watched her now and tried to get the measure of her.

Beatrice was standing with her mother near to the church door. Her hands were demurely folded before her. Her eyes glanced down from time to time, showing she was a little reserved, and she also looked to her mother for reassurance often. But she was nothing like Margaret had been as a young person, desperately shy to the point of infuriating Queenie. With Beatrice it seemed more a kind of watchfulness, taking it all in and working on it in her mind. There was something very intelligent in the girl's eyes.

Now the girl was looking at Benjamina, her step-grandmother. Beatrice had a weakness for fashion, that was clear. Her outfits were a little fussy and flouncy for local tastes; it must be the French influence. Beatrice seemed to be looking at Benjamina's vulgar black creation today with interest. She wore a frilly black bonnet with a veil, a lacy mantle and embroidered gloves. *The grieving widow*, thought Queenie wryly, inspecting Benjamina. *Ha!*

She remembered her own relief when her cruel husband had passed. But this one was still young – by Queenie's standards anyway. Benjamina had been seventeen when Ralph had married her and now she was free and rich at only forty-two, with no children to encumber her. Queenie wondered what she would get up to next. *Let us hope she finds another wealthy fool and leaves us alone*, thought Queenie. She had noticed in the past few days that Beatrice, despite liking Benjamina's clothes, soon ran out of conversation with her. Benjamina was tedious and had little to discuss other than fashion and dogs.

Queenie looked away from her in disgust and focused back on Beatrice. Something else had caught the girl's attention now; Cyril was taking the coffin on to his shoulders, but was saying something, loudly.

'Watch out, there!' he cried, in his petulant voice. The King family butler, Busby, shouldered the opposite corner to Cyril. The coffin swayed dangerously and tipped, but was soon righted by the butler who kept his decorum at all times, unlike the idiot Cyril, who huffed and puffed and shot evil glances around, blaming everyone but himself, as usual. Queenie looked back at Beatrice, who actually grimaced and looked away. Queenie could see from the first day that Beatrice was repelled by Cyril. What an excellent judge of character the girl must be. Each passing day, Queenie grew more and more fascinated by her.

There was a tap on her arm and Queenie's reverie was interrupted. It was her faithful lady's maid, Jenkins, who nodded her head towards the church.

Queenie acquiesced. Jenkins could always be relied upon to keep her eyes and ears open. She entered the church, Jenkins leading her to her place of honour in the front row. Queenie watched as the coffin bearing her son's corpse was lifted into place before the meagre congregation. *I wonder if he'll haunt me, like the other?* she thought.

∞

Later, at the wake at Southover, Queenie's feet were beginning to ache after all this standing about.

'We sincerely commiserate with you for your great loss at this difficult time.'

I wonder if they know how much I disliked my own son, thought Queenie, but said aloud instead, 'Thank you most kindly.'

Her son's wake was nearly over, thank heavens, but there was still a good deal of tasty food remaining, so some of the greedier guests continued to gobble it down. Queenie nodded politely as the wife of a local tile manufacturer wittered on about the cost of black silk these days. These types of people were the only reliable ones they could find to attend Ralph King's funeral, business associates of his – mostly of Queenie's to be frank as Ralph was never any good at running the business. He was the male figurehead of the King fortune, but everyone knew that it was herself who ran it all and had done for twenty-odd years. Her grandson Cyril had done his bit, visiting the works from time to time and chivvying on the foreman and suchlike. He wined and dined the other brickmasters and made connections in the counties beyond with other industrialists. But he had no true business acumen. It was Queenie alone who ruled the King businesses and she did so with an iron fist.

The wife was still talking to her and Queenie was nodding sympathetically and hoping she wouldn't be required to respond to any particulars, as she hadn't heard a word of it. She was watching Beatrice again, who was now standing near to the window and gazing out of it, with rather a lost expression. The poor girl must be bored to tears and feeling very alone at this gathering of strangers, all from England, from Shropshire, speaking of things Beatrice knew nothing about, and gathered for a man Beatrice had never known.

'Mrs Elkin,' Queenie interrupted the wife who stopped abruptly, mid-flow. 'Have you met my great-granddaughter, Beatrice?'

'I have not had the pleasure,' simpered the Elkin woman, while Queenie swept past her, gesturing her to follow. She advanced towards Beatrice by the window, who turned to notice her approach. Queenie was greeted by a dazzling smile, which delighted her.

'Beatrice, this is Mrs Elkin.'

'Delighted, I'm sure,' said the woman.

'And I too am delighted to make your acquaintance,' said Beatrice.

The girl speaks well, thought Queenie. *More than well. Her English is excellent.*

'May I offer my condolences for the passing of your . . . grandfather?'

'Yes, my grandfather. Thank you. I never had the fortune to meet him, but I understand he was a great man.'

Queenie raised her eyebrows a touch. She was impressed by Beatrice's diplomacy. How many girls her age would be arch enough to play that game so well? But Queenie was eager to steer clear of discussing her son.

'Beatrice, I should explain that Mrs Elkin's husband manages a decorative tileworks along the river.'

'Decorative tiles?' said Beatrice to the wife. 'Are they very pretty?'

'Oh, yes! Very pretty they are. I cannot pretend to understand the business itself, but I know a pretty thing when I see it. These decorated tiles are the latest thing. We have them all over the front of our house. It is like a show house, you see, to show off our wares. You must come to see us one day for afternoon tea, Miss Beatrice.'

'I would love that,' said Beatrice. Queenie's pleasure at the girl's social skills grew with every word. She could not be more different from her mother at that age, who had always cowered and hidden from every social opportunity.

'Oh and this is my husband now,' said Mrs Elkin, gesturing to a short man of broad girth who had manoeuvred past a range of snacking guests to appear at his wife's side.

Introductions were made and Queenie continued to watch as Beatrice responded to this dull couple so deftly.

Beatrice said, 'I understand you make beautiful tiles, Mr Elkin.'

Husband and wife smiled at each other and Mr Elkin attempted to laugh it off, but was clearly charmed.

'Well, I say, I find them so, as does my wife. Just recently, my tileworks has specialised in producing a range of encaustic tiles, with elaborate designs. Quite lovely. Exquisite, some might say.'

'And where do you sell such lovely things?' said Beatrice. 'We all know the world needs bricks, but where do you find your customers for such fancy work?'

'Why, all over the country, Miss Beatrice. All over the world, if I have my way! We do such fine work, it is a joy to behold. Very attractive. The ladies love it. You must come and see our house.'

'I said the very same thing, Edwin,' added Mrs Elkin. 'We'd be delighted to have you, my dear.'

Queenie watched Beatrice as she went on with the conversation, talking with these two stuffed shirts as if she'd known them for years. The girl had managed to flatter them, appear interested and even knowledgeable about a business she surely knew nothing about and had garnered an invitation to tea from both husband and wife in just a few utterances. Queenie was delighted her first impressions of the girl had been correct, that she was not shy but instead watchful with a busy mind. Her company was as lovely as her appearance, an excellent coupling in society. But she was no mere society belle, practised in the art of small talk. She showed real interest in Elkin's business. They were talking of which clays they used in its manufacture now. Queenie stared at Beatrice as she negotiated each turn of the conversation with ease, and at that moment, Queenie made a decision. She vowed that she would take the girl under her wing, introduce her successfully into society and teach her about the business. Her son Ralph and grandson Cyril had been such disappointments when it came to running the King businesses, whilst her one hope, Margaret, had run off with an artist and forfeited her place. Now here was a bright young woman who possessed a true spark of life. This girl would be her protégé and Queenie couldn't wait to get started on her. With the right influence Beatrice might even one day lead the King family.

Chapter 4

Beatrice was taught the waltz first. Madame said that the galop and polka would come next, with the mazurka last, as it was the most tricky.

'You are coming of age at the most thrilling moment in the history of dance!' exclaimed Madame at the end of her first dance lesson. 'Dancing closely with a man is now the fashion. Lucky you, Beatrice! Ah, to be young in 1858.'

Beatrice smiled uncertainly as Madame fanned herself in dramatic fashion with one hand, while touching her forehead with the back of the other. Maman had told her that Madame was actually called Mrs Prescott and was Shropshire born and bred, yet had taken the name Madame and a fake French accent to attract more pupils. When introduced to Madame, Beatrice had begun speaking in French, glad to speak it again after a couple of weeks of only English. But Madame had looked at her somewhat aghast and Beatrice realised that her dance teacher did not speak a word of French.

'Are you not excited by the thought, my dear?' said Madame.

'The idea of dancing with a young man?' said Beatrice. 'Why, yes!'

'Well, I can't see that the huge crinoline under my skirt would allow me to get closer to a man than an arm's length, or even further!' laughed Beatrice.

But Madame did not appreciate this and pursed her lips with disapproval. For a fake Frenchwoman, she certainly seemed to disapprove of any nod to Beatrice's slightly risqué sense of humour. She ignored the comment and went on, 'Are there are any young men you have had the pleasure of meeting here in Ironbridge?'

'I am newly arrived and have not yet had the pleasure.'

'Well, there is not much choice hereabouts. Shrewsbury would suit you much better. Some lovely young men there. But around these parts, you'd better seek out the masters' sons. Ironmasters, brickmasters, coalmasters. They are all educating their sons these days and I teach them all to dance. The gentry on the country estates have their own dance teachers, of course. But for the rich in town, like your family, then I am the one they come to. You are lucky I managed to fit you in, my dear. I am so busy. So very much in demand!'

And so Madame went on, rattling through stories of her first dances back in the day, which boys made eyes at her and how many hearts she broke and so forth. Beatrice listened with a polite, fixed smile but inside her stomach was groaning and all she could think of was finishing this dance lesson and meeting Maman. She would ask if they could visit a tea shop and have cake.

English cake was her new obsession, especially the sponge sandwich with jam and cream. She had not eaten since luncheon and it was now late afternoon and she felt ravenous. Beatrice's attention began to wander. She did not find dancing particularly interesting.

And it was not only dancing that bored her; the whole idea of being a debutante, of 'coming out' – something her grandmother and now her mother seemed obsessed with – it all seemed rather silly to Beatrice. In Paris she walked to the local shops alone, she met friends in the street and chatted, she ate snacks when she felt like it.

On arriving at the Kings' beautiful house, she was bowled over by the furnishings, the clothes, the servants. This last confused her the most. She had been expressly told by her great-grandmother that the servants were there to serve, no more and not to be friendly with them in any way. But Beatrice was used to talking to everyone, to anyone. There was a girl, her own maid, called Dinah. She had round pink cheeks and a shy smile, a nice soft voice with that local lilt of the Shropshire accent that Beatrice found so lovely, like music. When Dinah came to Beatrice to help with her clothes or hair, or to clean her room, or make up her fire, Beatrice would ignore the rules and try to engage Dinah in conversation. But it hadn't worked yet. Dinah was not only shy but she adhered to the house rules admirably – or disappointingly, for Beatrice. She was not used to this, this lack of conversation, this stiffness. It was the thing she disliked most about England.

But her favourite thing about England so far was her great-grandmother. She could see that some might find her a difficult woman, but with Beatrice Queenie would sit for hours telling her stories of the family – of Margaret as a shy girl and Cyril as a naughty boy and of her own sister Selina who sadly died young. She told her about the Kings, their history and their place in society. Queenie's eyes sparkled when she told these stories and Beatrice was pleased to hear them, her hitherto shadowy understanding of her background coming into the light and seen in sharp focus, a whole world of family she'd known little about until now.

Her other favourite thing about England were mealtimes. Such hearty meals, of several courses, cooked for you and brought to you at the table. But she had to wait so long for each mealtime and there was no opportunity to wander into the pantry and grab an apple or pop opposite to the *boulangerie* and have a croissant, as at home. Here everything was orchestrated at set times, with no exceptions. The formality of it all was beginning to grate. She had so much more freedom in Paris and virtually none here. She would have to be met by her mother after this class to be escorted home, even though it was only a short walk up to the house from town. She had admired Benjamina's clothes immensely but now her mother was at the dressmaker ordering some outfits for both of them and she wondered how restrictive the English styles would be; Benjamina never looked relaxed or comfortable, but perhaps that was her way, rather than her corset.

If Beatrice were honest with herself, she was confused by her new life here. She loved being spoiled, being waited upon, the richness of clothes and bedding, the bath by the fire filled for her by a maid. She loved the way her great-grandmother sought her out every day and talked to her. She was happy too to see her mother rest for once, at last, after years of work and struggle. It was a joy to see her being indulged, taking an afternoon nap, with no pupils to bother her, no bills to pay, but Beatrice missed home, its freedoms and their friends. She did not want to tell her mother that, as she seemed so happy here. Despite her new privileges, Beatrice secretly preferred her old life.

The window in the dancing room was ajar and through it came the savoury scent of freshly baked goods, which made her insides twist for food even more. She followed her nose and glanced past Madame's shoulder, through the window to the back yard outside. There, she saw a young man had come to the back door, carrying a basket covered with a cloth. He was tall and had yellow hair. The thin April sunshine caught it in that light and made it shine golden. A servant came out and questioned the young man. He lifted the cloth and showed her his wares, a batch of pies. Beatrice's stomach groaned in return. The servant was shaking her head at the young man and having words with him. Beatrice could hear the shrill tone of the servant and it caught Madame's ear too, who simply spoke more loudly, droning on now about the correct use of fans.

At last, Beatrice said, 'I think it is time, Madame. I must go and meet my mother now.'

'Ah indeed, our time is up. See you tomorrow for your next lesson. Send the next one in, will you? If she is there, that is. That girl is always tardy.'

Beatrice gathered her bonnet, shawl and purse and headed out into the corridor. Instead of going right to the front door, she took a glance behind her, then went left instead, towards the back of the house. She found a door to the outside and opened it. There was the young man and his pies and the servant still arguing with him.

'I ordered only four pies, Owen Malone. I dunna care what yer mother says.'

'But she has made five and she expects the money for five,' said the young man.

Beatrice spied the pies again, each one identical and beautifully turned, each one small and individual, perfect for one person to hold in their hands.

'I shall buy it from you,' said Beatrice.

Both faces turned to her in shock, the servant crossing her arms, the young man staring.

'How much for the pie?' she asked, reaching into her purse.

'There y'are,' said the serving woman, taking the four pies and piling them two by two on her arm and disappearing behind the door, which she kicked shut.

The young man did not speak, simply stared at Beatrice as if she had landed that very moment from the sky.

'Please, I really am ever so hungry and those pies look very good,' she said.

'Then you must have it, miss,' he said and held out the basket towards her.

'How much?' she said.

'Try it first,' he said, the corner of his mouth turning up. He was nervous but he was finding his way now. 'Then you may judge how much it be worth.'

Beatrice smiled and took the pie. In Paris, they often ate street food. But here in Ironbridge, the Kings only ate at the table with a full set of cutlery dazzling in its complexity, one of the many new things Beatrice was having to learn. It was good to take food sealed in its own container and simply bite into it, no napkin, no knife and fork, no decorum to speak of. She took a big bite, at which sight the young man's eyes grew even wider. As Beatrice chewed, the tastes of pork, onion and a hint of sweetness enveloped her taste buds. It was still slightly warm, so must have been freshly baked that afternoon.

'Hmmm,' she said as she polished off her mouthful. 'It is magnificent! Pork and apple, is it? What a lovely combination.'

'It is a fidget pie.'

'Fidget pie? What a curious and charming name! What can it mean?'

'Some say it is from the shape, being somewhat five-sided. Fidget can mean five round here.'

'How delightful! And your mother bakes these fidget pies?'

'Yes and makes a pretty penny selling them.'

'Please tell her from me that it is the best food I've eaten in England yet.'

'In the whole of England?' he scoffed.

'Well,' she said, desperate to take another bite but enjoying the conversation too much, 'I have only seen Ironbridge so far and some places en route from the port. But this is by far the best, in that limited experience.'

'You are from off then, miss?'

'From where?'

'Not from round here. An incomer, as they say? You dunna sound local. And you dunna look like an Ironbridge lass, if you dunna mind me saying.'

Beatrice laughed and said, 'Indeed no. I am "from off", as you say. I come from France.'

His eyes were wide again. Beatrice took another bite and savoured the delicious taste. He watched her with amusement as she wiped the crumbs from her mouth. She wondered what he thought of her.

'You sound English though, miss.'

'I learnt both languages growing up in Paris, as my mother is English. Oh! My mother! I forgot all about her!'

She glanced around and saw a wooden gate that she guessed led out into the street.

'Where is your mother?'

'She's coming to meet me out at the front of the house.'

'Here, miss. I'll show you. It's just through there.'

'Thank you so much,' she said and took another bite. He opened the gate for her and they both stepped into the street. The young man looked both ways, then something caught his eye down the road. Two men were walking their way and the young man must have known them, as they nodded to each other as they passed, staring at her and glancing back at him, their heads falling close.

'I'll show you to the main street, then be on my way, miss,' he said.

'Your name is Owen, is that right?' said Beatrice.

'It is,' said Owen and looked curiously at her. 'But how . . . ?'

'I heard the maid at the house call you that.'

'You have sharp ears, miss,' he said and smiled.

'My name is Bea.'

'Bea? Like the buzzing kind? Or like the letter?'

'Just Bea. With an A.'

He touched his forehead and nodded with a simple gallantry. 'Charmed, Miss Bea with an A.'

She took another bite of the pie as they walked up to the main road. There was no sign of her mother yet, so she walked up to the steps of Madame's house and turned to see Owen turn the other way.

'But are you not going to say farewell?'

Owen looked about him and replied in a low voice, 'I dunna think you want to be seen talking with the likes of me on the main street.'

'I happen to like talking to the likes of whomever I please, wherever I please,' she said and smiled.

It must have been infectious, as Owen smiled back. 'That the French way, is it, miss?'

'Perhaps. Or maybe it is just my way, just Bea's way.'

'I inna sure that Ironbridge is ready for Bea's way quite yet,' he said and she smiled. He was teasing her.

She laughed and said, without thinking, without pausing, 'I don't think I really fit in here. I don't have any friends here yet. I feel rather lonely.'

Owen's face was hard to read. She immediately regretted her honesty, as it seemed to have embarrassed him, this lad, this pie-seller. But he was kind to her and had such a friendly manner. And such a nice face.

'It must be very hard,' he said quietly. 'Leaving your home behind. And everything you know.'

'It is!' she said. 'Nobody understands that. Until you.'

There was a moment where they looked at each other and she felt her cheeks warming. She looked away, taking one last mouthful of the pie to cover her embarrassment, not wanting to look at him, though she wanted to very much at the same time.

'Farewell then, Miss Bea,' she heard him say.

'But the pie,' she cried as he turned away. 'How much for the pie?'

Owen glanced back and said, 'The pie is my treat. Take it as a welcome to Ironbridge.' And with that, he turned and strode off down the street, his basket knocking against his hip as he went.

'Beatrice!'

And there was Maman.

'I'm so sorry, *chérie*. The dressmaker took so long finding the silk we wanted for ... But what is that around your mouth?'

'Fidget pie,' she said dreamily, as she wiped her mouth and stared down the road, her eyes searching. But there was no sign of Owen Malone. He had been swallowed up by the crowds of folk going to and fro about their business.

The girl from the coach. It was surely the girl from the coach. Those same dark eyes, that same chestnut hair, even more shiny close up. Newly arrived in town. Her clothes, so curious, so different from the local girls. And she loved fidget pie. She loved his mother's fidget pie and ate it in the street, the crumbs dropping all over her shoes. Pink shoes.

'Malone, mon! Watch yerself!'

'He's in a dream. He's dreaming of the King girl!'

He turned in shock to see the two mates from the brickyard he'd spotted in the street earlier. It was Royce and Brain, two lads from the brickworks. Royce was around the same age as him and mostly worked as a labourer who dug out the clay. Brain was Royce's cousin or second cousin or something, and was as tall as Owen, though only being twelve years of age. Brain did a variety of jobs around the works, whatever he was bidden to do. They were all right lads, not too bright. Brain was thick-headed, which caused great hilarity due to his name. Royce was cleverer but not as genial as his cousin, more dour and even a touch bitter was Royce. But both were generally good to work with. And loyal, to the workers and to the yard, particularly to cousin Adam. They did anything Adam said and listened rapt when he spouted forth about workers' conditions. But what was it Royce just said?

'The what girl?' said Owen, stepping out of the flow of people on the pavement.

'Who you were chunnering with. That's the new King girl,' said Royce.

'She's a King?'

'You didna know? It's the talk of the town. The King daughter came back from France, after running off there with 'er fancy man all those years back. She brought her own darter back with 'er.'

'That's her? She's a King?'

'What did she want with the likes of you?' said Brain.

Owen stared off up the street, as if the girl from the coach might appear like magic before him. Bea, she said her name was. Bea. So, she was the Beatrice he'd heard tell of, the King. He'd heard the gossip, paid little attention to it. He wished he'd listened more now. She was . . . something he couldn't put into words, clear thoughts eluding him. She was so many things, so new and astonishing, it confounded his mind. But there was only one thing that sounded clearly in his head like a knell, she was a King.

'What did she want, mon?' insisted Royce. Owen looked back at them. He felt momentarily embarrassed by his distraction. They were smirking at him.

'She bought a pie,' he replied and knew that it was a lie, but a small lie. What did it matter, if she bought a pie or he gave her one for free? That was his business. But he suddenly realised with a jolt that he'd have to account for the lost coin to his mother and what would he say? *I'll tell her I ate it*, he thought.

'What would your cousin Adam say to see you talking with the enemy, eh?' said Royce.

Owen focused back quickly. 'I just sold her a pie, that's all. Making money inna a crime now, is it?'

'Depends whose money it is,' said Royce, an allegation hanging in the air. 'Listen, we're going to a meeting at the tavern now, with Adam and the others. Come with us. We'll be talking of the strike.'

'Arr, come with us, mon,' said Brain cheerfully, as if it were an invite to a picnic. 'It's at The Swan. The one on The Wharfage, not Lincoln Hill.'

Royce added, 'Adam'll want you there. It's a Sunday, you've got nothing else to do. You're needed there.'

'Not today, lads. Father is expecting me with this money. He has to pay a neighbour back who he borrowed from.' Another lie. Normally, he'd be excited at the prospect of a workers' meeting. But his parents had been rowing about it all more and more lately. And their arguments confused and upset him. He was not sure these days what he thought about the situation at work. He agreed with his mother's arguments that the masters were exploiting them, making coin while they went without and their children were forced into back-breaking labour just so their families could put food on the table. Something must be done, yet he understood his father's concerns too. The masters were in cahoots and had them tied up proper, with their price fixing and their stiff contracts. His father was worried about what would happen to local families if a strike came to pass; with no money coming in, essentials would soon be unaffordable. And strikes so often meant violence, as they'd heard of riots and trouble with the law in other parts of the country during strikes. So, his father maintained that nothing good would come of action. Owen agreed with parts of both, though his parents could not see an inch of common ground. He felt as if his home was battling itself, as well as his own mind.

'Another time, then,' said Royce and looked meaningfully at Owen. 'It would be good to see you more useful with all this. You believe in the cause, dunna you?'

'Course I do.'

Royce squinted at him. 'Your cousin leads us and I hear your mother is keen on action. But your father lets the side down.'

Owen bristled at this, though he knew it were true. 'Every man is entitled to his own opinion and must listen to his own conscience.'

'Arr, that be true,' said Brain, nodding. But Royce was not so congenial.

'Not when it comes to war. And that is what we are engaged in, mon. Make no mistake. We are skirmishing at present with the masters. But it wonna be long before it's war.'

'You'd be good on the stage, Royce,' said Owen. 'Natural flair for drama. Or a politician. You'd have to be good at lying though.' He had always liked Brain. But he had never been sure of Royce.

Royce narrowed his eyes at Owen and leant forward. 'Oh, I will lie and cheat and play dirty if needs be, when it serves our cause. And so will you, Malone. This meeting you had with that'un today could prove useful. I'll be telling your cousin that you've been seen talking with the King girl and ooh, how she did smile upon you and simper and blush like a sweet apple in your very presence! Most useful, that could be. We'll see what plans your cousin might have for you with that choice piece of news.'

'Tell him what you like,' said Owen and stepped aside from Royce's attention, too close for comfort. 'Brain,' he said pleasantly, nodding at him. The implications of Royce's words were beyond the likes of Brain. He just wanted to be involved, like a loyal dog.

Owen began to whistle a merry tune as he walked away from them and headed for home. But he knew it was fakery. Inside, his mind was churning like the river in a winter storm.

Chapter 5

'Wake up. Wake up, Miss Alice.'

Queenie fought the hands that held her shoulders, urging her to wake. Even half asleep, she knew it was Jenkins, her lady's maid, who was trying to wake her. Only Jenkins called her by her real name, Alice.

'What is it, for heaven's sake? Is the very house on fire?'

'No, the brickyard is.'

Queenie's eyes snapped open. Jenkins had lit a lamp and Queenie could see Jenkins's alarmed face, looking old, deep shadows beneath the eyes. 'What's this?'

'The foreman is here. Shall I send Cyril?'

Queenie's brain was still in a bit of a fog. But she knew what she thought of that. 'Lord, no. Don't send that idiot. Here, fetch my robe.'

'The foreman can't see you in this state, you silly old thing! What will he think?'

'I do not care!' insisted Queenie. 'Hurry or I shall face him in my nightdress.'

Queenie pulled herself out of bed while Jenkins did her best to make her presentable, helping her on with her robe and fixing her hair with a couple of pins. *Fire at the brickworks? Why was the foreman here instead of there, dealing with it?* Jenkins held Queenie's arm to walk her to the door, but she did not require it. She felt perfectly strong now.

'Enough, Jenkins. I shall proceed alone.'

She walked out onto the landing, to see the butler waiting for her, stiff as a rod.

'What is occurring then, Busby?'

'Mr Troon awaits you in the hall, ma'am. Shall I send him to your study?'

'No, the hallway will do fine,' said Queenie.

Then, a door off the landing opened and Benjamina appeared, a picture of languorous beauty in her dishevelled night attire.

'There is nothing to concern you here,' snapped Queenie. 'Go back to bed.'

'Is there trouble at the house?' she said in a fragile voice, a mock-feminine voice if you asked Queenie. 'Busby?'

Queenie hated the way Benjamina turned to the servants for answers when she herself refused. It only embarrassed them.

'This is business,' she said, and then to Busby, 'Lead on.'

'Yes, ma'am,' said Busby and swiftly turned to go below and tell the man to wait. He motioned with one quick sharp hand movement to a footman, who swiftly held up a lamp to guide Queenie down the stairs.

'Thank you, Grainger,' she said and followed him. She took pride in knowing the name of every member of staff, however humble. When she had acquired the brickworks a year ago, she had done the same thing with the list of workers' names. She insisted that the foreman, Troon, sent her updates regularly on who was hired and fired, so that she could keep a track of the families that worked there, where they lived, which family members they hired themselves and who came from outside the area. She had asserted that they try to keep to locals only. Those outsiders who came down from Lord knows where looking for brickmaking work were her last choice for workers. She wanted the tried and tested local folk the most. They were bad enough with their grumblings, but the ones who came down from elsewhere, they were the troublemakers, the drinkers and the talkers of uprisings and charters. Local people just wanted to make a living and that suited her fine. But there were not always enough of the locals to fill the skilled work, like the brickmoulders or the brick-burners. There was one from Liverpool, another from Manchester. She had told Troon to keep an eye on them. She didn't know if he did or not. She didn't know if she could trust Troon yet.

Troon was standing in the middle of the hallway, cap in hand, watching her come down the stairs as if he'd seen a ghost. Busby stood to the side, near the doorway to the drawing room, his hands folded before him, his eyes lowered, awaiting instructions. Queenie decided to keep him there. His stalwart service was comforting to her, especially at times of vexation, like this might prove to be.

'Troon, there is trouble at the brickworks, I hear,' she said to the foreman as she approached.

'I didna mean to wake you, ma'am. I thought it might be Mr King a-coming.'

'No, I am your superior here, Troon. Now, what is this business that requires waking me past ten at night?'

'There was a fire at the brickworks. But it's out now. Someone came in and set fire to one of the sheds. The kiln men were around and they saw two fellows running away into the woods, so they chased them but they eluded them, ma'am.' He was pleased with the word 'eluded', Queenie could tell. 'Then the kiln men put the fire out. All is well now and the damage inna too bad.'

'Was anyone hurt?'

'No, ma'am. Just some damage. No injuries.'

Queenie chose her next words with care. 'Is it possible, do you think, that it might have been one of the kiln men that started the fire? Perhaps it was . . . an accident.'

Troon looked affronted. 'That would never be, ma'am. They are good men, through and through.

Worked at the yard nigh on ten year. Trust 'em with my life, I would. All good men, at the King brickworks. All good men.'

'Then, who set this fire? And for what purpose?'

'That I canna say.' Troon's face was blank.

'You "canna" say? Or you "wonna" say?' Queenie narrowed her eyes at the man. He was a good foreman in his way, excellent with facts and figures, liked by the workers and always on time with their meetings. He knew the business inside out, had worked in it since he was a boy, carrying clay to his father's table. He was a tall, broad man in his thirties, family worked with him at the yard, quite handsome with a bit of a twinkle in his eye. But his face at times was so difficult to read and she had not found the trick of it yet.

'If I knew, I would surely tell you, ma'am. We dunna want trouble at the works. Why would we set fire to our own livelihood?'

'To make a point,' said Queenie, raising her bony finger and pointing it directly at him. 'I've heard tell of meetings in town, Troon. Seditious talk.'

'Workers grumble and talk, that is true. Always have. There is nothing in it.'

Queenie looked at him but again, the face gave nothing away.

'Thank you for coming to give me notice of this occurrence, Troon. It was good of you. I am most grateful to know that no one was hurt.'

'Ma'am.'

'Tomorrow, you should surmise the cost of the repairs and supervise the rebuilding of the shed. And I want you to look into this occurrence further. Talk to the workers and find out if anyone knows anything. Report back to me by evening.'

'Yes, ma'am.'

'I do not like this turn of events, Troon. I do not like it at all. And it is your job to keep order in that yard. Make sure you do so. I shall see you tomorrow. Get home to your wife and children now.'

'Ma'am,' he said again and turned to leave.

'Mr Troon,' said a voice behind her. Coming down the stairs, fully clothed and hair loose about her shoulders, was Benjamina. Queenie felt herself colour with rage. What on earth did she want, dolled up like that?

'Yes Ma'am?' said Troon, his eyes agog.

'What do you want here?' said Queenie, turning at the foot of the stairs to stand directly in between Benjamina and Troon. What on earth was she up to, interrupting them?

'I think the man deserves some refreshment, don't you?' said Benjamina, looking past Queenie and offering a dazzling smile to Troon.

'This is business and does not concern you,' snapped Queenie. Benjamina had never had as much as a sniff of business matters before now. Why was she involving herself?

'But I understand Mr Troon has had a terrible night of it,' replied Benjamina and stepped past Queenie, swiftly positioning herself beside him.

'As I said ...' began Queenie, dismayed that the woman was interfering with her meeting. But Benjamina interrupted her and continued to speak to Troon directly.

'Please accept our hospitality in return for your good service in coming all this way from the yard to tell us of the trouble. You must feel free to come to me with anything. With my dear husband gone, I know he would want me to step in, to ensure that the brickworkers are well taken care of. Busby, will you take Troon to the kitchen and furnish him with food and perhaps some ale?'

'Thank'ee most kindly, ma'am!' crowed Troon, who caught Queenie's eye then looked suitably chastised. Queenie saw too that Busby was appalled by the suggestion, yet had to follow the mistress's orders. He said gruffly to Troon, 'This way', and led him off.

Benjamina stood smiling sweetly at Queenie, who really wanted to slap the strumpet in the face. What was she thinking, interfering like that? Ingratiating herself with one such as Troon? Anyone watching might have felt that Benjamina was being kind. But Queenie knew better. That woman gave not one jot of care for those below her. Before Queenie could summon up the energy to give her a tongue-lashing, Benjamina turned and ascended the stairs languidly.

'I don't know what you think you're up to!' cried Queenie after her.

Benjamina turned and looked down upon her. 'Carrot and stick, mother-in-law,' she said enigmatically, then went back upstairs, too quickly now for Queenie to continue the conversation. Whatever did she mean? Oh, the damned woman. If she'd shown even a spark of interest in the business before, Queenie might have welcomed the help. But she'd known Benjamina for years, and while she was certainly clever enough, she was a schemer who was only out for herself. She'd squeeze every penny of profit out of the works to buy pretty dresses and fabulous jewels, but her inability to think outside her own interests would soon see the business fail. If she thought she was going to used Ralph's death to gain a place in the business she had another thing coming. The sooner she was gone, off with a new husband, the better. Queenie would have to seek one out and marry her off.

But something told her that would be a much harder task than it sounded, with this vixen to deal with. Queenie and Benjamina had never liked each other, but she had been easy to deal with when Ralph was alive. She'd never had any interest in anything beyond herself. This new development of Benjamina interfering with the business was a new addition to Queenie's daily stresses that she did not need.

The whole experience had greatly fatigued Queenie and she hauled herself up the stairs to find Jenkins waiting for her on the landing. Her maid put her to bed and though she lay awake for a minute or so wondering about this mysterious fire, she was soon fast asleep again.

∞

It was the witching hour. Queenie awoke with a start. It took her some moments to become aware that she was not in the dream, a dream of being lost in a crowded marketplace, jostled by people all around her, pushing and shoving. But she had pushed on, as she was frantic in the dream, looking for her lost child. A horrible dream, losing your child like that. It wasn't Ralph she'd been searching for in the dream; it had been her daughters. She dreamt of them often, yet always as little girls not as the babies that were gone. She thought, *If my girls had survived, all this would be different. They'd have been strong characters, like me. Not like the King men. All of them are weak fools.*

She felt a tear escape her eye and settle on her cheek. She wiped it away and suddenly felt forlorn, overcome with grief and worry. All her children were dead, and though she hadn't been fond of Ralph, he'd been her son.

'Jenkins,' she muttered. But her lady's maid in the next room would never hear that, even as devoted as she was. 'Jenkins!' she called and soon heard movement and the door opening.

'What now?' said Jenkins, looking a bit of a fright with her grey hair in a plait over her shoulder, the fringe sticking up at all angles, lit up like a spirit from the lamp she held up.

'Jenkins, you're getting old,' said Queenie.

'You woke me up at this hour, to tell me that? You stupid goose.'

'No, no. I had a dream. An awful dream of common people, all around me, manhandling me. It was atrocious!'

Jenkins came over and helped Queenie sit up by rearranging her pillows. She did look aged and tired. Jenkins had been in her employ for fifty years, coming to this house as a kitchen maid aged only nine. She was the person that Queenie relied upon for everything. Jenkins sat down on the bed and sighed, pushing her messy hair back from her face.

'You had that dream because of the trouble at the brickyard tonight. It's all about that, dealing with those scurrilous people. If we can call them people. Setting fire to things now, are they? Animals. No, that's too good for 'em. Monsters, they are.'

Queenie nodded and wiped her eyes again. 'I do not understand these people. We give them paid work, freedom to hire their own families if they wish. And still they treat us like the very devil.'

'Ungrateful, they are,' said Jenkins. 'And they will never learn. Now, enough unbroken sleep tonight. Get some rest. All this kerfuffle is aging me terribly. I cannot be doing with it at my advanced years. I need my sleep, woman!'

'I am sorry, Jenkins. Please forgive me,' she said, her voice catching in a little sob.

'Now, now. Don't upset yourself. Just sleep now. Nothing for you to worry your head about at this hour. We shall talk it all through in the light of day. I'm going back to my bed. Good night, Miss Alice.'

'Good night, Jenkins.'

Jenkins shuffled out of the room, taking the lamp with her. The room fell into inky darkness again. Queenie had never liked the dark. As a child, she and her sister had shared a room all of their childhood and most nights shared a bed. They had cuddled up together, sleeping like spoons, she stroking Selina's hair or Selina stroking hers, whispering secrets and stories to each other until sleep took them.

But their parents split the two of them up when Selina began acting strangely in her later teens. And then, Queenie was married off to Ralph King Senior and they took Selina away and put her in that asylum. That made it sound like a place of rest, a kind of hospital, but it wasn't. It was a prison for mad people. Queenie's new husband forbade her from seeing her sister in that place. She was found hanging there. Selina. Beautiful, clever and kind Selina had killed herself. It had broken Queenie's heart.

Since then, the only person she had given her heart to was Jenkins, but always in the back of her mind was the hard fact that it was a business arrangement, of course. She paid Jenkins to be with her. Yes, Jenkins was fond of her, she was sure of that. And Jenkins knew no other life or family, had left her own at such a tender age and lived here with Queenie ever since. But still, it was not true family, not true love, unsullied by money or duty. The last time she had fallen for anyone had been those few months before marriage, a kind of madness she thought of it now. Once married, she discovered the cold truth about her husband: that he had no capacity for love and that he wanted to bed virgin maids, not her. And so he did, regularly. Sometimes with tragic consequences.

She lay in her bed, determined to sleep, but the light was bothering her eyes. What light? She screwed her eyes tight shut, but still she could somehow feel it playing across her eyelids. She opened up one eye speculatively, determined not to be roused from her warm, cosy position. And there it was, a strip of light coming through the gap in the curtains. Surely she had not slept the night through and the dawn had come. She opened both eyes and stared at the light. It was not daylight. It had a silvery quality to it. And then, with a sinking feeling of nausea, she knew where she had seen that light before.

She stared at it, watching that same shifting shimmer she had seen all those years before, coming through her curtains, just the same as when the ghost had visited her after her husband's death. She had seen it again at the grave of her husband. It had spoken to her, cursed the family, the house, their future. She had believed it then. But since, she had come to think that it was just her nerves that caused that false vision, just a belated reaction to her husband's death. An imaginary thing concocted in her addled mind, twisted by grief. Though she had hated her husband, grief was an odd fish. Nobody knew how it could affect you. Seeing things could happen to anyone placed under great strain. And after all, none of the ghost's wild curses had come to pass. It was all nonsense. She had come to know this. She had convinced herself. She wasn't like Selina . . .

It was the ghost of Betsy Blaize who had visited her, beneath her window and beside the grave. Twenty-four years ago Blaize had died penniless on the iron bridge, her newborn child in her arms, taken in by someone. The baby on the bridge, they called it. The bastard child of Queenie's husband, conceived by violent rape upon that poor servant girl in their employ, young Betsy Blaize. She had visited Queenie in this ghostly guise those two times, foretelling disaster for the King family, '*This house will fall . . . Dark times are ahead . . .*'

Yet despite her fear then, nothing had happened to Queenie or any of the family to confirm this horrible fate. Yes, Margaret had eloped soon after, which threatened scandal on the family, but people soon forgot and moved on. The daughter of the house had at least married the artist, which Queenie ensured was reported in the local newspaper. Since those days, the King fortune had gone from strength to strength, acquiring land and businesses galore. They were now richer than ever. So, the flame of her fear had guttered and gone out over the years, replaced by disbelief that it had ever happened at all.

But now, eighteen years since she saw it last, that same flickering light was here again. But perhaps it was not a ghost. It could be moonlight. She shut her eyes with the thought and willed herself to sleep. But it seemed to burn brighter through her closed eyelids and she could not bear to keep them shut. It was brighter, almost white in its intensity now. She felt drawn to it, the mystery of it. But also, a dread in the pit of her stomach. She felt her body move almost without her will. She pushed back the covers and stood up from her bed. She walked over to the window and paused at the gap in the curtains. She felt as if the spirit were moving her, not herself. She pulled back one of the curtains and looked down, into the light.

Blaize stood there, in the family graveyard that Queenie could see from her bedroom window. The same bright white hair and skin, the same spectral blue eyes. She had dreamt of this vision many times since, but never seen it again with her waking eyes. And despite her determination over the years to disbelieve it, she could not deny its terrible presence there beneath her.

Just as before, its words came to her in her mind, without its lips moving.

'Have you forgotten?' said Blaize. 'Have you forgotten my words?'

Queenie thought, *You said the house would fall. But it has not.* Then Queenie grasped the handle to the window and opened it to the night air. She spoke aloud, 'I am not afraid of you now!' She had tried to be brave but her voice came out as a squeak.

'You *have* forgotten. I told you once, the crucible will purify. After the fire, I will come again. A baby will bridge the divide.'

Queenie had forgotten those last words. They were said to her by the grave in the second visitation. Somehow, over the years, she had blanked them out. Not understanding them at the time, she had simply forgotten them. But now, tonight, after Troon's visit and news from the brickworks, she felt a prickle of recognition. The fire. *After the fire, I will come again.*

'So, here you are again, after the fire.' Queenie spoke more steadily now. She felt stronger, more able to reason with this creature. 'What do you want this time?'

The spirit's eyes burned bluer than ever. They seemed to bore a hole in Queenie's gaze, so bright she wanted to look away, but could not.

'Justice.'

Justice? Queenie thought. *I have been a good woman. I have managed my family and my businesses well. My workers are paid fairly. What else can I do? Give all our riches to the poor? Ridiculous!*

The spirit answered, 'You lie to yourself.'

Queenie felt intensely uncomfortable. Blaize could read her mind, it seemed.

Suddenly, the ghost raised its arms and cried out, 'My baby! Where is my baby?'

The face of Blaize was horrifying, twisted in its misery and glowing whiter than snow beneath the sun. Its eyes seemed to expand, its black mouth too, gaping open. Queenie had to steel herself against this horror and keep her wits about her.

'I do not know,' said Queenie firmly, though it were not strictly true. She had heard rumours, from Margaret first back then, and more recently from Jenkins, that the babe was taken in by a local family back in '34. She knew no more than that. If it had lived, it would be a young person now with children of its own, perhaps. If it had lived. And she had decided long ago, that although the child were a King, a bastard child of the head of the King family, it had no place here at Southover. It had done well to escape the poisonous men of the King family. She was happy for it, just as she had been happy for Margaret when she escaped. She had seen that a wrong had been done to this girl, to Betsy Blaize the maid, raped from the age of twelve, pregnant at fifteen, dead at sixteen. It was a terrible wrong, but what could Queenie do for her now? It was all a long time ago and the child was lucky. It had

74

escaped not only the Kings but a life with an outcast for a mother, an unmarried mother. It should count itself lucky. 'What do you want from me?' Queenie asked.

'Find my child. Improve her lot in life.'

So, it was a girl then, the baby on the bridge. A girl that had been taken in and looked after by a local family. Queenie remembered what she'd said to Margaret, all those years ago, *It's a fortunate child that escapes the King family*. 'And what if she doesn't want to be found? What if she's happy as she is?'

The ghost said nothing. It had no answer to that. Queenie was emboldened by this and went on, 'And what can you, a mere spirit, do to me if I do not follow your instructions?'

Blaize's arms fell, her mouth closed. It stared at Queenie for what seemed like an age. Then it spoke again, quietly, almost a whisper, though Queenie could hear it as if the ghost were speaking into her ear, 'The fire will wash you clean. *All of you.*'

Chapter 6

'Brothers and sisters of the brickyard, I bid thee welcome. Our spare time when we are not slaving at work is precious and so I doubly thank'ee for meeting here today. Let us not waste this time with pleasantries. We must state our aims and draw our plans together.'

Owen glanced around the room at the men, women, children, infants and babes gathered there in the arched brick cellar of The Swan Inn. There had been smaller meetings in past weeks, but this was the largest yet by far. The majority of their number were women, as female workers made up the bulk of the brickmaking force. Most brickmoulders were women, though some men had made it their skilled trade as well. Men did the heavy digging and brickburning, and operated the machinery. Child brickworkers were numerous too, with boys and girls hired equally as clay carriers and to do other odd jobs around the site. Thus, the whole family could be employed as brickies. As Owen surveyed them all, it felt to him as if all human life was present, all the poor folk of human life at any rate. The men puffed on their pipes, the women held their babies or knitted. Always knitting to do and never a moment wasted, those women. Some men drank their time away in taverns but Owen never saw a woman in his community waste her time, though he knew some of the outsiders that camped along the river had just as many drunken women as their men. Not in his area though, where he lived. The women were the salt of the earth. Many here were nodding at Adam Jones's words. Some squinted at him, their faces betraying that they were unsure about him or perhaps they just required spectacles they could never afford. Everyone here was listening intently and the sheer number of people squashed into the meeting room in the tavern basement was enough to show the strength of feeling.

Adam went on, 'Afore the King family bought our brickyard a year hence, most of you will remember our old boss, Mr Cotterhill. Yes, he was a bit of a fool with business and yes, he sadly went bankrupt. Nobody can deny that. But he was a good mon and a good manager of people. He was fair and he was just. He could see the skill in what we do. He and his good lady wife celebrated champion brickmakers, rewarding those moulders who worked not only the quickest but with the highest quality, and even the child who lugged the clay on his head wasna below Cotterhill's attentions. He gave bonuses on a weekly rotation, so that every good worker received his or her due. He had plans to train his workforce to produce more fancy wares, decorative tiles and so forth.

He built houses for us and charged low rents. He organised a meal every Easter Sunday for the whole workforce at his own expense. And our children were hired by Mr Cotterhill himself. He paid 'em fairly and charged his overseers to look out for their safety. He was a good mon, a fair mon, a just mon.'

Owen saw the nodding heads increase and grunts of approval all round.

'But now we have the Kings. They believe we have no skill whatsoever. They believe we are the lowest sort of folk. Some of us have overheard Cyril King say as much in his rare visits to the yard. They have put up our rents, left our houses to fall into rack and ruin with no repairs, no maintenance. There is an end to the annual meal and to the bonuses the hardest workers enjoyed. There has been a simplification of our wares, so that all plans for expanding the works and the benefits of new training have gone. Our hours are longer than ever. They have introduced the unfair "back pence" system, whereby they withhold part of our wages until the end of the season, which is only paid if there have been no unforeseen incidents that year to reduce their profits. The Kings have also callously changed our contracts in another way, so that now the children are hired by the moulder him or herself, so that no legal responsibility resides with the Kings in respect of any child on the site. If a child is injured or overworked or hurt in any way, the moulder must answer for it. And this, when brick moulders are already engaged in producing a thousand bricks a day at a minimum, they are being asked to look out at the same time for the welfare of the dozens of children that work all over the site? This was once the responsibility of the owner and his foreman. But now each moulder must become an overseer with none of the pay to go with it. It is a nonsense.'

Each of these points was greeted with a disgruntled cheer, a cheerless cheer of angry agreement.

'And now, brothers and sisters, the latest degradation. There is talk of reducing our wages.'

Some men stood up at this point and yelled out a hearty 'boo', shaking their fists and cursing. Women were shaking their heads and patting their babies' bottoms furiously.

'I am sure you will agree that this is the final straw that will break our backs.'

Adam's head fell and he shook it slowly, then wiped a shaking hand across his eyes. Women frowned in sympathy, men puffed thoughtfully on their pipes and grimaced in solidarity. Owen recalled his dad telling him Adam should've been an actor, with all his theatrics. Owen had to agree. But at least Adam was putting it to good use, not using his dramatic skills to charm women or cheat working folk as a confidence trickster; he was using his charisma to help his fellow brickworkers. And Owen loved him for that. Worshipped him, if truth be known.

Adam looked up and scanned the crowd, his gaze seeming to fall on each face in turn. His next words were spoken so low, the crowd seemed to edge forward as one to hear them. 'But are we to be broken so easily?'

There was general muttering.

'Are we, my friends?' Adam said, louder.

There were a few cries of 'No!' and someone called out, 'We inna, by God!'

'Then it is time for us to join together. Just as the brickmasters are joined, so should we be. They conspire to lower wages. So we should combine to stand against them. All gathered here today and those not here due to other commitments must join together as one. We must form a union of brickworkers, with the same aims and objectives. Strength in numbers, brothers and sisters!'

This was met with a hearty cheer by many voices. A baby started to cry.

'No to lower wages! No to longer hours! No to poorer contracts!'

Each was cheered on by the whole assembly now and many were up on their feet, including Owen.

'Yes to respect!'

A great cheer.

'Yes to a fair wage for a fair day's work!'

An even greater cheer.

'Yes to the United Operative Brickmakers' Benevolent and Protective Society of Ironbridge, Broseley and Vicinity!'

A yet greater cheer, showing a hearty approval of the idea of a union of brickworkers, yet some confused muttering as to what a mouthful it was.

The meeting had been a wonderful success. A table had been set up near the door, manned by Owen, Royce and Brain, writing down names in a ledger and taking the dues of tuppence to join the society. Meanwhile, Adam stood beside them fielding queries and slapping men on their backs and leaning in to women with a smile and ruffling the hair on the heads of children. Almost every person in the room joined up and the air was filled with plans of when the next meeting would be, what would be discussed and what action might be agreed upon to be taken against the Kings. And the name of the Kings rang around the room like a curse to Owen's ears.

There was a light pat on Owen's shoulder and he looked up to see Adam looking down seriously at him.

'A word, cousin?'

Adam moved over to a darkened corner and Owen followed him.

'Owen, lad. Well, I suppose I shouldna call you lad any more, now that you are grown. It should be mon!'

'Yes mon!' laughed Owen.

'Now, to business.' The smiles were over and Adam was frowning down at him. 'I hear the King girl is sweet on you.'

'Oh well, I wouldna go that far or anything like it. I met her in the street and sold her a pie, is all.'

'I hear different. I hear she couldna take her eyes off you. All blushes and how-do-you-do.'

'That be from Royce and Brain, would it? I wouldna trust either of them to report a rainstorm even when they're drenched in it.'

'I see,' mused Adam. 'Did she seem well disposed towards you? Could you approach her again without a fuss, d'yer think?'

Owen felt his own cheeks start to flush at the thought of Beatrice and cursed himself for it. Adam didn't miss a thing and added, 'I see she's had quite the effect on you.'

'She is a pretty thing, there's no denying.'

'Well, dunna be fooled. All those Kings are poison. Your mother knows that more'n any. But we need someone inside there. We're trying to get to some of the staff working in the house, but it's proving tricky. If you could ingratiate yourself with Miss Beatrice, now ... that would be summat. Get to know her a bit, get her on side a bit. Find out what the Kings are planning. There's talk, but then there's knowing. Ask a few questions, find out a bit of this and that. She'd be interested to talk with you again, you reckon?'

Owen's thoughts were racing ahead. He had thought of little else but Beatrice since their meeting a few days ago. Of course, he hadn't told a soul. He had tried to find a reason to justify speaking to her again and had come up with nothing. And now a reason to talk to her was being handed to him on a plate, encouraged and required, even. He had licence now to pursue this girl, this marvellous girl. But it left a taste behind it, something slightly bitter. To see the girl and talk to her, to help the cause by doing so, yet at the same time lying to her by doing so. She was a King though, he must remember that.

'I do reckon I could do that. I am certain I could.'

'Good mon,' said Adam and put a rough arm around him, grinning and winking. 'I knew I could rely on family. And a good-looking lad like you'll have her eating out of your hand in no time. Report back to me once a week, whenever you can get away from your father. I think it best to keep your parents out of this, dunna you? Just between ourselves, like. Dunna want to upset them, eh?'

'Arr, wouldna wanna do that,' said Owen and nodded. *Secrets and lies. This is how they begin*, thought Owen.

Beatrice looked through the window again. Still no sign. Madame was droning on about the etiquette of the ballroom and how one should comport oneself in regards to the filling in of the dance card, but Beatrice wasn't really listening. She was waiting to see if Owen the pieman was going to turn up again. But the lesson was almost over and he wasn't there. Her disappointment was acute and surprised her. She had thought about the lad a few times in the past few days, but had put such thoughts out of her head. What was the point? He was not the sort of person anyone in her family would encourage her to make an acquaintance of, a door-to-door pie salesman. She had noticed that his nails had been grimy with grey dust and wondered how much of that muck went into the pies, but perhaps none, as the pie certainly tasted good. She ran her tongue over her lips and could almost taste it there, the savoury pork, the sweet apple. Delicious.

Madame was coming to an end and ushering Beatrice to the door. She was a little ashamed that she had listened to so little of what had been taught her and knew she would regret it once her first ball came along and she had no idea what to do. But she cared so little about such things, despite her mother's insistence that she must learn the correct protocol for 'coming out' – such a strange expression. Coming out of what? Into what? Childhood to marriage, she supposed. She did not feel ready to be married.

She left her dancing teacher's house by the front door this time, shut it behind her and descended the steps, glancing up and down the street for her mother. Late again. Her mother was the worst timekeeper. She sighed and considered going back inside, but she couldn't be bothered. Then she saw a figure walking towards her and smiling right at her. It was him. It was the pie boy.

'Miss,' he said and touched his cap respectfully.

'Owen!' she cried. 'I wondered if I would see you today, at the back door. But you did not arrive.'

She knew she was gushing, but she didn't care.

Owen had stopped before her, still with a smile on his face. Such a nice face.

'I inna selling pies today, miss. Day off.'

'Do you sell pies all over town, then? All over Shropshire, I wonder? They are such good pies, I'm sure they're in great demand.'

'Did you think I was a pie-seller? That it was my trade?'

He was still smiling, with an amused look in his eye that he knew something she didn't. 'Well, I thought . . .'

'Ah, well, you know what thought did.'

'What did thought do?'

'Followed a dust cart and thought it were a wedding.'

Beatrice stared at him, puzzled at this nonsense. But his smile got to her and she grinned broadly, then laughed aloud and so did he. 'I have no idea what you are talking about!'

'Neither do I, much of the time, miss. May I walk you to your destination?'

'Ah, I am waiting upon my mother again and do not know when she will arrive. She is always delayed by something. But we can talk here on the steps a while. And you must tell me, what is your trade, if it is not selling pies?'

'I just sell pies on a Sunday sometimes, to help out my mother. But it inna my trade. I'm a brickburner, just like my father.'

Beatrice looked more closely at him. 'You work at a brickyard?'

'I do.'

Was his the face she saw from the coach that day? It couldn't be. Could it? What were the chances?

'Not the King brickworks?'

'The very same. Your family are my bosses, so it probably inna the done thing to be talking to you like this in the street.'

She ignored that last comment – the done thing never really interested her – and put her hand to her mouth. 'But this is extraordinary. I saw you, I'm sure I did. The very first day I arrived in Shropshire. Our coach stopped beside the brickworks and Maman – that's what I call my mother – Maman told me that it belonged to the Kings. And I saw a young man and we looked at each other. Could it be you? Tell me it was you. How marvellous that would be!'

Owen's smile had gone and his cheeks were reddening. He looked away from her and muttered, 'I dunna think so, miss. I dunna make a habit of staring at young ladies.'

'Well, perhaps you could not see me clearly from where you were, but I saw you, I'm sure I did! How wonderful! And now we are met again, by chance. How strange the world is!'

He looked back at her now, not smiling, cheeks still flushed, his eyes meaningful. ''Tis a strange thing indeed.'

'Certainly. So tell me about life as a – what did you say you did? A brick something?'

'Brickburner, miss.'

'What does that involve?'

'I bake bricks.'

'Tell me more. I want to know. What is your average day like?'

'It will be tedious for a young lady like yourself, surely.'

'How can you say a young lady like *yourself* when you don't even know me? Once you do know me, you will find that I want to know everything. I am hungry to speak to every person who ever lived, if needs be, to discover the truth about the world and all that is in it. So, please, if you will tell me what the life of a brickburner is about.'

He looked taken aback by this little pronouncement – people often did, not expecting a girl to be interested in anything other than dances and little dogs – but he soon recovered himself and went on.

'I work in the kilns with my father. We are responsible for the baking of the bricks until they are ready. We have a great responsibility, as if we mess up our job then the bricks will be ruined. They have to be stacked just so, and the fires must be maintained just so. It is a job of some serious responsibility.'

'I can imagine,' she said, though she could not. And, as usual, her mouth ran faster than her thoughts. 'Actually, I cannot. I must admit I have never once in my life thought about the making of a brick. I have seen thousands of them, tens of thousands most likely. And never once have I considered where they all come from.'

'Like most people,' said Owen. 'When people look at a house, most don't even notice the bricks. But there's blood in those bricks.'

'Whatever do you mean?'

'Blood and sweat and misery. Long, hard shifts of boys, girls, men and women. Digging the clay from the ground, weathering it in great heaps for months, carrying it on their heads or in heavy, unwieldy handcarts, feeding it into the mills, to cut it and wet it and flatten it and make it easier to work with. Then moulding it into bricks on tables, a thousand a day. Then carried to the kilns and stacked and arranged just so and baked, the fires burning and watched like hawks do, for days and nights on end. Then carried and stacked again, transported by horse and cart and barge all over the county, the country even. Nobody thinks of all that, when they pass by a house, a row of houses, a whole street of 'em. The time it took to make each brick, the effort and the backbreaking hours and the accidents at the brickyard that took young lives. Like I said, there is blood in those bricks, every brick.'

Beatrice gazed at Owen. The whole time he had been making this extraordinary speech, his eyes had been on hers and she had felt paralysed by them, their blue intensity. 'You are truly an astonishing person, Owen.'

Now she had embarrassed him. He looked askance, nervous and out of sorts, but she did not regret what she had said. She meant it. Her great-grandmother, uncle and step-grandmother – her new family would probably have thought it akin to a crime to be standing here, talking to a brickworker. They saw their workers as objects, she knew that from the way they spoke of them, moving them about here and there like so many chess pieces. But this young man was no object. His mind was alive. It flowed out through his words and through his eyes.

'I ought to go, miss,' he mumbled. 'I've said too much.'

'No, I fear you have not said enough. I wish to know more, about my family's brickworks and what life is like for you there. Can we meet again, here next week? I will tell my mother I need a chaperone no longer and will walk home alone. I'm sure I can convince her. Then perhaps we can talk a while, on the way. What do you say, Owen?'

'I say yes to that, miss.'

'Won't you call me Bea?'

'Maybe next time, miss,' he said, and with that he smiled again at her, touched his cap and turned away. She watched him walk down the street but then he stopped. He turned back and looked at her. His smile was gone and he stared at her intently, a worried look upon his face. She raised her hand a little to gesture farewell, but he turned quickly back and hurried away. His face was like the weather here in Shropshire, constantly on the move and as predictable as a moth. She was sure he felt deeply about things, sure he thought deeply about things too. But how did Owen feel about her? That was the question left burning in her mind, as she saw Maman hurrying up the street to meet her, thankfully and gloriously late as ever.

On their walk home, she said to her mother, 'When you were a little girl, who were your friends here in Ironbridge?'

'I didn't have many,' said Maman, with a bit of a sigh. 'I was a loner and loved to read and play on my piano. I was schooled at home, as you know, so I did not have much of an opportunity to meet friends.'

'You did not have any friends, not one?' gasped Beatrice. 'Nobody like my Juliette or Ana?' Beatrice thought with a pang of her friends from home and reminded herself she must write to them. How she missed her dear friends and their laughter, their secrets and giggles. She wondered when she would see them again, when they would end this extended visit to England. Were they to stay for a month, a year? Forever? Each time she asked her mother, she had no answer but 'a while, Bea'. For the time being Maman seemed to be in no hurry to leave this place she called home.

'I did have one friend, yes. A dear friend. But . . . we fell out, sadly.'

'Why did you fall out?'

'It's a long story.'

'What was she called?'

'Her name was Anny,' said Maman in a small voice. Beatrice stole a glance at her to see that she was frowning. 'But that is enough about that,' she added, peevishly.

Beatrice knew that tone well. Maman did not want to speak about it any further. They walked on, along the street that led from the town square towards the hill that took them up to Southover. She watched the folk walk past, some well dressed, some poorly dressed, all consumed with their own thoughts and business and lives. It often hit her with a little shock how placid a person might look on the outside, yet inside their heads was a whirlwind of thoughts and memories, feelings and passions. Though she walked silently beside her mother, her own mind was consumed with curiosity into this friend of her mother's, Anny, about whom she had never heard a word mentioned. She kept trying to phrase and rephrase her next question about this Anny in her mind, to make it sound by the by, of passing interest, as if she didn't really care. But her mother spoke first.

'I'm sorry I snapped, *chérie*. It's being here, back at home. Makes me think of the past and I become maudlin. And I mustn't. It is all water under the iron bridge, long ago and long gone. Now, the future, that is something I'd much rather talk about. Tell me about your dancing.'

Chapter 7

'You've seen her then?'

Owen met up with Adam in the basement of The Swan. Adam bought him a pint of beer and the taste of it was good and earthy. He smacked his lips and answered, 'I have.'

'What is she like?'

'She is a talkative girl and not stupid – clever, in fact. And open to talking to anyone, it seems, myself included.'

Adam was pleased. 'She'll be easy to handle, if she's friendly and trusting.'

'She is that,' said Owen and in saying it, felt the truth of it and the distaste of how easy it would be to fool her.

'But how did it go, talking with her? Did you make any headway?' said Adam with impatience.

'It went well.' Owen sensed he needed to impress him further, adding, 'It went better than I could've planned.'

'How so?'

'She asked me – *she* asked *me*, mind – if I wanted to walk her home from her dance lesson next week and talk further.'

'That be sebunctious news, mon! I knew you'd manage it. Now, we need to know more about their plans. Do you think she'll talk about her family a bit? Or too loyal?'

'That I dunna know, as yet. I shall figure it out the next time. I aim to tread carefully.'

'Arr, tread lightly, agreed. But we have little time. The Kings will make their move soon, as they'll have had wind of our meetings and will want to curb it. The fire at the sheds will have unnerved them. Try to find out all you can but dunna look like you're trying to find out anything.'

'Yes, mon. Understood.'

'Now then, enough of that. Do you have your eye on any local girl?'

Owen was taken aback. His father's cousin had never shown an interest in him to this extent. He'd always been roughly affectionate with him, since he was a little boy lugging the clay to Adam's table. But he'd not sat with him and talked like this.

'None in particular,' said Owen, thinking of Beatrice. Yet another lie, then.

'Find yerself one, mon. Handsome type like you needs a girl. Take his mind off things. Seek some pleasure in this weary road to death we call life.'

'I suppose.'

'No suppose about it. And make sure she's the right sort. A girl like you, from around where you live. She'll understand you, listen to you. Her parents and your parents will know each other and get on. These things matter, lad. They matter.'

Owen realised that Adam was not so subtly warning him off any thoughts of Beatrice.

'After I lost my Judith, I thought I'd never want another. But when I met my Martha, I knew she was the right one. And her Quaker parents were good, kind folk and they approved the match. And now she is with child, I couldna be happier. It is a wonderful thing, to know you'll be a father. A settling thing. Secures a man's place in the world, to start a family.'

'Arr, you're right, of course. I shall keep my eyes peeled,' said Owen, to placate him. But the only girl who really seemed to understand him was Beatrice. The real him, the poet in him, same as his father, who'd been lucky and found a local girl who understood this about him. His mother would often speak of how thoughtful and interesting his father was. Beatrice had seen it, too, she had called Owen 'an astonishing person'. What local girl would ever say something like that? He was smitten; he knew he was.

A week later, Owen was waiting for Beatrice when she came out of her dance teacher's house and stood on the step. He saw from her searching eyes that she was waiting for him, too.

'Owen! I am so glad to see you. I was so hoping you'd come, but didn't know if you would.'

She was an open book about her feelings and thoughts. She didn't seem to care who knew it. *No fear in her*, he thought. *Not a bit of it.*

'Miss. Shall we walk?'

'Yes, let's. My mother agreed to no chaperone, as I know my way about the town now. Let us walk along the riverside and then I can take the woodland path home, up to Southover. I have explored the woods a bit too and find I adore them. I was brought up in the city of Paris, as you know, so woodland and countryside are all new to me.'

She did rattle on. But he loved to listen to it. Her accent was English through and through but there was a touch of the foreigner about it, something you couldn't quite put your finger on. She was from off, as they said around here, and however good her accent was, the foreign nature of her way of speaking and her dress, even the way she held her head to one side or flourished her hands while talking, all spoke of something exotic.

'What is Paris like?'

'It is a huge, smelly city. But it is my home and I love it. There are street vendors calling and singing their wares. There are boatmen on the River Seine, crowded and shouting, not unlike here with your River Severn. There was music everywhere, in our home, a singer with an accordion on the streets or a violinist two doors down. Artists painting, bakers selling sweet pastries. The best wine in the world. Yes, I have tasted a little,' and she smiled coquettishly at this.

They had crossed the road and gone down the steps below the iron bridge to the river path. This sunny May Sunday was the perfect day, apple and pear blossom snowing in wafts from the trees that lined the river, drifting into the water, muddied and lost there. Every word she said was like a sip of wine to him, delicious, bittersweet and intoxicating. But he must keep his wits about him.

'It all sounds a bit too good to be true.'

'Oh, I have only said the good things, for the most part. There is poverty, terrible poverty. Beggars on the streets, worse than here. People starving to death. I've seen corpses in the gutter with my own eyes.'

'People starve here too.'

'They do?'

'In the winter, a lot of the brickworkers are laid off, as there is not so much work to be done. They look for other jobs, the men in the iron trade, the women whatever they can find. But some find their way to the dreaded workhouse. And some never find work and they starve.'

Beatrice gasped. 'Is there nobody to help them, in this small, welcoming town? I thought it would only be the big cities of the world that cared little enough of their thousands of poor to let them starve. I assumed here would be different. Everyone seems so caring and friendly here.'

'Family help, friends help, where they can. But when you have precious little for your own, it is hard to share it with others. We do what we can. But we must live. We earn so little for our labours. It inna possible to spare even a penny some days.'

They walked on, Beatrice quiet. He glanced at her, the pretty profile in repose, biting her lip. He had to walk slightly behind her, her skirts too wide for the riverside path. It gave him the perfect opportunity to study that profile, the curve of her neck and the way her dark hair was swept up at its nape. One strand was loose and he could not take his eyes away from it.

'Owen, may I ask you something?'

'You can ask. No harm in asking.'

'Do my family treat you well? At the brickworks, I mean. Are the Kings good bosses?'

The girl was making it too easy for him! He was glad, knowing how pleased Adam would be at his progress. Then he swallowed down a lump in his throat and coughed. Pride and shame, in the very same moment. Never in his life had he felt so muddled.

'Do you want to hear the polite answer? Or the truth, miss?'

'Why, the truth, without a doubt.'

She had stopped on the path and stared at him, awaiting his answer.

'You might hear some things that inna to your liking.'

'Before you go on, please understand something about me. I was brought up with Maman and Maman alone. You have probably heard from gossip that my mother had run away from her family because they did not approve of her match. It was a great, romantic gesture. But what you may not know is that my father tragically died when she was with child. So, I grew up with a widow for a mother, who made her way in the world alone. We never had pomp and finery when I was a child. My mother taught pupils at our small home, which never brought in riches. I was not raised a King. And I had no concept of family, other than my mother. So I am not a King and do not wish to be. I am Beatrice Ashford. I am myself and always will be. Anything you say to me about the Kings, I will listen to without prejudice. I merely want the truth, from my friends, my family, from the world. I want to *know*. So, if you please, go straight ahead.'

He had watched her mouth and eyes as she spoke. He wanted to take her by the shoulders and kiss that mouth. What was he doing? What was happening to him? He wanted to say so much. He wanted to tell her the truth, about Adam, about his role as a spy. He almost said it. Who could resist such a pure, simple appeal to truth? But unlike her, he did not stand alone. He had loyalties, deep ones, rooted three hundred feet down in the Shropshire earth, down in the layers of Ironbridge clay.

'The Kings dunna treat their workers well.'

'But how? What do they do?' She stared at him, her eyes welling with tears. She could be so moved, by only this? He could not look her in the eye any longer. Her straightforward honesty shamed him.

'Let us walk on, miss. I'll tell you how.'

They fell back into walking, but slowly now, his words slowing to match their pace, thoughtfully chosen, carefully.

'We had an old master before the Kings, who treated us well. Fair contracts, good hours, useful training to better ourselves and solid housing, well maintained. Now we have lost all of those.'

'Who is responsible? My uncle? My great-grandmother?'

'Both, I believe. We do not see the elder Mrs King, but Mr Cyril King appears down the works from time to time. And it is never a good day when he comes around.'

'I am sorry to say that I concur with that,' she said, her voice small. Perhaps she had a little loyalty to her family after all, but could not help but speak the truth. 'I do not like him.'

'Few do, miss. You inna alone in that.'

'I have not fallen foul of him myself, but there is something in my belly that tells me he is a cruel man.'

'That he be, miss. That he be.' He thought on his feet and felt it might be the right time to push a little further.

'Does he speak of us? Do they discuss such things as us poor folk at home?'

'Oh yes, well, from time to time. I have overheard things. And I am not pleased by what I hear. Uncle speaks of workers as "things".'

'Things?'

'Yes, objects. Things. I heard Cyril say once, "A worker is a damnable thing."'

'*Things*,' he repeated. 'I am not a thing. My father is not a thing.' He thought of his conversation with his father, that the masters saw only money when they looked at them. He assumed it were true. Now he heard it from the horse's mouth. They sickened him, the Kings.

'Oh, indeed not! I know that. You believe me, don't you?'

This girl though, she was not one of them. And yet she was part of them, the youngest of them and with the pig Cyril having had no children, she was the heir. The heir to the King fortune. And she was walking beside him – Owen Malone, brickburner – sharing confidences with him. A stroke of luck for the brickworkers' union, a blessing and a curse for him. He was torn between kissing her and betraying all of her confidences.

'I do believe you,' he said, then added with a small smile, 'I think.'

'Oh, please believe me. Maybe I could even help.'

There she went again, laying his path so conveniently for him. She was too kind, too rash. Too lovely.

'Do they talk of the brickyard?' he said. 'Of their plans?'

'What kind of plans?'

Had he pushed it too far? Perhaps he should have saved this for another conversation. He did not want to spook her, as a young horse must be coaxed into having a man on its back and only in its own time.

'Oh, nothing particular. We worry, that's all. About the future.'

'The future of the brickworks?'

'No, not as such. Bricks are needed everywhere. People need houses. We line shafts and tunnels in the mines with bricks these days, over timber. On farms, barns are being built in brick, as well as stables and other outhouses. We need bricks. We need clay too. Think of all of the stuff men dig up from the ground. Which would be the most precious to mankind, do you think? Gold? Or clay?'

He glanced at her to see her face had changed from cloudy to sunshine.

'Now you've explained it so well, my answer must be clay. But until then, I would have said gold, I think.'

'Why gold?'

'Well, now that I think of it, there is no worth in gold. It is not ideal for making anything but something pretty and decorative. It is swapped as a thing of value, but is not particularly useful in itself.'

'So which is more precious? Gold? Or clay?'

'I would say you have proved your point admirably. It is clay, of course!'

'I would say so, miss.'

'The more one thinks of it, the more things one finds that are made of clay. Why, clay has contributed more to our comfort and well-being than gold ever did, or perhaps any other substance, save coal.'

'You are quite right. Coal, clay and iron. We dig all three from the ground round here and all three power the world.'

'What you do is mightily important, Owen. I hope you are proud of that.'

'I would be more so, if our wages were higher.'

There came the clouds across that pretty, pale face again. Had he done it again, ruined the moment, startled the filly?

'I heard them talk of wages the other day. They say . . . I heard them say . . . the wages of the brickworkers were to be lowered. I heard my great-grandmother talk of it, and Cyril and Benjamina. They were arguing but it was decided in the end.'

And there he had it. What he wanted. Exactly what he wanted. Adam would be pleased as punch with him, for wheedling that information out of the girl. But all he felt was sick, sick with the knowledge that their pay was soon to drop and how hard that would make his life, his mother and father's lives, all of their lives, sick with betraying this girl who told confidences so easily.

Now they had reached the woodland path. There was a moment of complicit understanding that he would not proceed further with her than the river. This path was open and peopled by passers-by. But the woods were hidden and shadowy. A respectable girl would not be seen alone with a young man there.

'You are silent, Owen. What say you to this news? Have I helped you by telling you this? I do hope so.'

What could he say to this? The girl was too good, too nice. Was there ever such a girl, so honest and true? And could such a girl really be a King?

'We suspected it,' he muttered, intending to say no more, to play it down and leave her now, not wanting to pry more from her, to leave her be. But he couldn't help himself. 'I have never . . . I have never met such a person as you, miss. Most of the rich care nothing for us. What makes you interested in us? In the brick-works? In clay and the people who work it? Why do you care?'

Beatrice cocked her head and gazed into middle distance. How lovely she was when she was considering, the deep brown eyes darkening with thought. 'I suppose it is because I was not raised in wealth. I am new to it. It is as foreign to me as your Shropshire words, your dunna and inna and so on.'

She laughed, a clear, sweet laugh like water tumbling over smooth pebbles. But her face clouded again and she looked closely at him.

103

'But also, Owen, I do care. I am part of the King family now and I do not wish it to be part of something cruel. There's good in my family . . . I want to visit the brickworks and see more. I want to speak to the other workers and hear their views.'

Owen couldn't have that. He was supposed to be gaining information. If she demanded her family take her to the yard they would start asking awkward questions and Adam's plan would be over before it even began. 'It wouldna do any good, miss. If you came, it would be announced beforehand and everyone would clean themselves up and speak only good things to you. Troon the foreman would make sure of it. He is a lackey of the bosses.'

'Then, I shall come unannounced one day. You shall see.'

'I do hope not, miss. It is a filthy, smelly place. Much worse than your Paris, I'm sure.'

'We shall see,' she smiled that kittenish smile again, playful and inviting. 'I may surprise you.'

'You do surprise me, Miss Beatrice,' he said and they both laughed, good-naturedly. 'Well, you best get going or they'll be sending out a search party for you. Will you make it through the trees with that . . . that contraption on?'

Beatrice looked affronted but laughed at the same time, showing she took it in good humour.

'I see you do not approve of the crinoline! Is it because we women are taking up more room in the world? We command more space in one of these and push the men to the side! Is that your objection?'

'I just like to see a woman's natural form, is all. There's nothing finer.'

There was a moment of quiet between them.

'Meet me next week, same time, same place?' she said, as she turned to ascend the forest path to her home, the big house on the hill.

'I wouldna miss it for the world,' he said, taking off his cap with a flourish. He watched her figure move lightly through the trees, until all that was left of her was the tread of her footsteps through the bracken and the warning sounds of little birds that foolishly fled as she passed them by.

Chapter 8

Beatrice stood outside the kitchen door holding an empty pillowcase, listening intently. She was wearing her travelling dress, the simplest garment she now owned. She heard someone chopping and someone else gossiping about their neighbours. They seemed to be fully occupied. She glanced up the corridor, to ensure nobody was coming. As quietly as she could, she opened the cupboard door before her. Inside were stored piles of clothes. They belonged to the servants who did not live in with the Kings. They walked to the house in their own clothes, then changed into their smart service uniforms on arrival. Beatrice had spied them coming and going and discovered this place where they stored their home clothes. She recognised her own maid Dinah's chequered shawl and took the whole pile and stuffed it into the pillowcase. She looked down at the base of the cupboard and grabbed a pair of boots that looked about her size. She would only be gone an hour or two and she'd replace the clothes exactly as she found them. Nobody would need to know and no harm would be done.

Off she scampered, out of the back door without seeing anybody, thank heavens. She didn't want to have to explain the pillowcase she carried conspicuously. She felt like a thief in her own home and all of it was thrilling. She slipped unseen from the garden into the woods. Once the house was no longer visible, Beatrice found a likely tree and quickly undressed, laying her clothes out on the branch and pulling out Dinah's, a calico shirt with woollen skirt and shawl. Once redressed, she stuffed her own dress into the pillowcase and stowed it in the hollow of the tree, mightily pleased with herself for this cunning plan.

The walk through the woods was easy enough. Beatrice could remain unseen there until the short stretch of road she had to walk along, before turning once again into the cover of the trees behind the brickworks. On the way, she rubbed her hands in some dust and smeared it across her face, as well as running some dust through her hair, hoping to disguise herself further as a working person. She made sure that the grime was lodged beneath her fingernails too. She could not roughen up her hands to mimic years of manual labour, but she had done enough of their household washing in Paris to make her hands not as smooth as other debutantes her age. Though dusty, her hair still had the lustre of someone who had it washed often, but she had used Dinah's cotton mob cap to cover it, tying its frayed ribbons tightly beneath the chin to make sure the hair did not slip out and show. All the way, she kept looking down at her garments, unable to get used to their fascinating newness to her. She knew from seeing people of all classes in town that perhaps she was even too well dressed for a girl looking for brickwork, which is what she intended to be. Dinah's hobnail boots, which walked her between her home in Jackfield and the King house seven days a week through all weathers, were suitably worn and muddy. But Dinah's clothes, Beatrice noticed, had been carefully mended in several places. Dinah took pride in her appearance and, Beatrice realised, could not afford to buy new ones when her clothes ripped.

She came to the back of the brickworks through the trees, seeing the great shadow of the weathering heap loom up before her. There was no fence as such, just a shallow trench dug around the site to mark its boundary here. She clambered across it, thankful the ground was dry and crusty due to a recent lack of rain. She came up behind the huge heap of clay and edged around it to get a good look at the yard that spread forth beyond it. As she loitered, she saw the workers engaged in their various tasks, too wrapped up in their business to notice her. There were tall, broad men digging into the weathered clay heap, their spades portioning huge lumps which were dumped to one side. A series of children, boys and girls, of a range of ages from twelve or thirteen down to some very small ones. Could they be as young as five or six? Or maybe, Beatrice grimaced, they were so underfed as to be older yet with stunted growth. All of the children were grey with the clay that stuck to their bare arms and legs.

She could see that she was indeed dressed far better than the majority of these children, many of whom were half naked. On their heads, they all wore caps or scarves of some sort, upon which they balanced a lump of clay that looked far too large for those small heads to accommodate. They would squat down without bending their bodies and take another lump in their arms, the clay mass shoved up against their stomachs, and then they would stagger off. She watched one girl with thin bandy legs and a stumbling gait, walk with difficulty carrying her double load, down the incline of the yard, past a variety of buildings and workers coming to and fro, all the way to a three-sided shed, and disappear inside. Within moments, out she came again, free of her burden and trudged her way back up to the heap again, her head bowed and her shoulders sunken. The girl moved in a strange, unnerving way, an awkwardness in her step, as if her muscles and joints were not on speaking terms. Beatrice could only imagine that this was the result of years of the same debilitating work rendering her growing body malformed in some way. When the girl looked up at the heap of clay before her, her cheeks were pale and there was a deadness in the eyes that chilled Beatrice. The girl took up her double load again and off she went. Beatrice watched her make the same trip three times, before she guessed that this is what the girl must do all day, every day and by doing so must walk for miles and miles and carry tons and tons of clay on her head and in her arms every single shift.

The sight of these children made Beatrice's heart lurch. She had seen dire poverty on the streets of Montmartre, begging orphans in rags hanging around in miserable clumps. But there was something about these grey children slogging through life with no rest, no hope, that seized her sympathy and shook her to the core. And to know this was her family's business, it removed any distance that she might have kept between her and those Parisian children. She didn't have the means to help back then and now the fine meals she enjoyed were paid for by the work of these poor waifs.

She wanted to see more. She came forward and was spotted by a clay digger, who stared at her with amazement, as if she had stepped down from a cloud. Perhaps her disguise was not enough, perhaps they knew what the new King girl looked like. She sincerely hoped not. She gathered her courage and said boldly, 'Looking for work.'

'Down on yer luck? Got yerself in trouble?' said the digger, smirking, looking her up and down in the way only a man could.

'Who do I talk to?' she said.

He pointed downhill. Which building or structure that indicated, she could not tell, but she stepped forward as if she knew anyway and turned her head away from him. 'Miss Hoity-toity!' she heard him say and laugh at her. She carried on walking as if she knew exactly what she was doing, but with every step she felt less and less sure of her rash decision to come here. More than anything, she hoped she would not see Owen. The thought of it had excited her on her walk, but now she was here, she felt how ill-advised her plan had been, to spend a morning playing at brickmaking. Inwardly she cursed her folly and regretted it sorely. What had she been thinking? She decided to ask one of the brickmoulders briefly about work then turn and leave as soon as she was able.

While walking down to the shed where the brickmoulders stood, she saw yet more young children, taking the bricks from the benches and delivering them to another shed, where she guessed the bricks were dried out. Men came and went from the drying shed, one man was leading a horse down towards the gate, others carrying tools into a building where she could hear some sort of machine at work. Further along, she saw more children coming and going from another structure, a round building dotted with a range of entrances, out of which each child was carrying four or five finished bricks at a time in their arms, their neck muscles straining, whilst their bowed legs looked about to snap. She turned her attention back to the open-sided shed, where the brickmoulders stood in rows, each one standing before a bench.

There must have been around twenty or so. At first she thought she saw one or two women amongst their number. But then as she looked more closely she realised that most of them were women, made sexless by their uniform grey colour and turbaned heads. Beatrice caught a quick glance at the dexterity of one moulder, who dashed the clay into the mould, pummelled it with a stick, threw a piece of cloth onto it and beat it with a stubby bat, then smoothed it off with a sweeping motion, using a tool that seemed the union of a cheese wire and a bow. And there, the brick was done. She whacked the mould on the bench to release the brick, which was taken up by a waiting child and removed from the bench. And now the next lump of clay was deposited and the moulder did her magic again, so quick, so skilful.

Beatrice could see that the moulder job must have been sought after in the brickyard hierarchy, as though you'd be on your feet all day, at least you didn't have to carry the clay or bricks and did not move from your bench. It seemed to her that those least able to do the heavy work were forced into that very role, with hideous and tragic consequences. The children she saw there looked more like creatures of nightmare arisen from the mud, ghoulish and haunted. One such boy who was coming down to deposit his clay on a bench lagged behind the others and she watched as a woman stepped out and swiped at him with one huge flat hand the size of a paddle, hitting him so hard he fell flat on his back. Not a word was spoken, as the boy struggled to his feet and the moulder carried on her work.

'Leave him alone!' cried Beatrice, before she thought to stop herself. Almost as one, all heads turned in her direction. She saw the boy staring at her, his mouth open in amazement. 'Are you all right?' she asked him. He shot a glance at the woman who'd hit him.

'Friend of yours?' the woman said to the boy.

'No, Mother. Never seen her afore, I swear!' he cried, then hobbled off uphill as fast as his spindly legs would carry him.

'That is your *son*?' said Beatrice to the woman, aghast.

'Who's asking? The Queen of Ironbridge?'

That raised a laugh around the workers and attracted the attention of an overseer, who turned sharply and stormed over towards Beatrice. 'Get on with yer work!' he shouted at the others as he approached, then turning to Beatrice, he lurched towards her face and yelled, 'Stop loitering there!'

'I came to ask after some work,' she said and felt her face turn hot.

'What manner o'work?' said the man, squinting at her. 'You dunna look like you ever done a day's work in yer life.'

She did not know what jobs they did at such a yard and suddenly heard how different her voice was from all those around her, how unmarked by toil she must look. *What a fool I've been, coming here, trying to fit in,* she thought. But others were staring at her and she had to say something.

'I was a teacher once. Fallen on hard times.'

'Teacher?' scoffed the man. 'That inna work. What good would yer be round here? Get away.'

'All right,' she said and jutted out her chin, defiantly. 'I'm going. But you better mind that your workers treat those children better. Or I'll report you all. Just you see if I won't!'

And with that, she darted away from the man, whose eyes had grown wider with every word and she'd feared he might strike her at the end of her little speech. She half ran, half stumbled up the incline, past curious looks and sniggering laughs, back out into the woods again.

The walk home was long and tiresome and with each step she repeated the scene at the brickyard in her head. She'd been foolish to think she could pass as a brickworker, but still she was glad she had seen the state of the yard for herself. She went down to the riverside and managed to scoop up a bit of water to clean the worst of the mud from her face and hands. She found her clothes in the pillowcase and managed to get them back on, but her hair once the mob cap had been removed was a fright, she could feel it. If seen, she would have to face the music and make up a story. At the edge of the garden, she waited a while to see if anyone had appeared at a window to see her passage, but there was nobody there. She whisked across the garden and into a back door. Upon opening it, she found herself face to face with Jenkins, her great-grandmother's lady's maid. Jenkins stared at her, dumbfounded.

'I got lost in the woods and could not find my way home. I followed the river but the wrong way. Silly me! What a fool I am! I was caught by the vegetation and it messed up my hair a bit. But I am all right. Please do not concern yourself with it, or bother my mother or great-grandmother. I have learnt my lesson and will not go exploring any further.'

All of this was said in a tumble of words that Jenkins appeared to regard with smug amusement, also eyeing with interest the pillowcase Beatrice grasped in her hands. Beatrice did not wait for a reply and instead dashed up the servant staircase, remembering halfway up that Jenkins would wonder why on earth the daughter of the house was taking that lowly route. But it was too late to go back down now, so she ran up the last few steps and across to her room. Once inside, she rebraided her hair, then took out Dinah's clothes and folded them neatly. Later, she'd have to find a time to replace them in the cupboard, but for now, she was exhausted and could not face leaving her room and bumping into Jenkins again, or anyone else.

She sank down onto her bed. Again, visions of what she had experienced filled her exhausted mind, like scenes from a night terror. But despite the misery of it all, she told herself that something good had come of all this. She was appalled at what she had seen, what those brickworkers had to endure, day in, day out, just to earn enough to live. With every passing moment, her disgust at her family's complicity deepened and by the time she heard the gong sound below for luncheon, she was resolved. Something had to be done.

Chapter 9

Queenie had tried to put the vision of the ghost out of her mind for weeks now, but with little success. She had told no one about it, yet the morning after the visitation, fresh from the ghost's plea, she had asked Jenkins to find out what she could about the long forgotten baby on the bridge. Jenkins had not approved, but in the end had agreed.

That had been weeks ago and nothing had been said since. But now she was watching Jenkins pin her hair up and she pressed her on it. 'You have said nothing about the baby on the bridge. Have you forgotten?'

'I'm not losing my mind. I don't forget things. I was waiting until I had all the information.'

'So, you have some information then? Oh, do not be tiresome, Jenkins. Tell me what you have discovered thus far.' Queenie was eager to hear of it, but tried to cover this fact.

'I spoke to the old school mistress, Miss Millington, who hears most of the gossip because the children tell her things. She said the baby was taken in by a Quaker family, but she didn't know which one or if they still lived. She thought the midwife Mrs Lunt might know, but she's been away from town this month visiting family up north and has only just returned. I was planning to go into town this morning and ask her. Satisfied?'

Queenie nodded respectfully and said, 'Yes, thank you, Jenkins.'

'I still think raking over those ashes is a bad idea. Leave them dead and cold as they are.'

'I am aware of your opinion on the matter and do not wish to hear it again. Leave me now. I shall finish my own hair today.'

Once Jenkins had gone, she looked hopelessly at her pins on the dressing table and thrust one in somewhere at the back of her head to feel that she had done something. How helpless she would be without Jenkins. She was not capable of even managing the hair on her own head.

She was annoyed at Jenkins for withholding information that could have eased her mind these past weeks. She guessed that Jenkins had done that on purpose, because she didn't approve of Queenie's interest in the baby on the bridge. But she was not about to admit to Jenkins the truth behind why she was really asking about it, and worse still, what she had seen from her window. She was haunted not only by the spirit of Betsy Blaize but also the ghost of fear that clutched at her about her sister. She'd told Bea that Selina had died young, but not that she had spent her final years in an asylum. Queenie feared that Selina's fate of madness and suicide would afflict her too, that it ran in families and she was losing her mind, seeing ghouls like that. She would not admit that to anyone, even Jenkins. It was the thing that frightened her most and kept her awake at night, even without ghostly manifestations to disturb her sleep.

'Enough of this folly,' she told herself in the mirror. Patting her hair uselessly, she stood up and made her way downstairs to her study.

It was one of her favourite rooms in the house, the walls lined with French novels that Queenie had no intention of reading. But they had belonged to Margaret, who had pored over them as a child and left them all behind when she eloped to Paris. After Ralph's death, Queenie had taken over his study, changing the décor and some of the furniture to suit her own taste. She had had the books moved in there from the library and all of her son's tedious magazines and journals removed. Having Margaret's old novels all around her gave her comfort. She liked to be surrounded by the happier memories of Margaret as a child, when things were easier and she had company in the house, someone to play cards with, other than Jenkins. She had failed Margaret all those years ago, but she was home once more. Now she smiled to herself that she had Margaret back and now Beatrice, her joy. Such a sweet girl and such fun to talk to.

Queenie felt better already and went to her desk, scrupulously tidy with dustless inkstand and blotter before her, and she sat down. She glanced at the clock and saw it was ten minutes before the hour. She liked to take her seat and prepare herself mentally and physically before any planned event and always insisted that Jenkins checked her hair and tidied up any stray strands and made it perfect. She saw any hint of messiness in a woman's hair as a character flaw. There, she was ready now, waiting for Troon to arrive for a meeting about the brickyard.

Busby the butler was as fastidious as she was about timing and as the clock in her study chimed the hour of eleven, she heard footsteps approach her room. In he came and said, 'Mr Troon and a Mr Jones are here to see you, Ma'am.'

'A "Mr Jones"?' repeated Queenie with disdain. 'Whoever is that?'

'I believe he works at the brickyard with Mr Troon. He introduced himself to me as Mr Adam Jones, a brickmoulder. Shall I send him away?'

'No, no. Troon must have a reason to bring him, I surmise. Show them in, Busby.'

In came Troon, that handsome face marred by a poorly disguised sneer sneaking about his lips, Queenie felt. And behind him this Jones chap. He was stocky and ill-shaven. Black sideburns, black moustache, black eyes. He had made an effort to wash his arms and face, as well as wearing a clean jacket. But his boots were caked in clay and Queenie knew the maids would be cursing him for traipsing it through the house.

Queenie spoke first. 'I was expecting you, Mr Troon. But not this other . . . gentleman. Please indicate your reason for attending this meeting today, Mr Jones.'

Both men had taken off their caps. Troon fingered his cap but Jones stood stock still and looked directly at her.

'I am a brickmoulder at your yard, ma'am. I am also the General Secretary of our union.'

'Of your *what*?'

Before Jones had a chance to answer, a knock came at the door and then it immediately opened. Her grand-son Cyril's red-cheeked face appeared. He strode across the room and stood beside Queenie's desk and turned to address one and all, as if he had been expected, as if he were wanted, which, Queenie thought, he decidedly was *not* on either count.

'I hear there are brickworkers in the house,' he said loudly. How Queenie hated his strident voice, pitched rather too high and with an edge of sarcasm about it, as if the world were a great joke to him. 'So I took it upon myself to invite myself to the proceedings.' He then flicked the tails of his brown frock coat and sat down upon a chair to the right of the desk, crossing his legs and folding his hands across his stomach, showing off his royal blue waistcoat and purple cravat, the height of informal morning wear.

Queenie was about to tell him to get out, when she stopped herself, aware that Troon and this Jones fellow would see it as a weakness that the family were quarrelling. So she swallowed her rage and addressed the two workers standing before her.

'Mr Jones,' she said imperiously. 'Your appearance here is unorthodox, without prior arrangement. However, I will hear your concerns.'

'I wish to inform you of our union of which I spoke earlier. Us brickworkers have formed a union. I have come today to advise you that we intend to negotiate with you on the rates of pay for all brickworkers under your employ.'

Queenie saw Cyril shift forwards in his seat and unfold his arms. She wished to keep this meeting brief and civil, yet if Cyril got involved with all his customary bluster, she feared things would take a darker turn. She was about to explain her position to Jones, but Cyril was younger and swifter and he got there first.

'Egads! The impertinence of the new breed of worker! This one has the look of a gypsy, don't you think, Queenie?'

Could the fool not be quiet for even a moment? He'd have this man up in arms before they even began talking. And to use her nickname in front of outsiders. But again, before she had a chance to reply, the Jones man was speaking yet again.

'Personal comments are unnecessary, Mr King. I come in the spirit of justice for all to inform you that we are united, that we speak with one voice. And we say to our masters, all we ask for is fair pay for a hard day's work.'

'Mr Jones,' Queenie began, raising her voice a notch to cut off a brash response from Cyril, who appeared to be winding himself up for one. 'We appreciate you coming here to inform us of your union and your concerns. Unfortunately we have a full meeting today. If you could speak to Mr Troon about your concerns in the first instance, that would perhaps be best.'

'And if I may ask, ma'am,' Jones said with a deferential nod of the head. The man was trying to show respect at least, thought Queenie. 'There is a rumour that a deal has been struck between all of the brickmasters, to lower our wages, and that this is to come into force imminently.'

Queenie was annoyed that Jones had heard of this. The brickmasters had agreed that the pay would go down at the beginning of the next month. *Nothing is secret in a small town like Ironbridge*, mused Queenie. But there was no way she would confirm it before talking to the other brickmasters. She began, 'This is not a matter . . .' but was shouted over by Cyril, who was now on his feet.

'You are absolutely correct in that and your new rate of pay per thousand bricks will be far more than you deserve. Of course we must lower pay, when you and your cronies work like lazy sluggards, always loafing off down the public houses. I hear you get tramps to man the kilns at night, so you can sneak off down to the inns and get drunk. Yes! I keep my ear to the ground too, you know.'

Cyril was utterly infuriating! Queenie glared at him. What was he thinking? All the other brickmasters would hear of it and think her a traitor for letting the news out before their set date. But she had to tread carefully; there was no way on earth she could let Jones and Troon know she thought her grandson was an idiot.

'Mr Jones,' she said in a conciliatory voice. 'Be aware that no final decisions have been made at this time, despite my grandson's ... enthusiasm. We regularly look into the cost of wages and materials to ensure the profitability of our business. Brick prices rise and fall and we must move with the tides of change. Our main interest is to ensure that this brickyard remains open.'

'Yes, indeed!' cried Cyril. 'And let that be a warning to you, Jones or whatever you call yourself,' said Cyril, taking a threatening step forward, as if readying himself for a fist-fight. 'Any talk of strikes and such foolery will be met in severe terms. The harshest of terms, man. Do you hear me?'

Troon took a step forward too – at which Cyril took a stumbling step backwards – but Troon had his hands out, palms down. 'Nobody has spoken of strikes, Mr King, ma'am.'

'I'm no fool,' spat Cyril. 'I've heard whispers about town of secret meetings and plans to strike. Deny it, if you dare.'

'There is no secret about it,' said Jones, jutting out his chin. 'We make no secret of our union, hence my visit here this day. We have not mentioned strikes but be aware, that if pay is to be cut in any way for any workers, then we *will* strike and it'll be on your head, let me warn you.'

Cyril continued, 'And allow me to warn you, you . . . you ruffian! Remember that a great many of our workers live in housing provided by this family. If you whip them up into insurrection and call a strike, every one of them will be summarily evicted. And if you're one of them, be assured you will lose your home and it will be the workhouse for you and everyone you care about.'

Cyril had gone too far! Queenie felt quite ill at this turn of events. She wanted to retract what her grandson had said. Evictions was a trump card to be used much later on in the process, if necessary. To threaten it now was idiocy. But she could not show division in the family. It would be a sign of weakness. While she wrestled with what to say next, she looked at Jones. He stared directly at Cyril and showed no sign of wavering. He spoke again, just as plainly and coolly as before.

'I am one of your tenants, sir. My wife and I have lived there together these past two years.'

'Then you'd better watch yourself or you'll be out on the street!' said Cyril, his voice raised.

'With all due respect,' continued Jones, 'let me remind you that we have our union. We shall look after one another. We have no fear of a strike and no terror of the workhouse. But Mrs King, Mr King, I must say this meeting has not proceeded in the manner in which I had hoped.'

'Listen to the gentleman!' scoffed Cyril. 'Speaking like a Lord!'

Jones ignored this and continued, 'And my wish to negotiate seems to have fallen on deaf ears. Please let me finish by saying that I have worked hard for this brickyard for twenty years, that I am a highly skilled brick-moulder who contributes daily towards the success of the King brickyard. I value my work and my colleagues, and do not wish to cause trouble unnecessarily. I hope we can talk again in the future in a more productive manner. Thank you for your time. I will take my leave of you now.'

With that, he made a short bow, turned and left the room, closing the door gently behind him.

Troon looked shocked and Cyril laughed. Queenie was left infuriated by Cyril. She was also impressed by Jones. There was intelligence in him, to be sure, and he had spoken sense and attempted to be respectful towards the end. It was clear that, if Cyril's rumours were to be believed, Mr Jones had the ear of all the workers and he was charismatic enough to lead them all against the King family and never give in. She would have to be careful with this one. He would take cautious handling.

'I do apologise for any offence caused, ma'am,' said Troon, his voice polite yet oily. 'It was my understanding that Mr Jones was coming here today to introduce himself as the union leader. I didna sanction any talk of strikes, nor do I at the yard neither.'

'Understood, Troon,' said Queenie. 'You are not to blame. Thank you and please take your leave. I shall see you again tomorrow, when tempers are cooler.'

'Yes, ma'am, sir,' said Troon, bobbing his head twice, then leaving quietly.

'Well, well,' said Cyril in a tone that showed how mightily pleased with himself he was. 'I knew something was going on with those blackguards.'

Queenie turned a cold eye on her grandson, who looked at her, pleased with himself, until he saw her thunderous expression.

'How dare you inflame the situation so! What were you thinking? What possessed you to pepper your speech with such inflammatory terms as "strike" and "eviction"?'

'Well, I must say, I'm surprised at you. You've always been tough as old boots with these types. Are you going soft in your old age?'

Queenie sighed and put her hand to her head. It would be easy to dismiss him as a fool, but she felt she must attempt to explain it to him, to prevent another such embarrassment. Cyril was in his late thirties now and not a young man any more. Although he was usually napping or supping or otherwise engaged, he did show some interest in the business and could be useful to carry out site visits and suchlike. She had to try to make him understand, at least.

'It is not a case of weakness. Negotiation must be handled with great care. Think of it as a politician might, when a great battle looms on the horizon. Attempts must be made to avoid it before letting slip the dogs of war.'

'I don't see why. They are but a rabble of rag-tags, half drunk much of the time and plotting our demise the rest, so people say.'

'What people? And what talk have you heard of this around town, Cyril? And why have you not brought it to my attention before?'

'It was only rumblings. But they're saying that the brickworkers meet in the basement of inns hereabouts and talk of sedition. I had no proof, only some drunken gossiping.'

'I see,' said Queenie. 'But this does not forgive your rash behaviour here today. You must curb yourself in future. I shall pursue matters from here on. I shall think on it.'

'But there is no thinking to be done. We must stamp on them. We must dismiss that Jones, immediately.'

'It is not that simple,' snapped Queenie, suddenly very tired of him and the whole situation. 'These things are delicate and need to be handled cleverly.'

'Delicate? What rot! Dismiss the lot of them.'

'Just like that! And where do you presume we shall find a whole brickyard's worth of trained workers, at a moment's notice? It would cost us a fortune to halt production and find a whole new workforce. That would be the last resort, or at least a threat to hold over them later in the process. Can't you see, that we must play our cards cleverly?'

'Nothing clever required with that lot of scoundrels.'

'Oh, do shut up, Cyril!' she cried. 'You have no idea what you're talking about. You are no help at all, just like your useless father.'

She walked past him, noting the lack of response as she went through the door and into the passageway. A wave of exhaustion came over her, tinged with guilt. She shouldn't have said that to Cyril, but he made it so hard to respect him.

Once in her room, she closed the door behind her with relief. It would be lunchtime soon and she would need to face the family. She made the decision to have her lunch sent up to her. She was about to ring the bell to summon a servant to give her luncheon instructions, when a knock came at the door.

'Saving me the trouble,' she muttered to herself and called, 'Come in.'

But it was not a servant. It was Beatrice.

'My dear, you do look tired. And very serious. What can the matter be?'

'I've had a very trying morning,' she said.

'Come and sit with me on the bed,' said Queenie and patted the covers. Queenie pushed her pillows up so she could lean against them and make herself comfortable.

As shattered as she was and as much as she longed for rest, she could not resist Beatrice and wanted to hear every last detail of whatever it was that had happened. Beatrice sat down opposite her, at the end of the bed, her feet curled under her. 'Now, tell me everything.'

Beatrice looked down and sighed. 'I have a secret to tell you. But first I ask that you must not be angry with me.'

Queenie was immediately rapt, but could not imagine the child could do anything that would make her angry. So she replied, 'I will listen without prejudice.'

Beatrice bit her lip. 'I do hope so . . . I went to the brickworks this morning.'

This was the last thing Queenie expected to hear. 'And how did this come to pass? Who took you there?'

'Myself. I took myself there. Indeed, I took it upon myself to dress up in the clothes of a working woman and go to the brickyard to see it for myself.'

Queenie was on high alert now. 'Were you seen? Were you recognised?'

'I was seen and spoken to, but I believe that my disguise worked and I was not recognised.'

'You believe?' probed Queenie. The scandal, if it were discovered! How humiliating for a King to be found dressing up as a commoner and rattling around with Ironbridge working folk. This was the opposite of what was needed just before Beatrice was about to be launched in society. Queenie was trying to keep her temper. The child had surprised her. As before, with Margaret's elopement, she was half shocked and horrified, half secretly pleased that the girl was showing spirit. But this, this madness? What on earth could the girl have been thinking?

'You are not angry, Queenie?'

'Why did you go, my dear?'

'I wanted to see for myself. I had heard bad things about the yard. It is owned by my family. So I felt I ought to know the truth.'

Queenie bridled at this, but fought to remain calm. She would come back to the accusation of 'bad things' presently. 'But why not request a formal visit, with me or your uncle, or even your mother? Why this theatrical subterfuge? Why lie and dissemble?'

Beatrice sniffed and looked blankly at her. 'I knew that if I went openly, the truth would not be shown to me. Everyone would be on best behaviour.'

'I am impressed by your reasoning. Now, tell me everything that happened, from beginning to end.'

'I saw the children there, half clothed and exhausted, lugging lumps of clay about that look twice as heavy as they are themselves. Some were deformed, it seems by the backbreaking work they must do. A child was struck viciously.'

'Well, what you may not know is that most of those children are working for their own families.'

'Yes, it was the mother who hit her son.'

'There you are, then. The moulders are at liberty to hire their own kin and how they treat them really is their own business.'

'But the whole place is riven with misery and want. If they were not worked so hard, were not in such dreary circumstances and were not driven by desperation to stay in such a job, perhaps they would not act so. The children are so downtrodden and pathetic, they tear your heart in two! Their faces are like that of old men, placed on young, weak bodies. And some of them were no more than five or six years of age. What of their schooling? What of their minds? What possible parents can they grow up to be if this is their education? But none of them have such choices, if they are worked into the ground in such a place. If I hadn't gone there myself and seen it with my own eyes, I never would have believed it were possible, in this day and age, in England, in this fine county, in our family business! Queenie, I do believe—'

But Queenie had heard enough. It was time to rein this one in.

'My dear child, you are young and passionate, but in one trip to the brickyard you could never begin to understand what it means to run a business. I'm sure you think you saw something, but we have people in place to manage the brickworkers, people trained to run the business. Your decision to go incognito to a King-owned business was rash and foolhardy. If anybody there discovered that

132

you were a King, we would be laughing stocks. Listen now. I am learning that you have a fine mind, that we can put to use in the business one day, I am sure of it. But you are still young and callow. What you did was rash and badly thought out. Luckily, it seems that you escaped without being recognised.'

'But, Queenie! Did you know these terrible things were occurring in your own brickyard? Did you?'

Queenie bristled at this. From anyone else, she would not have stood for such insolence. She could forgive Beatrice most things, but the girl was sailing close to the wind on this one. 'My business is to make a profit for our family and our shareholders. My fore-man's business is to oversee my brickyard. Your busi-ness is to profit from all of this and to sleep in a warm bed, eat your fill at mealtimes and wear the prettiest dresses in Shropshire. Please do not tell me my busi-ness, child.'

Usually this kind of Queenie pronouncement formed the end of most discussions. But Beatrice was not to be stopped.

'But you are the owner. You should know what is going on with your own workers.'

'What they do is their business. I am no foreman and I hope you are not suggesting I drag my skirts through the brick dust in my silk shoes and shout at people.'

'No, of course not. But you are guilty by omission! You are culpably unaware of the goings-on in your own brickyard. The children are being worked to death. It is a place of neglect and misery and violence.'

'And that is because of the brickworker breed. Coming from France, you may not be aware of this. But if you read our newspapers and the thoughts of our foremost thinkers, you will find that the brickworker in particular is not well thought of in any vein of society, including their own. The brickworker is known universally as the lowest type, the lowest of the low,' pronounced Queenie, sure this point would end this insufferable argument.

'That is not true,' returned Beatrice, tenacious in her dispute. 'As with all people, there are good, bad and indifferent. I was brought up in a small, narrow house without refinement or privilege.'

'That is not the same thing at all. Your mother was educated and taught you well. And she had the best of breeding, coming from my line, and the King line. It was born in you to be refined.'

'But not all educated, privileged people are refined. Look at Uncle Cyril! And not all brickworkers are like the one I saw strike her child. Some are the most wonderful, intelligent, even poetic people.'

'What drivel! How could you possibly know that from looking at them?'

Beatrice looked askance. 'I know one, personally. He is a friend of mine.'

'He?' gasped Queenie. This was going from bad to worse! 'Who is this "he"?'

'I bought a pie from a young man of around my age. He turned out to be one of our brickmakers. We have become friends. He is everything I claim. He is good and kind and clever. He would never raise a hand to a child or a woman. He reads and is well-spoken. I am proud to call him my friend.'

Queenie's alarm bells were pealing at full volume. She steeled herself for the lecture that was to come. A young male brickworker that reads, friends with her Bea? Never! 'Now listen, my girl. Only trouble will come of that. Ask your mother. It was that business with Anny that caused all the trouble years ago.'

Beatrice's face lit up. 'Ah! Mother has mentioned Anny but won't tell me any more. What happened between them? Was Anny poor?'

'Ask her,' said Queenie, with venom. 'Ask your mother what befell that friendship and all who suffered because of it. All I shall say is that your mother knows full well that friendships between the classes never work and will end in disaster. Mark my words, girl!'

'But this is about more than him. It is about the whole brickyard and the fate of its workers. I have heard that plans are afoot to lower their wages. Just yesterday, I heard you say that the price of bricks is on the rise. Could we not afford to pay our workers a reasonable wage? Should our workers not share in our success?'

'That is not how business works, Beatrice. Brick prices rise and thus our profits rise. We then invest that

135

money back into our businesses to grow them evermore. The brickworkers are used to their old brickmaster's ways and he was inefficient and became a bankrupt. We must tighten our belts when it comes to wages, or our profits will fall and eventually our business will fail. Then everyone will be out of work, including your friends the brickworkers and this fine house here and everyone in it.'

'I do not believe it is that simple. There must be a way to run a successful business and still take care of your workers. Great-grandmother, I beg you. Please do not lower their wages. Please, go down there and see them for yourself.'

'I will do no such thing, Beatrice!' Queenie was about to launch into a final sermon to end this madness, but the child had boundless energy for a fight and would not stop.

'But how can you stand by when those who rely on you suffer? You must do what you can. You must strive to improve things for them. It is your duty to improve their lot in life.'

A chill clutched at Queenie's throat.

'What did you say?' she murmured.

'I said you must improve their lot in life. Have I said the phrase wrongly? Maman says it, a good English phrase I think. Their lot in life.'

'Stop saying that!' cried Queenie and realised her hands were shaking.

'Queenie, what is it?' said Beatrice, visibly distressed. She moved towards her great-grandmother and took her hands in her own, massaging them gently.

Improve her lot in life, the ghost of Betsy Blaize had demanded for her child. Was the spirit working through her nearest and dearest now?

Queenie snatched her hands away. 'Leave me,' she said. 'You have upset me greatly.'

Beatrice looked guiltily away, stood up from the bed and walked slowly to the door. 'I am sorry for upsetting you. I am very sorry for that.'

Queenie was glad to hear it and waved her hand feebly to signal her acceptance of this. But the girl was not finished.

Before she left the room, Beatrice said quietly, 'But I am not sorry for what I said, as it is the truth. All of it.'

Beatrice went out and shut the door. For the first time in years, Queenie feared she might actually weep. The child had upset her so, with cruel accusations and worrying news. But the stress of hearing the spirit's words come from the mouth of her darling girl was too much.

'Jenkins,' Queenie said, knowing that her faithful servant was not there. 'Jenkins,' she said again, for comfort. But as if the call had summoned her existence, the door between their bedrooms opened and there she was, dressed up in her bonnet with the cloth flowers and her beige day dress, from her trip into town.

'You don't look right,' said Jenkins, coming over quickly to Queenie and taking her wrist, feeling for her pulse. Simply the touch of Jenkins's dry, firm hands was a relief.

'Must I be beset by troubles at this time of my life?' sighed Queenie. 'I ought to be seeing out my autumn years in peace and relaxation.'

'Winter years, more like,' said Jenkins, but then cocked her head and peered at her. 'But this is not like you. What's been going on?'

'Miss Beatrice has been playing merry hell with my nerves. I shall tell you all about it later. I want to stay up here for lunch. Tell them in a moment, will you? I've had the very devil of a morning. But first, Jenkins, news. News from you and then I must rest. What news from town?'

Jenkins undid the bow beneath her chin and removed her bonnet. She liked to delay her revelations, to draw out the drama. She did love a bit of gossip, did Jenkins.

'I have news. The Quaker midwife told me the baby was called Martha, brought up by the Beddoes family, good people. Both the Beddoes are dead now. This Martha – the baby on the bridge – she is now married to one of our very own brickmakers called Jones. They are with child, the midwife says, as she's visited them already.'

She knew that name. Oh no, could it be? The man who had stood in her study just that morning, the union leader, the cause of all her troubles at the brickworks? But it was a common name thereabouts, very common in Shropshire. There could be any number of Joneses.

'Did she say the man's Christian name, this Jones?'

'Now, let me see. Yes, she did. Adam. Adam and Martha Jones, she said. A brickmoulder at the King brickyard. Now then, you have your news. You know where the baby on the bridge is. Happily married and her own baby on the way. I'd say that's the matter closed, wouldn't you? Now, let me sort luncheon. Tongue sandwiches today, I think. You need a bit of meat in you. You look so pale.'

∽

Queenie slept that afternoon, shattered after her day of strife. She was hungry and ready for something good and filling to eat as the dinner gong sounded its hollow ring downstairs. She left her room and saw Benjamina appear, dressed up in a blue silk gown with bell-shaped sleeves trimmed with broderie anglaise. It was a fine ensemble, Queenie had to admit, but surely a tad over-dressed for a simple family dinner. Benjamina was pulling the door to gently, shutting her dog Louise in.

'You are the sweetest thing,' said Benjamina to the dog, who was wriggling through the gap in the door, trying to come out and join her mistress for dinner. 'Yes, you are. Yes, you are. The most loveable, most pretty, most sweet, most wonderful little creature that ever did live! But you must stay here. Mama is going for dinner now. I shall see you in less than a shake of your dear little tail.'

Queenie rolled her eyes. Benjamina managed to shut the dog in and turned to her, nodding and simpering that fake smile of hers.

'Benjamina,' said Queenie and walked forwards, assuming the lead, of course.

'Are you well?' came Benjamina's voice behind her.

'Quite well, thank you.'

'You do look a little pale. I do wonder if you take on too much these days.'

Queenie stopped on the landing halfway down the stairs and turned to Benjamina, who was still smiling that smile, with an overly concerned look in her eye. Queenie had never got on well with her daughter-in-law, but recently, the woman seemed to be up to something. Whatever it was, Queenie was keen to ensure that Benjamina knew her place, which was well down the pecking order from herself.

'Not at all, my dear. I have never felt stronger in my life.'

'If you're sure, Queenie,' said Benjamina, touching the blue ribbons in her hair, as if to adjust them, although they were quite perfect just as they were. 'We wouldn't want you to suffer under too much stress and vexation. Not at *your* age.'

Queenie ignored the remark and descended the stairs with a quicker step than usual. She swept into the dining room at quite a pace. Seated at the dinner table, she listened with distaste while Benjamina uncharacteristically filled in time by making conversation with the others. She began with indulging Beatrice by asking about her Paris friends, flattering Margaret by asking her favourite pieces to play on the pianoforte and next she came up with a topic she seemed to know would annoy Queenie.

'The old brickmaster's house,' Benjamina said. 'It's still boarded up. Shouldn't we open it up and use it? It is such a lovely location in Benthall Edge Woods, just along from that pretty church. I would be delighted to take over its renovation. It'd be a marvellous project to get my teeth into. If we are honest with ourselves, one would say it is a finer house than this, being built much more recently. Cyril agrees with me, don't you?'

'It is a good, solid house,' he said, with his mouth full, not letting that stop him. 'But too secluded and far away from town for my liking. I prefer it here, up on top of the hill, looking down at everyone.'

'Which house is this?' asked Beatrice.

Margaret answered, 'The Kings took over the brickworks when the old brickmaster went bankrupt and the house came to us. Is that right, Grandmother?'

Queenie nodded, finishing her mouthful. She did not deign to look at Benjamina, who again was sticking her nose into things that had never been her business, trying to reorganise where they lived, for heaven's sake.

This woman was definitely up to something, jostling for position since the death of her husband. Well, Queenie was having none of that. She dabbed the corners of her lips before answering. 'There is no question it is a fine house. But if Benjamina thinks we can afford to run two large houses with a full staff in the same environs, she's lost her reason. We shall sell it at some point, I'd imagine. But I haven't decided its fate quite yet. When the time comes, as head of the house and the company, it will be my decision and nobody else's.'

That put an end to that. Queenie glanced round the table to see Margaret looking blank, Beatrice looking thoughtful, Benjamina smiling an infuriating little smirk, and Cyril looking bored. But he caught her eye and said, 'Ah Queenie.'

'What is it, Cyril?'

'I forgot to inform you this afternoon. You'll be proud of me, as I have finally taken some initiative in the family business and shown those ruffians who's the boss.'

'What have you done?' Queenie said in a low voice.

'I've had eviction notices served on all of the brickies who live in King housing. Imagine their surprise when they finish their shifts and discover they must vacate our properties by tomorrow evening. That should sort out the blackguards once and for all. Now they'll know who they're dealing with. It'll take the wind out of their sails.'

Queenie could not believe her ears. After everything she had tried to explain to this fool, he had done this?

She was about to rain fire and brimstone down upon him, when she was interrupted.

'How could you!' cried Beatrice.

'How could I? Quite easily, my dear. I marched down to Brotherton's office and gave the order.'

Queenie could hold back no longer and with a great voice that scratched her throat and seemed to make the very walls quiver, she shouted, 'You *imbecile!*'

But there was no time for reaction, as in came Busby and approached her. He whispered to her that Mr Troon was here to see her. The door was opened roughly and there was Troon. Busby looked round, horrified that an outsider had passed the threshold to the inner sanctum. Would Busby try to manhandle him? It was unthinkable, a kerfuffle in the King drawing room. And Queenie knew that Troon's arms as sturdy as a sailor's would make quick work of the wiry, middle-aged butler.

'News has reached us of the eviction of all brick-workers from King housing,' announced Troon, standing at the foot of the table with his arms crossed. 'So I have news for the King family. Every last worker at your brickyard has downed tools and we have put out the kiln fires. From tonight at seven of the clock, we are officially on strike.'

Chapter 10

Owen was waiting for her on Madame's steps the next morning, as usual. They looked at each other without smiling.

'I am glad you're here,' Beatrice said. 'I didn't think you'd come.'

'Course I did,' he said and tried to smile, but it didn't quite work and came out as a smirk, then a grimace.

'I thought they'd tell you not to see me anymore.'

'Who?'

'Mr Troon and the other brickworkers.'

'I follow my own path,' he replied and smiled properly this time.

'Last night, my great-grandmother told me I was not to speak to you again.'

'You'd told her about me, about . . . us? Our friendship?' He looked nervous.

'Only that I knew a brickworker as an acquaintance. After we received the news about the strike, she found me upstairs later in my room and said I was forbidden to "fraternise" with anyone from the brickworks.'

'I see,' he said and fiddled with his cap he held in his hands.

Beatrice glanced up and down the road, checking her mother or anyone else from the house wasn't about to spot them. She leant in and whispered, 'But I know a place we can meet later.'

～∞～

Back at home, luncheon was a quiet affair, sitting only with her mother. Benjamina was indisposed in her room with her yappy little dog, Louise, while Queenie and Cyril were ensconced in the study all day having meetings with some of the staff. Four visitors arrived and were shown in to join the meetings, local brickmasters, apparently. Beatrice could hear raised voices coming from that room, when she loitered near it, but could not make out what they were saying. After lunch, Beatrice told her mother she was going for a walk along the riverside that afternoon with Madame. Her mother did not question her, as she seemed very pleased to see her daughter exercising. She did harp on so about Beatrice's waist these days, but never had in Paris. It made her feel quite low, this hint that she was plump and ought to do something about it. Maman had said, 'When you wear tight silk across your back, one can see a little roll of flesh bulging atop the line of the corset, which won't be seemly when you attend balls.' *Well*, thought Beatrice, *the flesh has got to go somewhere!* Also, it seemed more sensible to Beatrice to have the silk cut so that it wasn't so tight. Of course she was happy she had been given a whole new wardrobe, but she felt like she was wearing somebody else's clothes, outfits that never quite fit or sat right on her body. That morning, she had looked at a milkmaid in town carrying her wares on a yoke and thought how pretty she was, how pleasing her round cheeks were and her large bosom and hips that curved like hillsides. This obsession with the tiny waist was tiresome and silly. It seemed so unfair that women were not encouraged to look like women, but instead like a cool hourglass without feelings, breath, flesh or character.

Beatrice asked her maid the way to the old brickmaster's house and Dinah kindly drew her a little map to get there, which impressed Beatrice with its fine detail. She made sure she mentioned to her maid that it was beautifully done. Once out of the house and alone, Beatrice felt giddy as she hurried down the hill to town. Passing along the main street, she delighted in the sights and sounds of ordinary folk going about their business. There were sheep, cows and geese to be seen, chivvied along by their owners. Animal noises merged with the hubbub of chitchat and sellers calling out their wares. She smiled at everyone, receiving some pleasant looks in return, whilst others looked surprised to see a girl so nicely dressed walk among them, beaming at everybody. Some days here in England she felt so out of place, as lonely as a single boot on a roadside. But today she

146

felt part of the world, a piece placed in the giant puzzle of humanity. Her friendship with Owen had somehow linked her with everyone in this town and at last she felt a connection with her mother's home.

Walking up from the bridge she passed the halfway point marked by a waterwheel. She heard it before she could see it, the sound of rushing water growing louder as she approached. She expected something the size of a carriage wheel, perhaps a little bigger, but rounding the path and beholding it for the first time, she gasped at its size. It towered above the brick house beside it and was turning at a great pace, the splish-splash of water spraying from its spokes as it went around, catching the sun in twinkling cascades. There were a couple of well-dressed visitors looking and pointing up at the wheel, nodding appreciatively. Beatrice wondered if they had come especially to see it, a wonder of the industry that made this place so remarkable.

She remembered her mother telling Beatrice that her father, Jake Ashford, had come to Ironbridge to paint the industries and that is how they had met. Her mother never liked to talk about him. Beatrice had accepted this, growing up. That was just the way things were. She wondered sometimes if it were her mother's grief that prevented her from discussing him. But being here, in the place where her father and mother had met, she began to yearn for more information. She wondered if her father had stood here, gazed up at the same waterwheel and sketched it, all those years ago, before she existed. She must ask her mother. She would like to see his drawings, if any survived. If she had her father's skill – which she had definitely not inherited, drawing stick figures or horses that looked like dogs – she would sketch this magnificent waterwheel.

The final part of her walk was undisturbed in that part of the woods, away from town and the sounds of industry. It was so quiet there, she saw a deer, standing alert in a narrow clearing, which leapt away from sight in the blink of an eye. This was an animal she'd never seen outside picture books and it thrilled her.

She reached a fork in the path and looked at the map. The right-handed way was the one to take and it took her closer to the river. Its constant murmur was comforting, punctuated by the odd splash of a fish leaping. At that moment, she realised that it would be very hard to leave this place and return to the city. Its beauty had crept into her heart, curled up there and made itself comfortable. As she walked on, she heard the river grow in sound, the water rushing over something, probably a small weir beyond the trees. The sound was joyful and crystal clear. She listened to it and loved it. She wondered if she had come into existence in Maman's belly before she had left Iron-bridge, wondered if she had been surrounded by these woods or even heard a glimmer of the wandering river beyond her mother's frame and that's why it felt like home, despite the fact that Paris was where she had grown up. The woods, the river and the bridge over it had cast a spell over Beatrice. Ironbridge tugged at her heartstrings as if it had full claim to do so.

A house came into sight. It was not as large as Southover, but was more interesting to look at – Benjamina had been right about that. It had two tall brick chimneys, one on either end and many windows all along the two floors. There were rounded bays surrounded by wisteria that grew rather wildly and drooped over the windows, covering some of them completely. It needed taming. Beatrice approached a downstairs window and looked inside, to see a couple of items of furniture, swathed in white sheets. Other than that, the house seemed mostly empty of furnishings, all carpets, rugs and wall hangings having been removed. It had a sad air about it, as if the previous owners had left suddenly and the house longed for company. Beatrice wondered if there was a door that might be unlocked. Or at least might be easy to force open.

Then, footsteps on the path made her turn and stare, alert as she was to being alone. As she saw Owen walking towards her, framed by the swaying trees, she suddenly felt a strange certainty that she would never return to Paris. It frightened yet exhilarated her alike.

When he saw her, his face lit up. She was suddenly very aware of her solitude in that place, with this boy. She knew what they were doing was wrong. But she did not care to think about that.

'Afternoon miss,' he said and removed his cap with a flourish, at which they both laughed.

'Please, you must call me Bea. We are good friends now.'

'Bea,' he said simply.

She wished she could spend the whole day with him, but she wasn't sure how long she could stay away and this walk had taken far longer than she expected just to get there. 'So, the brickworkers are on strike.'

'Yes, we are.'

'Is that what you wanted?'

'It's more about need than want.'

His face was serious now and even more handsome that way. She felt a little unsteady – perhaps it was the long walk or simply the excitement of seeing him again – but she pushed on. She must tell him what she had planned to say.

'Owen, I have a confession to make. I have been to the brickworks but I came incognito.'

'In a what?' he frowned.

'No,' she smiled gently, 'I came in disguise. I borrowed my maid's clothes and came pretending to look for work. I did not want to be lied to or have the truth covered up, as it would have been had I come in my normal attire. I wanted to see the truth.'

'When was this? I never saw you there.'

'Yesterday. I did not see you either and I am pleased I didn't. It was terrible.'

'Terrible? How?'

'I saw a child struck viciously there and I defended that child to its mother and to a man who was some sort of overseer. They didn't seem to care.'

'Well, it's quite normal for folk to give a good clout. It happens all the time at the yard.'

'I can see it happens all the time. I saw it with my own eyes! How can you live like that?'

'Like what?' he said and narrowed his eyes at her.

'Amid such violence! How can you defend such actions? To strike a child so violently! It is criminal. And these are your colleagues. Explain yourself!'

'Explain *myself*?'

'Yes, you must give me an explanation. I am on your side. I have already spoken to my great-grandmother about improving things there. I have told her she must do something. But these are your people. What are *you* doing about it?'

'Me? It inna me doing the beatings!'

'But you've said it happens all the time, around you. Do you stand by and do nothing? What kind of people are they, that will beat a child, a child so malnourished and weak and beaten down by life already? It is monstrous!'

Her blood was up too now and she did feel faint. *This damned corset*, she thought. She glared at him, not afraid, not willing to back down, ever. These were his people behaving in this awful manner and she wanted him to explain it to her. She was already taking sides against Queenie and her own family. Now she needed some hope that it was the right thing to do.

'Listen here,' he said. 'You know nothing. You understand nothing. These people have been brought up in this life, the brickmakers' life. Most of 'em were born to it, carrying clay as soon as they were able, at five year, some of 'em. And most have never had a day of schooling. They're worked until they're ready to drop. But when they're done they dunna go home to some mansion and eat a three-course meal. No, they go home to a small house, where they sometimes sleep three to a bed, head to toe just to make room. And their supper? If they're lucky, they might get a good price on a sheep's head for a thin stew, so that tomorrow they can do it all again. Malnourished and weak, you say? You're right. And if the whole family dunna work fast enough then malnourishment slips over to starving. So they push their children to work harder. And your family has done all it can to make matters worse. Our cottages leak and mould grows up our walls, our wages drop and we have even less to eat. There inna time to think about what's right. My mother insisted I went to school every day for years, but we were the lucky ones. Most canna afford to have a child not working for any length of time. Education hasna played no part in their lives so they see no part of it in the lives of their young'uns. But I want change, I want reform. I want all children to go to school, of course I do, so that the little'uns are able leastways to read and write afore they are dragged into this way of life. But for that to happen, the brickmakers need higher pay and shorter hours, they need decent contracts and homes and conditions, so that they can send their child to school instead of being forced to hire them to make ends meet. It's the system that needs changing and then the people will change right enough with it. And *that* is in the hands of the brickmasters. They are the ones with the power to change for good. That is why we are on strike. Like I said, it's need, not want. What do you say to that, Miss King?'

She had watched his face twist into fury as he spat out the last two words.

'I am not a King. I am an Ashford.'

He was breathing heavily and glaring at her.

'If you're not one of them, then prove it.'

'How?'

'Help us.'

'I am trying to do just that. It's why I went to the brickyard.'

'You'd be more use to us at home than dressing up. Keep your eyes and ears open. Tell us what the brickmasters are planning. Speak up for us. Will you do that? Will you help us?'

She would be a spy – that's what he was asking. Could she do it? Did she want to?

'I want to help, of course I do. But I am no natural liar. I am not practised in the art of spying or dissembling.

But I will do what I feel is right. And you have right on your side. Yes, I will help you. Together, you and I could make a marvellous team!'

'I believe you're right about that,' he said and they smiled at each other. Then, their smiles faded as the intensity between them grew. His blue eyes became the centre of her vision. The world and all its troubles faded behind them. She reached out and grasped his hand.

The touch of her hand on his rooted them both to the spot. He looked down at their hands and stared at them, as if they belonged to somebody else. Then he moved his hand gently, letting his fingers slide between hers and lock the two of them together. He lifted her hand slowly to his lips and kissed it, his eyes closing.

She stepped towards him and then they kissed, mouth to mouth, her hands reaching up into his hair – how she had longed to touch it! So fair and now she knew, so soft. She felt his hands around her back. Her eyes were closed and the whole world had vanished into this one moment, this one kiss. She never wanted it to end.

But end it must, as they came up for air, gasping like dreamers rudely awakened. Owen was trembling, she saw, which astounded her. She had never imagined a man could be affected like that, especially by her. But she knew the strength of her feelings for him and hoped – no, she knew – that his were just as potent. He kissed her again.

When they stopped and came to, the life of the forest around them seemed to hold its breath, the whole world seemed to. They held hands and looked at each other. Their happiness was overflowing and they could not help but smile, then laugh. It spilled out of them like the bubbling water she could hear, frothing over the weir beyond. They looked into each other's eyes, searching for something there, some certainty perhaps, as she felt as if her legs were standing on a coracle in the river, whirling round and round. But now he frowned, he looked down and shook his head, still squeezing her hand tightly.

'Is this wrong?' he whispered. He kissed her hand tenderly and then kissed her mouth again and they held on desperately, as if they drowned in the air.

'It is not,' she said breathily, into his ear, then kissed his neck and heard him groan. 'It is right. I know it is right.'

He had to walk to the inn at Broseley, but he was walking on air and never wanted to arrive. He had seen her to the edge of the wood, making sure she went on to the main road safely. He wished he could have walked her home, like a local girl, seen her to her door, tipped his hat to her parents, noted their interest that a local boy had walked their daughter home, seen her blush as she crossed her threshold into her cottage. But this girl was not a local girl, the girl he loved. She was a stranger to Ironbridge and she did not smell of clay or iron but the scent of flowers and powder and money. He could not walk with her through town, hold her hand, kiss her on the cheek or take her to a dance. He could not bring her to his mother and father and watch them become acquainted with her ways, her frankness and curiosity, her kindness and her temper. He was a Malone and she was a King, whatever her father's name was. She was one of them and she was the enemy.

His lips felt bruised with desire, tingling and heavy as if stung. His insides churned and a heat emanated from deep within and flushed his entire body. He felt as if desire was written all over his skin that everyone could see it, it felt so alive to him. He had taken a liking to local girls before. But nothing like this, nothing like her. Beatrice. Bea.

He was coming up to the Jitties now, the rabbit warren of lanes and alleyways where poor folk lived in higgledy-piggledy squatter cottages, the names of each lane representing the names of families who'd lived there or old folklore. He walked along Spout Lane, past the pipe out of which poured spring water and by a woman carrying two buckets of water on a yoke back to her house. He went on down Quarry Road, left onto Carters Jitty, down Mission Jitty, along Simmonds Jitty, down Crews Park, then turned onto King Street, seeing the King's Head tavern before him. He stopped and almost turned back. He could not face what was to come, not right now. He wanted to run to Bea. Then, he cursed himself for his weakness. To lose your mind over a girl, and the enemy at that? But she had agreed to help him, to help them. Perhaps they were no longer enemies, perhaps they could even have a future. But he was still lying to her. How would she feel about him if she knew he'd courted her from the start for Adam's rebellion?

Head down, hands shoved in pockets, he stalked across the road and went into the tavern, seeking out the meeting room and hearing the hubbub of noise drift up the stairs as he descended. It was full of his fellow brickmakers and their children, talking excitedly, some angrily. A table was set up at which people queued to sign the open book. They were paying the subs that would help to see the worst affected families through the strike days ahead. Owen hoped that it would indeed only be days and no longer. He feared what would happen to those families that were poorest if the strike lasted longer than the weekend, let alone weeks on end. The pennies they collected in subs wouldn't last long if that were the case. Surrounded by his people, his desire dissolved like river mist in sunshine.

Adam saw him across the room and caught his eye, gesturing him to come over. As he made his way through the crowded room, Owen glanced about to see if his parents were there, but he couldn't see them. He knew his father was against the strike and wouldn't want to come, but he'd wondered if his mother might force him. Once she made her mind up, she was difficult to refuse.

'Owen,' said Adam and took a puff on his pipe. He looked grim and tired. Owen nodded at him. 'Have you been with her?'

'I have.'

'Any news? What did she tell you?'

Owen thought of her lips and swallowed hard, trying to erase the memory.

'She told me she came to the yard dressed up like a poor lass.'

Adam looked incredulous, then laughed. 'She didna! Did she?'

Owen took up his laugh, but it rang hollowly to his ears. 'Arr, she said she came to see what the brickworks was all about and she got the shock of her life.'

'Danker me! What possessed the wench? Why didna she come with her family?'

'She wanted to know what it was truly like. She was angered by it. She wants to make things better, I reckon. For us. For all the workers. She's already spoken out for us. Asking her family to improve conditions.'

Adam listened carefully and watched Owen as he spoke. Owen could feel his true feelings for her simmering over and believed Adam could see right through him.

'Is she sweet on yer, lad?'

Owen willed himself to be stony-faced. 'I reckon so.'

'And she wants to help us, you say?'

'Arr, I believe so. I know. She said as much. She said she'd help us in her own way.'

Owen waited while Adam puffed thoughtfully on his tobacco and blew out a stream of blue-grey smoke. Then, he grinned. 'You've done a fine job! The daughter of the house following you about like a puppy and all in a fluster as to how she can help the common folk. I couldna planned it better myself. Well done, lad!'

Owen felt a hearty clap on his back from Adam and he grinned back at him, but it was fakery and inside he felt sickened by it all.

'Thank'ee,' said Owen, having no other words, as he just wanted to get out of there and get away.

'Now then, the next time, see what you can wheedle out of her about the other brickmasters, what they're up to, what the Kings might be leaning towards. We need to know their intentions if we are to outrun them and win the day. See what you can find out, lad. But be careful, be wary. Dunna give away much about our side. When do you see her next?'

'We agreed to meet tomorrow afternoon. Now I'm not at work, there is more chance to see each other.'

'But where? You canna be seen with her.'

'Dunna werrit, we have a secret place.'

Adam raised his eyebrows in wolfish approval. 'Good lad. Good lad! Come see me after and report the latest.'

Owen walked home slowly. If his legs had been in charge, they would've run all the way to the old brickmaster's house and taken his girl in his arms again and kissed her. But she would be gone, back to the King house and he was due back at his own. The impossibility of what they were doing assaulted him – the stupidity of it! How could he have let himself be beguiled by a King? But in the same moment he condemned himself in one ear, a voice in his other told him she was a good person, a lovely girl, a beauty too and mad for him. But then the nausea came again as he remembered that he was a spy, that he had fooled her into trusting him and she had responded faithfully. But his feelings were true. He did not have to tell her the truth about the spying. He could keep that to himself until . . . forever. Why not? And then, in the future, when this was all over and they could . . . could what? It was exciting to meet in secret, to fool them all and steal kisses in the shelter of the forest. But what would come of it? Secrets never lasted long in Ironbridge. Everyone knew everything about everyone. And one day their secret would come out. What future was there for the brickmaster lass and the brickburner lad? But she could help them, help all of them. Maybe, just maybe, it would be the making of them. Secretly, he and Bea could hatch plans to bring the two sides together. She could persuade the Kings and he could persuade Adam and the rest. Could it work?

So consumed was his mind, he had barely noticed the journey his feet made to take him home. He was coming around the bend and up the incline to his house, when he saw his parents standing outside it, his mother in his father's arms, smiling at each other. It was strange to see them so happy, when all around was fret and worry. The strike was making everyone else grumpy and scowling. His father saw him first and his face broke into a great, big smile.

'Son! There is news!'

'What is it?' he said, breaking into a trot to reach them.

'I'll let your mother tell you. It's all her doing.'

'With a little help from you, Peter Malone,' she said and smiled at her husband. 'Owen, I am expecting.'

Owen almost said, Expecting what? But then the meaning of the words found him.

'You mean . . . ?'

'Yes, lad!' cried his father. 'Another little Malone is on the way. After all these years. Can you believe it!'

His mother laughed and came to Owen, taking his face in her hands and kissing him on the forehead. The touch of his mother's rough, dry hands was like balm, calming him and making him feel that all was right with the world.

'It is a marvel, is what it is!' he said and went to hug her, but held back, looking down at her belly. He saw that there was indeed a bump there and said, 'I must have been living in a daydream not to have noticed it before.'

'Maybe you thought I was just getting fat!' she said.

161

'You have been in a daydream these past weeks, son,' added his father in a solemn tone. 'Time to wake up. There's a babby on the way and all the extra work that will mean, for all of us. Hard times are ahead.'

'Oh, let's not think on that today. Only happy thoughts today!' said his mother. 'You know, Owen, I never thought I'd have another. I lost three babbies, after you. You never knew. My mother was the same. She had only me, then no more. I thought I'd be the same as her. But now, this one is clinging on and there have been no signs of trouble. He's a strong'un, that's for sure. I have high hopes for him.' Her face was full of faith and it squeezed his heart to look on it.

'Me too,' said Owen and kissed his mother's cheek. She beamed at him, her face filling with laughter lines, yet looking younger than ever. Expecting a nipper agreed with her. But Owen felt ten years older. Now, the strike took on a different colour, a threat to his family rather than a triumphant act. With a baby coming, they'd need their wages more than ever. His mother needed rest, not to work harder to compensate for their lack of pay. Now he must focus on her and not on anyone else, certainly not on the King girl. The old loyalties to hearth and home were pulling at him. He felt an awful tug inside him, as he looked at his dear mother and thought of all she had suffered.

Owen didn't know she had lost babies before, or that his grandmother had too. He had never thought about why he was an only child. As a boy, he had asked his parents over and over if he could have a brother, not a sister – he didn't want one of those, and they would just smile at him and change the subject. To think, his lovely mother had been suffering all that time, mourning the loss of the children that never were. But she never said a word, never betrayed her grief to him. He looked at her dear face and realised how little he knew of what went on behind it. He thought about how little folk really knew of each other, of the people they live with every day. They thought they knew them so well, because their faces, their hands, their movements and habits were so familiar. But the inside of someone else's head was as mysterious and unreachable as the moon. Only the moon knew its own secrets and the same went for the mind of every person living and every creature that crawled upon the earth, swam through the water and flew against the sky. The world was alive with secrets.

Chapter 11

Queenie lay in bed listening to the house creak on Monday morning. She had had Jenkins inform everyone she was to spend the morning in her room, alone, with no interruptions. Her fury of Saturday night had only abated after a drink of something strong and acrid, given to her by Jenkins, which helped her sleep. She had not asked what it contained. She had slept through the night, with no dreams she could recall and no visitations, thank heavens. She had awoken on Sunday in a bit of a fog but once she had eaten her porridge with honey and had drunk down a strong pot of tea with plenty of sugar, she felt human again. She had immediately sent word to the other brickmasters and they had come later that day. After a day of vexatious meetings, arguing amongst themselves as to the best course of action, she had gone to her bed late, exhausted. She had awoken with an idea at the back of her mind and wanted the morning to mull it over.

She dispatched Jenkins to take a message to Brotherton. He and his wife had worked for the family for nearly thirty years now and they were wholly loyal. In her note to Brotherton, she had asked for the address in Ironbridge of a particular brickworker and his wife.

When Jenkins returned with Brotherton's reply, Queenie sat up sharply and said, 'I will go out this afternoon.'

'Not one of your wisest ideas. You need rest, woman.'

Queenie smoothed the covers over her lap and sat up straighter. 'I feel quite well now and moreover, needs must. I will be visiting the home of Mr Adam Jones and I will need you to accompany me, of course.'

Jenkins shot her a glance. 'Jones? Not the union fellow, Jones?'

'Yes.'

'The baby on the bridge's husband? *That* Jones?'

'The very same,' pronounced Queenie, holding Jenkins's fierce gaze.

'What in all that is holy do you want to do that for? That is the worst idea I ever heard!'

'I have my reasons. And if I succeed, this strike will be over before it's properly begun. And what's more . . .' But Queenie faltered, aware she was about to mention the curse of Betsy Blaize. She had nearly let it slip to Jenkins – how clumsy! She had known Jenkins longer and in more depth than any other person living and she knew this woman's character was built on the rock of hard facts. If Queenie gave a hint of the supernatural or a curse or anything of the like, Jenkins would scold her and not hear another word of it. She must keep it her secret. Yet Queenie's fears over Blaize's curse had intensified since the weekend's events. The baby on the bridge was to be evicted, the wife of a union leader, an enemy of the King family. How could she improve her lot in life now?

'And what? What's more?' said Jenkins.

'Then, amends will be made. I will reverse Cyril's eviction order, save their home and Jones will be so grateful, he will capitulate and end the strike.'

'Just like that?' said Jenkins, folding her arms, her face smug with sarcasm.

'Yes, just like that. I can be very persuasive.'

Jenkins shook her head and came to sit on the bed. 'Miss Alice,' she said, knowing the power of Queenie's real name to tug at her heartstrings, 'I'm telling you, do not do this. Everything you've built over the decades, everything you've fought for . . . in all those years, you've never kowtowed to anyone, not once. If you see this Jones now, on his home ground, you will weaken your position so much, this strike will likely last for months.'

'But why will it do that? Why?' demanded Queenie. She could only see the positives in going to see Jones personally, a show of good faith.

'Because he'll see your weakness. He'll think he can hold out till you give in. But he doesn't know you like I do. He doesn't know yet that you'll never give in.

So you and he will dig your holes deeper and deeper until you are both buried. Families will starve, the brickyard will go under. Nobody will win. Everyone will suffer. And the King name will be damaged, probably beyond repair. Is that what you've struggled all these years for?'

Jenkins looked at her closely. But she did not press it further, raised her eyes to the heavens, then went out to fetch what was needed for Queenie to get ready.

Once she was prepared and her hair a picture of control, she asked that Jenkins summon Beatrice, who appeared looking radiant. A strange way to be when all around was trouble.

'You look well, child.'

'I am well, thank you,' said Beatrice and beamed at her.

'Come and talk with me, you on the stool and I shall sit here, in my favourite armchair.'

Beatrice came and took her seat.

'I was going to ask if you were upset about our disagreement the other day, but you seem to have got over it.'

Beatrice nodded and her radiance faded a little. 'Yes, of course, I have been worried. I hate the thought that we should ever fall out about anything.'

'Please do not concern yourself. We are family and we support each other, mm? I may disagree with your actions but I can see that your heart was in the right place. You are a good person, Bea. You are my dear girl and I love you very much.'

'And I love you, too and I always will,' she said and gave Queenie a sweet peck on the cheek.

'I am glad to hear it, child. Perhaps there is a way you could prove the truth of that. I need to ask you a favour and I very much hope you will accept it.'

'Of course I will!' she cried. 'Anything! Name it.'

'First, I must have your word that nothing of what we shall discuss will be repeated to another living soul.'

Beatrice looked intrigued and energised by the thought of such a secret. 'Of course!'

'Even your mother? You must not speak a word of it to her either. It must only be between the two of us. Will you agree?'

Beatrice frowned slightly, her hand tensed against Queenie's hands. But then she seemed to make some internal decision and said, 'Agreed. Just the two of us.'

'Good. Today I will make an unannounced visit to the leader of the strike, Adam Jones. I will attempt to talk him round by assuring him that the eviction notice was not of my doing and is to be immediately revoked. You will accompany me, Beatrice. Your presence will soften proceedings, from a confrontation between masters and workers to a more social call. And your friendship with the brickworker you mentioned and your sympathy with him will help us to provide a reasonable front to this man and show a more human side to our negotiations. I want you to know that I am no monster, Beatrice. I do what is right for our business to flourish, yet at the same time I do wish for my workers to be provided for appropriately. Agreed?'

Beatrice had listened to all of this with a growing smile. 'Oh yes, indeed. I would be thrilled to accompany you. I will do my best to help, but I will take my lead from you. Thank you for asking me! Thank you most of all for listening. And for trusting me.'

∽

When Jenkins saw Queenie was to go out with Beatrice, she gave Queenie a queer look. It looked like a mixture of scorn and envy. Queenie ignored it and enjoyed the walk out with her great-granddaughter, climbing into the landau together and holding hands, cuddling up on the seat. Queenie had never met a young person so affectionate. It was utterly disarming. She had not told the child everything – how could she? Instead, she had given her an edited version of events. She had said that Adam Jones was the leader of the strike, a fact. That his wife Martha was found as a baby on the iron bridge, another fact, her mother dying the same night, also a fact. That her dead mother had once worked as a maid at the King house, true. That since Martha's mother had once been employed by the Kings and Martha had been through enough difficulties in life, the Kings should not be the cause of any further hardship, also true. Beatrice had agreed wholeheartedly with all of this and looked delighted that Queenie was proving how kind she could be, after their horrible argument. Beatrice did not seem to have it in her to look smug, but Queenie could see it gladdened her heart to be on this mission of mercy with her great-grandmother.

'It's all so colourful and romantic!' cried Beatrice after hearing these facts. 'A baby found on a bridge!'

Queenie smiled at her girlish notions of romance. However, as they trundled down the hill to the centre of Ironbridge and through its bumpy streets to the poorer part of town, the facts she had omitted whispered their secrets in her ear. That the dead mother had been raped by Bea's great-grandfather, when she was still a frightened, powerless child. That Queenie herself had dismissed the girl when she started to show and Queenie had done worse before that, much worse. She dismissed these distressing thoughts. *Rome was not built in a day*, she decided. This was a good start and it would have to do, for the moment.

The landau took them through the town and over the bridge to the street that the Kings owned, taken over when the previous brickmaster had gone bankrupt. These were the dwellings not far from the brickworks upon which Cyril had served eviction orders the night before. The ten houses were built from the local brick, a row that shared walls all the way along, so the whole street looked like one house with ten doors and twice as many windows. Queenie could see that several of the cottage doors were open, with people toing and froing, carrying all manner of domestic items out into the street and loading them onto handcarts. There were stools and settles and other bits of plain furniture piled up in the small square yards in front of each house. The residents had answered the eviction order already, wasting no time. Queenie had thought they might resist it. She felt a tightness in her chest at the role she was about to play, the bountiful owner come to reprieve the workers. As the carriage trundled slowly along the short street, she saw every one of those folk in the road turn and stop to look, unaccustomed to such a fine carriage appearing at their doorsteps. The landau pulled up outside the fourth cottage along, the Jones's house.

Queenie said, 'Out you get first, child. Then give me your hand and help me descend.'

Their coachman opened the door and Beatrice descended first, turning back to offer her hand to Queenie, who stepped gingerly into the muddy road. She looked up to see that several people in the road were still staring, now at her. On every face was a look of recognition. And hatred. Queenie linked arms with Beatrice, for comfort more than support, and lifted her chin, ready for anything. She considered making a speech to these people right then and there, telling them that the eviction order was quashed. But her innate dignity stopped her from making pronouncements in the mucky road and instead she turned towards the Jones's cottage. He could tell them all after she had spoken with him. That would be far more fitting.

As Queenie and Beatrice approached the door, it opened. Out came Jones, not seeing them at first, turning back briefly to say something to a figure behind him, presumably his wife. Then, he looked back and stopped. Queenie was a good reader of faces. His expression was that of triumph. Perhaps Jenkins had been right. Perhaps this was not a good idea.

'May I speak with you, Mr Jones? Inside?'

Jones nodded, said not a word and disappeared inside. Queenie looked at Beatrice, who swallowed nervously.

'Come, child,' said Queenie. They entered the dwelling. There was one room downstairs, L-shaped, with a pantry in the smaller part. The room was dominated by a range against the wall and in one corner was a steep narrow staircase going up to the room above. Standing before the stairs was a woman, her hands resting on her rounded belly, a few months pregnant with a little time to go. Her face was pale, her hair hidden beneath a greyish cap, but those large green eyes, staring in shock at her unexpected visitors, shone out in the gloomy room. Queenie was assaulted by the resemblance to her late husband and it made her feel faint. She glanced about the room, looking for a seat to sit on, but the room was empty, all the furniture gone. With nothing to obscure the walls, Queenie could see that mould blossomed blackly along each wall from the floor upwards. How she wanted to turn tail and flee, to sit down, to lean on her great-granddaughter's arm at least, or even merely pull out her handkerchief and hold it to her nose. But she did none of these things.

'Come to gloat?' said Jones.

All pretence at professionalism had left him, Queenie noted. *It is time to change this tune*, she thought.

'Not at all, Mr Jones. I have come to meet the family. Now then, Mrs Jones,' she said, looking directly at Martha, the sight of those green eyes still bothering Queenie, they were so like her husband's. She swallowed her discomfort and pushed onwards. 'We have not been acquainted before now. Allow me to introduce myself. I am Mrs King and this is my great-granddaughter Beatrice Ashford. Please forgive us descending upon you with no notice, but time is of the essence, I see.' She gestured vaguely behind her.

'Ma'am, miss,' said Martha and bobbed a slight curtsey, then glanced nervously at her husband.

'What do you want with us?' said Jones. 'We are leaving in a matter of minutes. You could've sent a lackey to see this. But I'm supposing you wanted to enjoy the sight of it yourself.'

Queenie heard the anger in his voice and saw defiance in his stance. 'You do me a disservice, Jones,' she said and smiled, which seemed to increase the fire in his eyes. 'I am here to overturn the eviction and inform you that you may stay. All of you. The whole street. The eviction order was not sanctioned by me. It has been a misunderstanding.'

She awaited the gratitude and the turnabout of their chilly reception. But the Joneses simply stood and stared at them. Martha glanced at Adam, but nobody said a word.

'I hope I have made myself clear,' tried Queenie. 'The eviction is overturned. You do not have to leave these dwellings, any of you.'

Jones said, 'That may be so. Tell the neighbours if you like. I shanna be living in a King house no longer.'

'Mr Jones,' Queenie began. 'It would be pure folly to . . .'

'Dunna try to persuade us. We have a place to go, Martha 'n' me. A place where we are welcome and wanted. Unlike here. And they'll be expecting us. So, if you dunna mind . . .'

Jones held out his hand, to show them the door. Queenie stuttered, 'But . . . but Mr Jones.' She glanced over at his wife, hoping to appeal to her reason instead. 'Surely, Mrs Jones, in your condition, you do not want to leave your home.'

But Martha was silent and tight-lipped.

'Please, may I say something?'

It was Beatrice. Well, if the girl could make them see sense, it might help.

'Of course, my dear,' said Queenie.

'Mr Jones, I am friendly with Owen Malone.'

Jones said nothing, but glanced downwards at the floor. *An odd reaction*, thought Queenie.

Beatrice continued, 'He had told me of the conditions at the brickyard.'

Oh no! thought Queenie. The girl was not going to admit she'd been there, was she?

'I was unhappy to hear that things were not good there. I spoke to my great-grandmother about it. And I know that my great-grandmother came here today to make things right. I am sure that we can all work together to end this dispute.'

At least the girl did not admit her humiliating incognito visit to the brickworks. But she was rushing too far forwards, with these ideas of conciliation. Queenie must interrupt her before she weakened their position. But Jones got there first.

'You're saying the Kings will meet our demands?'

'The eviction is the pressing matter,' said Queenie, attempting to delay answering that question or anything like it, until she had a more formal setting in which to discuss terms. 'Please be assured that you are welcome to stay in these houses. They are your homes, you and your neighbours.'

'Not much of one.'

It was Martha, speaking up for the first time. Queenie turned to look at her.

'Look at the walls,' she went on. 'The damp grows and grows and never stops, however much I scrub it. Like a black, creeping death. I dunna want my babby exposed to it. We tell your man about it every month, when he comes to fetch our rent. We tell him about the hole in the roof too, where we have to put pots and pans upstairs to catch the rain when it comes in. But he hasna done a thing about it. After two years of telling. Not a thing.'

Queenie glanced at the black mould creeping across the walls and felt a shudder of disgust, tinged with shame. 'I will admonish my man for not responding to your requests and not informing me of these necessary repairs. It will be addressed on the morrow and all necessary repairs paid for by my family. We will make this a home fit for your baby, never fear, Mrs Jones.'

'Too little, too late,' said Jones. 'We do not wish to discuss housing with you. We have made our plans and are now delayed in carrying them out. All I wish to know from you is the question I have already put to you. Will you meet our demands?'

The man was a dog with a bone. 'We are not going to discuss such things now, here,' said Queenie sharply.

'Then, our conversation is over.'

'Please, Mr Jones,' said Beatrice. 'I am sure we can come to some arrangement, Great-grandmother? Can we at least discuss pay?'

'Yes! Pay. Tell me the wage per thousand bricks will not go down.'

Queenie regretted bringing the child with her now.

'I can make no such promise. The brickworks must remain competitive. Do not forget, Mr Jones, that the previous owner went bankrupt and nearly caused the closing of the brickyard. The Kings saved the business and we must run it as we see fit, in order to make it a profitable enterprise. With our competitors lowering their costs, to remain competitive so must we.'

'But you have the power, the standing in this community,' said Jones. 'You could stand alone from them, if you saw fit. You're rich enough, by God.'

'And where will it all end?' cried Queenie, exasperated. 'A penny today, a guinea tomorrow!'

'And why not?' spat Jones. 'We work ourselves to an early grave for it. Why should we not be paid in gold for our sacrifice? Without workers this country would crumble and fall in a week. And where would you be then, without your servants and your brickies and all the poor folk who prop up your comforts?'

'These are the rumblings of sedition, Mr Jones. And I will not stay to hear them.'

Queenie turned and looked at the open door. Through it, she saw that all of the neighbours that had been filling their carts with their possessions were now gathered in a silent, grey crowd outside, listening to every word, blocking her exit. Panic rose in her throat and she feared she would faint.

'Beatrice,' she said, summoning her last ounce of dignity. 'Please lead the way to our carriage.'

She felt the girl's arm link with hers and a warm flow of vitality flooded back into her from her beloved

Beatrice's touch. She lifted her head and fixed her eyes at the cloudy sky above the heads of the little mob at the door, allowing Beatrice to make the excuses to part the throng and get her safely into the landau. She sat back onto the carriage seat and did not look up as they left. She and Beatrice did not speak as the carriage laboured up the hill, homewards. Queenie did not wish to explain herself and the girl seemed to be keeping quiet out of embarrassment. Queenie spent the whole journey staring at her own gloved hands. Only when they came up the gravel driveway to Southover did Queenie lean forward to see the welcome sight of her own beautiful house, thankful to be back, away from the world and all its filth. But she glimpsed the family graveyard and it chilled her for a moment, before she heard her inner voice answer the request of another employee of the King family, long ago dead and now haunting her with its demands.

I did my best, Queenie said in her thoughts, to the spirit of Betsy Blaize. *I went to them on their own home ground and said they could keep it, for heaven's sake. It is not my doing that they rejected sense. I did try.*

Not hard enough, came the ghostly reply.

Chapter 12

They came at night. Nobody knew about them until a tramp who used to mind the kilns was passing the brickyard, bemoaning the fact that the kilns were cold and gone were his nice warm nights. And he saw them filing through the front gate, dozens of them, walking up the incline to the huts where it looked like they might be sleeping for the night. He'd heard them talking. They spoke English but with a strange accent. Irish maybe? Scottish or somewhere north? He had never left Shropshire, so did not know the accents beyond its boundaries. He'd run back to Broseley and told a brickie friend of his and then word spread fast.

Word arrived at the Malone residence early the following morning. Owen was asleep in his new position on the floor by the fireplace. It'd been all change in their house to accommodate the new arrivals. Martha slept in with his mother, both pregnant women deserving and needing the best bed, of course. Adam and his father shared Owen's bed, top to toe. Sometimes one would tire of the other's snoring and settle on the floor instead. It wasn't ideal, but at least the men weren't working these days, so they did not desperately need every moment of sleep like they had before. Owen was closest to the front door when the knock came. He heard the others muttering as he leapt up and ran to it, so urgent the knocks became.

It was the boy Brain, eyes agog and breathing hard.

'What is it?' said Owen.

'The Kings got in scabs to break the strike!' cried Brain, overexcited.

'How do you know? Have you seen 'em?' said Owen, regarding much of what Brain said with scepticism.

'Not me but word come from old Furlong the roadster. He saw 'em going in. Speaking in a strange tongue. They come from off. Maybe Irish'uns.'

Owen's father and Adam were up now and approaching the door. Adam got there first and reached out, shaking Brain's hand, much to the latter's surprise.

'Good lad, Brain. Well done for coming with the news.'

'Thank'ee!' said Brain, delighted.

'Go find Marshfield, Lunt and Deeley. Tell 'em to call their teams to The Swan by lunchtime at the latest. We must hold a meeting this day.'

Owen noted his father hanging back, rubbing his eyes. Peter had followed the strike orders like all of his colleagues. He was no blackleg. But Owen could see that he did not like to get involved. His mother, Anny, on the other hand, was as militant as ever, appearing from her bed, wrapping a shawl about her and asking what was going on. Brain had gone by now and soon the family – with their new members – were seated around the table eating a breakfast of bread and dripping, with a few fried-up potato slices left over from dinner the night before.

'Only two weeks in and already they have shipped in scabs,' said Anny, shaking her head in disgust and serving up more potatoes onto a central serving plate from which everyone took their share.

'They have no shame,' added Martha, dunking some bread in her cup of tea.

'We all knew this would happen,' said Peter, quietly. There was no tone about his voice, no suggestion of 'I told you so'. He was simply stating a fact. But his words hung in the air, as the voice of fact against the voice of anger.

'Well, yes. It was expected,' said Adam. 'But not so soon, I must admit. I dunna think they're from across the sea. And I dunna think they're Irish. I've heard tell that Cyril King has connections in Liverpool. I reckon he got the scabs in from there.'

'What does it mean, though?' asked Owen. 'What happens now?'

He was looking at his father, out of deference, but it was Adam who answered. 'Now we stop the talks. Every meeting I've had with the Kings and the other brick-masters this past fortnight has got us nowhere. And now they have broken their word and got in workers. We will cancel our next talk with the Kings and instead we must proceed directly to the yard and start the next stage of our campaign.'

Owen saw his father grimace, then poke a finger in his mouth to pick his teeth. His sour face could have been at something lodged in there. Or it could have been distaste at what his cousin was saying.

'What will that be?' asked Owen.

'We must set about harassing these workers and seek to drive them away. We shall protest at the gates each day and night, all of the day and night. We shall take it in shifts. We shall never let up or give in.'

'Never!' cried his mother and Martha added, 'Nor ever!'

'Come, lad,' said Adam, pushing back his chair and standing up. 'We must get on to the tavern and be there to greet our fellow strikers before the meeting starts. You coming, Peter?'

Owen saw his father continue to pick his teeth, taking his time to answer, staring straight ahead and not at Adam or anybody. 'Not today,' he said. Owen caught a glimpse of his mother, her eyes falling, her mouth set in a hard line. 'Work to do round here. Ground won't weed itself. We'll need those vegetables to grow out there more than ever now.'

Adam said nothing and went to the door, pulled on his boots and grabbed his cap. Owen did the same and out they went. Part of him wished his father was coming too, as he felt embarrassed by his lack of commitment. But part of him was glad, as he had something to talk to Adam about, out of his father's earshot. The two of them set off at a good pace, eager to get to the tavern, see their comrades and make plans.

'I had a plan to see the girl today, in about an hour,' Owen told Adam.

'Good, good. Then you must go. Dunna fret about missing the meeting. You are doing our work yer own way. I'll make excuses if anyone asks and I wonna be saying you're doing housework neither.'

Owen sensed a dig at his father, but did not respond. 'I'll walk with you far as the bridge then turn off.'

'Not much chance to talk to you about her these days, being so much in yer parents' good company. Any progress?'

Owen thought of how to measure progress in his meetings with Bea over the last two weeks. He had moved from kissing to putting his hand in various places on her body where he had never before touched a girl. That was certainly progress in his book.

'Nothing about the scabs. She didna know about them. She'd've told me.'

'There be only so much use in the girl unless she can become a bit more of a spy. Can you ask her? She

183

must loiter about more and listen in on things. Other-wise, we are wasting our prize asset. Surely, she is useful already, being in the house. But the stakes are higher than ever now and we must make more use of her.'

'I see that, but to be fair, she is arguing our side with her elders every chance she gets. As for more spying, I'll see what I can do.'

'And make sure . . . well, how can I put it? There must not be any . . . complications.'

Owen watched their boots stamp forward as they walked along the river path briskly onwards to the bridge. 'Not sure what you mean,' Owen said and glanced over at him.

Adam was not looking at him, instead staring straight ahead with his hands in his pockets. 'I suppose you've been cwtching and so forth. Kissing and such foolery.'

Owen said, 'Summat like that.' He did not want to talk about this with Adam. But also, he couldn't appear as if he did not want to talk about it. All along, he felt he had managed to keep up the façade of a lad toying with a girl's affections, not taking any of it to heart. Adam would not be happy with the truth, that his heart was gone, given fully to Bea Ashford.

'Well, make sure it goes no further'n that.'

'Course,' said Owen, but was not entirely sure what he was agreeing to.

His uncertainty must have come out in his voice, because Adam let out a harried sigh and said bluntly, 'Dunna get the girl in the family way.'

Owen gulped down a lump in his throat.

'Course,' he said again, in a small voice.

'All hell will break loose if you do.'

Neither spoke further. There was a grunt between them as they parted ways at the bridge. Owen went on alone, ducking into the woods to follow the path to the old brickmaster's house, where he was due to meet Bea in a short while. There was nothing he wanted more than to lie with her and be with her in that way, to be unclothed and alone, skin to skin. To see her in all her glory and to feel her as nobody else ever had, closer to her than any had ever been. He had thought of little else these past weeks. He dreamt of it by night and daydreamt of it the rest of the time, picturing the scene and haunting his own body with imagined feelings. He had never done that with a girl and so did not know what it might feel like. He could only think it must be like heaven. What a miracle it was, that amidst the drab routine of everyday life, there was this secret rapture at the heart of every home. The act of becoming one with another body was as forbidden as mortal sin and yet as common as muck. And he wanted it, not when he had a wife to make it lawful, but now, with this girl, with the King heiress. Her money, his poverty, her family and his – none of this mattered when two bodies met. He was her Owen and she was his Bea. That was all.

As he rounded the path and the house came into view, he knew it was all hopeless. Adam was right. There was no way he could bed the King girl. A child would be a disaster. And however much he would give his right arm to make such a girl his wife, he knew they could never marry. So it would never happen. He had to swallow these bitter facts.

But here she came, hurrying along the path after him, calling his name. And he feared that the iron will he needed to resist her would melt like molten metal the moment she touched him.

They did not speak at first, their greeting consumed with passionate kisses.

Bea pulled away, her face aglow and full of excitement.

'Here!' she cried. 'I have the keys to the house. I stole them from Great-grandmother's office!'

She flourished a set of keys from a pocket in her dress and jangled them.

'What house?' said Owen.

'This one, silly! The old brickmaster's house. We can go inside.'

'Should we?'

'Yes, why not?'

He looked at the building and raised his eyebrows. 'Folk say it is haunted.'

'Ooh, do they?' she gasped and turned to stare at the house, her hand on one cheek and eyes wide. 'Now we simply must go in!' She grasped his hand. He let himself be pulled towards the house, feigning reluctance. 'Come, come! Let us scare the spirits away.'

She reached a side door and tried a key, that didn't fit. She tried another and this one caught. She turned the key in the lock. The door was large and thick, made of carved, dark wood. Beatrice walked in breezily. Owen had never stepped across such a threshold. The smartest building he'd ever entered was the church. He stepped in guardedly and found himself in a dim passageway leading to a corner. Beatrice had already disappeared around it. He followed, listening to the click-clack of her shoes ahead of him on the stone floor. He came upon a large hallway to the main part of the house, an elaborate pattern of tilework on the floor, in shades of terracotta, white and black. The tiles looked old, like a ruined floor of an abbey. The decoration on each tile was simple, like a kind of flower, yet together the floor created a complex pattern of light and dark that confused the eye.

'It's pretty,' said Beatrice, quietly.

'It's owd, very owd,' said Owen, also in a quiet voice. There was something about the house that made him want to speak in hushed tones. Every door that faced onto the hall was closed, giving the space a muffled, dense atmosphere. Beatrice strode over to the nearest door and opened it confidently, letting in light that streamed across the floor in a sharp-angled shape.

They went inside to find it had once been a sitting room. Largely empty, there were some chairs near the window shrouded in white sheets. Dust motes floated in the light, disturbed by their entrance.

She turned to him and said, 'I thought it would be fun to come inside. But actually, it feels sad.'

'It is a sad place. And for good reason.'

'What happened to the brickmaster who used to live here?'

'You dunna wanna know that, wench,' said Owen, stepping towards her and drawing her near, leaning in to kiss her, so they didn't have to talk about it any further.

'I certainly do. Tell me!'

'It is a tragic tale.'

Her face fell. 'But now I must know. What happened to him?'

'When he lost his business and all his money, he drank himself stupid at a tavern. The men tried to take him home, but he would have none of it. He was found the following morning, on the mud by the coracle hut. Drowned.'

Beatrice shook her head. 'That is awful. I'm so sorry.'

'We were sorry too. Everyone was. He was a good man.'

She turned from him and folded her arms, thoughtful. 'Is there no end to my family's crimes?' she said in a low voice.

'The old brickmaster lost his business himself, nothing to do with the Kings. He never was good with money, so they said.'

She turned back to him, her eyes bright. 'But the Kings still profited nicely from his misfortune, did they not?'

'That they did.'

She looked at him searchingly. 'Do you blame me, for my family, making life so hard for you all?'

'Of course not. You've done nothing wrong.'

'I profit from them though,' she said, looking down at her dress. 'My things, my luxuries. Living there with them. Even taking the key to come into this house. Now I know what was lost here, I wish I'd never brought you inside.'

'Why did you bring me here, Bea?' he asked softly.

'I foolishly imagined it would be an adventure. But also . . . I thought . . . we might have some privacy. Was I wrong to do so?'

Her face was serious, her eyes searching his for an answer. He wondered if she had any idea what a man and a woman might do, when they are alone in a house.

'I canna stay here, Bea. I'm sorry.'

Her face fell. 'Why? Must you go?'

'No, I can spend a little time with you. But we shouldna be in here.'

'Is it because of him, the old man, and what happened?'

'No, it inna that. I shouldna be in this house with you, alone. It inna . . . right. Or safe.'

'But, whatever can you mean? What isn't safe? The house is perfectly well made. Benjamina was even talking about us moving in there.'

'No!' he raised his voice and it took her aback. 'I'm sorry, Bea. It inna that neither. Listen, if I stay in here with you, I fear what we will do. I fear what will happen between us. Dunna you?'

Bea glanced at her feet, then lifted those beautiful brown eyes up to him, twisting his insides like wringing a sodden cloth. 'I was hoping something might happen,' she said, quietly. 'Is that very wrong of me?'

'Yes,' he said, firmly. Then, at the sight of her forlorn face, added, 'I mean, no. It inna wrong. I mean, it is because we are not husband and wife. But I know I want to . . . lie with you. But we might get you . . . into trouble.'

'Nobody will find us here,' she said.

'No, Bea.' Was she really this innocent? 'You know what happens when a man and a woman lie together? A child might come of it. And we canna have a child.'

'Why not?'

He was perplexed now. Was it not innocence of the facts, then? Something else?

'Why not? Because we inna married.'

'Then let's get married!' she said and smiled. 'Let's run away together.'

'What?'

'My mother did it and started a new life in Paris. All right, it didn't end too well for her, but we would not be like that. We would make it work. We love each other so much, don't we? And that is all that you need in this world. Love.'

So, perhaps she wasn't so innocent about the sexual act. Instead, she was innocent about the world.

'There is more at stake than that.'

'Than love? Nothing is more important.'

'Bea, I canna run away with you. This inna no storybook. This is my life, my family, my friends. We are fighting here for our very lives.'

'I know that. I don't really mean it. I know we must stay and fight to make things better for you, for your family and for all the workers and children at the yard. But sometimes, I confess I feel selfish. My love for you makes me feel that way. There are times when I think of nothing else but you. Aren't you the same, sometimes?'

'Yes, but no. Thoughts of you fill my mind, it's true. But I do not have the same leisure to think as you. I must earn for my family and strive for them and for my people.'

'They are your people, yes. As the King family are mine. But we are more than that, we are individuals in our own right. And you are my love. I love you and you love me. Love conquers all!'

How little she understood. It exasperated him, even as she stood there with her stunning dark eyes and pouting mouth, making him want to hurl aside this stupid argument and just kiss her again.

'It inna just my mother and father, though that is enough. I would do anything for them. They have been the best parents a lad can imagine. Dunna you feel like that?'

'About my mother, yes. She has been my heart and soul as long as I can remember. I would do anything for her. I would die for her.'

'Me too,' said Owen. 'But it's beyond only close family. You may not know this, but the strike leader and his wife are living with us now. The very centre of the strike is in our home.'

'Mr Adam Jones? And his wife Martha, the one who's expecting a baby? I have met them. Mr Jones has been to the house. But my great-grandmother and I visited them, at theirs after Uncle Cyril evicted the workers.'

'Yes, I heard about that.' He did not say more, as he had been told an account of the meeting by Adam and it was not flattering to either old Mrs King or to Bea. Adam had characterised them both as royalty forced to converse with the gutter. Owen had smarted at the description. He knew that underneath Bea wasn't like that, however she had come across to Adam Jones.

His feelings must have shown in his face, as she continued, 'It was a wise idea, I believe, to try to speak with him and his wife. We went to try to make them stay. But they would not.'

'No, they wouldna. For good reason.'

'But why are they with you, now? Of all people, why are they staying with you?'

'Adam is my father's cousin. Well, he inna his blood cousin. Adam was once married to my father's . . .' His words trailed off. He had fallen into the trap of sharing confidences with her, but suddenly recalled who he was talking to. The daughter of the enemy.

'To your father's cousin, was it?' asked Beatrice, guessing at the end of his sentence. Was she simply interested or digging for information? His own spying had made him paranoid. Surely Beatrice was not engaged in the same pursuit as him. Was she a spy for the Kings as well? Had he been duped, all along?

'What is it, Owen?' she said and reached out to touch his arm. He flinched at it and she withdrew, hurt flickering in her eyes. He steeled his heart against it and chose his next words carefully.

'Listen. You must listen. This strike is killing us. There are children of brickies hereabouts grown dangerously thin. They dunna have enough food to eat. We get money to them, whatever we can, but there are too many and not enough food for us all. We must fight to end the strike as soon as possible. But for that, I need you. Only you hold the key to solving this crisis. Can you help us further, Bea?'

'Anything! Ask me and I will do whatever I can, you know that.'

'Speak to your great-grandmother again. Ask her to get rid of the scabs and get us back to work on our usual pay. We can talk about other conditions, but we must go back on the old pay. Nothing else will do.'

Bea frowned but nodded. 'She is a tough old bird and that's for sure. She is hard to persuade of anything. But I shall see what I can do.'

'Good!' he said.

'If I manage it, to get the strike ended, is there a future for us?'

So, this was what was at stake. The community's future rested on the strike outcome, as well as his family's. But even closer, his own happiness with the love of his life. Could it work? His mind raced forward, madly imagining a possible future, where the strike was done, the workers were back at good rates of pay and everyone's lives were better. And beyond that, himself, standing beside this beautiful girl, in a white dress with blossoms in her hair. It was madness, surely. Or was it?

'I cannot promise that, though I wish it with all of my heart. All I know is, once the strike is over and we are back to work, and nobody is starving, then we can talk further and make plans.'

'I will do it!' she cried.

Her face lit up with hope. It was a delight to see and he kissed her joyfully. Then, they kissed more deeply and joy gave way to a melting bliss, that flowed through his body like warm honey. He pulled away and they gazed at each other. All happiness was subsumed in passion now, serious and utterly compelling.

'You see the effect you have on me, Bea?'

'I know,' she said and pulled in close, her head beside his, resting her cheek on his shoulder. 'Me too.'

'And that's why we must be careful.'

'Yes,' she said and stepped backwards. 'But now we have a plan. We have a future, Owen!'

She moved to the door and beckoned for him to follow. She ran across the hallway, the dust flying in swirls as she passed through it. He ran after her and they came out into the day.

She locked the door and gave him a peck on the cheek. 'I will make things better. I will make it work. You'll see!'

And with that, she blew him a kiss, turned and trotted off up the path, homeward.

I hope to God she's right, he thought.

❦

Beatrice tried. She really did try. But Queenie was having none of it. Beatrice hardly saw her these days anyway, for she was either ensconced in her study with a variety of angry men coming and going or she was in her room, not to be interrupted, resting after the exertions of the day. The latest news was that two of the other brickyards had gone on strike too, and it seemed that some of the masters blamed the Kings for starting it. Beatrice could hear the arguments through the walls and floors of Southover, creating a constant air of disagreement in the house. The strike was not easy on anyone. What's more, the late June weather was unseasonably wet, with sweeping rainstorms for over a week, swelling the river and swamping the banks. Beatrice heard that houses were flooded and thus some of the poorest, scraping a living along the riverside, were worse off than ever. Out of work and now, out of house and home. The rain also meant an end to the excuse of walks for Beatrice, and with it, no opportunity to meet up with Owen. They had an agreement to meet at midday at the brickmaster's house every Tuesday, Thursday and Sunday, when they could manage it. But with the awful weather, Beatrice had missed three of these days and was pining for Owen so deeply, it felt like an insatiable hunger. She found herself seeking out food from the kitchens more often than ever, to fill her churning stomach.

She felt like a prisoner. At Southover, the day's proceedings were timed like military manoeuvres, under Queenie's strict regime. As much as Beatrice loved her great-grandmother, with no escape to soften it she felt disagreeably frustrated and took it out on her mother, griping at her over cards or at the breakfast table, when yet again the day promised nothing but rain. Her failure to deliver what Owen had asked of her was breaking her heart and her worry for the plight of the brickworkers only grew. But she could tell nobody here, which made it worse. Since she'd seen him last, she had tried on four different occasions to engage Queenie in a debate about the strike, trying to ease her way in through asking Queenie how it was going for her, for the Kings and the masters in general. But every time she tried to open a conversation about it, Queenie snapped it like a twig. She would not discuss it with her. Beatrice wondered if it was down to the fact that Beatrice had made it very clear how she felt about the brickworkers. Her dressed-up visit to the yard still remained a secret between the two of them and every time Queenie looked at her during these brief forays into the subject, Beatrice saw the accusatory stare of betrayal in Queenie's eyes. She wondered if her great-grandmother blamed her, too, for the meeting with Adam Jones not ending well. Thus, their discussions would end before they had really started. The feeling that they had joined forces to solve the crisis together had waned as the strike had progressed and relations between masters and workers had deteriorated further. Beatrice got the sense that battle lines were being drawn.

One Sunday morning, at breakfast, Beatrice took another slice of bacon, avoiding the smoked fish her mother was so fond of. Chewing away thoughtfully and staring over her mother's shoulder at the window beyond, she saw the first patch of blue sky she'd seen in days. Her dance lesson was due that day, which recently she'd been taken to in the carriage, due to the bad weather.

'Maman, look!' she said, pointing to the break in the clouds. 'I can walk today, yes? There is no rain.'

'Oh yes, so it is, *chérie*. Do walk if you prefer. I shall meet you there afterwards.'

'No, Maman!' she said urgently, then continued with a false brightness in her voice, 'I mean to say that last week Madame and I arranged that we would go for a stroll together after my lesson, as she had no more pupils after mine today.'

'Splendid,' replied her mother. 'Though it is worrying to hear that her day is not filled with lessons. I do hope Madame has enough pupils to make her way.'

'Indeed,' murmured Beatrice, thinking of how useful these weekly lessons had been to her and Owen. She had learnt very little about dancing, but had bought her freedom with the one regular chance she had to escape the house.

'And it's not long now until we shall be looking for an opportunity for you to have your first ball. You'll be coming out! Just think of all the excitement! Meeting the sons of all the masters in the area. I wonder who you'll fall in love with, my darling.'

'I wonder,' echoed Beatrice and hastily jammed her last piece of bacon into her mouth, before asking to leave the table.

After breakfast, she left by the front door, tying her bonnet ribbons as she hurried down the steps and onto the gravel. But the moment she'd left the house, she felt a drop of rain on her hand. She looked up to the sky, to see a dark mass of clouds above, but beyond it was more blue sky. So she hoped the rain would not last long. She decided to turn about and fetch her umbrella, just in case, then remembered that she had left it in the carriage under the seat the last time they'd been out. She crossed the driveway and walked around to the back of the house, where the stables and the coach-house were. There was a boy loitering near the horses but the coachman or grooms were not about, so she went in without having to speak to anyone about it. She opened the carriage door and found her umbrella, stowed under the seat and still damp. She grasped it, then shut the door, glancing outside to see the rain falling more heavily. She tutted and held out the umbrella before her. It was a pretty thing, with a mother-of-pearl handle and a pale pink canopy. She pushed it open and shook it out, drops of old rain flying off it in arcs.

'Oh no, miss!' came a cry.

She lifted her umbrella to reveal the stable boy had appeared in the doorway, staring at her, mouth open.

'What is it?' she said, annoyed but also a little alarmed.

'You mun open no numbrella indoors. It be the worstest bad luck.'

'Well, I'm not really indoors. The coach-house doors are open, see?'

The boy was shaking his head in horror. 'You mun never risk it. You'll be dead before the year be out.'

'Oh, what rot!' she scoffed and flourished her umbrella towards the boy, who fled. 'Superstitious nonsense.' Her umbrella was her friend today, allowing her to walk to her destination with some protection.

She walked out into the rain, her umbrella doing its job well. A movement in the corner of her eye caught her attention. Thinking it might be that superstitious boy again, she prepared to shoo him off, when she saw it wasn't him, but two other children. They were sneaking across the yard towards the back of the kitchen. There was no other way to describe it, as they were on barefooted tiptoe with their shoulders hunched and arms curved out, pattering along until they disappeared behind the kitchen wall. They did not work at Southover, that was for sure, as they were dressed in rags and as Beatrice had already spotted, they had no shoes on. Whatever were they doing here? She found herself sneaking along the wall too, to follow their route and peek around the corner of the building. But a spoke of her umbrella scraped against the wall as she came round and the two children looked up anxiously, ready to run, a boy and a girl. They were standing over a mound of rotting matter, old vegetable peelings and skins of fruit and other kitchen scraps. They both had what looked like potato skins in their hands and protruding from their mouths as they chewed voraciously.

The moment they saw her and clocked her rich clothes, they bolted.

'No, please!' cried Beatrice, as they ran. 'Please come back. I'll give you meat!'

They stopped dead in their tracks. The girl said something to the boy, but the noise of the rain obscured it from Beatrice. She called again, 'I mean it. I shall find you some bacon. Would you like that?'

The girl came forward nodding, while the boy hung back a little. As they approached, she saw more clearly how thin their arms were, how drawn their faces. They had those same young-old faces she had seen at the brickyard, children grown ancient before their time. They were shivering in the rain.

'Here,' she said and held out the umbrella to the girl, who was closer. The child stared at it, held out her hand and took it warily. Beatrice supposed she'd never held such a thing in her life. She grasped it awkwardly with both hands and held it high above her head. The boy came up and nestled under it, close against the girl. Beatrice looked down at their bare feet, so white they stood out like baked cod against the russet tiles of the yard floor. She glanced behind her at the coach-house and beckoned to the children, who watched her move over to the door and gesture through it. Another word or two passed between them and they decided to follow. Once inside the coach-house, the girl still held the umbrella up and Beatrice reached out, taking it gently from her.

The act of closing down the umbrella and placing it against the wall seemed to fascinate the two, as they gaped at Beatrice's every move.

'Wait here,' she said. 'I will fetch you something good to eat.'

The girl nodded. Beatrice went over to the kitchen and opened the door. Cook was there and two kitchen maids. Cook's face went from surprise to disapproval in a second.

'There inna anything for you here, miss,' said Cook.

'Oh, but it's not for me!' she cried, then realised that she hadn't meant to say anything about the children to anyone.

Cook narrowed her eyes and replied, 'Arr, of course it inna. It be for the fairies.'

Beatrice took a step forward confidentially and said, 'Please, Mrs Guest.' Cook look impressed that the daughter of the house had remembered her name, but Beatrice had learnt from Queenie that it was always wise to know the name of every servant. 'Please. I need a little food. It doesn't have to be anything fancy.'

Cook looked more amenable, but was still torn. The two maids watched with interest. 'Miss, you know I love to feed you up but your mother has made it most plain that I am not to give you food outside of reg'lar meal times. I canna go against Mrs Ashford, I canna.'

'Listen, please. There were two children outside eating potato peelings.'

'There wasna! Little ratlins!' cried Cook and went to go towards the door, presumably to chase them off.

'No, please, Mrs Guest. They were starving. They had only rags to wear, no shoes. Their faces were sunken. I have them waiting in the coach-house. I could not square it with my conscience if I did not give them some meat before they go.'

The maids looked at each other with raised eyebrows, but Cook was not moved. 'If you give 'em a scrap, they'll be back in their hordes tomorrow. There's a thousand like 'em all along the river and through town and the next town and the town after that. Feeding one or two wonna ever cure that.'

'You're right. I cannot cure poverty and misfortune. I have not the power. But I can do this one small thing to improve the lot of two children we have on our very doorstep. Can we not offer them a hand of kindness, this one time?'

Cook shook her head but gave in. 'Just a scrinch, mind. Girls, help Miss Beatrice.'

She was given a lump of cheese, a couple of cold rashers of bacon left from the breakfast plates and a hunk of hard bread from a stale loaf Cook had been saving to make breadcrumbs, all wrapped up in a cloth. Cook tutted throughout the procedure. 'Dunna give 'em my cloth!' she called to Beatrice as she left the kitchen. 'I want that back.'

Beatrice went back to the coach-house, half expecting them to have gone, as if she had imagined the whole thing. But there they were, standing in the exact same spot she'd left them, shivering and holding on to one another for more warmth. At the sight of food, all decorum left them and they threw down the umbrella and fell upon her hands, shoving the bacon into their chomping mouths first. Then they ate cheese, which the girl grabbed first and the boy grasped a chunk of before it disappeared behind her teeth. Then they ripped the bread apart and ate that noisily too. It was all gone so quickly, Beatrice felt ashamed she had not brought more.

'Have you no parents?' she said, softly, so not to frighten them.

'Yes,' said the girl, still finding crumbs about her mouth or down her front to pick at. The boy was crouched down and dabbing his fingers on the ground, securing more crumbs and licking his filthy fingers to get at them.

'You do have parents? Or you don't?'

'We've parents,' said the boy, not looking up from his work on the floor.

'What do they do? Do they work?'

The girl nodded. 'They be brickies.'

The boy stood up and smoothed back his wet hair. 'They be at your yard. Or they would be, if it wonna filled with Irishmen.'

The girl said, 'Shush!' and pushed the boy hard on the arm. She turned back to Beatrice and said, 'Thank'ee for the bait.'

'Come back tomorrow,' said Beatrice. 'Come every morning and I shall give you food.'

'Yes'm,' said the girl, but the boy grabbed her hand and ran off, dragging her with him. The little girl kept looking round at Beatrice, before the two of them disappeared into the woods behind the house.

Beatrice stood still for a moment. She looked up at the sky to see that the dark clouds were passing and the rain was almost gone. She knew that the sight of those waifs devouring that food would never leave her. She had used the word 'starving' before, to complain to her mother that she needed a snack, because she was a growing girl and nobody knew how constantly hungry she was. She now knew what it looked like to starve, to actually be starving. And her past words sickened her.

She returned Cook's cloth, then retrieved her umbrella, just in case, and walked out onto the yard. At that moment, the two kitchen maids appeared from around the corner and one lifted her chin and shouted, 'Louise!' The other one followed suit. Beatrice stepped back, so she was out of eyeshot and heard them gossiping about Benjamina, saying such things as 'We're always looking for that damned dog. Why does she let it run wild? It inna our job to look after it like a mollycoddled babby', and so on. Beatrice smirked as she listened, then their voices lessened as they disappeared behind the coach-house wall, but she could still hear them shouting the dog's name over and over as they went.

She stepped out and was ready to leave, at last, eager to get on and reach the old brickmaster's house. The thought of seeing Owen again, of touching him, made her cheeks go hot and she gasped at the strength of it. But someone was shouting behind her. It was the high, piercing voices of the kitchen maids. She so wanted to walk onwards, ignore whatever it was, some domestic disaster in which she had no interest. But their voices were shrill and she could not help but turn round and listen. One of the maids appeared and spotted her, her hand over her mouth.

Beatrice called across the yard, 'Whatever is it?'

'Oh Lord!' cried the girl and pointed behind her.

Beatrice walked quickly towards her. 'What? What is it?'

'Dead,' she said, her mouth gaping. 'She be dead as a doornail.'

'Who is?' said Beatrice, horrified to hear what was coming next.

But the maid was off, running into the kitchen. Beatrice raced off around the corner, in the direction the girl had come from. There was the other maid, staring at something on the ground. Beatrice ran up behind her, to see her step aside. There, on the ground, limp and pathetic, was Benjamina's little dog, Louise. Its veined eyes were wide open and its tongue stuck out, thick and dark.

The maid said, 'Oh, we shall be blamed! She will say it is our fault, all our fault. But how can we watch for a dog with all our chores to do? Oh, what will become of us!'

'Do calm yourself,' reassured Beatrice, staring at the poor dead dog, so grateful it wasn't the brickie girl, her first terrifying thought. 'I will take the dog. I will say I found her.' She put on a brave face and leant down to pick it up. The body was stiff and hard to the touch. She stood up straight, the body across her hands. As she stared at it, she realised the last thing anyone who loved this animal would want to see was its red eyes popping and its black tongue. She passed it to the maid, who took it with disgust.

'Find a sack for it and hide it, for the moment. I shall tell Mrs King.'

As she walked back towards the house, she knew she would not be seeing Owen today. She knew too that something terrible had happened here, beyond the death of a beloved pet. The animal had no blood upon it and no bite marks. That dog had been strangled.

Chapter 13

A week had passed since Louise's death. Beatrice had not been allowed out of the house at all since. That horrible day, Beatrice had told Queenie first, who looked dazed and then distinctly off-colour at the news, but soon recovered and said she would inform Benjamina. Since her arrival at Southover, Beatrice had seen that there was no love lost between Queenie and her daughter-in-law, but now she saw that Queenie was disgusted by what had happened to the little dog and was not looking forward to telling its doting owner. Beatrice went to her mother afterwards in her bedroom and told her what had happened. Maman was shocked to the core that 'such a cruel thing could be done to such an innocent'. At that moment, Beatrice thought of the two famished urchins that had devoured her food and she felt the phrase applied equally to them. Surely children were worth more than dogs. But the fact remained that her mother was right, the dog was innocent and had been deliberately killed to cause upset and fear.

Their talk was interrupted as they both heard a cry from the room across the hall, an inhuman wail that hollowed out the house. The strangeness of it left them both quiet and shaking their heads. Benjamina had not appeared from her room since, apart from the afternoon they had found Louise, where a solemn burial took place in the pet graveyard, alongside the bones of previous King dogs. Benjamina had insisted that no words were to be spoken, so she, Queenie, Margaret and Beatrice had watched the small wooden box the gardener had knocked together lowered into its resting place. Cyril was nowhere to be seen, Beatrice suspecting he had no time for the concept of dog funerals. Benjamina's face was unreadable, blank and pale. The little grave was marked with a posy of flowers, yet Queenie said Benjamina had ordered a gravestone with the inscription 'My beloved Louise, taken too soon by vengeful Death'.

The atmosphere in the house was stifling. The rains of the previous week had given way to muggy, cloudy heat that made the enforced curfew even more oppressive. Sometimes, to escape the house, Beatrice would take a turn around the gardens with her mother. They would talk of when Maman was a child and would tread the same walk. Maman told her how Benjamina had always had a little dog for company, but had loved this one the most. Sometimes, they would see Benjamina sitting at her window, staring out. Her large eyes in the white face were unsettling to look at and Beatrice would turn away. She

209

was filled with guilt and confusion. It felt as if her family had been attacked and yet her loyalties lay more with Owen than the Kings. Her feelings were swirling so violently, she felt nauseous with the puzzle of it all. The worst of it was that she had nobody to talk to about it. She could not reveal the truth about her and Owen to anyone. And even with him, she could not discuss the strike properly, as he was wholly partisan, as anyone in his position would be. She guessed that Owen's people, the strikers, had killed the dog. Everyone said it was so. It was a sickening, despicable thing to do. But she also knew that some of the strikers' children were starving. She had seen it with her own eyes. She would screw her eyes up to rid herself of the sight, squeezing her mother's arm more tightly.

'I know it is a distressing time,' her mother said on one such garden stroll. 'But it will pass. There were similar times when I was a child, dark times. But they passed. The fire of people's anger burns less brightly, cools and dies. It will turn to ashes and be swept away, you'll see. All will be well.'

'I do not think it will be well, Maman.'

'Have a little faith. You are young and time passes slowly for you. See it from my perspective and this is simply another bridge to cross. But we will get to the other side.'

Beatrice nodded, but was not convinced. Her hopes for a life for her and Owen beyond it all seemed further out of reach as every day of the strike passed, with no resolution. But her love for him burned brighter with each passing moment. The life she wanted and the life occurring around her were moving in opposite directions, pulled by forces beyond her reach. Maman was watching her and there was a moment where their eyes met and her mother stopped walking and looked at her; above her head the treetops of the woods beyond waved lazily in the thick air. 'You know that you can speak with me about anything. You've always known that, haven't you, Bea?'

'Yes, Maman,' she said and forced a smile. 'I know that.'

Her mother stared at her a while longer, waiting for Beatrice to say something. But Beatrice changed the subject and asked Maman if she would like to go inside and cheer themselves up by playing a duet on the pianoforte. Maman smiled her consent but looked concerned. There was nothing Beatrice would like more than to pour her heart out to Maman. She had always told her mother everything. But this was beyond anything she could share. She knew loving Owen would be met with not only disapproval, but now – with Louise's strangling – she was loving the enemy, pure and simple.

But then a thought occurred to her, something that had come from her lessons with Maman's pupils. Their lessons had revolved around the teaching of the English language. But sometimes, with the older pupils, talk strayed into other subjects, such as English customs, manners and habits, as well as English history, inevitably including the many wars between England and France across the centuries. Beatrice always felt that sitting there, discussing and learning with these French children and she herself, being a child of an English mother, were great proof that society was moving in the right direction, that talking, getting to know each other, was the way forward for any civilisation. And the only way to prevent such wars happening again was through knowledge first and then its offspring, understanding.

'Maman, may I play duets with you another day? I have not spent much time with Great-grandmother in recent days and I feel remiss.'

Maman smiled at her and cupped her cheek in her hand. 'What a good, kind girl you are. Run along, then. Take a pack of cards. How she loves to play cards!'

Beatrice left her full of fizzing energy, bolting up the stairs and arriving at Queenie's door, breathing hard from the exertion. She calmed herself, then knocked lightly on the door.

'Enter,' came Queenie's voice and in she went.

Queenie was sitting up in bed, awake and rested from her after-lunch nap. She had been distant these past weeks, but her gladness to see her favourite was obvious and she reached out her hand to Beatrice, who rushed across the room to take it and give it a peck.

'How *are* you?' she asked Queenie, earnestly.

'I am quite well, my dear. And how are you? All of this must be very upsetting for you. I am sorry for it.'

'I am quite well too, Queenie. Please don't worry on my account.'

'But I do, my sweet. You came here to Southover to take your place in English society and have the joy and excitement of coming out. And I worry it has been ruined by all this trouble.'

'It is the trouble I wish to talk with you about.'

Queenie looked disagreeable and took her hand away, putting it firmly on her lap and looking straight ahead. 'I fear it will cause us to fall out with one another and I do not wish to do that,' she said.

'I think that we can strive to discuss important matters without resorting to anger, don't you? And I must tell you something I know, that I have seen with my own eyes. Children are starving. I have seen brickworkers' children eating potato peel, ravenously hungry. We cannot allow this strike to continue any longer while children are starving.'

'Where did you see them?'

'Here, at Southover. They were foraging from the heap of scraps outside the kitchen.' She omitted the part where she gave them food, assuming Queenie would disapprove.

'Yes and the very same ragamuffins most likely harmed poor Louise!' snapped Queenie.

'Impossible!' cried Beatrice. 'They were too skinny and underfed to have the strength. They were shaking and shivering. No, these children were closer to their own death. So, we must protect them from this fate. We must come up with a way to end the strike as soon as we can.'

Queenie let out an exasperated sigh and closed her eyes. 'You see everything in black and white. You have no idea of the complexity of the situation.'

'Teach me, then. Explain it to me. I am eager to learn.'

Queenie opened her eyes and gave Beatrice a long hard stare, then seemed to soften. 'My hands are tied. I cannot offer better terms, as I have signed an agreement with the other brickmasters. And even if I did, my weakness would be seized upon by these union types and then we would have strike after strike, on any occasion where there was something they didn't like. There would never be an end to it. Thus, I cannot end the strike. The workers we brought down from Liverpool have gone. They could not withstand the pressure from the other brickworkers hurling insults – and in some cases, real brickbats! – day in, day out. So now the yard is closed again and we are losing sales and goodwill with our clients. If the strike continues beyond the weekend, then I have decided that we will close the brickworks for good.'

Beatrice listened intently to every word. It was clear to her now that there was no way on earth that Queenie – and those she did business with – would ever budge. All of this gave her plan more credence. 'Then, I have a solution for you.'

'Really, my dear?' said Queenie, sounding tired of the whole thing and distinctly sarcastic.

'Yes. I have told you that I had a friendship with a brickworker named Owen. Now, hear me out, please.

Owen's family are related to Adam Jones, did you know that?'

Queenie narrowed her eyes. 'No, I did not. But how do you know of it, child?'

Beatrice hadn't thought that far ahead. But her mind skipped and found a solution swiftly. 'I hear things. The servants gossiping. I've heard them talking about it. Owen's father is Adam Jones's cousin or his first wife's cousin or something. Anyway, they are staying with Owen's family, in their house, since they left their home.'

'All very fascinating, my dear, I am sure. But what of it?'

'I have an acquaintanceship with Owen, as you know. And yes, I am well aware you disapprove. But listen, what if I were to use this friendship to visit Owen, at his home, and speak to Mr Adam Jones. Perhaps, I can persuade Mr Jones to change his mind or at least to speak with you again. It is worth a try, is it not?'

'It is out of the question!' said Queenie, eyes agog. 'How could you imagine I would agree to such a thing?'

'But why?' cried Beatrice, irritated. 'You and I went to visit the Joneses at their house. How would this be any different?'

'Yes and remember how badly that went,' said Queenie.

'But things have changed since then.'

'Yes, for the worse! These people are monsters! How could I agree to send my great-granddaughter into that den of wolves?'

Beatrice hung her head and took strength from a deep breath.

'They are not animals, Queenie. They are people. They are fighting for a better way of living. And the Kings are fighting for their business, I see that. But whatever they have done, we have done. Whenever the strike comes to an end, whatever the outcome, the damage has been done and crimes committed on both sides.'

'And what crimes, pray, have we committed? As far as I am aware, we have not burnt down anyone's sheds or murdered anyone's dog.'

'Yes, but our family has done its fair share of wrongs. The conditions at the brickyard. Allowing children to work at these damaging jobs, watching their lives drain out of them, when they should be growing and learning and laughing. It is so wrong. Think too of the desperation of the people now there is no money coming in. Children are starving. It would break anyone's heart to see them, if that heart were not made of stone.'

'You need to see both sides if you are ever to understand the nature of profit and loss. One must be hard-hearted to make a business flourish.'

'Maman said to me that people's anger would burn out and all that would be left was a pile of ashes. But I think there would be a solid lump of hatred left in those ashes, hard as rock. We must find a way to reach out and join the two sides. There must be a shift on both sides. Surely that will be better for everyone, the business included. People make this business work. Surely we must appeal to them as people, for that is what they are.'

'People who would murder a dog?'

'And what of people who would let a child starve?'

'These workers chose to go on strike. We Kings did not want it. Nobody forced them to do it. They are letting their own children starve!'

'How can you say that?' said Beatrice with exasperation. 'What parent would ever choose such a thing? Their conditions at work and their poverty at home have forced them into a life with no choice. Are you so blinded by profit you cannot see that?'

Both Queenie and Beatrice sat with their chins jutting out, their eyes defiant. They had reached an impasse.

'We are very alike,' said Queenie, the ghost of a smile about her lips. 'As chalk and cheese as we may seem.'

'Let me go and talk to Owen and his family. Adam Jones will probably be there if I go at teatime.'

'But what would you say to them? What could you say? Everything that can be said has been said, with no progress.'

'At the very least, I can take him the fact that you are about to close down the brickworks if the strike does not end. That gives him one last chance to change his mind and those of his workers. They won't listen to you or the other masters and certainly not

Uncle Cyril. But I am a girl, softer in their eyes, not so threatening. They may dismiss me at first, but I can speak well. I believe I can make them hear me and make them listen.'

'You certainly have that gift,' said Queenie and considered her for several moments, looking at her face, her hair, her hands, then her eyes, as if taking in all that Beatrice was to her. *She'll never agree*, thought Beatrice. *She won't let me risk it, not me.* Then Queenie breathed in sharply as if coming to a sudden decision. 'Do it then.'

'Truly?' gasped Beatrice, genuinely surprised.

'It might just work. And it might get us out of this mess. If you can change my mind, you can change anybody's.'

'Ha ha!' laughed Beatrice. 'I will do my best!'

'But my dear, you must take someone with you. It's out of the question that you be without a chaperone in such a place.'

Maman would immediately see that Beatrice was sweet on Owen. She had that ability, to read Beatrice's face like a book. 'I cannot go with my mother.'

'Yes, it is probably wise to keep her out of this. She would not approve of the whole enterprise. We must keep it from her. Well, there's nothing for it but to take Jenkins. She will keep you on the straight and narrow. Go tomorrow. I'll say Jenkins is taking you on a nature walk, teaching you about the flora and fauna of Shropshire.'

Beatrice grasped Queenie's hands and kissed them. 'Thank you!'

'Thank *you*, my dear. Your initiative and passion to help may just be our saviour in this unholy chaos. I have never met a child so selfless.'

∽

The following morning, after a restless night bedevilled with nervous excitement, she heard an unfamiliar knock on the door, a staccato pattern. The sun was up, but the house was quiet. Beatrice dragged herself from her bed, went to her door and opened it to see Jenkins standing there, fully dressed.

'Chop, chop, Miss Beatrice. I'll send Dinah up to see to you. Choose your dress carefully. Nothing too fancy. We'll be walking a way and then visiting in a place that doesn't expect a crinoline. Keep it simple today, hmm?'

'Oh, yes, I see. Of course. Thank you,' stuttered Beatrice, half asleep but also a little afraid of Jenkins. She was the most senior female in the house, save Queenie herself, and had such an imperious manner, she demanded respect and awe from everyone beneath her. Beatrice included herself in the latter group. But then Jenkins did a funny thing, she winked at Beatrice, very deliberately, with an amused expression on her face. Then she turned and bustled off. Perhaps Jenkins was not so very fierce after all. At the very least, she seemed to be enjoying this subterfuge. Beatrice shut the door and turned with excitement back to her room. She went straight to her wardrobe to pick a suitable gown for the day. Not too showy and flouncy for the Malones and the Joneses of this world, but again pretty enough to hug her figure in all the right places, so that she looked her very best to see her darling again. It was a delicate balance, finding the perfect dress, and one she waited impatiently for Dinah to come up and assist her with, as she flicked through her choices, dismissing each one with mounting nerves.

After breakfast, the morning was spent twitchily, playing cards with Queenie for a while, playing duets with her mother too. Cyril came in and out, usually reading a magazine of some amusing sort. Benjamina stayed in her room, as usual. Lunch came and went, her mother and Queenie retiring to their rooms for a rest, to appear again at around three o'clock. Shortly after, Queenie announced to all that Jenkins would take Beatrice for a nature walk and they would take a picnic tea prepared by Cook. Jenkins knew the way, leading them through the woods, carrying their picnic in a basket. 'Nearly there now,' said Jenkins. 'When we arrive, I'll knock on the door and I'll introduce you. Any idea what you're going to say?'

'Some idea,' said Beatrice and gulped. She'd thought about it all night and all morning, but now all her speeches had flown out of her mind, like crows at the sound of a gunshot. The alarm of nearing Owen's cottage had unsettled her. She slowed her step.

Jenkins turned to her and said, 'Changing your mind? You don't have to do this, you know.'

Beatrice looked nervously at Jenkins and tried to smile. She could end all this right then and there, turn around and go home, where it was safe. But the image of the two hungry children floated before her. 'I know I don't have to. But I will do it. Someone must do something.'

'Good girl,' said Jenkins and on they marched.

The woodland path broadened and led them nearer to the river, which moved along swiftly on this humid day, still high from the recent rains. Beatrice could see the watermark halfway up tree trunks, with a couple of huts on the opposite bank submerged to the window ledges. Someone's home or livelihood lost. They were passing by some cottages now, safe on higher ground above the river. People were out and about, tending to livestock or smoking a pipe, watching the well-dressed pair pass by, no doubt wondering what on earth their business was here. A woman called for her chickens, 'Chook, chook!', then stopped and gaped at Beatrice, as a flurry of hens pecked about her own feet. Beatrice looked straight ahead, chin up. She wanted to appear like someone who knew exactly what she was doing. Inside, her heart was pounding.

'It's the third cottage along, over there,' said Jenkins, who approached the front door and rapped confidently upon it. The door opened.

There stood Owen. His curious glance changed to amazement as his eyes fell on Beatrice. She smiled, so widely, she forgot for moment that she did not like the shape of her teeth very much. How exquisite it was to see him with her own eyes instead of in her mind's eye. How she wanted to reach out and touch him. She had to pull herself together now.

'Mr Malone,' she began.

Owen was still staring at Beatrice, struck dumb. At that moment, a sound tore through them. It was a woman screaming. It came from within the cottage. Owen flinched as if struck, then stepped forwards, pulling the door to behind him.

'We cannot see anyone now,' he said. 'There is a baby coming.'

'Is it Martha Jones?' said Beatrice.

'Yes,' said Owen.

'Is the midwife there? Mrs Lunt?' said Jenkins.

'Yes, she's here,' replied Owen. 'But it inna going well.'

'How so?' said Jenkins.

'Martha's been at it for hours and hours now, since last night. The baby is stuck.' Owen pushed a hand through his hair and Beatrice saw his hand was shaking.

Jenkins said, 'Let me go in. I've seen more births than most. My mother was a midwife. Let me talk to Lunt.'

Owen stepped back, exhausted and in no fit state to argue. Jenkins put her basket on the ground next to the front door and went inside. Beatrice lost sight of her as the door swung back towards them, leaving it open only a crack. Beatrice turned to Owen.

'Are you well?' she whispered to him. How she wanted to reach over and touch his face. He looked older than when she last had seen him.

Owen glanced over her shoulder, chastened by the neighbours' inquisitive loitering behind them. 'Miss Ashford,' he said, a little louder. 'On any normal occasion, we would be honoured by such a visit. But today we are . . . we are . . .'

'Indisposed?' she tried.

'Yes, that,' he said. 'And I am sorry to say that now inna a good time.'

'Owen, let me help. What can I do? Can I fetch someone to help?'

Owen looked back at the door behind him, staring at the gap as if it had all the answers. 'The midwife . . .' he murmured.

Then the door opened. It was Jenkins. 'The woman needs a doctor.'

'We canna afford any doctor!' cried Owen.

'I can,' said Beatrice.

Owen looked desperately back into the house. They all heard another cry from a room to the side, the anguished cry of a woman in pain. Beatrice spotted three people inside, all talking in low voices, their faces drawn and worried. One of them was Adam Jones, whose arms were up, his hands at his scalp as if he were about to literally tear his hair out.

'No time to argue,' said Beatrice. 'We are going to fetch the doctor. Come, Jenkins.'

She did not look at Owen again before turning away. Jenkins led the way, down onto the river path, which they hurried along towards the bridge.

'What is happening with Martha?' Beatrice asked, breathlessly.

'I canna talk 'n' run!' snapped Jenkins. They went on, side-stepping passers-by who gawped at them. Under the bridge, up the steps and into the town. Across the square, around the back and along the street. Number ten, the brass plaque outside announcing the occupant's illustrious profession: Doctor Spencer Fitzpatrick, Physician.

Jenkins banged on the door with her fist, breathing hard. Beatrice was gasping, too, unaccustomed as she was to hurrying anywhere. The door opened and there stood a woman in a frilly mobcap, a hard look on her face, obviously used to fielding urgent enquiries to the doctor within. Her expression changed when she saw who had knocked upon her door.

'Why, Rose. Whatever is it? Trouble at the big house?'

Beatrice was almost startled out of her panic to hear someone call Jenkins by her first name.

'No, but we need Spencer now. Now, I tell you. Two lives are in danger.'

The woman at the door nodded and turned away swiftly. They waited, listening to the sounds of her footsteps receding and knocking on an inner door. A muted conversation, more footsteps and there appeared a man, receding grey hair swept to the side, which he was smoothing by the act of spitting in his palm and pressing it down hastily.

'Rose Jenkins,' he said. 'I can see in your face there's an emergency of some sort.'

'Indeed, Spencer. A woman and baby will die without you, sure as eggs is eggs. The Kings will pay, but these are poor folk. Will you come?'

'Anything for you, Rose,' said the doctor, turning to the woman who had answered the door to retrieve his physician's bag, coat and pearl-grey top hat.

'You have forceps?' said Jenkins.

'Yes, yes,' said the doctor.

Jenkins led the way, Fitzpatrick followed, glancing at Beatrice as he went down the steps, touching his hat briefly. She nodded and said, 'How do you do?'

'Charmed!' he said. 'And you are?'

'She's the Ashford girl, the King heir,' barked Jenkins as they went down the street.

'What on earth is she doing here?' he said.

'Enough of that and listen,' said Jenkins. They walked hurriedly together, Beatrice tagging along behind, trying to listen to everything, but missing the odd word or phrase here and there as they went. 'The baby is back to back . . . hours on end . . . Lunt has felt the bones in the skull . . . bad presentation . . . baby is stuck . . . mother in distress . . . Martha Jones, down at the Malones' cottage.'

Beatrice did not understand everything she was hearing, but it all sounded bad. They had rushed as quickly as they could, but she felt a sharp fear as they went along the riverside that it would be too late when they got there. Nobody was talking now, just striding forward, dodging obstacles, heads down. Three people on a mission to save two lives. This was not how Beatrice had imagined this day would turn out.

They came upon the cottage at last. As they approached, Beatrice watched with surprise as the doctor opened the door without a knock and walked straight in. Jenkins went after and though Beatrice felt nervous about entering without invitation, she followed Jenkins inside.

It was a one-storey house with one main room and one other off to the side. This room contained a large kitchen table and stove, a fireplace with chairs around it and in the corner a bed with a ragged rug beside it. Owen stood before the fireplace, staring at her, arms folded about himself, as if for comfort. His blonde hair stood up on end, clearly the victim of lack of sleep, and worried fingers trailing through it. Beatrice was about to go to him, say something to him, though she knew not what, when raised voices snatched her attention. The doctor had not yet reached the other room, where she could hear the mother-to-be moaning. A short, fat woman had appeared at its door, an apron and cap on. *That must be the midwife*, she thought. There were three other people by the kitchen table – Adam Jones sat slumped in a chair, looking as if the wind had been punched out of him. There was also another man and a woman, standing beside him. Those must be Owen's parents, the Malones. One of them was shouting.

'It's out of the question,' Owen's mother was saying. 'No doctors here.' Fitzgerald was trying to reason with her, but she was having none of it. 'There is no way on earth that people like us can afford you, sir. So please leave.'

Jenkins said, 'We've told you, Mrs Malone. We shall meet the doctor's bill.'

'Who, you? On a maid's pay?' she scoffed.

'Not me, the Kings will pay. Miss Beatrice here has assured it.'

All eyes turned on her. Beatrice saw Adam Jones, who looked at her blearily, a man who had clearly had no sleep, squinting at her, perhaps recognising her from that disastrous visit to his old cottage. But he seemed to have no strength to have an opinion on the subject. Next to him stood Owen's father, tall with thick, muscled arms, a kind face topped with fair hair, curious, looking her over with intelligent eyes. Then there was Mrs Malone, wavy red hair pulled back into a messy bun at her neck, scored through with a grey streak at her temple. She stared at Beatrice as she might at someone who had brought a dead rat into her house, disgusted and determined to get rid of the intruder.

Owen's mother spoke in a low guttural tone. 'We shall never take King money,' she said, spitting out the words as if they were a bitter herb in her mouth.

Jenkins said, 'Your husband and your son take King money every week.'

'Against my better judgment!' cried Mrs Malone.

Now Fitzgerald stepped forward. 'There is no time to be lost. Let me by to help this woman.'

Jenkins reached out and touched Mrs Malone's arm and said quietly, 'Please, Anny.'

Anny? Beatrice thought. She remembered that name. Her mother had had a friend called Anny when she was young. It had ended badly. Could this be the same one? It was a common enough name. And the woman must be about her mother's age. Surely it could not be. Could it?

Jenkins added, 'Let bygones be bygones, just this once.'

Anny Malone was still staring venomously at Beatrice, who felt acutely uncomfortable under her harsh scrutiny. Beatrice looked over at Owen, who was gazing at her too, but how different his expression was to his mother's. It was full of love and longing. She took strength from it. 'Please, Mrs Malone,' said Beatrice. 'Let us help Mrs Jones.'

'That's right,' said someone. It was Adam Jones, aroused from his stupor, standing up from his slump in the chair. 'It's my wife and my decision. I'll take it. I'll do anything for Martha. Go through, Doctor. Save my wife and child.'

'I shall do my best,' said Fitzgerald, walking onwards to the side room. 'Though we may be too late.'

The midwife said, 'Bleeding just started.'

Beatrice heard the doctor mutter, 'Oh Lord, the placenta, is it?'

The midwife went in first, followed by the doctor, who was backed up by Jenkins. Adam Jones turned and went in too, but was told forcefully to wait outside. The door was shut on him and he went back to his chair and resumed his collapsed position, staring into space.

Anny Malone turned away from them all and went over to the stove. She poured a jug of water into a kettle and placed it over the fire to boil.

'Miss King,' said Mr Malone, his face kindly yet embarrassed.

Beatrice said, softly, 'It's Miss Ashford, actually.' She hoped this would help the atmosphere. She wanted to reassure them that she was not actually a King, if that helped. 'My father was Jake Ashford, the artist.'

She heard Anny take a sharp intake of breath, then shake her head and stare pointedly at the ceiling. *What have I done now?* thought Beatrice, hopelessly.

'Would you like . . .?' Mr Malone began, then trailed off, looking about him, perhaps for something to offer her, though it seemed he could find nothing appropriate.

'I'm making tea,' snapped Anny Malone, but would not look around at anyone.

'Oh, the basket!' said Beatrice. 'We have a basket out-side with a picnic in it, that we haven't yet consumed on our walk. Please, let us share it with you all.'

'We have no need of your vittles,' retorted Anny.

'But it would be my pleasure,' said Beatrice, looking at Mr Malone for support, who shifted awkwardly from foot to foot.

'I'll take Miss Ashford outside,' said a familiar voice to her right. It was Owen, whose hair seemed neater now. He must have smoothed it down when she wasn't looking. 'It is a warm day and there'll be a welcome breeze out there, I'm sure.'

Mr Malone nodded, then glanced round at his wife and frowned as she stood facing the wall. 'Good idea, son.'

A cry came from the other room and everyone froze. Owen moved forward and ushered Beatrice outside, shutting the front door behind him. They were alone at last, except they weren't alone at all. A little group of neighbours had gathered nearby, watching the house.

'Any news on Martha?' said one woman, a baby sleep-ing with its mouth open on her arm.

'Nothing yet,' said Owen.

'We be praying for 'er,' said the woman, now staring with unashamed interest at Beatrice.

'Thank'ee,' said Owen and nodded. He glanced at Beatrice and gestured towards the river. They walked across the yard and along the path a little. Beatrice could feel many eyes burning into their backs. The house was still in sight and there was an overturned log there, ready to sit on with a view of the river beyond. Though she was worried for Martha, it was still nice to be next to Owen. She sat down and Owen sat beside her. To be so close to him and yet to be unable to touch him was exquisite torture.

'We are being watched,' he said quietly.

'I'm well aware,' she answered.

'But they canna hear us here, if we speak softly.'

'Good,' she said.

She was afraid to look at him, but she could not resist. All this time she had longed to look upon him and she risked it. He was watching the river, sitting bolt upright, stiff and awkward. He glanced at her and his eyes softened, his head tipped back a little and shoulders slumped, as if the sight of her had instantly melted the ice in him. 'It is a wonder to see you,' he said, breathlessly.

'For me too,' she whispered. They smiled meekly at each other and inspected each other's faces, drinking it all in. She heard voices nearby and a couple of pipe-smoking men passed by, eyeing them with amused curiosity. Both she and Owen stiffened their stance again and looked forward at the river.

'Your mother doesn't like me,' she said.

'Dunna take it personally. She dunna like any of the Kings.'

'She seemed even more annoyed when I told her I was an Ashford.'

'Well, I dunna know why that should be. Listen, why did you come today? How did you manage it? I was that shocked to see you, I thought I was dreaming!'

She laughed.

'And who was that old battle-axe you were with?'

'Oh, she's no battle-axe. She's my great-grandmother's maid. She's rather wonderful, actually.'

'She seemed to know my mother. She called her Anny.'

'Yes, I noticed that. Owen, my mother said she had a friendship with someone called Anny when they were children. She said it went wrong somehow, but she wouldn't say any more about it. Was it your mother?'

'I dunna have a clue,' he said, shaking his head. 'I dunna know much about those days. All I know is that Mother was falsely accused by the Kings of stealing and sent to the gaol for a time, but she came out later. My nana and also Father nursed her back to health and they fell in love, married soon after. Also, my mother's father died at the King ironworks. Some say it was an accident, others say it was negligence. That's all I know. I know naught of friendship between the two families, only dislike. Only hatred, to be honest with you. And it inna very likely, is it? Best of friends, Miss King and Miss Woodvine? That's what her name was back then, before she met Father.'

'Well, we're not very likely either, are we? And yet, here we are. Side by side, on a log.'

They glanced at each other and laughed, breaking any vestige of awkwardness that remained.

'Why *did* you come, Bea?'

'I came to try to end the strike. I knew Adam Jones was staying with you and I hoped I could talk to him, try to come to terms. Queenie has told me she cannot budge an inch, that her hands are tied by an agreement with the other brickmasters. She said they'll have to close the brickworks on Monday if there is no resolution. I had hoped to persuade Mr Jones to call off the strike and get everybody to go back to work.'

'I see,' said Owen and looked back at the river thoughtfully. Despite being a little way from the cottage, a piercing cry came from it that they could hear clearly. They turned to look, as did everybody nearby, stopped in their tracks, then came a shaking of heads and going on about their business.

'I do hope that quack can help our Martha,' said Owen.

'I'm certain he will,' said Beatrice.

They sat silently for a while, listening to the flow and splash of the river beyond, watching the swallows dive down to it, hunting for bugs in the dense summer air. The afternoon was waning and evening was on its way. The door of the house opened and out came Mr Malone. He was carrying two cups and saucers, balanced on what looked like a wooden chopping board. Owen jumped up and ran over to him. Beatrice heard him say something about not having a tray. She stood up and walked over to meet them.

'Thank you,' she said, taking the cup and saucer gratefully. All her exertions had left her feeling parched.

'Where will you put it?' said Mr Malone, worried about etiquette of which he had no knowledge.

'I shall hold it and drink it. It won't last long, I assure you. I am quite in need of refreshment,' Beatrice said pleasantly. Mr Malone grinned at her and Owen took his tea, smiling approvingly, perhaps at the tea, or perhaps at her attempts to put his father at ease. 'Mr Malone, the basket down there, by the door – it is full of good things to eat. Please do share it amongst your family. It would be my honour to help at a time like this.'

'Thank'ee, miss,' he said, gently. 'You have helped us beyond measure already. But please, do eat your picnic yourself. You must be famished. The hour is getting on. I am wondering if Owen should be sent to fetch someone from your home to take you back there.'

'With all respect, I do not want to leave until I know the outcome.'

'Any news?' Owen said.

'Miss Jenkins just told Adam that the doctor is going to try delivering the baby with forceps. There was some bleeding. There is a lot of noise but no further news.'

Another cry came from the room, a screeching rasping kind of cry that was unearthly. Beatrice thought, *At least Martha is still alive. That is something*.

'Take Miss Ashford back to your seat and do have summat to eat. We shall call you when there is any news.'

But then, a call came from behind him. 'Mr Jones!' It was Jenkins's voice. Mr Malone turned quickly back into the room. Owen put his cup and saucer roughly down on the ground, the tea sloshing over the side and Beatrice did the same, then followed him inside. Jenkins was standing at the door to the other room, her bonnet off, her white hair half unpinned from its usual tight bun, greasy strands hanging limply down. Suddenly, a high-pitched shriek came from behind her, the unmistakeable sound of a newborn baby. 'It's a girl!'

Adam jumped up from his chair and said fearfully, 'Martha?'

Jenkins replied, 'She will be fine. She is weak now. She will need plenty of rest for many days. Lots of looking after. But the forceps did the trick and now the baby is out, Martha has a good chance of a full recovery.'

Adam whooped and clapped his hands, suddenly alive after looking like a half-dead man since the moment Beatrice had arrived.

Mr Malone clapped his hands too. 'Sebunctious tidings!' he cried.

Anny Malone had her hands over her face, tears streaming over her fingers. She shook her head with relief and sank down into a chair. Mr Malone went straight to her and crouched down beside her, putting an arm about her and whispering reassurance. Beatrice turned to Owen, who had tears in his beautiful eyes. Without a thought, they threw their arms about each other and hugged and hugged, the feel of his body so strong and warm and comforting, joy and relief coursing through them both. They were laughing and crying at the same time. When they finally released each other, they saw that everybody was looking at them, shocked. But too happy to let the break in decorum spoil the mood, the moment passed and Adam rushed in to see his wife and child. Beatrice remembered the basket and went outside to get it. She brought it over to the kitchen table and started unloading its goodies, tongue sandwiches, fresh tomatoes, chunks of cheese wrapped in wax paper, fruit scones and a punnet of raspberries.

'Please, everybody must help themselves,' she said.

She expected Anny Malone to complain, but she seemed too exhausted by the day's events to move, let alone speak.

'That is very kind of you, miss,' said Mr Malone, warmly. He patted Anny on the shoulder, who looked up briefly and nodded, the slightest of nods, but a definite acceptance of Beatrice's gift. 'It all looks delicious,' added Mr Malone, feasting his eyes.

'But I'd much rather have one of your fidget pies, Mrs Malone,' said Beatrice.

Anny raised her head at Beatrice, looking her in the eye for the first time. 'How on earth do you know about those?'

'Owen gave me a pie once. That's how we met.'

'You two . . .? You know each other?'

Owen looked a bit queasy but forced a crooked smile. 'I sold her a pie. Once.'

'Well, I tried to buy it, but you were so generous, you gave it to me. And then we became friends,' said Beatrice.

There was a heavy moment of silence as this fact landed in the midst of them all. But the spell was broken when in came Adam Jones, proudly carrying his newborn daughter wrapped in a chequered blanket. His eyes were dead tired, but his smile beamed.

'Here she is, the one that's caused all the mischief. Meet Hettie Jones.'

Every person in the room made a sound, a soft, breathy, marvelling sound reserved only for the arrival of tiny new things. Beatrice felt her eyes fill with unexpected tears. She blinked them away to look in awe at the baby, its little face screwed up with distaste at its new world, miniature fists curled by either cheek. Beatrice glanced at Owen, who was crying too. He looked at her and smiled, a laugh of relief and wonder catching in his throat, causing a tear to roll down his cheek as he gazed back at her, lovingly.

In her whole life, Beatrice had never felt such pure and utter bliss.

Chapter 14

The girl had gone now, thank heavens, gone off with the doctor and the old hag's maid. When Anny first saw the girl, she had the most awful shock. Those eyes. They were Jake Ashford's eyes. To see them again, after all these years. After staying up all night by Martha's side, then bleary with lack of sleep and wracked with worry, to see those eyes again, it nearly toppled her. The girl looked so much like Jake, it was hard to find any of her mother in her. But as Anny had looked more, in secret glimpses, she saw that she had Margaret King's mouth and chin. She had spent so many hours with Margaret when they were young – Peggy, as she called her then – she knew that face as well as her own. The eyes of Jake Ashford – she had gazed at them so much, she'd know them again anywhere. And then, when she was carted off to prison, she had dreamt of them often enough. Until she had heard of his betrayal with Peggy. The double betrayal was almost too much to bear, her best friend running off with the man she'd thought to marry and coming so soon after the death of her dear father. Her only consolation was that they had left the country and Anny wouldn't have to watch Peggy and Jake parading around Ironbridge, rubbing Anny's face in her own defeat. There was a stretch of sea between them and Anny had hoped that she would never have to lay eyes on them again.

But then gossip told her that Margaret was back, all these years later, with a daughter in tow, the artist Ashford's daughter. Rumour had it that Ashford had died of the pox, years back. A lucky escape for Anny, she had thought. But it was not so simple to recover from your first love. She had not seen Peggy and her girl about town, thankfully. She did not wish to. She did not trust herself not to walk over to Peggy and slap her across the face.

It sickened her to see that girl here, in her own home, proof positive of the betrayal of two of her most beloved people in the world, back then. And to discover that somehow, in some ridiculous twist of fate, the girl was already friends with her own dear son? But it looked like so much more than that. The way they'd thrown their arms about each other when the baby came. She had watched the two of them through the window when they sat on the thinking log by the river. She saw them talking, smiling and laughing. They were so easy together, as if they had spent a lot of time in each other's company. There was something rotten going on there.

After the unwelcome visitors had gone, Martha was sleeping. The baby was asleep too, after its first feed, wrapped up in a blanket and lodged in the top drawer of the bedroom dresser. Adam, Owen and Peter were sitting at the table, finishing off the last scraps of supper in a worried silence. Owen had just told them all the news the girl had brought, that the Kings were to shut the brickworks the day after tomorrow if the strike didn't end. Adam had been deep in thought ever since, staring at the tabletop.

Anny did not know what Adam would do about all that. It was a weighty matter to be sure, but more pressing to her at this moment was what on earth was going on between her son and that girl. She knew she should hold her tongue, that there were more vital things to deal with. But every time she looked at Owen, she wanted to scream. She stood now, watching him, wringing a cloth angrily about in her hands.

'I never thought I'd see the day when I was glad to see a King!' mused Peter.

'Me neither!' said Adam and shook his head. 'The girl brought terrible news about the strike. And heaven knows what I shall do about it. But thank God for 'em, too. As Martha and the littl'un would be dead now without 'em, I'm sure of that.'

Owen was nodding at this. 'Strange that they sent the girl to deliver such important news,' said Anny, staring at her son. He glanced up, saw her eye on him and looked away. Anny went on, 'Why would they do that, do you think?'

'I've met her before, the girl,' said Adam. 'She came with the old hag when they threw us out. Maybe they thought we'd be nicer to a girl.'

Owen was still not looking at her.

'And what were the two of you talking about all that time outside, eh, son?'

He still would not look at her. 'This and that. She couldna stay in here, with all that business going on in there. We passed the time of day.'

His nonchalant tone infuriated her. 'Don't you lie to me, lad. I'll put you across my knee! You aren't too old for it.'

'Now then, Anny,' started Adam, glancing sidelong at Owen. That look meant something, she was sure.

'And what do you know about it? Are you two in cahoots, or something?'

Owen said, 'The girl and me. We are acquainted, is all. I sold her a pie once, that's all.'

'Leave the boy alone,' said Adam. That was the last straw.

'Don't you tell me how to speak to my son, Adam Jones,' she snapped. 'Something is going on here and I want to know what. Owen, what is it between you and this girl, eh? Spit it out!'

Owen looked sick as a dog. But it was Adam who spoke again.

'Dunna torture the lad. I told him to do it. He's been on strike business.'

'What?' said Anny, exchanging a confused glance with her husband Peter, who obviously had no knowledge of any of this either.

Owen was staring at Adam now, who carried on, 'I told him to do it. Since the girl was sweet on him after this pie business, I told him he should cultivate it. Find out what he can from her. Ask her for information. He's been at it for weeks. He's been spying for us. So, now you know, all of yer. Now you know. She's fallen hook, line and sinker for him.'

Peter said, 'Is this true, lad?' His voice was flat and tired, tinged with disappointment.

Owen nodded but said nothing.

'So, leave him alone. He's a hero for the cause,' said Adam, standing up and pushing his chair back, striding over to the room where Martha rested, going in and shutting the door behind him, as if that put an end to it. A heavy silence hung in the air, thoughts racing, words forming.

'I'm going out,' said Owen, standing up and pushing his chair back, just the same way Adam had done it.

'No, you are not!' cried Anny.

Owen looked at her then. 'Yes, Mother. I am.' They'd had their little rows in the past, mother and son. But never had he looked at her with such defiance. Then, as she glared at him, his face softened. 'Dunna fret, both of yer. It inna a bad thing. We are friends, is all.'

'Didn't look like friends to me,' said Anny. 'All that hugging and longing looks. Adam said she'd fallen for you. Have you fallen for her?'

'No, of course not, Mother. I'm no fool. She is a means to an end, that is all. Try to have some faith in me, eh? I've been doing all I can to end this strike and if that meant I had to pretend to befriend a daft little rich girl, then I did it and gladly.'

Anny reached out and grasped at his shoulders. 'Don't lie to my face, son. You're in love with her. It's as plain as day.'

'For God's sake, leave me alone!' he shouted, stepping back roughly from her grip. She stumbled forward and his eyes switched to concern. He reached out to her, looking at her belly. But she backed off, crossing her arms and glaring at him. His eyes fell and he let out a long sigh.

Anny turned to her husband, who was not even watching, picking at the last morsels on the wooden board before him.

'And what do you make of all this, Peter Malone? Our son, whoring himself to the Kings for the good of the workers?'

Peter met her eye and said coldly, 'You told me once that anything was justified when it came to the strike. Why do you think I want no part of it? Now you see the results of that loyalty to . . . to *anarchy*. Everybody turns liar and cheat in the end. Nobody wins.'

His gaze fell again to the table and he went back to dabbing uselessly at the crumbs.

'Try not to take on so, Mother,' said Owen, fetching his cap. 'Dunna you think we've got bigger problems to worry about? I'm off down the tavern.'

'Owen,' she tried one last time. 'If you love that girl, if you love a King, why . . . it will kill me, son.'

'Enough of this now. Dunna get yourself in a terrible state. Think of the babby. We are friends, that is all. It's nothing for you to fret about. Anyway, with the threat of the yard closing, it'll all be over soon. Everything will.'

He left. Peter stood up too and started to clear away the feast. Seeing that girl place all that luxurious food on her own kitchen table had made Anny want to smash it all up with a brickbat. It was just like the girl's mother had done, all those years ago, at their second meeting in the forest, when Peggy had brought a picnic. She had devoured it then, noticing how Peggy ate little, but she herself was hungry, always hungry and had taken King food and loved it. That's what the Kings did, giving you things, winning you over with money and things and lies. It was all poison to her now. To think of the years wasted on that friendship, the long talks, the visits, the letters they hid in the fairy tree – the old lime tree with the hollow in its trunk.

The memory of it gave her an idea.

First, she'd need a snack. There were only plums in the bowl. No pies these days, as she could not afford the ingredients to make them, as nobody could afford to buy them. Two or three plums would have to do. Then, she needed paper and pencil. She found some in the drawer beside the bed. She wrote quickly, not as neat as her hand had been in younger days, when she had delighted in writing. She hardly ever wrote now, had no use for it any more. She wrote a note, with instructions on it. It was not a request. It was an order. She folded it up tightly.

Her husband was washing the dishes, an uncomfortable silence between them. Anny slipped outside. She saw a neighbour's child, a likely boy who was usually up for an errand with food as payment. She called him over and told him what she needed him to do and handed him the fruit, which he took with hungry eyes, licking his lips. It was evening now, but still light. It wouldn't take him too long to get up there and back. She said not to come and tell her anything afterwards, just to go home. She couldn't risk the others overhearing. She would crawl into bed beside Martha soon and try to sleep.

That night, the baby woke them up regularly, as babies do. Martha was still weak, so Anny fetched little Hettie. She cooed and shushed her for a moment, hoping she'd fall back into her infant dreaming. It was so good to hold a babe in her arms again, a small, warm package of life. Her own child was growing lustily inside her body and the excitement of that fact overcame her, after the fear she'd suffered these past hours when she thought Martha and the child would die. It terrified her to think of Peter and Owen, alone with her gone, or with a new baby to bring up without her. But all had turned out all right in the end, thanks to that blasted girl and the doctor her money had bought, but still. How Anny had longed for a daughter, all these years of trying and nothing to show for it but blood. Maybe she was carrying a girl now, who knew? She watched Hettie's dear face chronicle its babyish thoughts and fears, before her fists balled up again and she cried out for milk. Anny took her to Martha to feed. The men slept soundly in the next room, as she climbed into bed beside Martha and fell back into slumber, listening to the sound of Martha's voice humming a lullaby.

In her fits of restless sleep, Anny was visited by a dream Jake Ashford, young and dark-eyed, a gypsy air about him, as he always had. She told him in the dream, *You are dead and gone*. He gazed at her and said, in a ghostly whisper, *It is all dust and ashes without you*. In the morning, she found it difficult to look her husband Peter in the eye.

She dressed quickly and quietly, speaking to Peter in low tones so as not to wake the other sleepers in the house.

'I'm going for a walk in the woods to clear my head.'

'You should be resting, love,' he said, with a worried face.

'No, I need to stretch my legs and get a bit of peace. I'll be back soon.'

Owen and Adam were still fast asleep when she left. Adam had fretted till the early hours about what to do about the strike, but had come to no answer before he took to his bed. Owen had come home late, curled up in his place on the floor and slept like a log. Now he looked innocent as a babe, lying on his back with his mouth open.

Yesterday he had assured her they were just friends, him and the girl. But Anny would not be fooled so easily. She knew young love when she saw it. The very idea disgusted her. Fate was laughing at her, that was clear. Well, she had defied fate before and she would do it again. All this must be stopped. The boy must be told.

But she knew what children were like. The minute you tell them not to do something, they want to do it more than ever. If she shouted again at Owen, laid down the law with him, he would be more determined than ever to see the girl. That's how their minds worked, your children. You had to be cleverer than that, sneakier. You had to let them think they'd got away with things, sometimes. She had another notion in mind. She would seek out support for her plan, from the unlikeliest of quarters.

She made her way slowly to the fairy tree, enjoying the peace and freedom of a woodland walk, away from home, its responsibility and strain, its surplus of people, bursting the seams of their tiny home. Five adults and now a new baby was enough to tear at anyone's nerves. She liked Martha and Adam, and had offered herself to have them when that forsaken bastard Cyril had evicted them.

But now, to discover that Adam had led her son astray, into this nasty business, left a bad taste in her mouth. Using Owen like that, making him fool a girl into loving him, even a King. It didn't sit right with her. Anny had always got on well with Adam and could see that he and her son were thick as thieves, which she'd supported, as Owen was showing his full commitment to the cause. Peter had disappointed them all, with his lack of support for the strike. He had gone along with the union rules, but would not take part in any of the protests, preferring to stay at home and garden or clean than stand at the barricade and harry the scabs. But his defiance of these expectations was carried out so quietly yet firmly, that she couldn't help but admire his resolve. He had always made it clear to her that the strike was not in their interests and he would take no part in it, beyond stopping work as his comrades had done. And as things were turning out, Peter had been right, hadn't he? The strike dragged on, the masters wouldn't budge and along the river children were growing thinner by the day. The whole thing had turned sour and hopeless. It was always thus, the masters stamping on the workers, like earwigs.

She'd said that to Jake Ashford twenty years or so ago. And it was still true.

As she walked, she recalled the route she used to take every day from her parents' old house up the hill through the trees to the office where she had worked for Mr Brotherton, the Kings' estate manager. Proud and happy she'd been, taking that joyous walk each day. Cyril King, with his wiles and his threats and his disgusting designs on her had ruined it, then shattered her life with his tricks and his lies. She saw him sometimes these days, loafing about town, going into the taverns for daytime drinking. He was so wrapped up in his own selfishness, he never noticed her, a downtrodden, tired, middle-aged woman, her once fiery red hair he had so admired now faded to a russet brown lined with grey. He never noticed the woman whose life he nearly destroyed; the woman whose father was struck down in his prime by the furnace explosion that took him and other good men; the woman whose mother died soon after in penury, despite Anny's attempts to save her from the fever that took her one hot summer night. The Kings had paid each family recompense eventually, but too late for her. The money came two days after her mother died, when who knows, perhaps it could have been used to pay a doctor to save her – but it was too late.

These painful, bitter memories swirled about her head like midges in the summer heat. At least here, beneath the swaying trees, it was cooler and it was quiet. She took comfort from the swish of branches, the soft rattle of leaves, the calls of birds above and the endless flow of the river beyond. She was so weary, she considered sitting down right here and now and sleeping on the forest floor. But there was business to be done.

She steeled herself for the meeting she had arranged. She expected to get there first, as rich people always had a leisured attitude towards time, being able to buy it so easily. But as the spot where the lime tree stood came into view, Anny looked ahead to see a woman in fine clothes standing beside it, her back to her, a fashionable bonnet covering her hair and face. Anny knew that willowy, fine figure anywhere. It turned about to look at her. It was Margaret King, all grown up and middle-aged, like her. It was Peggy.

'Hello Anny,' she said, quite softly. There was no hatred in those eyes, just a kind of weary acceptance that, somehow, this meeting was inevitable.

'This is not a social call,' said Anny. 'I do not want to be here at all. And for the life of me, I cannot fathom why our lives seem to be so knotted together. However much I want to escape from the grip of the Kings, I always seem caught by you people, like a fly in your web.'

Margaret seemed at a loss for words. They stared at each other, both taking in the sight of their old friend. She said simply, 'How are you, Anny? I see . . . you are expecting?'

Margaret nodded towards Anny's bump, quite large and obvious these days. But Anny would not be swayed into an exchange of small talk. 'Like I said, this is not social. I have no interest in you or your kin. But something has come to my attention and it needs sorting. Your daughter and my son.'

'You have a son? How lovely. Wait . . . my daughter?'

This lack of knowledge of her family was either a prideful lie or typical of the Kings' ignorance of anyone beyond their narrow circle. 'Yes, I have a son. Owen. And he is sweet on your daughter. And she is sweet on him.' She certainly had no intention of telling Margaret the whole truth, about the subterfuge and the spying. But she did not want her son to be wrapped up in any of this anymore. And despite what Adam and Owen claimed, she knew what she had seen with her own eyes. Their children were deeply in love with each other.

Margaret frowned, uncomprehending. 'But how can this be? How can they have met?'

'Something to do with pies. But that's not important. The fact is they were at my house together yesterday, with Jenkins. They brought a doctor to help our friend have her baby. All much appreciated, I'm sure.'

'Jenkins? Yesterday?'

Had Margaret lost her reason in the past decades? She looked dazed, as if she'd bashed her head. 'Oh, do keep up!' Anny snapped.

'But they were going on a nature walk, Beatrice and Jenkins. They came home late, as they lost track of time.'

'Well, the girl's been lying to you. For quite a time, I reckon. I watched them yesterday, your lass and my lad. This was no chance meeting. They've been close for quite a while, I'd say. They were all over each other, as much as prudence would allow. I know first love when I see it. And they've got it, all right. They've got it bad.'

Margaret's thoughts flitted across her face. Anny guessed she was analysing many things that had been said to her, now putting a whole new slant on all of them.

'You have certainly surprised me, Anny. I thought I was here to talk about the strike.'

'Why would I want to talk with you about that? You are in no position to affect a thing.'

'I have the ear of my grandmother,' she retorted, some conceit in her voice. 'If there were a message you wanted me to relay, from the workers, I would be happy to deliver it. It's a nasty business, this strike.'

'I have nothing to do with any of that. I employ myself and run my own businesses. But while your family eats meals of many courses in your fine dining room, there are children hereabouts who are starving for want of a few pennies. A strike is the only way people like you would listen.'

Margaret glared at Anny, who raised her chin in defiance. Anny was finding this whole encounter increasingly satisfying. She heard her voice quavering, aware that there was twenty years' worth of resentment building up behind the wall of her self-control, ready to flood at the slightest provocation. But that was not her business today and she must get back to that.

'Listen, I could rail at you all day for the crimes your family have committed. A whole week of it would not be enough to list it all. But that is not why I have come. We must stop this foolishness between our children. I am certain you are as disgusted at the idea as me.'

'Nothing good could come of such a liaison,' said Margaret, imperiously, looking and sounding more like her grandmother than ever. Gone was the sweetness of her youth. Anny saw only a tired, aging woman, who had fallen back into her old ways of luxury.

'I ask for your help to end it, now. Speak to your daughter and warn her off. I will do the same with Owen. Lie to her, if you must.'

'I think there have been enough secrets and lies, don't you? I shall be telling her some choice facts. She knows nothing of our pasts, of what really happened. Does Owen?'

Anny wanted to scream that it was none of her damned business what her son did or did not know. Even hearing a King mention her son's name made her want to vomit. But, inwardly, she had to admit that it was time to tell the true story of their past. Only the truth could make them understand. Margaret was right about that, but she wasn't going to give a King the satisfaction.

'Tell her whatever you deem fit. This cannot be allowed to continue. Are we in agreement?'

Margaret nodded firmly. Anny had made her point. There was nothing left to say. She turned to walk away, her legs weak, her hands trembling. It must be because of her lack of sleep the last two nights. Yes, that was it.

'Anny? About Jake . . .'

Anny stopped dead and turned back. Her face must have looked like thunder, for at the sight of it Margaret flinched. 'I do not wish to speak to you about that, not now or ever.' Her voice shook with emotion. This would be the crack in the dam through which the torrent would soon come.

'He turned out badly. I left him.'

'I said speak no more!' shouted Anny, her rage boiling over now. She dug her fingers into her palms to stop herself marching over to this damned woman and strangling her.

'He died of syphilis.'

So the rumours were true. But to hear her speak of that man was more than Anny could bear. 'I am glad of it. You both received your just desserts.'

'I know you hate me. You have that right. Except there is much of which you are wholly ignorant. Did you know it was I who saved you from prison? Yes, that's right. I approached my grandmother and father

254

with the help of our maid Lucy. Remember her? She saw Cyril commit his crime against you, placing that money in your bag. She and I joined forces to blackmail my father into dropping the charges against you. She was too afraid to speak alone, but I persuaded her. Without me, you'd still be rotting in that cell.'

Anny's head felt light and the ground seemed to swell beneath her. What was this? Margaret had saved her?

'I knew nothing of that,' she muttered.

'Well, now you know.'

'I suppose I must thank you for that, at least,' said Anny, though it was hard to say.

'You are welcome. But that is not all. There is more you need to hear. The truth is we were both led in a merry dance by Jake Ashford, you and I. He was lying to us both. He was a drunk, violent liar. Yes, I ran away with him, seeming to have taken the grand prize from you. But it was a poisoned chalice and he led me a sorry life, before I left him, fat with child as you are now. I went out onto the streets of Paris alone and never saw him again. I had to make a life for myself and my daughter, with no man to love and protect us and none of the King money to keep us safe. And I did it, through sheer hard work and determination. You are the one who found a good man, by all accounts. You have a home, a son and another child on the way. The truth is I envy you all of that. If it were ever a competition between us, be assured that you won. You won, Anny.'

Anny stared at Margaret. She had given this woman such a high pedestal of hate for so many years, she had loomed large in her imagination as a mighty villain. But now, these revelations and the sight of her standing there, looking far older than her years, diminished her old foe into something far smaller and more human. But it was not so easy to erase years of loathing in only a moment.

'You still took him from me. Worse, you left me. When I needed you most.' Anny's eyes were filling with tears and she cursed her weakness. She must not cry in front of Margaret King.

'He was a liar and a womaniser,' said Margaret softly. 'And he hit me. It was a lucky escape for you. Think of all you have now. And be satisfied.' And with that Margaret turned and began the walk back up the hill

For a moment Anny stood frozen in place, then overcome with emotion she sank to the forest floor and the tears came flooding out. She sobbed, rubbing her quivering hands over the mound of her belly to soothe herself.

'Shh,' she told herself, as if pacifying the babe inside her, not herself. 'Dunna fret.'

She stayed seated, sniffling and rubbing her eyes till she saw stars. She felt like a mad woman, grovelling on the ground like this. She thought she had pushed all of this deep down, the misery, the envy, the anger at Margaret King. Now it was bubbling up again violently, threatening to overcome her. And it was mixed with confusion, that her dearest friend Peggy had helped her, had released her from hell. It had been hard to carry hate for all those years, but somehow it seemed harder now to release it. She felt as if her mind would capsize and her body would be dashed against the rocks. But no, she would not allow that to happen. Everyone needed her. She was the iron backbone of her family. Everyone relied on her to be strong. When your sleep was stolen, this is what happened. She remembered it now from when Owen was a baby. You felt as if you were losing your mind. She was just tired, that was all. There would be no rest at home, not with the house full of needy folk. Anny pushed herself up from the ground and staggered over to a broad tree, which she leant against with one hand. She slid down and sat beneath it, her back up against its trunk, one arm cradling her bump, the other resting on the forest floor. It was comfortable there. *Just for a moment*, she thought. *Just a little rest*. She closed her eyes and listened to the lulling whisper of the woodland.

Chapter 15

When Margaret had left her daughter that morning, she had been playing cards again with Queenie. This was something Margaret had done regularly with her grandmother years ago, yet there the resemblance ended. When she had played Old Maid with Queenie, they had largely sat in companionable silence, their thoughts wandering and their interest directed at the game itself, which both of them had loved. But watching Beatrice play with Queenie was utterly different; they chattered and gossiped all the time, making each other giggle like schoolgirls. Margaret hated to admit it to herself, but she was envious of her daughter, jealous of the intimacy she had established with Queenie so quickly. Beatrice found it easy to make friends with anyone. It was something of which Margaret had always felt proud. She loved the way that people loved her daughter so easily and Beatrice loved them back, giving her love away like surplus bon-bons to all and sundry. Yet she always felt that Beatrice's truest love had been reserved alone for her, her mother. It was her privilege and her joy to have this person who adored her above all others. But since returning to Iron-bridge, Margaret felt she was losing that special position. Beatrice was withdrawing from her, in subtle ways, she had thought. Until now, until this revelation from Anny. Now she knew that there was nothing subtle about it. Beatrice had given her heart away to someone else. And not just anyone. Anny Woodvine's son.

During the walk back from the fairy tree, she'd considered her feelings at seeing Anny again. She was still beautiful, her hair darker now but just as glorious. Her crowning glory, she'd told Anny once. How she had been jealous of Anny's red hair, often feeling her blonde locks were too similar to Cyril's to be attractive. She was shocked to see Anny's pregnancy, telling herself how fortunate she herself was not to be married and having another child at their age. But if truth be known, when she'd seen Anny's bump, a shiver of envy had taken her.

Yet as she approached Southover from the woods, saw it loom above her and thought of the life of ease it now afforded her, she felt a spurt of happiness at it. One could blame oneself forever for the woes of others. But she had paid for it, twenty years of working alone, raising her daughter alone. Anny might be angry with her still, but Margaret knew she had more than paid her dues in her life. Now it was her turn to be happy. First, she must ensure her daughter did not throw away her life for nothing. She did not want Beatrice to make the same mistakes she had made, all those years ago, forsaking everything for first love. Knowing Anny, she was sure that her son would be a fine young man. But the idea that Beatrice might be with such a man, of his sort . . . that was ridiculous. And it must be quashed. Of that, she and Anny were in perfect agreement.

On entering the house, she heard no talking emanating from the drawing room, so went upstairs to Beatrice's room. Before knocking on the door, she heard chattering from inside there instead. She opened the door. Sitting on her bed was Beatrice, whilst beside her sat her maid, Dinah. Heaven knew what they were talking about. They both whipped round at the sight of her. Dinah scrambled up from the bed and rushed behind Margaret to the open door, a quick nod of the head, then out onto the landing, disappearing down the servants' staircase at great speed.

'You frightened her!' cried Beatrice, mock-alarm on her face, but still laughing.

Margaret closed the door and sat down beside her daughter, who immediately gathered something was up and composed herself.

'*Chérie*, you know how much I love you.'

'Yes, Maman, of course!' said Beatrice and hugged her. Margaret took the hug stiffly. She would not be put off.

'And everything I do and say is for your own good.'

Beatrice's eyes were now wary. The knowledge that her daughter had been lying to her, for months, made Margaret falter.

'What is it? You look sad.'

'I am saddened, I'll be honest with you. I have discovered something today. I know that you have been keeping something from me and it saddens me that you did not feel able to share the truth with me. I thought we were the best of friends.'

'Oh, we are! We are!' she cried and went to hug her mother again, who gently pushed her back this time, much to Beatrice's surprise.

'I know about Owen.'

Beatrice's face fell. She looked away sharply, showing her mother the back of her head. Margaret had dealt with tantrums before with her daughter, arguments that so often were like summer storms that passed by quickly, followed by the sun coming out again. They had been a team and never had a serious disagreement about anything. She supposed there had to come a time when Beatrice would begin to draw away from her and make her own life. She thought back to herself at Beatrice's age. If she shouted at Beatrice, she would receive only resistance. She had to be shrewder than that, if she wished to win her over.

'Tell me about him.'

Beatrice turned back to her, clearly surprised. She had tears in her eyes, which gripped Margaret's heart. But she had to stay strong.

'Maman, he is a good, kind person. He is intelligent and thoughtful. And full of . . . I don't know how to explain it. He is full of love! It brims over in him!'

Her eyes were shining now. *She's head over heels*, thought Margaret. This was going to be more difficult than she'd imagined.

'How did you meet? How did all this come about?'

'He gave me a pie, one of his mother's. He was selling them at Madame's house. We started talking. And we got on so well, as if we'd known each other forever! Quite extraordinary really.'

'*Chérie*, why didn't you tell me about him?'

Beatrice looked down at her hands. 'Because . . . you wouldn't understand.'

'Is that the only reason? Remember I eloped with your father. You know that. I think you knew I would understand that part of it, about falling in love.'

'That is true . . .' said Beatrice, biting her lip.

'So, what was the real reason you didn't tell me?'

'I . . . because of . . . well, I didn't think you'd approve of him. Because of his . . . class.'

'He is a brickmaker. The enemy, as far as your great-grandmother is concerned.'

'Yes,' she said, perking up. 'But the strike and all that didn't come about till later. And we were friends by then, close friends. We didn't . . . fall in love till after that. And then, it all seemed hopeless. And it's been terrible ever since. We haven't been able to see each other or talk or anything. And I have missed him so much. We have both missed each other. It's been like torture. And I know we are from different sides, from different classes, from different . . . everything. But love, love does not choose sides. Love is all that matters in the world, isn't it, Maman? Love conquers all!'

Beatrice's eyes were glistening with emotion and usually Margaret would take her in her arms to comfort her. But not yet.

'And I know another phrase about love. Love is blind. You are blinded by your desire for this boy. There are many truths that you are unwilling to see. It goes beyond your class, your stations in life, beyond even the brickworks and the strike. Firstly, there is the matter of money.'

'But we have plenty now!' cried Beatrice, cheerfully.

'No, we do not. I have virtually nothing. The comforts we enjoy here are courtesy of your great-grandmother. But Queenie will never endorse this relationship with this boy.'

'Then, we will go back to France. The three of us. Things are much easier there, much more understanding of love and freedom, surely.'

'I cannot afford to take us back to France! I have not a penny to pay for it and not the energy to earn it when we get there.'

'Then Queenie will help us. She adores me!'

'It is true that Queenie is fonder of you than anyone I've known, excepting Jenkins perhaps. But there is no way on earth she will ever consent to paying for us to leave her, to go back to France and fund our lives there, just so you can be with a brickmaker's son. Could you really imagine that would happen?'

'She'd do anything for me.'

'Oh child, not this! We are here in England to stay. We must make the best of this and do what Queenie wants, which is also what I want for you, too. That is, that you should make a good marriage and eventually, take over the family business with your husband. That is what we have planned and what you must do. That is how we will secure your future.'

Beatrice stared at her, her lips turned down, her cheeks reddening, as if her face had just been slapped.

'But I don't want any of that. And money doesn't matter to me.'

'Money isn't everything, but it keeps a roof over your head, your belly full. You are young and naïve. You don't understand what it is like to worry about money every moment of your life and compare it with this life, which is safe and secure.'

'But I do understand that perfectly. I lived alongside you all those years in France, watching you count every *sou*. I do know the difference. And I am prepared to give that up for Owen.'

Margaret could not contain her 'wise mother' tone any longer and heard herself raise her voice with frustration, before she could stop it. 'You'd live with a brickworker, in a filthy hovel?'

Beatrice looked narrowly at her then and stood up, walked to the window, her resolute back to her mother. Margaret regretted raising her voice but it was necessary. Beatrice had always been precocious in her speech, learning to talk early and easily. And this quality caused her mother to forget sometimes how very young and naïve she really was.

Beatrice's voice was small when she said, 'I had not thought much on how we would live. But I did have a little cottage in the forest in mind. With roses about the windows. And perhaps a goat to milk and make cheese.'

It was worse than she thought, this ridiculous vision of woodland harmony, like something from a fairy tale.

'That is not how it would be. Brickworkers earn a pittance!'

Beatrice turned angrily to her mother then and said, 'And whose fault is that?'

'Not mine, I assure you! *Chérie*, you must see that the very idea of you, Beatrice Ashford, heir to the King fortune, living with a brickmaker, is madness. It will never happen.'

'Only because of people like you, and Great-grandmother, who cannot see beyond your own prejudice. And imagine yourself superior to everyone who has not money and position.'

'That is not true. You and I lived on meagre earnings and amongst very mixed society in Paris, all of your life till now. I gave up this comfortable existence for love. This is not about snobbery, not on my part. This is about reality, the world in which we live.'

'I don't care for a world that does not accept our love. We shall make our own way!' cried Beatrice, her fist clenched with determination. Margaret could see the fire in her eyes and knew that no amount of reasoning would dim it. In fact, she understood Beatrice's resolve only too well. She remembered her own passion for Jake and how nothing could sway it. If her daughter loved this boy even half as much as she herself had loved Jake Ashford, then she pitied Bea with all of her heart. But gone was the time for sympathy. Now was the time for some harsh medicine.

'Beatrice, please sit down beside me.'

'I will not sit down!'

'Please, *chérie*. I have some truths to tell you, things you know nothing about. They will not be easy for you to hear. But hear them you must.'

Beatrice looked concerned, her resolve deflating a little. Then she sat herself on the end of her bed, her arms folded, her face turned away from her mother.

Margaret began, 'I will tell you what you know: your father and I eloped from Ironbridge. We were madly in love. We came to Paris to make a life for ourselves. But there is something you do not know. Something

I shielded you from, to protect you. Please, let me explain. Listen to the whole story and hopefully then you will understand why I did what I did. When I met your father, I had a best friend. Her name was Anny Woodvine.'

Beatrice turned to look at her. 'Woodvine? Anny Woodvine?'

'Yes, that was her name then. She has since married.'

'And her name is now Malone!' said Beatrice. 'I knew it!'

This wrongfooted Margaret. Had she discovered it from Owen? Or Queenie even? 'Yes, but how . . . ?'

'Owen told me what happened to his mother, that she was accused of theft and was in prison for a time. You said about a friend called Anny. I wondered if it could be her, but Owen said he couldn't imagine it, that the Kings and the Woodvines hated each other.'

'I see. Well, there is much more to it than that.'

'Tell me.'

'Anny was my best friend for many years. We kept it a secret at first, as we knew nobody would approve. But then we both met Jake Ashford, your father. Anny and I both fell in love with him. We were rivals then, though I hated the thought of it. I was torn between my best friend and the man I loved. But it was more complex even than that. Uncle Cyril was in love with Anny. He wanted to marry her. But she hated him. We all did then. He wanted to force her to love him. After she rejected him, he framed her for theft. She was sent to prison and later released when I persuaded Queenie and my father to drop the charges.'

'Was she not grateful to you? You saved her! Were you not reconciled?' Margaret could see Beatrice's mind working, that if there was reconciliation between the families, perhaps all was not lost.

'No, we were never reconciled. Because I left with Jake, and Anny had loved him. What I did not know was that he had played us both, that he had made her fall in love with him too, to make me jealous. That he was only after my fortune and when I refused to go back to Ironbridge for him to claim it, he beat me.'

Beatrice was frowning now, pulling back slightly from her mother, as Margaret leant forward to drive home the point of her story. Her voice had changed, as her old bitterness from the past was seeping into her throat.

'*Chérie*, this next part of the story will be very hard for you to hear. But now is the time to tell you and you must hear it. Your father beat me and told me he had never loved me. He drank all the time and he had ... been with other women. He had not only romanced Anny, but had been with others. He told me all this the night before I left him, with you in my belly. I knew it was not safe to raise you with such a man. I packed my things and left, never to see him again. I never heard from him. A friend heard of his death, around four years later.'

Beatrice was slowly shaking her head, a look of disgust on her face. 'Why would you tell me such lies?'

'They are not lies. The story I told you as a child of your father and me, that was the lie. I told it to you to protect you. You were too young to understand it. And I did not want you to grow up hating the memory of your father or thinking that all men were like this. I wanted you to grow up with sweetness and light and beauty and love. I wanted you to feel that the world was full of possibility, not ruined by betrayal.'

'You lied to me, for years, all my life,' said Beatrice, her voice a dry whisper.

'I did. But I have explained my reasons why and I stand by them.'

'My father was alive, until I was four years old. He was alive when I was a child. I could have met him.'

'I know, *chérie*. I know. It's a hard fact to comprehend. But I was protecting you from him. If he could treat me so badly, I was determined he would not do the same to his child.'

'But it should have been my choice, not yours, if I wanted to know my father. It should have been his choice, not yours, if he wanted to know his child.'

'It sounds so simple, when you put it like that. But you were an infant and I had to protect you. As for him, he had lost all rights to you when he beat me and betrayed me. I protected you from all this so that you could grow up surrounded by love and light, not bitterness or regret.

I tell you now so that you will not make the same mistake I did.'

Beatrice's eyes were filling with tears now. She turned her head quickly to her mother and a fat tear sprang from her cheek and landed on Margaret's hand. 'You are saying that I was a mistake?'

'No! Never, *chérie!*' Margaret reached out and grasped Beatrice's hand and kissed it. 'You are the one good thing I have done in my life. No, my mistake was to rush blindly into love, to believe that love justified anything, that love would conquer all. That was my greatest blunder. It was proven cruelly wrong, in every way it could be. And I cannot allow you – my darling, my heart and soul, my life! – to commit the same foolish error.'

Beatrice wrenched her hand away and sat slumped, staring at the floor.

'Owen is not like that. He is not like . . . Jake Ashford.'

Margaret's heart broke, as she heard her daughter call him by his name, instead of her own name for him, Papa. She was beginning already to come to terms with the loss of the father she thought she'd had, to the man she now knew he really was. *Should I have told her? Should I have perpetuated the fantasy?* Margaret agonised. *But she had to understand. I am only being cruel to be kind.*

Margaret put her hand on Beatrice's shoulder, who flinched at her touch. '*Chérie*, he may not be. If he is like his mother, he may well be a good person, through and through. He may never have told you a single lie. But consider too that he has far more to gain than you in this relationship. You are a prize, a rich heiress, the daughter of the house of his enemies, not only the enemy of his family but of all his confederates at the brickworks. His intentions may not be . . . honourable. He may have told you all sorts of lies to make you love him.'

'He does not lie. I would know if he had,' Beatrice said breathily.

'It is very easy to be lied to and believe it, when one wants to believe it.'

'Yes, it surely is,' she said sarcastically and shot a look of loathing at her mother.

It was like an arrow to her heart. Her daughter had never looked at her so coldly. Margaret swallowed her feelings and continued, 'But whatever Owen's motives, surely you can see now, that it is impossible. There is too much water under the bridge between the Kings and the Woodvines. We are enemies and always will be. Nothing you can say or do will ever change that. And if you defy it, and run away together, one day you will find that you have thrown away your life for a man you barely know. And heaven help you then, for all will be lost.'

Beatrice put her hands over her face and cried into them. Margaret took her daughter in her arms and held her as she sobbed. 'My darling, *ma petite chérie*. I am so sorry. So sorry.'

She let her cry it out for a while, holding her through-out. Then Beatrice pulled away, wiping her face with a handkerchief her mother had given her. She blew her nose noisily and passed it back.

'Thank you, Maman,' Beatrice said quietly, staring at her shoes. Then she turned, smiled stiffly at her mother and said, 'Thank you for telling me the truth. I can see now that you are right, about everything.'

Margaret smiled back at her daughter, but the turn-around seemed too quick, the consent too ready. 'It is a lot to digest. It will take time for you to comprehend it all.'

'I don't need to think about it. I have learnt my lesson. I will stop seeing Owen Malone.'

Still, there was that stiff smile on her daughter's tear-stained face. *If only I could read her mind*, she thought, and not for the first time.

Chapter 16

'Your mother's been gone for hours,' said Peter, coming into the house from the garden, where he had been working on their patch of land.

'Maybe she went to chapel,' said Owen, sitting despondently at the table, feeling lazy and moody that sultry afternoon.

'Even so, it's a long time past that now. Will you go into the woods and shout for her? Have a look around for her? I've got chores around here to finish.'

'All right,' said Owen, but felt his father was fussing a bit. Mother could look after herself. His father must have seen his reluctance, as he added, 'She's in a delicate condition. Better to be safe than sorry.'

What an idiot he'd been to forget that for a moment. 'Course, yes. I'll go. I'll find her, dunna fret.'

As he left the house, Adam appeared, approaching from the path to town. He had been to talk with some other strikers about the latest news, that the Kings would close the yard tomorrow if the strike did not end. He'd asked Owen to go with him but Owen had said no, for once. He'd said he was tired. The truth was his mind was filled with confusion and he could not face a long conversation with Adam that morning about the strike or about anything really, especially not about Beatrice. Owen nodded at him and called out, 'Going to look for Mother.'

Adam nodded back, his face clouding with some concern.

Owen hurried off. He took the path worn by years of working people's feet taking their shortcut through the trees. Where had his mother gone for all this time? Perhaps it was just thinking time she wanted. Was it planning time? Or had she been to see someone about . . . things? She had the ability to read his mind from his face. She guessed about him and Beatrice at first glance; he saw it in that first look she gave him, when the girl had come in and smiled right at him.

He continued on, mulling over his thoughts. He raised his head and immediately saw something that shocked him so much he stopped walking and stood motionless. There, beneath a tree, was a figure. It was a woman hunched over, her lower back against the trunk. It was his mother. He broke into a clumsy run and sprinted up to her. He stopped dead for a moment, staring down at her form in shock. Was she breathing? He fell to his knees and said, 'Mother! Mother!' and stroked her hair.

A small groan came from her and he felt faint with gratitude.

'Mother? Are you well?'

A longer groan came and she started to uncurl like a fern frond, stretching out her arms. He looked at her dress for any sign of injury or blood. But there was none. She opened up her eyes blearily and looked about, startled. Then she focused on him.

'Oh, my son!' she said and smiled. 'Oh, I must've fallen asleep here.'

'Oh, Mother! We didna know where you'd be. You've been gone hours. Why are you sleeping here?'

'Hours, is it? Well, I must've needed the rest. Things lately . . . well, you know, they've been so busy at home. No rest, no peace. It's been taxing to say the least.'

'It has indeed. I'm just so glad to see you are all right and all is well,' he said, nodding at her bump. She smiled at it and ran a hand over it.

'Yes, all is well. Here, son, help me up. We shall take a leisurely stroll home and I shall rest on your arm like you were a proper gentleman.'

He did as she asked. It was good to feel her lean on him. She worked so hard and had always been his support. It felt right that he should be the one to do the same for her now. The shock of seeing her on the ground like that and fearing the worst had brought a tear to his eye, reminding him how much he loved and needed her. And with a pang, how much he regretted keeping the truth from her. He would not hide from her any longer. He owed her that and much more.

'Mother, can I speak to you about summat, in confidence?'

'Course you can, son. About any old thing. You know that.'

'It's about Beatrice Ashford,' he said and glanced round to gauge her reaction.

'I thought it might be,' she replied with a rueful smile. He took courage from that. At least it was not anger. 'I could see you two were singing out of the same book. A mother knows these things.'

'It started as we said, with her wanting a pie. Then Adam said it was useful and I should cultivate it. I did so and would report back to Adam anything I'd learnt. But then I . . . I started to . . .' Here he hesitated, not knowing how to frame it, how to explain such emotions to his mother, when he could barely articulate them to himself.

'Tell me how she made you feel,' she said, reading his mind, as ever.

He thought for a moment, picturing her standing before the old brickmaster's house, a shaft of sunlight beaming down on her through a gap in the treetops. 'Like the bright centre of the world,' he said. 'I knew she felt it too. We knew it was madness. But we couldna help ourselves. We . . . we have fallen in love. Completely and totally in love.'

They walked in silence for a time, listening to the sounds of the woodland around them and the dull crunch of their steps on the leaf litter underfoot.

'What are your plans for this girl?' she said.

He frowned and his head ached again. The thought of her had acted as a momentary painkiller, but the troubles ahead brought the soreness back with a thump. 'We anna thought that far ahead. I suppose we've been living moment to moment, if you know what I mean, Mother.'

'I do know exactly what you mean,' she said and sighed. 'As hard as it is to believe, I was once a young girl in love.' He imagined his parents as young folk and smiled at the thought of them courting.

'Owen, I have some tales to tell you now and you must listen well. It concerns our past, all of us. Me, your father, your girl and her mother. When you've heard it, you will see that whatever future you have half imagined for you and this girl ... well, suffice to say, son, you will feel differently than you do at this moment. I am sorry for it, but it must be done.'

He expected a tale of woe about the prison, the Kings and their dastardly ways. He prepared himself to give a speech in defence of letting bygones be bygones, of mending the old feud. He would explain that the strike would come to an end soon and Beatrice had done all she could to help their side, that she was the bright future of the Kings and one day, who knew, perhaps society would accept their love and they would forge a new path together. But nothing had prepared him for what his mother was about to say. She stopped walking and looked away from him, staring down the incline they walked beside, down into the edges of the river, which lapped languidly against its banks.

'My first love was Beatrice's father, the artist Jake Ashford. He promised himself to me, said I should wait for him until he had made his fortune. I loved him with all of my heart, with my very soul. I imagined a great future for us, him painting his great scenes of industry, me a clerical worker in a fine office in Shrewsbury, maybe a lawyer's office or something illustrious like that. My future stretched before me like a shining path, just waiting for me to take my first step on it, arm in arm with Jake. But Cyril King had his eye on me, wanted me for himself. He found out about Jake and was madly jealous. He attacked me here, in these woods, trying to force himself upon me. He wanted to marry me and I rejected him most forcefully. I told him I'd rather die. He took me at my word. In revenge, he made it seem I had stolen money and I was sent to prison, as you know. Margaret King, Beatrice's mother, was my best friend. We had been secret friends for years. She came to the prison and swore she'd help me. The next time I saw her there, she told me my father was dead in an accident. But I knew he was killed by Ralph King cutting corners with the safety at the furnace to save money. My father was the dearest man in all the world to me. His death nearly ended me.'

His mother's head drooped forwards and she covered her face with her hands. He took a step towards her, but she lifted it again, wiping her eyes and shaking off her emotion, determined to continue.

'And that wasn't all Margaret delivered to me. She said too to forget Jake Ashford, that he would not be visiting me in gaol and that it would be better for everyone if I put him out of mind. I guessed why – she wanted him herself. I cursed her and her forsaken family. Then she betrayed me with Jake and they ran away together to the continent. Eventually, I was released from that hell-hole and made my way home, very ill and weak.' She paused, thinking about what she had just learnt from Margaret. But that was neither here nor there in terms of what Owen needed to know. Anny took a breath and continued, 'You may think you know that part of the story, but you do not know the details, the truth of what it was to live through that terrible time. I nearly died in that place. It was the site of the lowest degradation and brutality you can only imagine. It broke my body and it nearly broke my mind. Your father and his mother saved me. They nursed me back to health, in my body and in my mind. We married soon after. Then you came along. You know the rest, because you lived it. My life began again when yours did. I became a whole person again when you came into the world.'

He watched her staring into the flowing water below. Every ounce of devotion he owed to her surged in his chest and threatened to burst its banks. 'I didna know . . .' he began, clenching his fists with a rage that was brewing there too.

She turned to him, her face pale and eyes wide and white. 'I did not want to taint you with it. I wanted to escape those dark days of my youth and start afresh with you, my boy. You were all new, my perfect, pure, untouched, unblemished baby. I would not let the memory of the Kings' betrayal stain our life together. But the poison they poured into me flowed in my blood forever more. Surely, it slowed to a trickle as life went on and our happiness grew and grew, despite our poverty. But when the Kings took over the brickworks, the venom resurfaced in me and would not let me breathe freely. I felt choked by it more and more each day. Again, the Kings were directing my destiny and those of the people I loved. It was unbearable to me. Now you know the cause of many an argument with your dear father. He understood my hatred of the Kings, of course he did. He knew how I had been wronged. He saved me and made me anew. I loved him for that and for everything else that is in him. He is the great love of my life.'

His mother took a step forward and held out her hands to him. He took them and she squeezed them tightly, looking searchingly into his eyes.

'Do you understand now what I said to you yesterday? That if you love that girl, it will kill me?'

Her eyes were brimming, her face looked years older, drawn and thin. How could a son tell that face, those eyes, that he would willingly break her heart? Maybe another son could, another man, a lesser one. But Owen Malone – with his soft poetic heart he inherited from his father – could not.

When they returned to the cottage, Owen's father and Adam were waiting for them at the door, puffing on their clay pipes. Peter's face relaxed the moment he saw them. He popped his pipe in the corner of his mouth and came over to Anny, putting his arm around her, asking after her. She wouldn't have any fuss and went straight inside, the others following. Sufficient explanations were given and his mother was helped to sit at the table and tea was made and bread was sliced and spread with butter and jam, to put some colour back in his mother's cheeks. Martha was up and about, looking wan but much improved on the previous day. Baby Hettie slept on her arm and they all drank the tea down and were comfortable together, for the first time in a while. But inside, Owen's mind was aflame with a cauldron of emotions, new truths and old lies thickening the unholy brew. It was a great effort of will just to appear normal.

'We've been talking since you've been gone, Anny,' said Owen's father. 'Things need to change around these parts.'

'Oh, not more change, Peter,' sighed Anny with a smile. 'My head is spinning already.'

'Change for the better this time,' he replied. 'You've been doing far too much around here and taking too much onto yerself. You need more rest, with the babby on the way. Owen and I will be helping you more around the place. And Adam has summat to say on the matter too.'

All eyes were on Adam, who nursed a mug of tea in his large scarred hands and stared at the table top.

'I have decided that the strike must come to an end.'

The news fell upon silence. Nobody gasped, nobody said a word.

Adam went on, 'With this news come from the King girl that the works is to be closed tomorrow otherwise, I've been talking to the others and folk are telling me they canna afford to lose the works altogether. There is no appetite left amongst the workers for resistance. What's more, I've heard today that two more brickworks have gone back to work, Cooper and Colley's works and Heighway brick and tile too. That was the last straw for most folk. Most everyone I spoke with said the same, that it was time to go back. For myself, with a wife and child to support, I have no choice. And we've lived under your roof and relied on your kindness for too long.'

Anny spoke up, 'You know you're welcome as long as you need it, Adam.'

'I know that. But you need your home and your rest, and now the babby is here, we need our space too. We shall go back to our house, still empty I understand it, and take the old hag on her word and have our home again.'

Owen saw Martha nodding thoughtfully at this.

Adam continued, 'We must take the cut in pay and go back to work. I have called a meeting for four o'clock this afternoon, then I shall walk up to the big house this evening and tell 'em myself.'

A shocked silence followed, interrupted only by the drowsy grizzling of baby Hettie, unaware of the gravity of the situation. Owen imagined that each person around the table had their own differing reactions to the news, but nobody had the will to voice them or the vigour to dispute. The whole thing had staggered on for too long, now dropping by the wayside in a defeated heap. There was dejection in the room, but also a sense of relief. The strike was over and they had lost. Back to work it was, on far worse terms than before, but at least the strike was over.

The silence was broken by a small sound that came from Adam's throat. A stifled sob, that brought his fist up to his mouth. Owen could see that Adam was fighting back emotion, determined not to let it overcome him. He cleared his throat, sat up straight and set his face firm. 'It has been a fight for good, a fight worth fighting. They know now we are united, that we will speak for ourselves and not be trod upon like creatures of the dust. I may have failed this time . . .'

Adam stopped, swallowing down his feelings.

'That inna true,' said Owen firmly. 'You anna failed anyone.'

'Yes, I bloody have,' snapped Adam, then contained himself once more. 'But despite my failings, our cause was righteous. And I say, let this be the first of many, the stirrings of working people against the tyranny of masters. We have lost this battle, but the war will be long. One day, working people will be heard.'

'I'll drink to that,' said Peter. The two men looked at each other, so often at odds these past weeks, and a passing understanding was exchanged and they nodded.

꧁꧂

Owen went with Adam to the union meeting. There were far fewer people there than previous ones and a similar air of defeat. A few mouthy ones grumbled against it, but Owen noted that everyone looked simply exhausted with it all, a mirror of those around his own kitchen table. People shuffled away after, saying little. Such was the lot of the working man and woman, their rounded shoulders seemed to express. There had been light and hope and much talking and jostling in their community for a while, but now it was time to return to real life. Adam had gone off to Southover to tell them the news, insisting he do it alone. Owen guessed he wanted no witnesses to his shame.

The next day they were all up early, his mother preparing as hearty a meal as she could for the three men, with the meagre provisions they had left, some eggs from the chickens out back, some porridge with milk from a neighbour's goat. There would be money coming in at the end of the week, less than ever, but at least it would be something and they could afford to get some meat. His mother said that she and Martha would pack up their things and get some boys to help them take their bits and pieces back to their old house. His father and Adam said they'd do the heavy bits when they came home. The three of them trudged the walk to work in silence, heavy feet and heavy hearts.

As they approached the yard, Owen watched as their fellow brickies traipsed in beside them, as if the whole place was a weak magnet, drawing them in slowly but surely, unwilling and gloomy. Clothes were more ragged and filthy than ever, the children shoeless of course, as they ever were. The adults looked similarly dishevelled. There was a meeting with Troon and everyone gathered to listen to his instructions. Owen could see that there were far fewer workers than before the strike. Some had moved away, looking for other work in neighbouring counties. Some had gone into the workhouse. Some had starved, some had succumbed to illness. It was a ragged congregation, appearing more fit for admittance to a hospital than a long day's labour.

Troon was assigning new roles for many, now that the workforce was depleted. As well as being his father's assistant brickburner, Owen would now need to help out at the pug mill, checking the equipment and keeping it running smoothly, as well as loading the clay into the machine, where the wheels and knives inside it sliced and mixed it to produce the right consistency. It was a step down for him to be doing that job and also extra work, on top of his existing duties at the kilns. Troon said that now pay had gone down by thruppence per thousand bricks, everyone would want to work harder to make up the shortfall, as well as make back what they'd lost during the strike. So, there it was, more work, for less pay, for longer hours. The faces of everyone around him registered the miserable truth of their situation. There they were again, worse off than ever. There were a few daggered looks thrown at Adam, who kept his head down. He had been their hero and saviour once. But people always looked for someone to blame, when things were wrecked and ruined.

Days passed in echoes of each other, long, shattering days of toil, lacking definition between one and the next. Owen worked and slept, worked and slept. He dreamt of Beatrice. He would wake up shaking and sweating, as if weaning himself off some dreadful addiction. He developed a cough and his mother wrapped warm poultices about his throat each night, which he threw off in the July heat. At the end of the first week back, everyone arrived again at work with eager anticipation of the pay that would be handed out later, this promise buoying up their flagging vitality, helping them to push through this last day before their one day of rest on the morrow.

Owen left his father at the kiln to check on proceedings at the pug mill. It was a huge contraption, towering above them, a barrel-shaped machine topped with a wide horizontal wheel which had a diameter about the length of a tall man. This was driven by a cog wheel that in turn was driven by a steam engine beyond. The hopper was below the wheel, where the clay was fed in, made malleable by the rotating knives inside. At the base, the reduced clay came out, ready to be taken by children over to the moulding tables. An engineer called Tinsley was in charge there, a bully of a man who liked to give the young'uns a clip round the ear for little or no excuse. Owen hated him and so was even more depressed to have been assigned to the pug mill. Brain was working in here now too. Good old Brain, just turned thirteen and taller by far than Tinsley, who was a wiry little man, bitterly resenting anyone that towered over him and punishing them for it. But Brain was immune to such hostility. He looked cheerful and happy to be back, full of gusto, despite his family nearly ending up in the workhouse these past weeks, saved only by a few pennies from the union fund and the ending of the strike. He seemed more like a jovial dog than ever, his hair long at the back, stiff and straggly with sweat and clay. Owen thought the pug mill was not the best place for Brain, being of such a simple turn, that labouring at digging up clay suited his mind better than all this machinery. But he was very glad to have a friendly face around.

Brain turned when he saw Owen coming in and called over, 'Ow bist, Owen? Ow bist, me owd butty? Pay day today!'

'Shut yer trap, yer drearing great lump,' snarled Tinsley. 'Oil that pinion wheel like I told yer. No time for socialisationing.' After Tinsley spat out that last mouthful of a word, annoyed that Owen had witnessed it, he stomped away, pushing Owen's shoulder roughly with his own as he passed. Owen was knocked off one foot and swayed to steady himself, turning to Brain to have a laugh with him about miserable old Tinsley.

In the moment he looked at Brain, reaching up under the moving wheel to oil it, Owen shouted, 'No, Brain! From above!'

But there was no time for Brain to listen, to hear that it was mortally dangerous to oil the wheel from below. There was no time because Brain's hands were already caught in the cogs and in one terrifyingly swift moment, his whole frame was jerked upwards, pulled in up to the armpits, his arms mangled in the wheel and his body thrown against the wall behind the machine. The force of it jammed him between the wall and the end of the pinion shaft.

Owen ran to him, screaming, 'Stop the machine!' The wheel was blocked, straining to go about its circular journey. Brain's face was white as a china plate, a thin line of bright red blood trickling from the side of his mouth. He uttered a high, wheezy whine. Thank God, he was still alive. Owen kicked over a barrow and jumped atop it, so that he could stand face to face with him.

'Brain,' whispered Owen, his hand hovering by Brain's face, afraid to touch it. 'Brain, we're gonna get yer out.' He looked wildly about the equipment, trying to fathom how to extricate Brain from the mess of it.

'Owen,' he murmured. His eyes were closed, tight shut, as if he were hiding from something. His lips were open, a row of crooked teeth visible, lined with red.

'Dunna speak,' said Owen.

'Owen, me owd mate,' Brain whispered, a bubble of blood appearing on his lower lip then bursting.

'Hush, Brain. We'll soon have yer out.'

'I didna know.'

Owen stroked his cheek now with the tips of two fingers. 'I know, Brain. I know. It inna your doing. It inna your fault. Hush, hush now.' Then, he jerked his head round and shouted, his voice cracking, 'Turn that bastard machine off!'

The wheels at once loosened and Owen grasped at Brain's back, afraid he would fall. Men were running in, swearing and gasping. Two came up behind Brain and took his weight. Owen felt a hand patting him firmly on his shoulder but could not turn his head from Brain, whose eyes were beginning to open a sliver, at the touch of men at his back.

'Owen,' said a familiar voice and he twisted his head to see his father's face. 'Come down, lad. They need to move the wheel a bit to free him. Come down out the way.'

But Owen could not move, frozen there. Peter took his shoulders firmly and guided him down off the barrow. Owen felt his legs give away, his arms flailing. Then his father caught him, saying, 'Now then, son', and dragged him up to lean against him, steering him away from the mill and out into the fresher air. Owen felt his feet stumbling beneath him, glad of the strength of his father's arms about him.

'He didna know what he were doing,' he cried. 'Tinsley never showed him properly. He'd never worked the pug mill before. He shouldna been in there at all.'

His father was hushing him now, as he himself had hushed Brain moments before. Owen suddenly felt a fool, for collapsing like that, when Brain was the one who was injured, not him. He pushed his father away and stood up on shaking legs, forcing himself to stand tall. He turned from him and marched back to the scene of the accident, to find that they had managed to get Brain out, who was now lying on the ground, someone's coat over his front, covering up his grievous injuries. Troon was there now and Adam. They were talking about getting the doctor and a boy was sent off running.

Troon said, 'It's hopeless, though. Look at him, mon.'

'Doctor can sew him up. He can . . . he can . . .' Adam said, gesturing vaguely towards Brain, 'Take off the arms. He'll be a cripple but . . .' His voice trailed off.

Owen looked down at Brain and saw Royce was there now, sitting on his haunches, his arms resting on his knees. He was staring grimly at his friend. He reached out a hand, then withdrew it, his hands joining together, wringing shakily. He dropped down to his knees and sat there, watching his friend's grey face. Owen stood observing them both, his arms hanging loosely by his side, his ears registering sounds around him of complaint and pity, the cries of women weeping and children sobbing, the voice of Tinsley defending himself and men arguing with him. Everyone knew that no amount of talk would bring Brain back and no doctor could save him now. Time washed over Owen, irrelevant, meaningless, as unstoppable and uncaring as a flowing river over a drowning man's head. All he could do was stand there and watch Brain die.

Chapter 17

Beatrice had never played card games before she came to England. Now she was addicted to Old Maid, played sometimes in fours with her mother, her great-grandmother and her step-grandmother, and it occurred to her that around the table, all the women playing, in one way or another, had something in common with the maid of the title. Three of them were widows, with no man propping them up. And the fourth, herself, was most definitely a maid, though she did not intend to remain one for long. The object of the game was to make a pile of pairs and avoid being the one left with the singular queen. But she was torn about this and, though loving to win, she also felt special if she was the one left holding the Old Maid. She thought the queens painted on the playing cards were beautiful and also mysterious. They had the allure of power about them, women in high places who could rule over others. She wondered if this was why Queenie loved the game too. Mostly it was played by just the two of them, sometimes for an hour or two or more. They never tired of it. For Beatrice in the days during the strike, it had served as a distraction from the constant frustration of being separated from Owen and worry about how everything would turn out for their families.

Now the strike was over and the brickies had been back at work for six days, Beatrice had been allowed out of the house again, if she wished to go. But the freedom she had longed for seemed a cruel trick on her now. She had kept to the house this past week, citing the heat or tiredness or a headache. The truth was that her mind was in turmoil. Her mother's revelations about the past had hit her hard, a cruel and unexpected slap in the face. The romantic vision she had grown up with of her parents' elopement to Paris had been shattered and in its place was a tawdry story of her father – the drunk, the womaniser and the wife beater. Such news might turn a girl against men for life, but all it did was serve to highlight Owen's qualities more than ever, as she knew in her heart that he was none of these things and would never be a man like that. He was good, through and through, and despite her protestations to her mother, inside she yearned for him desperately.

The story of his mother and her mother affected her deeply too. She understood her mother's motives in all of it, and sympathised with her. But she was ashamed to admit to herself that it was Anny who she empathised with. Such terrible things had been done to her by this family, it sickened Beatrice to be a part of it, though she loved her mother and her great-grandmother dearly. The wrongs that had been committed hung over her like a black cloud. She marvelled how the Kings could carry on so easily after destroying someone's life like that. It left her feeling conflicted about Queenie. How could she reconcile the great-grandmother she loved with the woman who had stood back and let a life be destroyed? It made her feel proud of her mother's flight to France, for at least she had the decency to go away and make her own life, away from the Kings and all that they stood for.

The atmosphere at home was cheerier for those around her. Benjamina had emerged from her room, perfectly turned out each day, seeming much more like her old self and talking about procuring a new puppy. Queenie was visibly happier, relieved that the strike business was finally over and done with and things could get back to normal. Cyril was restless, it had to be said. He'd seemed to enjoy the intrigues of the strike and now it was over and familiar routines had resumed, he was bored and fidgety. Beatrice's mother seemed content in a quiet way, yet Beatrice noticed her watching her from time to time, no doubt wondering if what Beatrice kept saying to her was true, that she was over Owen and never thought of him. Nothing could be further from the truth. Yet, on the surface, peace had been restored at Southover and everyone seemed better for it.

But then Troon came, on the Saturday afternoon, just before teatime. Beatrice and Queenie were in the midst of an Old Maid marathon, when Busby came and told his mistress that Mr Troon was here to see her. Beatrice saw Queenie's face fall at the news.

'Oh, will I never be free from these brickmakers? I've half a mind to close the place if this is how it's going to carry on.'

'Queenie!' said Beatrice, shocked to hear it after everything everyone had been through. 'You don't mean that!'

Queenie scowled and shook her head. 'Of course not, dear. But it's tempting.' She sighed and said to Busby, 'Show him in here, Busby. I am comfortable and do not wish to disturb our game.' Busby nodded and withdrew. Queenie went on, 'And anyway, Bea, it'll be useful for you to start taking an interest in the business. Maybe you'll take it over in the future, if I have my way.' She said this last with a twinkle in her eye.

'I don't know what I want for my future, really,' sighed Beatrice. 'But do you really think I have it in me to run all . . . this?' she said with a flourish of her hand.

'I do not *think* it,' said Queenie. 'I *know* it. You have the right kind of mind for it. You are confident too and easy with people. They relax in your company. You have a clear sense of what is right, which is what this company needs going forward, I believe, as long as you temper that with business sense. This can be taught, if you are willing to learn. The overseers like Brotherton can deal with all the administration. But you, my dear, with a good husband by your side, would make a fine heir to my role. It is what I hope for.'

Beatrice smiled at her great-grandmother and nodded her interest, but nothing like her assent as yet. Could she do what Queenie had done, step into her shoes? Queenie was formidable and Beatrice did not feel she would ever be so impressive. Or could she? She imagined herself, making decisions, holding meetings, reading reports. It was vastly preferable to a future of indolence, such as Benjamina had. Thoughts of the power it would afford her crept into her mind too as she pondered it all, when the door opened and Busby returned and after him, Mr Troon.

Troon's face was disturbing to look at. He had dark shadows under his tired eyes. He looked like a man with nothing good to say. Beatrice saw Queenie noted it too. They both placed their cards on the table.

'What is it, Troon?' said Queenie, her voice tinged with apprehension.

'I am sorry to report . . . an accident at the yard. A very serious accident.'

'Not Owen Malone?' cried Beatrice.

'No, miss,' said Troon, looking at her quizzically. Beatrice's heart had been clamped in terror at the news, but now she could rule out the worst of it, at least.

'What's happened, Troon?' said Queenie, with some irritation.

'It's a death, madam. A lad got his arms caught up in the workings of the pug mill. The doctor was sent for but the lad died at the scene. Nothing could be done for him.'

Queenie grimaced and said, 'A regrettable incident,' with a suitably sombre tone. 'Where is ... the body now?'

'Doctor arranged for it to be taken by cart to his dwelling for examination. Said he would need to establish cause of death, for the coroner.'

'Of course. Was anyone else hurt?'

'No, madam. The workers are shocked and saddened, as you can imagine.'

'Was any equipment damaged? And is the brickworks up and running again?'

Beatrice stared at Queenie, incredulous of what she was hearing. A boy had died, in the most gruesome and unnatural way. And Queenie wanted to know if the business was still running. If this was what it took to be in her place, then Beatrice wanted none of it.

'Yes, all is in hand.'

'Very good. We shall speak again on Monday. Arrange for Brotherton to be informed and he should bring me the boy's details. I shall write to his parents. Thank you, Troon.' Queenie turned away from him, signalling that the audience was over.

'Madam, miss,' he nodded gravely at them both.

'Mr Troon,' called Beatrice as he began to turn away.

'Yes, miss?'

'How old was he?'

'Just turned thirteen, miss.'

'What was his name?'

'Brain. Harold Brain. But everyone called him Brain. He wasna too bright, you see. His brain ... well, the Lord hadna finished him, if you take my meaning. So we all thought it funny, his name being Brain. He thought it were funny too. Never took offence, mind. So that's what we all called him. Brain.'

'Harold Brain,' murmured Beatrice.

'Yes, miss. And curious you should mention Owen Malone, for they were friends, in actual fact. And Owen was there when it happened. Saw the whole thing and stayed with him till help came. He'll be needed by the coroner, no doubt, as a witness.'

'That'll do, Troon,' said Queenie, quietly. He nodded again and left them, trudging across the floor and closing the door with care.

Beatrice stared at her great-grandmother, who picked up her cards again and studied them.

'This is terrible,' said Beatrice.

'Yes,' said Queenie, rearranging her hand of cards, pointedly not looking at Beatrice.

'It is *frightful*.' Her mind was filled with the image of Owen, seeing it all, staying with Harold Brain, talking to him. How the poor boy must have suffered ... What did arms look like when they were 'caught up in workings'? It was ghastly and unthinkable. The agony of it. The horror Owen must have seen.

'We must do something,' insisted Beatrice, willing Queenie to look up from her cards.

'We will be doing something. I shall send my condolences to the parents.'

'A letter they probably can't read!' scoffed Beatrice.

Queenie looked sharply up at her. 'It is the way it is done. I cannot become too involved with it until the inquest is heard. This has happened at *my* brickworks. We must hear the evidence and then make our decisions about what is to be done. There is a matter of blame, of fault. It is not as simple as a tragedy.'

'But it *is* a tragedy!' cried Beatrice. 'A boy is dead. Killed by a machine. His arms, they must be . . . mangled. The pain! It must have been . . .' She could not find the words. Nothing seemed adequate.

'And this is what you must learn as the first rule of business. Never become emotionally embroiled in such things. Someone has to remain objective, until the evidence is gathered and the hearing has been held.'

'Do you have no softer feelings for these people? Can you find no kindness in your heart, as I do?'

'Twice I have followed your lead in such things and where has it got me? I visited the Joneses and was sent away with a flea in my ear. I paid the doctor's fee for them at your request and have I received a word of thanks or even acknowledgement? No, I have not. Nothing. These people do not understand kindness. And all that softness does is lead to weakness.'

'I don't understand you,' said Beatrice, coldly.

Queenie looked down at her cards, reordering them yet again. 'One day, you will understand. If you run this business, you will.'

Beatrice was gathering her words wildly, ready for a verbal attack. But she was interrupted by the entrance of a maid bringing the tea things.

'Time for afternoon tea,' said Queenie, sounding grateful. She placed her cards on the table.

Beatrice said nothing, turned away from her great-grandmother and looked out of the window. As tea was served, Beatrice stared at the green mass of trees beyond the drive, still as a painting in the breezeless day. She could leave, right now. She could go into the conservatory, out of the glass door and run into the woods, follow the river and go straight to Owen's house. But he would not be there, only Anny Malone would be there. And she would have no time for Beatrice, for Anny hated her, surely. She could run the other way then, down the driveway and into town, along the road and up the hill towards the brickworks, go find Owen there and . . . and what? How welcome would a King be there? They wouldn't care that her name was Ashford. She would be one of *them*, that was all. It didn't matter whose fault it was, the accident. The boy had been killed by King equipment. Owen might even hate her for that. The thought appalled her. If only she could go to him, right away. If only she could see his face, this instant, and know if he still loved her.

The door opened and in came Cyril, making a beeline for the cakes on the table.

'Don't mind if I do!' he said and stuffed one in his mouth, the crumbs cascading down his front and onto the carpet. Beatrice glared at him. Did he know what had happened? She shot a look at Queenie, who turned to him to speak.

'There is more bad news from the brickworks, I'm afraid to say.'

'What now?' said Cyril.

'A boy has died, caught up in the workings of the pug mill.'

Cyril grimaced. Beatrice watched his face. It was suitably sombre, but did not show what Beatrice would call suitable emotion.

'It is all in hand,' Queenie continued. 'But there will be an inquest and some unpleasantness, I daresay.'

'The workers will be itching for a fight again, no doubt,' replied Cyril, his tone a mixture of flippancy and tedium.

Beatrice glared at Queenie again, who gave her great-granddaughter a sympathetic look. Queenie had reacted coldly towards the news, but at least she wasn't dismissive of it, as Cyril was.

'It is a tragic thing, the death of a child,' said Queenie pointedly to Cyril. 'It would behove you to remember that, when dealing with any of our workers regarding this business.'

Cyril sighed and threw himself down on the settee in a dramatic pose. 'I know that, of course. Ghastly business. But I'm sick of it all. Sick of the brick business. And I'm sick of Ironbridge and all its petty squabbles.' He sat up straight and looked Queenie in the eye. 'And it's made up my mind, actually, Queenie. You remember the fellow I know from Liverpool? The one who got us all the scabs. James Melton.'

'Of course,' said Queenie. 'We are indebted to him for that. Do you wish him to visit?'

'No, I do not. I wish to visit *him* and then accompany him on a bit of a jolly. Listen, this new-fangled thing in the iron industry that's being talked about. The Bessemer process? It's a new way of making iron, turns it into steel. Well, it's the latest thing and it's driving forward the iron industry into the future. I'm sick of all this brickworks nonsense. I know the iron industry has been on its last legs round here for a while, but this new process sounds just the ticket to me. Melton has invited me to travel with him to America. We'll be inspecting the industries of Pennsylvania, the coal and steel industries. He is going to go in a month or so. I wasn't sure I could be bothered, but I'm sick of it here. I need to get away from all this provincialism.'

Queenie took a sip of her tea and replaced the cup neatly on its saucer, placing both carefully on the table before her. She was clearly mulling over Cyril's words as she did so.

'Cyril, you should go to America. It will be good for all of us. You'll bring back new knowledge and improve the business. It'll give you something useful to do and, the Lord knows, there is a first time for everything on that account.'

'Jolly good!' said Cyril and bounced up from the settee. 'I'll make the arrangements forthwith! Let me know if you need any assistance with this death business.' He grasped another cake and left the room, trailing crumbs as he went.

'I wonder where your mother and Benjamina are? Lounging around upstairs, no doubt,' said Queenie and took another bite of cake. 'They are missing out on a good sponge.' Queenie glanced up at Beatrice, then looked quickly away again. 'And we do need to inform them of the sad news.'

Beatrice felt nauseous. The lack of feeling towards the boy who'd died was sickening her and she could not bear to pretend any longer. Yet she did not have the strength to argue about it either. She stood up and said to Queenie, 'I feel somewhat ill. Please tell Maman that I shall retire to my room for the rest of the day. Please do not call me for dinner.'

Queenie looked concerned and said, 'Dearest, do not let Cyril upset you. It's just his way. And do not concern yourself too much with this latest problem. I do assure you that once the inquest has settled things, I will look out for the boy's family. All will be well.'

Beatrice could see Queenie was trying to be kind, but she had lost some faith in her great-grandmother, particularly her ability to make anything 'well' for her workers.

'Yes, I'm sure you're right,' she said, turning to leave the room. But Queenie hadn't finished with her.

'And soon, my dear, we shall launch you onto the social scene. There is a ball, I hear, in a fortnight's time, organised by Mr and Mrs Elkin. You remember meeting them at your grandfather's wake? They adored you. I think it should be the occasion of your coming out. We can order a dress from London. That will be something for you to look forward to, shall it not?'

'Yes, of course. Thank you,' murmured Beatrice and left the room. She began to climb the stairs slowly, but then the tears came and she took the last few swiftly, hurrying to her room to weep in private.

She cried herself to sleep, taking a fitful nap, fraught with nightmares. Her dreams were a swirl of misery, leaping from one dark thing to the next. She pictured the boy and his accident, the crushing of his arms, the blood and gore horrific. She imagined Owen, sitting beside him, watching him die. She should be with him, comforting him. She tried to reach him in the dream, but could not walk towards him, her legs strangely bound. She woke up damp with sweat, her mouth as dry as cotton. She knew in that moment that she would never be able to obey her mother's wishes. Whatever she had said to her about trying to forget Owen, she knew it was folly. She loved him. She wanted to take her place beside him, for the rest of their lives. The boy's death was a brutal reminder that life was short. She did not want to waste hers in regret. But how could such a fate be achieved?

Then she remembered Queenie's words from earlier, that one day Beatrice would take over the business. What had seemed a daunting responsibility, suddenly began to whisper possibilities to her, that if she was clever and bided her time, one fine day, she would take over from Queenie, run the business and promote Owen Malone to a position of power and prestige. They could see each other in secret, then when the time was right, they could marry and run the business together. With her common touch and the business knowledge gained from Queenie, and his industrial knowledge and understanding of the workforce, they would make the ideal team. Only that morning, it had seemed ridiculous, an impossible dream. But now, hope filled her heart. Her stomach grumbled and she realised how hungry she was. Perhaps she would go down for dinner, after all. She would need to eat to keep her strength up. She had plans to make. Her first must be to figure out a way to see her beloved Owen again.

Chapter 18

Beer was so comforting. It was liquid but it had body to it, a bit like soup, Owen mused. He downed the dregs and thought about getting another. A couple of days had passed since Brain's death and they'd arranged a hasty funeral. Most of the other mourners had gone home now. Brain's mother had cried all the way through the church service and family members had taken her home before the burial. She wasn't fit to stay. The brickies had clubbed together to pay for a headstone but the stonemason said it wasn't enough and nobody had any more to spare. Brain was buried in a pauper's grave. There were already a few bodies in there, the uppermost being very small, a baby of indeterminate age. The air was foul about the hole and nobody stayed long. It was best his mother didn't see where her son had gone to rest. Nobody let her see his body on the day of his death either. No mother should see their child like that.

Owen ordered another beer. His father had warned him not to stay too long and drink too much. His mother had said to leave him be, let him work it out his own way. His father had looked annoyed, like he knew that something had been going on between mother and son that hadn't included him. But just before they left, his mother had whispered in his ear not to get too drunk, as he'd regret it in the morning and the shifts were longer now and he'd need his wits about him. He was ignoring their advice, as was often the case these days. His father plodded on with work without question, which infuriated Owen, but he had not the energy to argue with him. And what would be the point anyway? Nothing would change.

As for Owen's mother, she was struggling with the pregnancy and looked so tired all the time, he had not the heart to discuss anything with her about the old truths she'd told him. He did not want to upset her by bringing all that up again. He just wanted his mother to be well.

Brain's mother relied on her son's meagre earnings as she was herself a widow and not of a hale and hearty constitution. Owen wondered what would happen to her now. He hoped there might be a relative somewhere to take her in, though he had not heard of one. Imagine having Brain as your comfort, he thought. Such a jolly soul. And then imagine losing him and having nothing and nowhere to go. Harold, his name was. Owen had learnt that at the church service in his memory. Harold Brain, the vicar had said, and Owen realised he'd never known Brain's first name, everyone calling him Brain from the day he started at the brick-works aged six. *Harold Brain*, thought Owen. *Harold. Did his mother call him Harry*, he wondered? *Or Hal?*

He closed his eyes and wished a man could wipe his thoughts clean, like a slate at school. Well, a few more of these beers and he could effectively do that, for a short time anyway. But the moment his eyes were shut, he saw Beatrice. He imagined her standing before him, her face a picture of concern, her hands reaching towards him, to comfort him. She put her arms about him and kissed him. The relief of feeling her again, the want of her was like an unquenchable thirst. The misery of Brain's death would never leave him completely, but it would be soothed by her presence, her touch, her love.

He snapped open his eyes. It was late, gone ten at night. She'd be in her bed now. A thought came to him and he shoved it away. He took another deep draught of beer. He ought to be getting home. But the thought came back, of walking the other way from the tavern, of going along the river path, then up through the trees, up to the house on the hill. If he could see her one more time, just one more time, then that would be enough. Then he could say goodbye and leave her forever. Just one more time would do it. That was all he wanted, wasn't it? Then he could give her up for good, as his mother wanted.

But he knew he was lying to himself. One more time would never be enough. It would only make it worse. It would only serve to sharpen his longing. He shook his head to rid it of the stupid notion. He finished off the dregs and did not order more. He was going to remain relatively sober tonight and he was going to walk straight home, as his father wanted. He would not be going to see Beatrice that night. He would be going straight home instead. Indeed, he would. He turned and set off, walking at a fair pace.

It was a warm, sticky night. The air was heavy with it. There had been cloudy skies all day and they had not dispersed, trapping the heat between heaven and earth. He stopped before his destination and stared at it. He leant against an oak tree and gazed at the King house across the lawn. Then, a yellow square of light appeared, flickering invitingly. The rest of the house was obscure and silent. He nearly turned away, went back along the dark whispering woodland path home, to where his parents would be waiting, hoping he did not come home too drunk this time. He remembered he would stink of beer and suddenly regretted it, imagining what Beatrice would think if he came to her smelling like a brewery. But he was not going to see Beatrice, of course, so it did not matter. How would he find her anyway? He had no idea which room was hers or how to get to her. The whole thing had been a fool's errand. He should turn and go home, this instant.

That is what he told himself as he stared at the lamplit window. Then, a figure appeared. Long, flowing hair, a white nightgown, pale as a spirit. But this was no spectre, this was flesh and blood, warm and real. It was Beatrice, leaning on her windowsill. He stepped over the lumpen roots of the oak tree and marched across the lawn. She saw him and her face lit up with a glorious smile. She beckoned and he broke into a trot, arriving beneath her window and gazing up at her.

'I cannot believe you are here!' she spoke in a hoarse whisper, her face lit up with delight.

'Nor I,' he said and grinned.

'I couldn't sleep. So I came to the window. And there you were! Am I dreaming? Can you be real?'

'You are not. And yes, I can. I am real. I am here, to see you!'

'Oh, my love!' she said and his heart lurched. 'But how shall we do this?' She peered behind her then turned back to him, biting her bottom lip. 'I might be able to sneak through the house . . .'

'No,' he said, looking about him. 'I shall come to you.'

'But how?'

Below her window was an ancient and sturdy wisteria. It clung to a trellis that was nailed to the brick. He could climb up the trellis and step onto the flat roof of the library beside it. Was it the beer that gave him courage or his need for her? Was it foolhardy? No, he decided. It had reason to it, if the trellis held. The angle between the flat roof and her window was sharp, but there was a ledge beneath her window that he could put a foot on and grab the gable. He wouldn't be relying on her to pull him in, but he thought he could make that ledge. He reached out and grasped the trellis, giving it a good yank to check its strength. It was firmly attached to the wall and he believed it would take his weight. He began to climb, the wisteria blossoms tickling his face as he ascended, filling his nostrils with a musky scent that was quite overpowering. He had to focus to keep his grip.

He reached the flat roof and climbed onto it. Her windowsill was more or less level with the roof. But the gap between the ledge and himself looked much wider now he was there. She reached out her hands towards him, but he shook his head. If he could reach the gable first, he could then get one foot on the ledge and pull the rest of himself over. There was nothing for it but to try. He leant out, glancing down at the ground that now seemed far below. He did not fancy landing on that gravel on his back. *Better not look down then*, he thought. He leant out, eased his hands along the bricks, then grabbed the gable, getting a firm grip on it before trying to hop a foot onto the ledge. It missed its spot at first and he pushed himself back onto the roof. But he had a better idea of where things were this time and he reached out again. Gable, ledge and his foot was there. He pulled his body up and hung onto the gable, his feet wedged safely on the ledge. He felt her hands on his legs and nearly let go, her touch affected him so. But he kept his wits about him and eased his way down, whispering 'Move back!' so that he could throw his feet inside and land on her floor.

Once inside, they both paused at the noise of his heavy boots landing on her carpet. No sounds came, nobody was the wiser. He was breathing hard from his exertions. He needed a moment to recover. He stood, his hands on his thighs, and stared at her. She was almost too beautiful to touch, but that did not stop him. All thoughts of the smell of beer and all commitments he made to never see her again were long gone, as he stepped forward and put his arms around her, drew her to him and they kissed, open-mouthed, deep, wet and glorious. He had never bedded a girl before, but he was certain in that moment that he would know exactly what to do. Her bed was beside them and he thought of it there, ready to take them, if she wanted him to. He wanted to. He wanted to very much.

Beatrice pulled away, buried her face in his shoulder and a little sob caught in her throat.

Owen whispered to her, 'Are you well?'

'I am well,' she said and smiled up at him. 'I am overcome.'

He kissed her again and ran his hands up and down her body, feeling her for the first time with only a thin layer of fabric between his hands and her flesh. His own body felt as if it would burst into flame, his whole being filled with an urgency to act that strained in every muscle. Would she let him? He would never force himself on her, on any girl. Would she invite him?

She stopped and took his hand. She sat down on the bed and he sat down beside her. But now she was kissing his hand lightly and smiling at him, squeezing his hand like a friend.

'Owen, I believe you can read minds.'

He hoped he could and he hoped also that she wanted the same thing as he did.

'Can I?'

'Yes, for I have been wracking my brain these last days, trying to think of a way to contact you safely and you managed it yourself.'

He did not want to talk. He wanted to kiss her again and pull her to him, lay her down and lie atop her. But there she was, talking.

'I thought of writing you a letter, but where would I send it? Your mother might see it and would guess it was from me, I thought. I could not think of a way around it. But you came to me!'

'I did.'

'I'm so glad you did. I'm over the moon!' she cried and squeezed his hand tightly. But then her face clouded. 'But I know I must not be so selfish as to be happy, when there are such sad things in the world around us. Owen, I heard about the accident at the yard. I heard about Harold Brain.'

'Yes,' muttered Owen and looked down, away from her face. He did not want to think about Harold Brain at this moment. Yet a series of gruesome images assaulted him and he looked back at her face to rid himself of the memories.

'I'm so sorry for it. So sorry.'

'That's all right. It's not your fault.'

There was a moment of silence between them, laden with questions. If the Kings were to blame, as they surely were, could she be included in that guilt?

'Troon told me you were with him at the end. That was so good of you. You are such a good man.'

'No choice. I was there when it happened. I saw the whole thing.'

'Oh, how terrible for you! Do you wish to speak of it? I will listen to anything you have to say. I am not a squeamish, silly girl.'

'I'd rather not,' he said, his desire ebbing as sombre thoughts filled his mind. The touch of her hand was comforting though and he squeezed it.

'I understand. Let us speak of other things. I have a plan, something that might sound mad at first, but it could change things around here, change them for the better. Please bear with me.'

He did not want to talk about anything, truth be told. He just wanted to rid his head of bad memories. But the night was long and maybe once he had heard this plan and discussed it sufficiently, he could stop her mouth with kisses and then ... She was explaining something about becoming the mistress of the King business, taking over from the old hag and running it.

That she'd make sure he was well provided for and that one day, when they were older and he was promoted, they would marry.

'Marry?' he said.

'Yes, marry. If . . .' Now she looked uncertain and looked at him with large brown cow eyes. 'Don't . . . you want to marry me, Owen?'

He had wanted to see her. He had wanted to kiss her and take her to bed. He had not thought beyond that, not for a long time now.

'Of course I do,' he said. 'It's just that . . . it never seemed possible.'

'But with my plan in place, it is just that. It is possible now.'

'But what of the past? My mother told me things. If you dunna know them, I am afraid to tell you. But you mun know.'

'I know it all, Owen. Everything. My mother told me too. Terrible things. My father beat her. Your mother loved my father. The prison, Uncle Cyril, all of it. It is awful. But it has nothing to do with us.'

Owen dropped her hand that still held his. 'It has *everything* to do with us.'

'No, no. It does not. Don't you see? The past is past. We cannot let their mistakes haunt us. We are new and . . . and we shall be free.'

'You are wrong, Bea. Life does not work that way. The past is everything. It holds us and colours us. We cannot

315

escape it. It lives in our bones and our blood.' She smiled at him, curiously. 'What are you thinking about, at this moment?' he said, as he realised, he never had a clue what she was going to say next, let alone what was going on behind that beautiful face.

'I was thinking that I love the way you speak.'

'Thank you, Miss Ashford,' he said and made a complimentary nod.

'You're welcome, Mr Malone,' she said. 'Being here with you, it is the most delicious treat to sit and listen to you speak! Better than ice cream, better even than *croissants aux amandes*, warm and fresh from the oven, spread with melting butter and *confiture d'abricot*!' He had no idea what that meant, but he did not care, watching her talk, drinking in the miracle of her face, her lips moving, her eyes deep and dark in the dim lamplight. 'We must keep talking, keep being honest with each other, share our innermost thoughts and feelings. If we always stay true to each other, we will weather this. Time will pass, our positions in life will change and society will change. And one day, one fine day, Mr Malone, you and I shall be together. Do you believe it?'

'I believe anything that comes from those lips,' he said, still transfixed by them.

'No, no, Owen,' she giggled. 'I am serious now. It will take time, much time. We can meet in secret along the way but we must both have patience. If we bide our time, one day, we shall marry and be together always. Do you trust me?'

'Yes, I trust you.' He did not have the heart to ask the same of her. Everything he was to her was based on a lie. Would she still feel the same if she knew he'd first courted her to use her an unwitting spy?

'Then, we shall say good night now. And you will come again soon.'

So tonight was done then. She thought they had a future together. But for him, it was just this one night only. The future beyond that was tangled up with the past, but this one night was theirs alone. But she did not know that, she thought it was the first of many to come. She was wrong and he could not tell her why.

'I dunna know when I can come again. My mother's babby will come soon.'

'Yes, of course! How lovely.'

'Yes, it is. But it means more work too and more help needed at home. And the yard since the strike, well . . . we have to work harder now.'

She looked down, perhaps with guilt.

'I am so sorry for that. I did what I could, for you and for everyone. But I failed.'

'It is not your fault. You did your best. It means much that you tried.'

'Thank you. I know times are hard. But promise me you will come to me here, at night, as often as you can. I cannot live without you, Owen.'

'Soon. I will come again soon,' he lied, knowing that he would have to make a choice, between his family and her, and it would be an impossible choice. 'I wish it were different, but wishing does not make it so.'

'It did tonight. I wished you to come and there you were, leaning against the oak tree. I know we will be fine. Everything will be fine.'

He grimaced then sought to cover it with a smile.

'What is it, Owen? Something is wrong.'

He turned away, afraid his face would tell more tales on him. 'Everything, of course. Everything is wrong.'

'But we love each other,' she said simply and reached out for him, drew him to her and held him close. It was not desire that held him there but comfort, pure and simple. The feel of her soft, warm body was a kind of luxury and he wished he could lie down and sleep with it, truly sleep, listening to her breathe until dawn came and woke him.

When she pulled away from him, he felt as if part of his soul had been wrenched and detached. She kept it and he had lost it. He looked at her, longingly.

'Your face . . .' he began, gazing at it. Words failed him. The beauty of it. 'Ducklings . . .' he began.

'Ducklings?' she whispered, quizzically.

'When ducklings are born, down by the river, they come out of the egg and they follow the first thing they see. It's usually their mother but you can make them follow you. They bond with it and love it, fall for it head over heels. They'll follow it anywhere. They fall in love, with just one look. That is how it was with me and with you. When I first saw you, your face appearing at the window of your coach, across the filthy yard. A pale face, lustrous hair, eyes like a tawny owl, round and dark. I saw you and I loved you.'

'You loved me?' she gasped, tears starting in her eyes.

'I love you,' he said.

'Oh, Owen! And I love you,' she said, placing her hand on his cheek. They kissed again and desire rose in him once more. She sensed it and pulled away. He wanted to pull her back to him, but he would not, unless she gave him some sign. 'We must . . . take care.'

He knew what she meant. 'Yes,' he replied, sharply disappointed but in agreement, in theory at least. 'We cannot afford to . . . complicate matters.'

'Indeed not, for then our plans will come to naught. A child now . . . would ruin everything. We must have patience.'

'It will be a trial,' he said, gazing at the creamy skin where her neck met her shoulder, imagining the curves and contours below it, beneath the thin cotton of her nightdress.

'We cannot meet in public now. But Owen, it is a hot summer and I leave my window open every night. Every single night. Come whenever you can. We shall talk further and make our plans. We have all the time in the world. We have the rest of our lives together.'

She smiled at him and kissed his hand, then led him to the window. Descending from her room was not as straightforward as its opposite. Clambering from the windowsill to the flat roof was a leap of faith and he was glad he had long legs to make the jump. He managed it, though a little winded, and climbed down the wisteria, his legs shaking, from the climb or from his feelings, he could not tell. He waved to her as she smiled down at him. Her long hair was hanging down about her face, the light from the window catching it, its ends glowing like embers.

He looked about him and went across the lawn, reached the trees and turned back. She was still there, one last wave between them, and he disappeared from her view into the woods. He stopped and took a glance back, saw her light go out and watched the window frame disappear into darkness. Then, he heard something behind him. It was the noise of bodies moving through the trees. Ready for fight or flight, he turned and clenched his fists. Who would be out at night in a forest, except lovers or thieves?

It was Royce and another bloke, Bolton, from the brickworks. He was a big lad. He dug out the clay and had thick arms and a broad neck. Royce's bulldog, Owen guessed. The sight of them there, so close to Beatrice's house, sickened him. They caught sight of him too and all three stopped, dead still, eyeing each other in the gloom of the woods.

'What the bloody hell are you doing here?' said Owen.

'Same question to you, mon,' said Royce, taking a step towards Owen, followed by Bolton. They stood in a shaft of moonlight and Owen could see them clearly now. Bolton's huge fists were curling and uncurling.

'Just walking,' said Owen. 'Couldna sleep. And you?'

'Just walking? Right past the King house, by some lucky chance?' sneered Royce.

'What business is it of yours, anyway?' said Owen, keeping an eye on Bolton's fists.

'King business is my business.'

'How do you figure that?'

'We're gunna do over the King house.'

'Do what?' frowned Owen.

'We're gunna pilfer some stuff to sell for money for Brain's mother. Not tonight, but soon. When they're all out.'

Owen shook his head and sighed. 'No, you inna.'

'We are, by God. They've got it coming to them, them Kings.'

'Big talk for a ratlin such as you,' said Owen, eyeing Royce's short frame up and down.

Royce lurched forwards, grabbed Owen's sleeve and said, 'We're gunna do it, Malone. And you're gunna help us.'

'Ha!' Owen gave a hollow laugh and wrenched his arm away. "Dunna be soft in the head. Just leave it. You inna robbing the Kings and I inna helping you.'

Royce said, 'You dunna think I can do it. Well, I've made my mark already. It was me killed the King bitch's dog.'

Owen scoffed, 'That was stupid. Why take it out on a creature? You just made things worse, you fool.'

Royce said, 'Dunna you care what happened to Brain?'

'Course I do,' Owen spat.

'Then prove it. We need a way in to the King house. We canna force our way in and be heard.'

'Then do it, if you mun. What's it to do with me?'

'We need you to find out from the King girl how to get in.'

'What do you know about that?'

'I know enough. I listen and watch. I know you were seeing her and she paid to save Jones's wife at your own house. I know things.'

'You dunna know a thing,' said Owen, the mention of Beatrice making his stomach lurch. 'Strike's over and all that business be done and over with.'

'Nothing be done and over with,' growled Royce. 'We want revenge on them Kings and by God we mun have it.'

'You're all talk,' said Owen with disgust and turned to walk away.

'Traitor.'

Owen stopped. He turned back. It had been Bolton's voice.

'What did you call me?' said Owen, his whole body tensing. Bolton was a head taller than Owen, but he didn't care. He'd give this one a good larruping if he ever called him such a thing again. He stepped towards Bolton and saw his blank face and small black eyes in the moonlight.

Royce said, 'Now then, lads. Let us not fight amongst ourselves. We are all on the same side.'

Owen said, 'If he calls me that again, I'll kill him.'

'Well,' said Royce, patting Owen's shoulder. 'Prove you inna. Help us.'

'Make me,' said Owen and squared up to Royce, inches from his face now.

How he wanted to punch Royce. But it would do no good. Together he and Bolton would thrash him black and blue and then he'd have all that to explain to his parents. He turned and left them. He thought they'd follow but didn't hear them. He stumbled through the forest, tripping often in the darkness and cursing everything. When he came closer to the river, the moon shone on it and lightened the last part of his journey. He came within sight of home and saw the thinking log. He threw himself down on it and hung his head with the shame and the muddle of it all.

He looked up and watched the moonlight dappling across the ever-moving river. Eternal things, moons and rivers. They had lived forever and would live forever more. Maybe he could learn something from them. Maybe he could step out of the tangle of his own time and see things as they do, across long swathes of time. Beatrice could do it, could look ahead, could see change coming. He looked back at his house. Soon, the new baby would come. His mother was hefty with it now. She would be caught up in a brand new life. She might see things differently. Maybe it wasn't so hopeless, after all. Maybe Beatrice would take over the Kings' business and make things better. Maybe they would ... marry one day? Was it possible? Just a couple of hours ago, it seemed as likely as reaching up and bagging the moon. But the way Beatrice explained it, it could happen. All they needed was time. And for things to heal. Perhaps then, anything was possible.

But one thing was for sure. If the King house was burgled by brickworkers, then all of their plans, however unlikely, would come to naught. And all of their lives would be worse for it. He had to stop Royce. But how? And who would help him?

Chapter 19

Ten days since she'd kissed Owen in her bedroom, Beatrice leant on her windowsill gazing at the woods, the trees barely moving in the heat of the summer evening, shadowy and eerie in the twilight. She'd done this every night that week, hoping and waiting, waiting and hoping. But he had not come back. In a minute, she would be called downstairs to meet the others before they all took the carriage to the Broseley town hall for the Elkins' party, her first ball of the season. Maman had helped her pick out a fine dress from the latest Paris fashions and they'd had it made in Shrewsbury and sent over this morning. It was utterly stunning. On any other night, at any other time in her life, she would have been overcome with delight to be sitting here, perched on the corner of her dressing table chair, her taffeta skirts about her. She stood up and twirled before her mirror. Her shoulders were bare, each sleeve gathered into a posy of silk rosebuds. The skirt was bell-shaped, sewn in four layers, with each layer accentuated by a line of ruffles, again formed from the same silken buds. The dress alternated pure white and soft pink. Her hair was gathered at the neck in two chignons, with a loop over each ear. It was a beautiful dress and she was delighted with it. But as she stared at herself in the mirror, all she could think was that Owen would never see her in it. What was the point of getting all dressed up, if Owen were not there to behold her? Everyone else in the world, every other word of flattery – all of it was hollow and held no music for her, unless it was from Owen. The poetry of his words had won her, as well as his blue-sky eyes and corn-yellow hair, golden in the lamplight. His strong arms about her felt like safety, yet the eagerness in his body felt like danger, a delicious danger she wished to throw herself into, like deep, inviting waters. She loved the way he looked, but she loved him for himself too, his kind soul, his humanity.

The call came. Dinah appeared at the door, all a-flutter at Miss Beatrice's beauty that night.

'Ooh, miss! You look so fine, all drawed out!' she had said earlier. This meant dressed up, Beatrice discovered.

Beatrice went carefully downstairs, her broad skirt skimming each step. The three King women and Cyril looked up at her, each face registering its preference. Margaret, proud; Queenie, approving; Benjamina, envious; Cyril, bored. He was staying at home, having said at breakfast that he'd 'rather stab a fork in his eye than spend an evening with those tedious Elkinses.' The four women were shown out to the landau by Busby. It was lucky that the other women did not go in for crinolines, as there would be only room for one in the carriage, and that was Beatrice's huge concoction. The coachman set off and they trundled down the gravel drive, the breeze from their momentum welcome in the stifling heatwave of the past few days. The weather had grown hotter and hotter, the wind dropping to nothing, as if the whole world held its breath, waiting for rain and relief. Out onto the tree-lined road, the coach picked up speed as it travelled towards town. All four women were lost in their own thoughts. To stop herself pining for Owen, Beatrice looked at them all, her mother beside her, whilst her step-grandmother and great-grandmother sat opposite, their backs to forward travel. Maman was lost in peaceful contemplation. Beatrice could only assume she was happy that her daughter was coming out at last. Benjamina sat in perfect composure, smiling complacently, as usual. But when she looked at Queenie, her great-grandmother's face gave her a start. She was staring at something behind the carriage, tilting her head this way and that, as if to catch sight of something that had been seen on the side of the road. Her eyes were wide and her arm moved unsteadily forwards, her hand forming a trembling point, as she stared fearfully behind Beatrice.

'Queenie,' said Beatrice. 'What is it?'

'Oh!' cried Queenie, shocking Benjamina, who turned abruptly to look. 'Oh, no!' she shouted, her voice strident and loud.

'Grandmother!' called Maman, reaching forward.

But Queenie's hands were about her face, shielding her from whatever she'd seen. And then she cried out again, a scream of horror that pierced the still night air. All in a rush, the horse behind where Queenie sat squealed with terror, long and loud, its back legs buckling and the landau throwing them all forward. The other horse neighed with alarm and the carriage tipped to the left, swerving towards the trees at the side of the road, whereupon the coachman yanked back on the horses and yelled something. The carriage finally came to a stop when its back end smashed into a tree trunk, leaving them listing at an awkward angle.

All four women were gasping and uttering sounds of distress. Maman turned to Beatrice and said, 'Are you well?'

'Yes,' she uttered breathlessly. 'I am well.'

She saw the coachman take a swift look behind him, to see that nobody was injured. He then jumped down and went straight to the horses, checking them both far more carefully than he had the humans in his charge.

'Queenie, are you well?' said Beatrice, reaching across and taking her hand, which was shaking and flailing about, as if swatting away bees.

'You stupid old woman!' shouted Benjamina, pushing Beatrice's hand aside and clambering over them both to reach the landau door. She shoved it open and stepped down into the road, went around the back of the landau and looked at the place it had struck the tree. 'The wheel is split in two. Ruined. We won't be going anywhere fast tonight.'

'Grandmother,' said Maman, reaching out to her too. Queenie was shaking her head from side to side.

'I saw her. I saw her,' Queenie muttered.

'Saw who?' Beatrice said.

'I've never seen her out here. She was pointing, back at the house. Pointing. With her long, white bony finger. Pointing to the house!'

Beatrice and her mother glanced at each other in confusion.

'Ellis,' called Benjamina, now walking around to the coachman, who was doing his best to calm the horses, who snorted and shook their heads, their back feet kicking at the landau once or twice. He spoke to them soothingly and they eased a little, the snorting changing to a blowing sound and eventually a gentle nicker.

Beatrice took his lead and spoke to Queenie, softly reassuring her. 'There, there. She's gone now, whoever she was. Whoever frightened you.'

'Yes,' murmured Queenie. 'Yes, she has gone now.' Her face crumpled and she hid it in her hands, shooing the others away who tried to comfort her. It was shocking to see her great-grandmother like that. Beatrice had only ever seen her in complete control, the very model of restraint. Whatever had come over her? It was baffling. Seeing that Queenie was shaking, Beatrice took off her wrap and hung it around Queenie's shoulders, then sat side by side with her great-grandmother, one arm around her to offer silent comfort.

Beatrice heard Benjamina and Ellis discussing the situation, formulating a plan. Benjamina came round to them, while Ellis continued to soothe the horses.

'Now then,' said Benjamina to them, pointedly ignoring Queenie's trembling body. 'This is what's to be done. Ellis will run back to the house and bring down the barouche and some extra men. Someone will take us on to the ball and men will organise what needs to be done with the landau. If they can fix it in the road, they will. If not, they shall arrange for a cart to bring it home and someone will lead the horses back. All understood?'

Maman said, 'A good plan in theory. But Grandmother is not fit to go out, Benjamina. Surely you can see that.'

'Quite right,' said Benjamina, looking at Queenie with annoyance. 'She must be taken home. Ellis, bring the barouche for us and Cyril's cabriolet for Mrs King senior.'

Ellis nodded, then said, 'I oughta unhitch the horses from the carriage, just in case they take it in their heads to bolt. Better it be just the two of 'em running down the lane, than dragging a broken landau along with 'em.'

'Yes, indeed, Ellis. Good thinking,' said Benjamina.

Once he had disconnected the horses from the carriage, he said to Benjamina, 'Someone needs to stay with 'em and keep 'em calm. They're proper jittery and we dunna want 'em to bolt if we can help it.'

'I'll stay with them,' said Benjamina, commandingly.

Ellis took one last look at the horses and went off up the lane, breaking into a run after a few steps. Beatrice watched all this skittishly, trying to concentrate on Queenie's distress, but wanting to see what was occurring about her. She saw Benjamina standing to the side of the horses, holding herself in as elegant a pose as she could on the side of a road after a traffic accident. She ignored the horses completely, who shuffled nervously.

While they waited, Queenie spoke no further, only whimpering from time to time, as Beatrice and her mother stroked her hands or patted her arms. Queenie sat with her head down, her hands over her eyes. Beatrice wanted to ask a thousand questions, but she could see it would only whip up Queenie again. The evening had started with her despondency at the window and now, with this latest twist, it had led to a moment of terror and now a gnawing worry. The only thing she knew for sure was that she did not want to go to the ball any more, if she ever had. She did not want to face anyone, be forced to smile or speak small talk. She did not want to be anywhere but home.

'Maman,' she spoke quietly, so as not to disturb Queenie.

'Yes?'

'I don't want to go to the ball.'

'Oh, *chérie*,' sighed her mother. 'Do not let this spoil things. I will stay with Queenie and look after her. You should go, with Benjamina.'

She looked at Queenie; her trembling had lessened, but she was still shaken. She couldn't imagine leaving Queenie like this, and all so she could spend an entire evening with the sons of brickmasters.

Her mother read her mind and smiled gently, adding, 'Yet if you felt too shaken by the accident to go on . . .'

Beatrice smiled wanly back and squeezed her mother's arm. 'You always understand me, Maman.'

A sound of clattering wheels approached and they turned to see two carriages coming down the lane, the larger barouche in front, the smaller cabriolet behind. As they came closer and eased to a stop, Beatrice was surprised to see Uncle Cyril clamber down from the cabriolet, dressed up in his finest dinner attire. Before him gathered a group of men from the house, stable lads and a couple of footmen, Ellis leading them for-wards to the scene of the accident. But pushing past them all and making a beeline for Queenie was Jenkins, dear Jenkins. When she reached Queenie, she put her hand on Queenie's arm and said, 'I am here.'

Queenie came alive and said 'Jenkins!' in a pitiful voice.

Jenkins looked up at Beatrice and her mother, at which Margaret said, 'We shall alight, so that you can sit with Grandmother.'

Jenkins nodded, then Beatrice and her mother climbed down from the landau. Beatrice saw Jenkins get in beside Queenie and put her arm tenderly around her shoulders, whispering in her ear and taking her hand.

Meanwhile, Cyril had marched over towards Beatrice and the others, eyeing up the side of the landau with astonished amusement.

'What a damnable mess!' he cried, clearly enjoying the drama.

'What are you doing here?' snapped Benjamina.

'Now, now,' he said, grinning. 'Is that any way to speak to your knight in shining armour? I am here to rescue you ladies and take you on to the ball myself.'

'But you had no intention of going to the ball before,' said Benjamina.

Cyril replied, 'Oh, come on, old girl. It'll be a last hurrah for me before I go off to America in a couple of weeks. Ladies, will you join us?'

Beatrice's mother replied, 'We three will return home. Your grandmother is in shock and needs to rest. I fear the same could be said of the two of us as well. None of us feel in a fit state to proceed to the dinner. We would all rather return home immediately. Ellis, can we take the barouche with you back home?'

'Of course, ma'am,' said Ellis.

'Well, if that's what you wish. Beatrice too? It is your first ball, my dear,' said Benjamina, languidly. Beatrice sensed that she said it because it was the right thing to say, not because she had any desire for Beatrice to accompany them.

'I feel rather shaken by all this myself. I'd rather go home, if you don't mind,' said Beatrice, politely.

'Come, come, then Benjamina,' said Cyril, cheerfully. 'We shall take my nifty little cabriolet. Let us climb aboard my steed. Nice and cosy for me and Mrs K.'

Benjamina shrugged, then took his hand and went to the two-wheeled carriage. Jenkins helped Queenie descend from the landau. She was much more composed now, looking more like the Queenie they knew. She had not spoken a word though. Cyril and Benjamina took off smartly in the cabriolet, while Beatrice and the others climbed into the barouche. Ellis took the reins and directed them round in a gentle circle; the last thing Beatrice glimpsed of the scene was the stable boy she'd once talked to about her umbrella, staring at the broken wheel of the landau, slapping his thigh and laughing.

They advanced at a slow pace up the lane towards home, Beatrice imagining Ellis felt it was better to take it as easily as possible for the three shaken lady passengers. The accident had been a shock for all of them. But just as alarming for Beatrice was Queenie, to see her in such a dishevelled state, shaking and gibbering like that. Beatrice would never forget her face, white as a sheet and slack-jawed, looking for all the world as if she'd just seen a ghost. She watched her closely now, reassuring herself that Queenie would be alright.

When they reached home, Jenkins took Queenie slowly upstairs, whispering to her as they went, about who knew what. Beatrice followed her mother upstairs too, suddenly weary, her dress feeling heavy and tight. She found Dinah waiting for her. Her maid fussed over her and seemed almost relieved to have something to do when Bea suggested she might like a snack. Dinah assured her she would bring some very good supper for her to eat from a tray in bed and went off to sort it, after helping Beatrice off with her dress and underclothes, and into her nightdress.

Once in bed and waiting expectantly for her plate of goodies, there was a small tap on the door. She licked her lips ready for food, to see instead her mother, now in her own nightdress and dressing gown, her hair in a long plait over her shoulder. She closed the door and came to sit beside Beatrice, taking her hand and kissing it.

'Are you all right, *chérie*?'

'Yes, Maman. Truly, I am quite well. It was rather exciting, in a way! But Queenie. What on earth was wrong with Queenie? Is she unwell?'

'I don't know. I really don't know,' said Maman, looking concerned. 'I'm sure she'll recover. She's safe with Jenkins now. It's strange. I've seen her confused before. I've seen her angry. But I've never seen her scared like that before. Never.'

'It was so odd. Who do you think she saw?'

'I really have no idea. I very much doubt she will enlighten us. Though if she were to share her thoughts with anyone other than her beloved Jenkins, it would be you, *chérie*.'

'Her face was quite a sight. White as a sheet. I've never seen her like that. I know she's quite old, but she never seems it. She always seems so strong. I wish I knew what had frightened her like that. Perhaps I'll ask her tomorrow or when she has recovered.'

'Perhaps. I would not push her for answers though. She is such a private person.'

'You're right. She's a difficult person to get to know. But I do love her.'

'I know you do. Now . . .'

'Not as much as I love you, though, Maman!' And she reached out and hugged her mother, who squeezed her back affectionately.

'I know that, silly! You and I are two of a kind, always have been. A perfect pair, since I first felt you move, fluttering away in my tummy like a butterfly. And now, here you are. A beautiful young woman. I was so proud of you, watching you come down the stairs in your gown tonight, *chérie*. You truly are a stunning young woman. I am sorry you had to miss out on your first event. Once Queenie is better, we shall sit down with her and properly plan for your season. A series of balls and so forth, to launch you properly.'

'You make me sound like a ship, Maman!' She laughed with her mother, but she was thinking how a season, and balls, and dances, and small talk with local young men, was the last thing on earth she wanted. Would it be the right time to tell her mother that now? Right now? Perhaps she could spill her heart to her mother. She hated keeping things from her.

As ever, her mother watched her face and detected something in it, which Beatrice had sought to hide. 'But you are worried about something. Is it what happened tonight? Really, don't concern yourself too much. Queenie has always been a bit unusual and I'm sure she will recover fully. I remember her saying some very peculiar things when I was a child. But that was twenty years ago and nothing terrible has happened to her since, so you mustn't worry too much.'

'All right, Maman.'

But immediately, Maman knew that was not it. She sighed and took Beatrice's hand again, lacing their fingers together.

'If you are fretting about coming out, about meeting these young men . . .'

'A little,' said Beatrice, looking down at their hands, knitted together. She did not want her mother to see her eyes, as she feared they would betray her thoughts, filled with the image of only one particular young man.

'*Chérie*, I am so proud of you, for moving on and accepting the way things are. After . . . that boy.'

Beatrice could not look at her. She felt her mother's hand under her chin, lifting her face towards her. Beatrice felt her eyes fill and saw her mother's sympathy as a tear rolled down her cheek and onto her mother's palm. Maman took her in her arms again and held her. Beatrice fought to suppress her emotions. She missed Owen so much and pined for him dreadfully. She had lied to her mother too and did not want her to see her guilt. All of this, as well as tonight's misfortune, made the tears flow.

'I know first love is powerful,' said her mother, stroking her hair. 'Believe me, I truly do know. But these things pass. It seems they are solid as rock and will last forever. But instead, they are sand, washed away by the tide.'

'Yes, Maman,' she whispered to her mother, who drew back and wiped her tears away with her sleeve.

'Now then, perhaps a new plan of action might be in order.'

'What kind of plan?'

'If you do not feel ready to enter the social season here in Shropshire, perhaps you might prefer a change of scene.'

Beatrice thought only of Owen, that any time spent away from Ironbridge meant another week or fortnight or more where she could not see him.

'I'm very happy here, Maman.'

'I know that, but I think a break from this place might do you good. Get away, meet new people, see new sights. I'm wondering if you and I should join Cyril on his trip to America.'

'What? I thought you disliked Cyril. I know I do!'

'Yes, but he would merely be a means to an end. He would be our chaperone as we travel, yet upon arrival, we could go out for trips alone, the two of us. Visit places of interest, see the countryside. Imagine all the fascinating places that must be there. It would be good to broaden our horizons. What do you think?'

America was across the ocean! She would be away for months! It was out of the question.

'It is a very long way to America. And I do hate the sea.'

'I know but you are young and strong. You will cope. Think on it, *chérie*. It could be an adventure for us. And it would be good to get you away from . . . memories.'

Then came a knock on the door.

'That'll be Dinah with my meal,' said Beatrice, saved by the tray of food that her maid now carried in.

Her mother stood up, leant down and kissed her cheek.

'Think about it,' she said, smiling.

'I shall, Maman,' she said, reaching eagerly for her tray. Dinah had done her proud. Thick slices of ham, cheese, cucumber and buttered bread sat on a plate beside a bowl of cherry pie with cream for dessert. Dinah left a glass of warm milk on her bedside table.

'Goodnight, my beauty,' said Maman, lingering by the door.

'Night,' mumbled Beatrice as she bit down onto the bread, her stomach grumbling. Before Maman turned to go, Beatrice saw her framed in the doorway for a moment, her hair streaked with grey, her face wrinkled with smiles, yet also fatigue. The trip to America would be too much for her mother, she was sure. She needed to stay here and have an easy life. Maman was only trying to get her away so she didn't mope around about Owen. Beatrice would just have to act more carefully, convincing her mother that she had no need of being spirited away in order to forget her first love. She would have to be convincing. Perhaps she should even agree to meet a young man or two, just to put Maman off the scent. She resolved to start doing just that tomorrow. Yes, she'd have another talk about it all with her mother, tomorrow.

Taking a slice of ham and placing it on the bread, she took another large bite, then looked around at her open window. She prayed Owen would come to her, late tonight, so they could discuss more plans. She was sorely tempted to suggest they elope, to escape this American proposal. But she knew how badly elopement had turned out for her mother and really, she knew in her heart of hearts that though she loved Owen completely, she did not want to be poor and without her family. She liked food too much and the other comforts, and she loved the idea that she and Owen could change Ironbridge for the better. So, she would stay and stick to her plan. Her love for Owen was eternal and thus they would have to be patient, as she had told him. She polished off her supper, took a swig of the milk beside her bed and placed the tray on the floor. She turned down her lamp but left it dimly burning in the hope that Owen would see it and come to her. She snuggled down in bed, shoving off the covers as it was infernally hot in there. She lay still and waited, her eyelids drooping, though she fought to keep them open. Her last thoughts were about her mother, that whatever happened, whatever choices she and Owen made, her mother would still love her. Maman had always loved her more than anything in the world and Maman always would. The drama of the evening had worn her out and the heat lay on her like a heavy blanket. Within minutes, she was fast asleep.

Jenkins had only left her when she was sure Queenie was asleep. But Queenie had been feigning sleep, so that she might be left alone. It was horrid to be in distress and not be able to tell anyone – particularly her dearest ones – why she was in such a state. It was the ghost of Betsy Blaize she'd seen, standing beside the road as the carriage advanced, pointing back at the King house. Its white face had gaped open blackly again, as it had once before. It was a ghastly sight, enough to curdle blood. She had broken down in front of everyone, which was unforgiveable. But one would have to be made of stone not to in the face of such horror. The visitations were escalating and becoming more extreme. Either Queenie was losing her mind – something of which she would brook no serious contemplation – or the ghost was becoming more insistent in her demands. But Queenie had done all she could on that account. She had visited the Joneses at home and tried to make them stay. They had refused but now were back in their home, kept empty for them on Queenie's orders. She had been told by Jenkins and Beatrice of the need for a doctor to help at Martha Jones's childbed, and she had paid for the doctor and received no thanks. Surely this was enough; she had secured the safe passage of Blaize's descendants! What more could be asked of her? In fact, she had been convinced that was what the visits had been about. That the whole business had led to that moment, when, through Beatrice, she had been able to save Blaize's daughter and grandchild. Once the doctor's bill had been paid, she had been sure she would never see the ghost again. She had safeguarded Blaize's legacy. Why would she see her again now?

Queenie said aloud, 'Again, I say, I have paid my debts.'

Not all of them, came a ghostly reply.

Queenie's eyes snapped open and she shivered. A white light shone into the room through her open curtains, the window also left open to receive respite from the heat. It was silver like moonlight, yet bright like sunshine. She knew that unearthly light. She had felt braver the last time she saw it shining through her window, had been belligerent even with the ghost. But now, after seeing it beside the road, she feared it more than ever and trembled at the sight of that dazzling harbinger casting her room into stark white relief.

Come, said the voice. *Come outside.*

'I will not,' whispered Queenie, terrified yet with an ounce of defiance remaining.

Come to your husband's grave.

Queenie gazed at the light, tempted to stay safe in bed, but if she didn't nip this in the bud, it could go on forever. Steeling her spine, she pulled back the covers. She was Queenie King, she backed down from no one, man or ghost. Her feet were bare and made no sound on the floor as she approached the door and saw the key left in it, turned it to the right and opened the back door, stepping out into the night, the sky still coloured with the failing light, the woodlands about the house grey and obscure. There, across the gravel and beyond the low wooden fence, low enough to step over, were the neat rows of family graves, beyond them the collection of little gravestones to mark the dead family pets. Standing amidst them all was Blaize. Her white hair flowed like winter water and her eyes beamed blue, gazing into Queenie's soul.

She walked across the gravel, feeling the stones dig sharply into her bare feet, but she felt she had no choice but to proceed. She stepped over the low fence and approached Ralph King senior's grave. Betsy Blaize's spirit stood silently beside it.

You know what you did, said the spirit.

Queenie did not argue. She knew exactly what Blaize was referring to. Many times over the years the scene had entered her mind and each time it came she had shooed it away, unwilling to relive it. But as she closed her eyes to escape the sight of the ghost, the scene from her past replayed itself complete in her mind's eye.

She saw herself in a fine dress, a dark red gown with silver beading, one of her favourites from her fifties, when she still wore rich colours. Queenie recalled crossing the hallway, then seeing something amiss at the foot of the servants' staircase. There was a tray on the step, beside it a pile of broken glass and a puddle of liquor, which smelt like her husband's best whisky. She looked about for some explanation, but could see none. She walked onwards with displeasure, along the corridor to her husband's study, ready to complain to him of the state of the housekeeping these days at Southover, that it would not do, and that he must support her in beginning a new regime of discipline in the house. She recalled so perfectly her indignation at this latest outrage. Queenie had shown more interest in the business lately and the house had suffered. But why should it be only her that was responsible for the tenor of servants in the house? She went to see her husband with her grievances. She opened his study door quietly, wondering if

344

at this time of the afternoon he was taking a nap on his chaise longue, which he sometimes did when his work tired him. She went in softly, peering around the door to see if he were at his desk – no – then looked around to the day bed and saw him there.

He was lying face down on it. He was moving around, his trousers were shoved down so she could see his naked backside and underneath him, squirming and small, was a tiny figure, looking like a doll beneath his tall, oversized frame. Her husband's head moved to one side, burying itself in the figure's neck, and Queenie saw the large eyes of the new maid, Betsy Blaize, her little face white with terror, her eyes blinking wildly until they found Queenie, staring at her from the doorway, and they stared back. Queenie had hired the child herself. She was twelve years old. Her lips were moving. They mouthed, 'Help me.' The man on top of her began moving more vigorously. 'Help me,' said the girl again, staring straight at Queenie now, as she stood more than two decades older, remembering it in perfect detail. Ralph's large hand came into view and clamped itself over the girl's mouth. Queenie saw her younger self step backwards in horror, standing in the corridor outside her husband's study. She turned round swiftly as a footman came along and stopped, standing to the side and bowing, waiting for her to move on. She quickly brought the door to, then closed it very gently, turning the handle to close it securely. She said some angry words to the footman, pointed down the corridor and he hurried off. She stood there alone, her hands trembling, as she brought them up to her mouth and covered it, her eyes staring downwards, her head shaking slowly from side to side.

Queenie now felt the tears streaming from her eyes, so much so that the image in her mind seemed to blur and vanish. Now, she could not see anything except her misery and shame. She dropped to her knees, grovelling at the feet of Betsy Blaize's spirit.

You knew, came its words. *You knew.*

'I'm sorry, I'm sorry, I'm sorry!' cried Queenie.

I asked you for help.

'I know, I know.'

Why did you do nothing? Why did you not help me?

'I could not, I could not!' she said, tearing at her nightdress in her distress. Queenie looked up, wiping the tears from her eyes, frozen again by the blue scrutiny of the ghost. 'I had no power. I was my husband's possession, just as you were. We are both women.'

I was not a woman. I did not choose to marry. I was a child. A man forced himself into me, over and over, in your house, under your watch. You knew it was happening. For three long years, you knew. And you did nothing.

'I am sorry. I can only say I am sorry, a thousand times.'

It is not enough! cried the ghost, her voice magnified, so that it sounded like a wind, a hundred winds roaring, a whirlwind of sound.

'Tell me,' cried Queenie, shaking like a leaf in a storm. 'Tell me what I must do.'

You must pay.

'Tell me the price! I will pay anything! Tell me, I beg of you. Tell me what I must do!'

You . . . must . . . suffer.

Queenie stared at Blaize, whose whiteness grew in intensity until she could bear to look upon it no more. She covered her eyes and buried her head in her arms, curling up on the brittle grass, dry from the heatwave. She hid her face there until she could hear no more, see nothing but the inside of her eyelids and feel nothing but the sticky night air on her bare legs and feet. That was the last sensation she experienced, before a blackness took her and she passed out, deeper than sleep, darker than night.

Chapter 20

'I'm off out now,' said Owen, pulling on his cap. He did not need his coat, as it was still as warm as an afternoon out there, despite being well past nine o'clock at night.

'Don't stay out too late, mind,' said his mother, resting by the cold fireplace, her belly a high mound.

'I wonna be too long,' he said and smiled at her.

'Mind you're not. This little'un needs her big brother around.'

'A girl now, is it?' said Owen, smiling at her.

'Wishful thinking,' she said. 'Less trouble than you boys, always getting into scrapes.'

'No scrapes, Mother. I promise,' he lied.

'Good lad,' she said and looked away, running her hands over her bump. She looked sleepy but content.

His father was outside next door, chatting with a neighbour, puffing on his clay pipe. He saw Owen leave and raised his hand in brief farewell. Owen nodded at him, then turned away and walked down the path to town. He was a little late for meeting Adam at the tavern. Adam had been the only one he could talk to about Royce's plan. He'd gone to his house a couple of days before, seen Martha and baby Hettie and cradled the baby in his arm nervously for a minute or two. Then he'd motioned Adam outside for a private chat. He didn't tell him about his feelings for Beatrice, only explaining the damage Royce's plans would do to the brickworks. He believed the Kings would close down the works if there were any more trouble. Adam was convinced and said he would talk to Royce and warn him off. But just yesterday, he'd seen Royce again with Bolton in town. They were talking together in the tavern, heads down, looking like conspirators if ever he'd seen one. Owen talked again to Adam and they agreed, Royce couldn't be trusted. Adam had heard from a servant at the King house that most if not all of the Kings were going to a ball that night in Broseley. It would be the perfect opportunity for Royce and his cronies to burgle the house. So, Adam arranged with Owen that they'd meet in the tavern, then go along to the King house and keep an eye on it. They'd make sure nobody did anything stupid. Owen never liked lying to his parents, but it was necessary. Adam would know what to do and the two of them would be able to talk Royce and Bolton down, if it came to that. Adam was handy in a fight and he himself was sure he could beat Royce to a pulp if necessary. He had the fuel for it.

Adam must have grown tired of waiting in the tavern, as Owen came across him on the path from town.

They turned about and walked the other way, along the river and up through the woodland towards Southover. They talked a little on the way, about conditions at work, the longer hours causing such fatigue in everyone that more and more mistakes were being made each day. They knew it was pointless discussing it, that nothing would change, but they liked to hear themselves moan about it. It rid their heads of it, at any rate. As they approached the King house, Owen was surprised to see lamps burning in quite a few windows, despite the fact that most of the family were out at the ball. He guessed they were there waiting for the family's return, which Adam had told Owen was supposed to be well past eleven that night, so they had a couple of hours to wait. They had guessed that Royce and company would not risk breaking in while it was still light, so left it till now to come. All seemed quiet, to Owen's relief. They stopped by the oak tree he'd stood by before, watching the house in silence for a while. Owen stared for a long time at Beatrice's open window, wishing she were there, wishing his father's cousin was not beside him, wishing he could sprint across the lawns and leap into her room in one bound and kiss her. Then, they heard a noise.

It was the stealthy movement of feet through the undergrowth, many feet not just two or four. Adam and Owen swapped glances, then melted back into the shadows behind the oaks. Adam saw Royce first and silently pointed him out to Owen. Royce had appeared from behind a copse of trees at the southern side of South-over. Bolton was there, too, but then they saw there were three others. Owen cursed himself for not coming more prepared.

'Five of 'em,' whispered Adam and grimaced.

'What shall we do?' whispered Owen.

'We need to end this, now,' said Adam, and Owen nodded. They stepped out onto the grass and marched towards them.

'Oi!' called Adam. All five men froze. They were picking up something from the ground, clutching something in their hands. Bottles. Were they ginger beer bottles? They looked just like it, just as Owen had drunk from many a time. Ginger beer? But there was a stink of fish. None of it made sense.

Royce sneered, 'Look what we have here! Jones and his lapdog Malone.'

'What're you doing, Royce?' said Adam. Royce looked momentarily nervous. That was the effect their union leader still had on the workers. But it was only a moment and soon he was squaring up to Adam, flanked by Bolton and his other henchmen, all much taller than him and twice as broad.

Royce turned to his men and said, 'Put the bottles down, lads. Nice and careful. We have another job to do first.' All the men lined up their bottles on the ground, pushing them into the soil. It was then Owen saw that each bottle was filled with a thick liquid and had an oily rag stuffed in its neck. He knew that smell. It was whale oil.

'I said, what the hell are you doing?'

'What needs doing. You couldna get what we needed. So we're taking it into our own hands.'

'Taking what?' said Owen. 'This wonna get you higher pay. It wonna get you nothing.'

'It'll get us satisfaction,' said Royce.

'And vengeance,' added Bolton.

'It speaks!' sneered Owen.

Bolton squared up to Owen. 'Say that again, Malone.'

'Come on, lads. This is a nasty kind of mischief that wonna do anyone any good,' said Adam.

'Dunna stop us, mon,' Royce said. 'Or we shall stop you, permanent like.'

Adam raised his voice now. 'Stop this, Royce. It's gone too far. There are innocent servants in there, mon.'

'No, they inna! They work for the Kings. And anyway, most of 'em are out tonight. It's the King house we want to burn to the ground.'

In the shock of the moment, nobody spoke, but Owen had heard enough. He let his fist fly and punched Royce in the side, winding him and making him drop to his knees. It was a moment of sweet satisfaction. But the next thing he knew, a fist was making friends with his head and a wallop had come from the left into his ear. He staggered to the side, then righted himself just in time to see Bolton coming at him. He ducked then punched Bolton in the stomach, taking advantage of his momentary recovery to try and hit him on the head, but he missed and someone pushed him hard. He struck out and hit someone, though his view was obscured by wrestling bodies. He scrambled up and hit the first person he saw, before someone grabbed his arms and pulled him away, throwing him to the ground. Before he could get up, someone had kicked him in the back. The pain was bad and he covered his head, afraid of being kicked there too. Another kick came to his legs and sent him curling up. He tried to look out to see how many had him on the ground, and if he could grab their legs. He caught sight of Adam being punched in the side of the head by a big bloke, who shouted 'Traitor!' at Adam as he fell straight over like a skittle, out cold. Then a blow landed on Owen's eye and he clutched at it, feeling something warm and wet. He tried to open his eyes only to discover one was blinded by blood. The other opened to see the world at the skewed angle of a man on his back, looking up at the dark tops of trees. He twisted his head to see four pairs of legs walking over to the house. He tried to drag himself upwards to go after them, but a searing pain in his back stopped him and he collapsed on the ground again. He watched Royce use a rock to smash a glass panel in a door, then four men went into the house carefully and quietly, carrying their bottles, shutting the door behind them. Two legs appeared in his line of vision, grasped the unconscious Adam and threw his head back against the ground, just in case. The last thing he saw was Bolton's face leering at him, grasping him by the scruff of the neck.

'See this fist?' whispered Bolton, brandishing it at him. 'It speaks!'

He punched Owen in the face and that was that.

∽∽

Margaret was dreaming of Paris. She was turning the key in their front door, walking in to the little house in Montmartre and shutting it behind her. She could smell horse manure from the street outside, sweetened by the scent of baking bread. She could hear her neighbours chatting in melodious French. She saw her daughter, beautiful brown hair tumbling down her back in waves, sitting at the piano beside a pupil playing halting scales in a major key. Beatrice turned to smile at her. She had brought flowers home with her and found a vase on the windowsill, filled it with the flowers and water from a jug. She placed the vase on the table, where primers in English language were splayed open, layered with papers and pencils. It was evening and the sun was streaming through the window creating a yellow square on the table, criss-crossed by the shadows of the window leads. Her little world, her little life. Happiness.

But as she stared at the golden light on the table, it began to glow brightly. Brighter and brighter still, until it hurt her eyes to look at it. She put up her hand to shield herself and saw she could not find her hand before her face. Her head was surrounded by webs of grey, as if she'd fallen into a spider's web. She swiped at it to no avail, unable to see anything now but the dark grey and the blinding flash of light behind it. She fought to open her eyes and heard someone coughing. They were coughing fit to burst their lungs and she looked around wildly to find who it was.

When Margaret awoke, she heard the sound was coming from her own throat. She was choking. Finally, her eyes could open and she knew she was not in the world of dreams any longer. She was surrounded by smoke. She tried to call out, but only a hoarse scratch came. She realised her breathing was quick and shallow. She listened to it and tried to take a deeper breath, but that brought on the coughing again. She tried to sit up, but it made the coughing worse. She reached over to the bedside table and used it to pull herself out of bed and onto the floor, where she banged her arm and knee as she fell. She crawled under the bed, as there was not so much smoke there. It had been worse higher up in the room. She tried to call out again, but she had no voice.

'*Chérie*,' she uttered, a husky sound. She could see the door from under the bed and knew she had to get to it. Yet from here, she could see a line of bright light flickering at its base and it frightened her. She would have to get to the window instead. She pulled herself out from under the bed and there came the coughing again, wracking her chest until she felt nothing but a deathly exhaustion. She tried again to call out.

'Bea . . .'

It was a whisper now. She heard herself saying it aloud in her head, calling it along the street in Paris, where Bea would run off with her friends and look for snacks.

'Bea, ma *chérie* . . .'

But nobody came.

∽

Beatrice woke with a start. She was coughing and the room was hazy, grey wafts of smoke circling around the dim lamp, its fingers reaching into each corner. She was slick with sweat. There was a sound surrounding her, a roaring sound, as if wind were blowing through her brain.

Fire, she thought. *The house is on fire.* She tumbled out of bed and ran to the door, went to touch the door handle, but it was hot. It hurt her hand and she cried out. She did not want to open that door. Yet beyond it would be her Maman and Queenie. They would never have left without coming for her first. She must go to them. But the scalding handle and the flames that lay beyond it trapped her in her room, cutting her off from Queenie, Maman and who knew who else. She turned and stumbled to the window. The sight she saw was terrifying. Below to her right was the conservatory, filled with flames. To her left was the flat roof of the library. It was not on fire as yet. That would be her escape route. She called out, hoping someone, anyone might have got out. Most of the servants had the night off, but she knew Dinah and Jenkins were somewhere in the house.

'Help!' she cried and coughed afterwards. Nobody replied.

She looked feverishly at the flat roof. It had looked so easy when Owen had jumped on to it. But he was taller and fitter than her.

'Help me!' she shouted again, louder this time, the coughing worse. Her throat ached but she had no choice; she had to try to raise help. 'Maman! Help me!'

It was no good. Nobody was going to come. Where was everyone? Were they hurt? Trapped? She couldn't think on that now. She had to get out. She stared at the flat roof, trying to work out how far she would need to jump and what would happen if she missed it. There was the drop and gravel below. It would hurt. She might break her legs, or her back, or her neck. But if she stayed . . .

She lifted up her nightdress and clambered onto the windowsill, sitting on it, her legs dangling. At least it was less smoky out here. She coughed and coughed, feeling light-headed and weak. She forced herself to concentrate. She couldn't sit here forever. She levered herself up, holding onto the top of the window frame and putting one foot, then the other on the sill. As she turned herself around slowly, her legs shaking, she saw the smoke rushing in under the door to her room now, the roaring sound louder than ever. Soon the door would burn down, she was sure of that. She held on to the gable and craned her neck round to look at the roof. It looked impossibly far away. How on earth had Owen done it? She pictured herself over and over again, making the leap and failing, falling to the ground and breaking her neck. Her legs were rigid and she could not make them move. Fear had frozen her.

Then, a sound came.

'Bea! Dunna move!'

It was Owen's voice. How she'd wanted to hear it. It must be her mind creating it, wishful thinking. She clutched onto the gable more tightly. Thick white smoke was billowing from her room now in two streams, divided by her body. She could not see and she began to cough horribly.

'Bea! Bea! I'm coming! Dunna move!'

It was Owen's voice, near and clear now. Was it really him? She could not open her eyes. She could not move her legs. She felt weak from the coughing, tried to open her eyes but was blinded by the smoke. Her grip loosened. She felt she would fall. She turned her head to try to look towards the flat roof, knowing it was now or never. Through the swelling smoke, she thought she saw someone, two arms reaching, shouting something at her again.

Was it really him? How was he here? How did he know she needed him? Or was she imagining it? So many times she had sat at her windowsill and conjured him with her mind, pictured him so clearly appearing from behind the oak tree and coming to her across the lawn. Was he real now? Or simply a mirage, created by her panic and the swirling smoke?

⌘

He had heard her before he saw her. He had come to with an aching head, and aching back, aching everywhere. He'd been badly beaten up and felt like a cracked plate, held in place by stillness but as soon as he moved, he feared he would break into pieces. But there it was again, that voice, calling. He forced his eyes to open and looked up into the canopy. There was a thickness to the air, beyond the heat, something tangible and there was a stink of bonfires. He turned his head with care, aware of a soreness in his neck, to see the King house was ablaze. It was so shocking to see, spectacular in its way, the white smoke pouring out from windows, flames engulfing the room the men had gone in by. They'd done it. They'd set the house on fire. But then he heard the sound again, a plaintive call. Someone was calling. It was Beatrice's voice. Bea!

Owen's body moved without his volition. He had jumped up and nearly tripped over Adam, out cold on the ground. He shook Adam by the shoulders and said his name. Adam groaned. Then he heard the voice calling again and knew he had to leave Adam and go. He started running towards the side of the house where her bedroom was, without even registering the pain all over his body. He lurched forward, his focus only on that one thing – her voice. He skirted the burning conservatory at a distance and came upon her room, seeing the flat roof he'd climbed first, then looking upwards. There she was! Clinging onto her window and trapped there.

He called to her, told her to stay still. He could climb up there and get her. The smoke was thick here. She would succumb to it soon and fall. He threw himself at the wisteria that was singed, embers of petals drifting on the air with the hot smoke. He climbed rapidly, grasping with desperate precision, never missing a grip or a foothold. Within seconds it seemed, he was up on the flat roof.

'I am here!' he shouted at Bea. 'Jump, Bea. I shall catch you. Jump!'

Her face was buried in her sleeves. She seemed too frightened to move.

'Bea, trust me! Trust me, you wonna fall. Open your eyes, Bea and look at me.'

She heard him and started to turn her head. She opened her eyes and squinted at him, the smoke thick around them. Both of them were coughing, he holding his arm across his mouth.

'Jump, Bea!'

'I can't!' she cried. 'I'll fall!'

'I'm here. I shall catch you. Trust me. I know you trust me, Bea. Come on, my sweetheart. Come to me.' He reached out towards her.

She didn't look down, she didn't say another word. She let her right hand drop and she leapt towards him, launching herself from the windowsill, her arms flailing. He made contact and held on tight, pushing himself backwards to take her weight. They tumbled down onto the roof and landed in a heap, the pain of his back searing through him, but the relief of having her in his arms swept through him.

'Come on!' he cried, scrambling up and helping her. She was coughing again. He had to get her off the roof and away from the smoke. It was smoke that killed folk, he knew, before the flames even touched you. 'I shall climb first and you shall come after. That way, if you fall I shall be below you. Come now.'

He reached over to the trellis and held on with two feet and one hand. He beckoned to her with his free hand. Her eyes were wide now, terrified. He feared she would freeze again but she moved and grasped the trellis. He hoped it would take the weight of both of them. He began to climb downwards as she did, making a move that echoed hers, always one step ahead, beneath her, his right arm on her at all times, in case she fell backwards. Then, the ground came and they were on it. No time for happy reunions. He grasped her hand and ran her away from the building to the safety of the trees. He had done it. He had saved her. They held on to each other and she wept, coughing and sobbing and saying his name. He held her and let her cry, thanking the Lord, the stars and everything that she was safe.

'Thank you, thank you,' she said and looked at him, kissing him messily. 'How are you here?'

'How are *you* here?' he said, unable to answer her question easily. 'You're supposed to be at the dinner with your mother.'

'Maman!' she cried and wrenched herself away from him. She was running toward the house.

'No, Bea!' he shouted after her. She was running around the house to the left, heading past the conservatory that was an inferno now, keeping her distance but not slowing or stopping. 'Come back!' he shouted again.

He could hear her screaming as he came around and saw her pointing up at the window above the conservatory. It must her mother's room.

'Maman is in there! I must go in.'

'No, are you mad?' he shouted above the roar and crackle of the fire and caught up with her, holding her back. Now he saw there were people on this side, servants standing at a distance from the house, some running to and fro from the stables that were not yet ablaze, bringing buckets of water and throwing them uselessly towards the conservatory, the heat being too great to get near enough. The grooms were leading the horses the other way to safety down the driveway, the poor, terrified beasts pulling frantically at their reins. More onlookers were gathering around the perimeter of the grounds, pointing and staring. Nothing and nobody could save the house now.

Beatrice wrenched herself away from him and ran over towards the huddle of servants, throwing questions at them and pointing towards the house. People were shaking their heads.

Owen caught up with her. 'Bea, come with me, away from the house,' he said, desperate now to keep her back, she was so rash and unpredictable in her movements. He half expected her to run wildly into the burning house itself.

'My mother is in there!' she cried, feverishly. 'I saw her go to bed. Nobody has seen her since. Nobody has seen Queenie either!'

'They may've come out a different way. Stay here and I'll go around the outside of the whole house, see if they're somewhere else.'

'I'll go that way, you go this way,' she said, nodding.

'No! No, you are weakened by the smoke. You must stay here.'

'He's right, miss Beatrice,' said a female voice. It was a maid, young and short, her face smeared with grime from the smoke. 'You mun stay here with us.'

'But Dinah,' replied Beatrice, 'my mother and great-grandmother may be in there. Where is Jenkins?'

Owen said, 'Keep her here,' and nodded at the maid, who nodded firmly back. He ran off, skirting the house at a safe distance. Around the other side were a few other servants gathered, while at the edge of the woods more crowds of locals were gathering. He could not see anyone in nightclothes or otherwise looking well-dressed, until he saw a frail old thing in a nightgown standing by the graveyard, her arms in the air, her mouth open wide as she cried out at the sight of the burning house. She was being comforted by another woman in a nightdress, who was grasping at her flailing hands. He recognised her, it was Jenkins. And there was old Mrs King with her. He had no time to think on them more, as he had to get back to Beatrice. He came around the other side of the house to see he had skirted its entire perimeter and was coming back to where Dinah and Beatrice had been. But Beatrice was not there. The maid was shouting and running forward.

As he came about, he saw a white flash disappear into the front door of the house. It was Beatrice's nightdress, he knew that, and without a thought he followed her in. The hallway was flanked by a searing wall of flame on the right-hand side. He could see Beatrice heading for the main staircase, where flames licked the bannisters, yet there was a path upwards. He could hear the roar and creak of a house about to cave in on itself and madly rushed forwards, grabbed at Beatrice and caught the edge of her nightdress. She screamed and fell forward, onto the first steps of the staircase. He held on tight, yanking her towards him and forcing her up and into his arms. Her eyes were wild and she screamed, 'Maman! Queenie!'

He was not about to argue and manhandled her across the hallway.

She screamed, 'I can't leave them!' and pulled away from him again. He reached out and grasped her, shoving her hard in the direction of the front door. He saw her lose her footing and stumble forwards out of the door and sprawl onto the gravel. Safe, at last. Bea was safe at last. Someone rushed forward to attend to her. Owen took a breath and stumbled forwards towards the open door, and fresh air and freedom. But a great splintering sound came from above and he looked up to see the ceiling rippling with flames and a huge fissure appearing across it. The next moment the ceiling opened up like a cracked eggshell, beams, joists, plaster and all, splitting and subsiding, and down it all came upon him.

Chapter 21

Beatrice had been in this room before, she recalled, as she looked around the drawing room of the old brickmaster's house. It was only a few weeks past, but it seemed like years, like a lifetime ago. In a way, it was, as the old Beatrice who had stood in this room had been another person. She had stood beside this window, surrounded by space and floating dust, a few sticks of furniture about covered in sheets. She had stood here with her young man and she had run from the room, smiling, determined to change their futures for the better. She had been a young fool, innocent of the world and its wanton violence.

A new Beatrice had been born – a hard, flinty version of the girl she had once been – the night she lost Owen and Maman.

Just to think of her brought on tears. The loss of Owen had been like a knife in her guts, a sudden, painful tear in the fabric of her existence. But the loss of her mother was broader, deeper and all-consuming. It felt as if the Biblical flood had come again, but instead of water, Beatrice's world had been drowned in darkness, a thick, drenching sadness that felt as if it would never clear. There was a hollow in the centre of herself she felt would never be filled. In the days after the fire she had wept like a person who had lost all reason. She was cosseted by maids and Jenkins was often by her side. She was given draughts to drink from the doctor that only served to haunt her sleep with nightmares. In those chaotic days, she was hardly aware of what was happening around her, but she recalled being taken to a hotel and thence to this house, filling daily with new things to make it habitable. She saw very little of Queenie, who had taken to her bed. She saw more of Benjamina, taking over the new arrangements with a kind of delighted panache that sickened Beatrice. How could anyone in this family enjoy themselves after the disaster that had befallen them all? Cyril was around too, grimly assisting Benjamina, but loudly complaining about their new situation and the vengeance that justice would pour out upon the heads of those responsible. He talked loudly too of his imminent trip to America, his plans unchanged by the tragedy. It was clear he couldn't wait to get away. All this passed by Beatrice as a kind of waking dream, something from which she could not escape.

Today was the first day she had been fully dressed and downstairs. She sat now in a narrow, firm armchair, its florid pattern bright with newness. She was alone, looking out of the window in a stupor for an hour or more now. She did not feel ill any more. She had stopped taking the doctor's concoctions as they made her feel worse. She felt clear-headed and clear-eyed, apart from the tears that sprang there each time she thought of those she had lost. She turned from the window and looked behind her at the sitting room. Just there, she had stood, Owen beside her. He had kissed her there, right there. Oh, the visceral pain of imagining his mouth, his lips! Another stab in the guts. She allowed herself the painful pleasure of picturing him there, his hair yellow like butter, his eyes blue like a summer sky. So handsome, so young. An image leapt into her mind of how his body must have been after the burning. And then her mother's. Thus was her mind swept with sweet, sad memories and harsh, violent images of death these past weeks. She stared at the room and knew in that moment that she could not stay there. Not in that room, that house or even that town. Every day would be painful, every minute would be torture, walking through the site of her abandonment, by every bright hope and tender love she had valued most highly. If she stayed in Ironbridge, she would be haunted, every second that passed, every breath she took. She knew it in her bones. She could not stay there and she would not. It was the first decision she had made since becoming an orphan – and in her eyes – a widow. They may not have been married in law, but in her heart her future husband was gone forever, her hopes and dreams along with him. Now, she had to make a new life. And it would not be here.

She stood and walked across the room, every step stirring up memories like the dust that floated about them the day she and Owen had come here to be alone. She went out into the hallway, its rich tapestry of tiles assaulting her with more memories she wished to escape. She ascended the staircase and approached Queenie's door. She knocked briefly twice then opened the door and went in. Jenkins appeared at the door opposite, the entrance to her own room, just off Queenie's, where Jenkins could keep a sharp eye on her.

'Miss Beatrice,' said Jenkins in a hushed voice, glancing cautiously at the bed in which her mistress rested.

'I have come to speak with her,' said Beatrice.

'I am not certain she's strong enough yet,' said Jenkins. 'Another day, perhaps?'

'Is that you, Bea?' came a voice, throaty and dry, unused to conversation these past weeks. Beatrice looked to see Queenie's head turned towards her, eyes wide open.

Beatrice ignored Jenkins and went to Queenie's bed. She sat down beside her great-grandmother's prone body. Not for the first time, she thought of how the old woman was now in her late seventies and it seemed so unfair that an elderly life should continue when such young lives had been cut short. She hated to think of it that way, she chided herself for it, but the thought still came to her, that Queenie seemed to live forever, while others perished along the way. But of course, she was glad that there was one person left in the world who understood her, who loved her, as Queenie did. And Queenie remembered Maman and loved her too, in her own way. It should be enough, to keep her there, Queenie's love. But as Beatrice took her hand and patted it, and attempted to turn up the corners of her mouth to smile at Queenie, she knew that even her great-grand-mother's love was not enough to sustain her. She saw only hints of Maman in those eyes, those cheekbones. And it haunted her, just like the house.

'How are you today?' said Beatrice.

'I am feeling stronger, now that I have seen you.' Queenie's face wore a complex expression, a mixture of pity, compassion and desperation.

'Good,' said Beatrice and looked away. 'I am glad you are stronger. Queenie, there is something I must tell you.'

'No more revelations,' groaned Queenie. 'I may be regaining my health, but I have not the strength to hear more revelations of secrets and so forth. I really do not have the strength for it, my dear. Can't you see that?'

'Nothing like that,' said Beatrice, with patience. 'It is hard to say, though. But it must be said. I cannot stay here.'

'What do you mean, my love?'

Hearing the word 'love' made Beatrice pause. She had always had her mother's love and now that it was gone, she had but one person left in the world who truly adored her. But it was not enough to dent the hard shell she had grown since the fire. It would not stop her from what she felt she must do.

'I mean that I must go away. I wish to accompany Uncle Cyril on his trip to America.'

'But no!' Queenie sputtered. Jenkins must have been waiting nearby, as she came through the doorway and approached the bed, shooting Beatrice a testy glance, before taking Queenie's hand and saying, 'Hush now. Don't upset yourself.'

'Leave us, Jenkins!' snapped Queenie. Beatrice saw in that moment that Queenie had not lost her steely nature entirely. Jenkins was used to such rough handling and simply lifted her hands with forbearance and left the room, closing the door behind her. 'Now, Bea, listen to me.'

Queenie pushed herself up in bed and Beatrice went to help her, but was waved away by a dismissive hand. 'A terrible thing has happened. An awful, irreversible thing. You have lost your mother. She was the centre of your world, I know that. It will take much time to heal and you will always grieve for her, I know that too. I have lost someone I loved more than myself and I still think of her now, my dear sister. The loss will never leave you, it is true.'

Beatrice could feel the need to weep rise in her, but she forced it down. She had to remain hard now, if she had a hope of getting through this conference with her plans intact.

'Yes,' she simply said.

'But that is no reason to run away. One must face it and cope with it. Take all the time you need to grieve.

371

And after that period has passed, once we both feel stronger and more able to face up to matters, as we will, then it will be time to make plans and go out into the world again. And we will have many plans, I can assure you. Life will go on. Until then, the best place for you is here.'

'I cannot stay here,' said Beatrice, calm yet firm. 'I am telling you this with a clear head. This is not the grief talking. It is my survival. If I stay here, I will go mad.'

'Child, do not say that word!' Queenie cried. Beatrice saw true fear in her eyes.

'But I mean it. I surely will. This place is haunted.'

'What?' gasped Queenie. Her hands began to shake and Beatrice took one and stroked it as she went on.

'This house, this town. Everywhere I could go, I would see Maman in my memories. If I went back to Paris, it would be the same. And if I stay here, in this house, everywhere I look in this house I see him in my recollections.'

'See who?'

'Owen Malone.'

'The boy who saved you from the fire? Well, yes, that was a sad loss after he had been so brave to help you. But why on earth . . . ?'

'We were friends, I told you that. But it was more. We were in love.'

Queenie snatched her hand away. 'What nonsense is this?'

'It was not nonsense. We loved each other. We hoped to marry one day.'

'Over my dead body!' cried Queenie.

Beatrice suddenly felt very tired. She had no fight in her for one of their arguments about class and wealth and all that business. She saw the world through a different lens than her great-grandmother and she had not the interest or desire to educate this old woman in its use.

'It hardly matters now, does it? Now that he is dead.'

There was a silence between them. Beatrice imagined that Queenie's head was filling with feverish thoughts, while her own remained clean and clear as a glass of cool water.

'My sweet child, I am sorry to hear that you have lost not one but two people who were . . . dear to you. But let me say again that the answer to this is to cleave to those you have left, those who love you more than life itself. To me, Beatrice. Stay with me.'

'No,' said Beatrice, hearing the iron tone in her voice and surprised by it. 'I will not be staying. I will be going to America in three days. I will ask my maid Dinah if she is willing to come with me. And hopefully, if she agrees, we will travel on the ship with Cyril.'

'But you've never liked Cyril!' cried Queenie, seeming to pluck at any argument now to prevent her.

'That is true. But he is simply a means to an end. Someone to accompany me. A reason to be in America and not here, for a while at least, until I have blown all the cobwebs away and feel ready to return, rejuvenated. It is what I want and what I need. I am old enough to make my own decisions now. I am an orphan and a grown woman. This is what I have chosen and it is what I will do.'

Queenie turned her head away, but Beatrice carried on. 'I am sorry to sound so harsh, but I needed to make you understand. I am telling you in no uncertain terms that I cannot stay here.'

'So you have said.' Queenie's voice was cold.

'Great-grandmother.' There was no reply. 'Queenie, please. Look at me.'

Queenie turned and Beatrice saw the face she had known so well in their arguments of the past, which now seemed like a lifetime ago. Queenie's chin jutted out and her mouth was set in a hard line.

'We are very alike,' said Beatrice and smiled faintly at her. 'We are stubborn women. But we are strong. And we will prevail. We will survive this. And I will come back to you, renewed. But for now, I cannot stay here with you and you cannot come with me. I will go and you will agree it. Because you love me, as I love you.'

Beatrice saw her great-grandmother's eyes fill with tears and spill over, running down the rivulets of her face and into her white halo of hair. But Queenie shook them away and took Beatrice's hands, patting them firmly and nodding her head.

'Go then, if you must. Obstinate child. And make sure that when you return, you are ready to be the woman I need you to be. My legacy. My future.'

∞

Queenie was up and about. She had felt stronger that March morning than she had in months. Jenkins came in to find her seated in a stiff new wing-backed chair by the window of her bedroom, looking out upon the budding woodland surrounding the old brickmaster's house. Everything in the house was new and uncomfortable. Benjamina had seen to it all. Since the fire, Benjamina had been trying to poke her nose into the King business, making a hash of it at every turn. So she instructed her daughter-in-law to take charge of the renovation of the old brickmaster's house, to keep her busy and away from the business. In just over seven months, Benjamina had managed to organise the redecoration of almost every room, excepting the kitchen and servants' quarters. Queenie surmised that Benjamina had decided that those particular rooms could wait a while, could wait till doomsday if needs be, as she didn't care a damn for them or their lowly inhabitants. Queenie disapproved of this and knew she ought to take Benjamina to task for it, but she had not had the energy for anything but existing these past months. When Beatrice and Cyril had gone to America, Queenie left the business in the hands of Brotherton and his foremen. She had gone into a kind of stupor, staying in her bed for days on end. It was similar to her mourning period after her husband's death, but this was worse, much worse. She still could not believe that her granddaughter was dead and gone and that her great-granddaughter had left her.

Jenkins came in. Dear Jenkins, her mainstay, her saviour. Queenie had been found by Jenkins on the night of the fire, on the ground by her husband's grave. Jenkins knew that Queenie had wandered there before and came straight to her when the fire had started. They had sat together, Queenie sobbing and shaking, clutching onto Jenkins as they watched the house burn. Only later could Jenkins persuade her to stand and approach the ruins and the terrible truth of what had been lost there.

Jenkins came over to her, capable and calm as ever, holding a letter.

Queenie said with anticipation, 'From the child?'

Jenkins shook her head and passed it over, then left her mistress alone to read in peace. It was not the letter Queenie wanted from Beatrice, but something else she had waited upon and was glad to see. It was from her solicitor. Weeks before, she had instructed her solicitor to act for her, sending a letter to the judge appointed in the case of arson and sedition upon the house of Southover. She was sure that the majority of the brickworkers charged had been fully involved. But there was one worker there who had been sentenced to hanging and Queenie did not want that to come to pass. She wrote to the judge, informing him that a certain Adam Jones had been an honourable man. Although he had been the head of the brickworks strike, he was a good man with a wife and child, who had always acted within the law. It was said that he had been found unconscious some way from the scene of the arson, where he had clearly taken a beating. The other arsonists had said Jones had led the attack on the house and that it was his idea to set the fire. Despite the other men implicating him in their testimonies, Jones had always maintained his innocence and that he had been there to try to stop the crime, along with Owen Malone, who was unfortunately killed in the fire. Thus, Jones's only reliable witness to his case was already dead. Jones had been convicted and sentenced to hang along with the others. Queenie explained that the evidence lay in his favour, that she had respect for him and his word, that in all their dealings he had always acted responsibly and truthfully. In short, she believed him. The letter from her solicitor which she now read informed her that the judge had commuted his sentence to transportation. He was to be sent to Australia for seven years. The others were all hanged. Queenie had read the news with satisfaction. She had saved the life of Martha's husband and the father of her child. Surely, the ghost of Blaize would be pleased with her on that account.

She had seen Blaize every day since the fire and no longer was the spirit doomed to roam outside. Blaize would now appear in her room, on the stairs, in the hallway and, most distressingly, behind Queenie in her mirror. This always made her jump fearfully and nearly gave her away to Jenkins, who assumed it was all down to the shock of the fire and everything – and everyone – that had been lost. Queenie was careful to maintain Jenkins's ignorance of her haunting. Queenie did not want any sort of word getting about to Benjamina that she was seeing things. Benjamina was on the rise these days. She could use this knowledge to finally carry out the threat the King men had made to Queenie before, of sending her to the asylum. So, whenever Queenie saw Blaize, she did her best not to flinch, not to gasp, not to cry out. She had to force herself to become accustomed to this fearful visitor and make her peace with its presence. At least the ghost's appearance had softened somewhat in these recent weeks. Blaize's spirit now did not shine so brightly, looking more like the girl she had in life, though deathly pale with those spectral blue eyes. She did not speak, just stared at Queenie, watching her closely, looking for signs of something.

'You are checking to see that your curse has come to pass,' she said to the ghost one day. 'To see that I suffer.'

Blaize had made no response, either from her mouth or within Queenie's mind. Blaize simply watched her, scrutinising her. In a strange way, her presence was oddly comforting. Queenie was aching from grief and loneliness, with the loss of Margaret and the absence of Beatrice. She had slept most of the first fortnight or so, missing Margaret's funeral, attended only by Beatrice,

Cyril, Benjamina and a few local people. She had heard from her sickbed the daily noise of Beatrice's inconsolable sobbing, assaulting the peace of the old brickmaster's house like an unattended baby. And then Beatrice had left her, gone across the ocean. Queenie was distraught about it, feeling the distance like a rent in her heart. Jenkins reminded her that Beatrice had promised to write. One letter had come from Beatrice, but it was brief and cold. It told Queenie only that the ship had arrived safely and that she would write again with news of their activities and an address in New York to which letters could be sent. But that was months ago and Queenie had only heard once from Cyril since, a short missive with the New York address. And nothing more from Beatrice. Had they had some misadventure? Were they ill or dead even? Nobody knew. America was a world away. Queenie longed for word, simply a sentence to let her know Beatrice was alive and well. But the days stretched on and nothing came.

Queenie called for Jenkins and said, 'I am feeling better today.'

'I can see that. You've colour back in your old cheeks.'

'I wish to write to Beatrice. Bring me my writing instruments and lay them out at my dressing table. I shall write it here.'

'Is that a good idea? You know how upset you get when you think about the child.'

'She is not "the child",' snapped Queenie.

'But you always call her that!' cried Jenkins, annoyed.

'She is ... Beatrice.' Saying her name aloud was indeed difficult, and Jenkins could see this. She reached out a hand and placed it on Queenie's shoulder, who shrugged it off. 'And I wish to write to her. Now, get on with you and fetch my writing implements forthwith.'

Jenkins smiled at her and said, 'You *are* feeling better.'

As she waited for Jenkins to return, she pondered, what did she wish to say to Bea in this letter? What could she say to persuade the girl to come back, that her place was not across the blasted ocean, but here by her side? Somebody needed to unseat Benjamina and take this house and business in hand. In time, she knew she herself would grow stronger, but she needed help. Jenkins was not enough. She needed her strongest ally, her dearest one, her Beatrice. How could she say all this without sounding desperate? She had not begged for anything in five decades and she was not about to show that weakness now. At that moment, she glanced upwards and there was the spirit, behind her in the mirror, staring at her coldly. It made her jump, as ever, and she put her hand to her heart.

'Have I not suffered enough?' she muttered, dropping her eyes to the dressing table, unwilling to look upon the spirit yet again. 'Will you never leave me?'

I will, came the reply, inside her own head.

Queenie stopped and looked up. She turned around and Blaize stood close to her. It was the first time it had spoken to her since the fire.

'You will leave me, one day?'

Yes, came that inner voice again.

'When? When will you leave me?'

At the bright, good time, when sunlight will conquer moonlight.

'What does that mean? What do you mean?'

Blaize leant forward, her eyes hypnotic, her face so close now to Queenie's own. *The child will cross the bridge. The child will make one house from two. The child is the answer.*

Queenie gazed at the spirit, as she had never been this close to its beautiful face. She saw that it was transparent and subtly moving, as if its waterfall of white hair was wafted by warm air. She felt as if she could fall into its blue eyes and never stop falling. She wanted to touch it and reached out her hand, but the image of Blaize began to fade, subtly erasing itself until only a hint of its blue eyes remained and then they too had vanished.

The door opened behind the spot where Queenie had just a moment before looked upon the spirit of her dead maid. Jenkins came in and walked through the very spot Blaize had stood, oblivious to the fact. She placed the writing materials on the dressing table, then turned to look upon Queenie.

Jenkins frowned at her. 'Is this all too much? Do you wish for your bed again? You look a bit peaky, old girl.'

'No, I am well,' said Queenie, distractedly. 'I must write. Leave me now.'

'Very well,' said Jenkins and went, waiting at the door for a moment, at which Queenie gestured for her to go, so she did.

She filled out the necessaries at the top of the paper, then wrote, 'Dear Beatrice.' She thought about what she would say next. She would have to be clever in the way she framed it. She could not simply tell her great-granddaughter that a ghost had said Beatrice should come home and solve everything. Surely that is what the ghost meant, wasn't it? The child? What other child was there? Yes, Beatrice was the answer. Queenie just needed to word it with care, call up that prodigious vocabulary of hers and put it down in finely crafted sentences. She must persuade the child that her holiday in the New World was over and now it was time for her to come home.

❧

It was the first warm day they'd had in months. Spring flowers were blooming along the fringes of the woods near Anny's house. It was a good day to sit outside and feel the sun on your face. She had spent the winter in the house, nursing her baby and speaking rarely. Peter tried to talk to her, tried to comfort her. But she only had eyes for her little one. It had been a cold winter, snow piling up against the door. Money had come from the Kings in reparation, swiftly this time, within weeks of the fire. Anny had sent it back without a word. They now only had Peter's wage coming in, as Anny was not fit to work, drained from the baby's needs and exhausted from grief. They lived as simply as they could. Peter hadn't pressured her, not for a moment, but she knew that come the spring, she'd have to start working again, making pies and taking in washing and sewing. Her little boy was seven months now and eating well. He was bonny and bright.

'He's a proper boster!' said Martha, as she came up the incline from the river path, carrying her daughter in her arms. Hettie was ten months now and toddling. She put her down and Anny reached out to her. Hettie came stumbling towards her, giggling, and those bright green eyes like her mother's bright with intent, losing interest in forward motion and staring instead at her clever feet. She stumbled and fell forward, Anny catching her, whirling her up and placing her down beside her boy on the blanket she'd spread out for them.

'He really is,' said Anny, proudly, looking at her healthy, chunky boy. Evan was delighted to see his best of friends, Hettie Jones. He rolled over from his tummy and pushed himself up onto all fours. He was crawling now, but to his constant bewilderment, could only crawl backwards and looked at Hettie in confusion as she seemed to retreat from him ever further. She toddled after him and leant down, gave him a clumsy hug, then slumped down on to her bottom. Anny picked up Evan and placed him on his bottom too, then passed them both a hunk of bread to chew on, which they did, with studied attention.

'I'll fetch you a chair,' said Anny.

'No, I'll do it. You stay there,' said Martha and went into the cottage, coming back out with a kitchen chair and placing it beside her.

'Nice to see you,' said Anny, watching the children.

'First decent weather we've had in a while,' said Martha. 'Nice to get out.'

They sat in companionable silence. They had lived together and spent so many days together, they were like sisters now. Their children were like siblings too. They had both suffered and comforted each other in the dark times. Brighter times were ahead.

'I had news today, Anny. I wanted to tell you. But I didna wanna upset you. I know you dunna like to talk about . . . that night.'

Anny frowned and reached forward, picking up the bread Evan had dropped and putting it back in his chubby hand.

'You're right. I dunna wanna talk about any of it.'

'But there is news. Good news. The best news. Can I tell you, Anny?'

Anny looked at Martha. Her green eyes were shining with emotion. Good news, she'd said. The best news. The only kind of news Anny was interested in would be that time had sent itself backwards, that the moment her son had turned to her and said, 'I'm off out', she had grabbed him and forced him to stay home. That all the Kings would have died in that fire and her Owen would have slept through the whole thing and woken up in the morning. His heart would have hurt at the loss of that girl, but it would have mended. And she would have him here, playing with his little brother on the blanket, instead of six feet under in his cold grave.

Anny said nothing. Martha would tell her anyway.

'A letter came. I couldna read it but a man on my street knew his letters and read it for me. Adam is not gonna be hanged, Anny. He is to be transported instead. Mrs King senior wrote for him and spoke up for him. He'll be going to Australia. But he wonna be hanged.'

Anny did not look at Martha. She could hear her voice crack with feeling. Martha would feel gratitude, no doubt, to God maybe, to Mrs King Senior, to providence and luck and everything. Her husband was saved.

'That is good news,' said Anny and nodded.

'I had lost all hope,' said Martha, her voice shaking now. 'I canna believe it.'

'Good,' said Anny. 'Good news.' She reached out a hand and placed it on Martha's lap. Martha took her hand and squeezed it.

'They said it'll be seven years away. Seven years. Hettie will be eight. But it's better than nothing. It's better than hanging. Anything is better than death.'

Anny felt her throat tighten. She gulped hard, to stop herself from choking. Martha glanced at her in horror at what she'd said.

'Oh, Anny!' she cried. 'Anny, I didna mean . . . I'm so sorry, Anny.'

'No,' said Anny and squeezed Martha's hand. 'Dunna tread round me on eggshells. I am all right. And this is good news. Very good news. I'm glad for you. Truly, I am.'

She had nothing else to say and could not look at Martha. She meant it, really she did. It was just so hard to be thankful for anything, now Owen was dead. It was so hard to hear gratitude to anyone or anything. It was hard to breathe, in and out, in and out. Sometimes the grief came over her like summer floods, warm and deadly, stifling her. She would gasp in it and writhe, dreaming of him and waking cruelly, with him gone and never to come back. Peter would hold her and she would push him away. And though his grief was terrible – wracked him with nightmares and hours of staring, wordless, at Owen's carved chess pieces, which he would turn over and over in trembling hands – she could not comfort him. He could not comfort her either, not for a moment. They barely looked at each other for weeks on end. She somehow blamed him, though she knew it was not his fault, none of it. He was Owen's father, though, and should've protected him somehow. She blamed herself too, for not taking Owen in hand enough, for assuming he'd listened to her properly when she told him to give up that girl. She blamed Adam Jones too, for leading him unto that place of death, secretly, and letting him run to the girl while he slept on the grass.

Surely she hated the Kings and blamed them for the fire that destroyed their home, stoking the hatred in their workers. But if truth be known, nobody was solely to blame. And others had lost terribly too. Margaret had not deserved to die. She had set Anny free from prison, after all. Anny felt with a guilty pang that even she herself shouldered more than a small part of the blame for what had happened to her own son. If she and Margaret had let go of their feud, if Anny in particular had cured her own hatred of Margaret and the other Kings, then their children might not have resorted to secrecy and lies. And perhaps Owen might still be alive. Even Owen played his part – if he had not been so brave, had not run in to a burning house to save a life, he would be with her now. His heroism was a glimmer of goodness in this tragedy, but that didn't lessen the pain.

Jenkins had come to tell her, the next day. When Anny saw her face at the door, she knew a terrible thing had come to pass. She screamed at her when the news was spoken, flew at her in a rage and had to be held back by Peter. A sharp pain came inside and she fell to the floor. The shock had shaken her so badly, she started to bleed and was taken to her bed. They all thought she'd lose the baby, grief piled on grief. But the bleeding abated, the bedrest did its work and she recovered. Anny's littl'un came quickly, on a wild and windy October evening. Peter held her on the bed as the babe came out of her, bawling away like anything. A boy. They called him Evan, a plain, solid name. He came into the world with a mother and father who adored him, and a dead brother who he would never know and who would not look upon him or hold him or marvel at the boy that would be his only brother in the world. With a brother or sister, a person need never be alone again, thought Anny, forever saddened that she'd never had one of her own, an only child to her parents, both dead and buried. But now baby Evan's brother was gone. And he was alone in the world. But what a delight he was for Anny and Peter and how they held him tight and fretted over his every moment. They began to look at each other again, their eyes shining, their new life drawing them back to each other a little more each day, step by step.

Hettie had finished her bread and Evan lost interest in his as soon as he saw Hettie stand up. Martha stood and reached over to her daughter, holding her hands to steady her. Evan gazed at his friend with unashamed adoration. Hettie took two steps towards Evan and sat down with a thump beside him. They watched each other for a moment, their serious mouths turning into smiles. Hettie reached out and put her arms about him, squeezed him clumsily and patted him on the back. They both giggled and patted each other, patting and patting. Never had patting been so hilarious. They could not stop laughing and could not stop patting.

Martha was watching Anny's face, her own a picture of concern. Martha reached out and touched Anny's cheek tenderly. The tears rolled down their faces. They did not need to speak their feelings. There was both too much to say and nothing to say.

The little ones were still laughing, both sitting on their bottoms again, patting each other's legs and arms and faces. Anny and Martha looked at them and wiped their tears away, the laughter infectious, as they chuckled at their children.

'They are proper sweethearts,' said Martha. 'Maybe they'll marry one day.'

Anny gazed at her beautiful son. He could not find a sweeter girl than Hettie, a nicer mother-in-law than Martha. But no, that was not what Anny had planned for her son. Wherever his heart might lead him, she would not make the same mistake again. She would raise him to want more from life than this, than the work of his father and his dead brother, than the grind of daily servitude. She would raise him to turn his back on this godforsaken place ruled over by the cursed Kings and make a new life somewhere else, somewhere new, somewhere far away and safe from the secrets of Ironbridge.

Epilogue

7th July 1859

112 Summer Street
Brooklyn
New York City
New York State
The United States of America

Dear Queenie,

I hope this letter finds you well. I have missed our chats so much and our card-playing contests! The evenings feel lonely without you to keep me company. It is a strange new world here in America, but also one that is full of interest and excitement. I miss Ironbridge and I miss you very much, dear Queenie. Yet despite this, I am learning to see this new land as an opportunity for me to start again and its very newness allows me to do that, to move on and to put the past behind me. Grief is a terrible thing and, though I know the losses I've suffered will never leave me, I believe I heal a little more each day.

It was so good to receive your letter and to hear news from Ironbridge. It was almost as if we were once again seated around the card table, sharing gossip, with Maman just steps away, playing at the piano. I wish we could turn back the clock and all be together once more. Sadly, time does not move in reverse.

And I'm afraid this is the reason I must disappoint you. Your request for me to return to you and take my place beside you, running the business, is a kind and generous offer, and one that I do not take lightly, I promise you. But I feel as if returning to Ironbridge would be like trying to travel back in time, to capture something that is lost to us now. This is something I cannot do.

Maman brought me to Ironbridge to give me a better life and you, Queenie, offered me the same idea, a life of comfort and prospects. I love you both for only wanting the best for me, but wealth and comfort isn't enough to sustain the soul. I was in need of friendship and companionship. I was in need of a soulmate with whom I could share my feelings. I found it in Owen Malone. It is hard to write his name without weeping. But you see, I have no regrets about my feelings for him. I truly loved Owen. Not a fleeting, girlish desire. I loved him and wanted a future with him. But that was not to be.

I know you may now be recoiling in horror from such a statement. I know what you feel, and what my mother felt, about relationships between the classes. But I have to disagree with you, then and now. For I believe that class is something we make, we construct out of our own false ideas of what is right and proper. But that is all it is: a construct. Class is something we build to protect ourselves, to tell ourselves that those who have and those who have not are a different breed. This makes us feel better about being rich and allows us to dismiss the rights of those who are not. I now believe with all of my heart that this is wrong. You will say it is the French in me, the influence of that revolutionary nation in my upbringing. You will say I am like my mother once was, young and foolish. My mother felt she was proven wrong. But I disagree. I believe that the class system we live by has robbed us all of those we love. The treatment of the brickworkers, the strike and its aftermath, the crimes committed on both sides, the separation of classes into masters and servants. All of this creates a society of conflict, envy and hatred. And it has directly led to the deaths of those we love. Anny Malone has lost her son Owen. I have lost my mother and you your granddaughter. And now, I fear, I must tell you that you will lose me, now and for the foreseeable future, at least.

Here, in America, I see a different way of life. To be sure, there are the rich and the poor, and the gap between them is just as wide as in England. But there is a different idea about it here, a different way of looking at it. If you speak to people here about their lives, there is hope for change. There is an idea of what can be if one works hard and believes. In England I saw some of that spirit in the brickworkers when they went on strike. Yes, they were opposed to you and I sympathise with you on that count. I know how hard it was for you to run that business fairly and in a way that made a profit. But the wrongs that were perpetrated against those workers were unacceptable; they were crimes in their own way and had to be paid for. You lost those you love and your house. They lost their hope. I see hope for improvement all around me here, not only between the workers and the masters but between men and women and people of all races. For America is a mixture of all types and shapes and sizes and colours, more so even than Paris, and a thousand times more than Ironbridge.

You see, there are people here who are fighting for change. I am living in New York with Dinah — remember Dinah, my maid? She is my maid no longer and we live together as friends. She is a fine artist — did you ever know that about her? One day, she drew a map for me to the very house you live in now and it was a work of art. I love to write and she loves to draw. Some friends we met on our ship to New York were in the newspaper business. On our arrival, Dinah and I were invited to stay with them. Uncle Cyril has gone to Pennsylvania with his companion James Melton, yet I decided to stay here at the comfortable home of our journalist companions, who have made Dinah and me so comfortable and welcome. Encouraged by them, Dinah began sketching scenes from the streets hereabouts and I wrote descriptions to go with them, a visitor's views of American life. We now have these published in a New York journal called *Street and Smith's New York Weekly*. It is a charming publication, full of fascinating facts and amusing anecdotes. Dinah and I are now members of the profession of journalists! Yes, we are paid for our work and we love it. Just yesterday, we met a man at a gathering who was once a slave here in America. He spoke of the rights of negroes and the rights of women too. He publishes his own newspaper and his name is Frederick Douglass. The sub-heading of his paper reads thus: *Right is of no Sex — Truth is of no Colour — God is the Father of us all, and we are all Brethren.* To read these words moved me very much. I said to Dinah afterwards that there would only be one thing I would add to it and that is this: Equality is of no Class. Just as there are movements here to unite all people, whatever colour or sex they happen to be, I believe in the movement to unite people of all classes. I believe that mankind will not progress if we continue in our current unequal and unfair distinctions between rich and poor.

All of this must sound like heresy to you, I am sure. But it sounds like music to me. Times are changing here. There is talk of war. Many do not agree with me. Many agree with you. Others hate and will kill for their beliefs. I hope it does not come to war. But if it does, I know what side I will be on. And sadly, it will not be the same side as you, dear Queenie, or of any King. I am not a King. I am an Ashford. Though I love you, I cannot come to you. Though I wish you well, I will not live your life. I love you very much, Queenie, but I cannot accept the life that you live. There is a portion of my heart that will always be with you, that makes me yearn to return to you. But I know that ultimately I would be unhappy and that I would make you unhappy too. It would never work. It is a hard choice I make, but I must make it.

I will write to you often and share my new life here with you on paper. I wish to make my living through words and will use words to conjure up my life here for you. I hope you will do the same and keep in touch with news from Ironbridge. It will always be a special place for me and I am so very fond of it. Some of the best people I have ever met are Ironbridge folk. But it was never my home. It could have been, if events had not turned out as they did. Instead, I spent a few heady months there, ending in unimaginable loss. I am afraid that it has become the seat of my pain and I cannot bear to live there again.

Thank you for offering to make me the sole recipient of the King fortune. But I tell you now, I do not want your money. I do not want any part of the King way of life. I will never take a penny of that money. Once, a lifetime ago, I spoke with Owen Malone about brickmaking. He told me, 'There is blood in those bricks.' Now that you know about Owen and my love for him, you will understand that I believe there is blood in that money. I want none of it. If you make me your heir, I will give it all away. Thus, please do not give me your money. Find someone else deserving who wants and needs it more than me. Assist those you have wronged. If you want to make it right, you need to do something to modify both your business and yourself. I believe you have it in you, Queenie. I have seen the goodness in you.

As I write this letter, I realise that today is the 7th July and is Hettie Jones's birthday. Exactly one year ago, I stood in Anny and Peter Malone's cottage and heard that child come into the world. My Owen was still with us. It was one of the most precious moments of my life. If you wish to contribute in any way to my happiness, then do not offer me money. Instead, help that child and others like her. Small alterations in your own life can lead to huge changes in the lives of others; you can bridge the divide. Improve the lot in life of the poor, in Ironbridge, in Shropshire, in England and the whole of society.

I will live my life here from now on. I wish you all the very best with yours.

Love and hope always,
from your great-granddaughter,

Bea

Acknowledgements

Tony Mugridge, expert artisan brickmaker, for teaching me how to make a brick by hand and giving me access to his incredibly detailed knowledge of nineteenth century brick and tile manufacture. Thanks also to Fliss Burke, for making me feel so welcome.

Shroppiemon, for offering dialect advice at any hour, reading the final draft, and tagging me in a huge range of useful posts on the marvellous Memories of Shropshire page on Facebook.

Stephen Dewhirst of the Broseley Local History Society, for extensive help with brickmaking resources, including contemporary newspaper reports, as well as reading the final draft and his helpful comments.

Jim Dale of BBC Radio Shropshire for the fascinating and fun interview on brickmaking at Tony's house.

Joanne Smith, Museum Registrar for The Ironbridge Gorge Museum Trust, for help with brickmaking resources, including the Blists Hill brickmaking materials and suggestions of clayworker books.

Karen Young at the Shropshire Archives, for help with items on brickmaking in the archives.

Chris Blanchett of Buckland Books (now retired), for directing me to the British Brick Society.

Mike Moore of Moore Books, for help with brickmaking titles.

Becca Burnton, Jessica Ryn, Jean Fullerton and Theresa Therrien for invaluable help with midwifery and obstetrics questions.

Jayne McDermott, Lin Keska and Claire Powick Hainsworth for information regarding the Benthall Waterwheel, posted in Shropshire Tales, History and Memories on Facebook.

Early readers of this book: Sue White, Lucy Adams, Lynn Downing, Pauline Lancaster and Louisa Treger for your quick reading and wonderful support, as ever.

Megan Prince of the Ironbridge Bookshop, young and talented bookseller extraordinaire, for marvellous support for the books and perfect bookselling at events and beyond. Thank you for looking after me so well at the events too, Meg.

The Ironbridge Festival of Imagination, for asking me to take part in events at the bookshop and at the Meadow Inn, including Simon Fletcher for organising the super Country Voices event.

The Friends of the Ironbridge Gorge Museum Trust, for inviting me to talk to them about the research for the Ironbridge Saga. Particular thanks to Geraldine King, Judy

Mondon, David De Haan and Glyn Bowen. Special thanks to the audience, who made me feel so welcome and asked excellent questions, as well as giving me such useful information and advice about coal mining for the next book.

All of the Facebook Shropshire groups for continued support of the Ironbridge Saga, as well as advice on all things Shropshire, from bricks to coal to wimberries. Particular thanks to administrators Lin Keska, Marcus Keane, Chris Hughes and Margaret Ann Roberts.

Tara Loder, my wonderful editor, who always goes above and beyond and is such an expert on character and plotting; these books would not be the same without her magnificent input.

Everyone at Bonnier Books, with special thanks to Claire Johnson-Creek, Katie Lumsden, Ellen Turner and Sahina Bibi.

My excellent agent Laura Macdougall, who continues to support me and my career at every turn with such brilliance.

My writing friends in the author community, particularly those in the Prime Writers and on Facebook, who provide companionship, advice, support and laughs.

Bookbloggers and readers, who have shared their appreciation of the Ironbridge Saga, online and beyond. A huge thank you to all of you – too numerous to mention individually – for reading and talking about the books, attending events and coming up to talk to me, as well as for so many kind messages.

Colin and Poppy, for listening to me go on and on about Shropshire stuff and word counts and edits, and not falling asleep as I do so. Mostly, for understanding the writer's life and always supporting me through it.

My lovely family and dear friends, for being there always, through hard times and easy times.

·MEMORY LANE·

Welcome to the world of *Mollie Walton*!

Keep reading for more from Mollie Walton, to discover a recipe that features in this novel and to find out more about Mollie Walton's inspiration for the book . . .

We'd also like to introduce you to MEMORY LANE, our special community for the very best of saga writing from authors you know and love, and new ones we simply can't wait for you to meet. Read on and join our club!

·MEMORY LANE·

www.MemoryLane.club

Dear Reader,

Thanks so much for reading the second instalment in the Ironbridge Saga. I first had the idea for the saga when standing on the iron bridge itself and I've returned to the area many times since, not only for research but also for the love of it. Continuing the story of the Woodvines and the Kings was a wonderful experience for me, as I'd missed their company since finishing *The Daughters of Ironbridge*. I wanted to know what they were getting up to next! As with the first book, the research I needed to do was extensive. While iron was the main industry of *The Daughters of Ironbridge*, brickmaking became the focus of the second book. Since discovering the wonderful Shropshire groups on Facebook, I started by asking for advice there and was immediately recommended by several people to talk to Tony Mugridge. Tony is an artisan brickmaker and all-round expert on the history of brickmaking. Well, not only was Tony able to start me off in my research with various ideas, he also invited me to come to his workshop and make a brick myself. Of course, I agreed!

I visited his house in Madeley and met him and his partner Felicity Burke. They were both so kind and welcoming. Once in Tony's workshop, he showed me the lump of clay we were about to transform into a brick. He gave me a brick mould and showed me how to throw the clay into it, then beat it into the mould with a brickbat. It's like a short, stubby cricket bat and you could certainly do some damage with it. Once the brick was flattened down, he showed me how to slice off the top with a tool that looked a little like a mixture between a cheese-cutter and a bow for arrows. Lastly, we whacked the mould to release the brick and there it was, in all its glory: my very first brick! I was proud of it, as it actually looked brick-like. It took us several minutes to do it. But then Tony told me that a brickmaker in the nineteenth century would have had to produce around a thousand of these a day. A thousand!

At that moment, it truly came home to me what back-breaking work being a brickmaker was. Not only that, but also conditions at the brickyards were awful. The work was long and arduous, for very little pay. Small children were employed to carry the lumps of clay. The masters could drop wages and lengthen hours, whilst workers went on strike to improve conditions, some-times with but often without success. It was then I knew that I'd chosen the right industry for this story. It was full of natural drama. Also, the topic was something that everybody had experience of; all of us have lived and worked in buildings made from bricks at some point in our lives. Furthermore, it is a subject of which many of us may be quite ignorant – that is, the actual process it takes to make a brick, from digging the clay, to moulding the brick, to firing it in the kilns, then transporting it around the country. It's so vital yet so often we think nothing of it when we see a house. I wanted to celebrate the hard work of those people who created the bricks that have built houses in which we still live and work today, still standing firm due to their expertise.

My experiences working with this expert artisan brickmaker was another in a line of wonderful meetings I've had with local people in the writing of these books. Having come to the Ironbridge area four years ago for the first time, to visit my brother and his wife, I've had a lot of contact with Shropshire folk, particularly through the Facebook groups that celebrate all things Shropshire. What I've learnt is that Shropshire folk are truly special. Their generosity is exceptional and their love for their county is second to none. I feel honoured to have met and corresponded with such a wide range of Shropshire locals in the writing of these books. I will be forever grateful for their kindness and warmth.

I hope that my stories have helped in some small part to throw a spotlight on this beautiful part of the world. If you have never visited, I urge you to do so! And if you do, when you walk across the iron bridge, perhaps spare a thought for the countless poor folk who lived near it and worked all their lives to create the Industrial Revolution, the fruits of which we enjoy today. Without them, there would be no iron, no coal, no bricks and all the rest. We owe them so much and it's an honour to tell their stories.

Glossary of Shropshire Dialect Terms

All drawed out: all dressed up

Anna: haven't

Arr: yes

Bait: food, a meal

Blackleg: a worker who goes back to their job despite the strike

Chunnering: talking too much

Boster: healthy, chunky baby

Butties: mates

Canna: can't

Cwtch: a cuddle or a hug

Danker me!: I'll be damned!

Darter: daughter

Didna: didn't

Drearing: loitering

Dunna: don't

From off: from outside the local area

Gunna: going to

Hadna: had not

Hasna: has not

Inna: isn't

Larruping: beating someone up

Mon: man, often used as a term of address to males

Mun: must

Nowt: nothing

Ow bist: how are you?

Owd: old

Ratlin: runt of the litter

Roadster: tramp

Scab: an outsider brought in to replace striking workers

Scrinch: a morsel

Sebunctious: something particularly special or good

Shanna: shall not

Shoulda: should have

Shouldna: should not/should not have

Singing out of the same book: courting

Summat: something

The Lord hasna finished him: historical term for intellectual disability

Unket: lonely

Wanna: want to

Wasna: wasn't

Werrit: worry

Wonna: won't

Wouldna: would not/would not have

Yer: you

Wimberry Pie

Also known as Mucky Mouth Pie, wimberry pie is a kind of fruit pie that Anny makes for her customers, alongside her savoury fidget pies. Wimberries are traditional Shropshire fruit, picked on the hills and harvested in the late summertime. These berries go by many regional names around Britain, including wimberries, whinberries, windberries, bilberries, blaeberries, hurtleberries, fraughans, black-heart berries and myrtle berries. If you can't find wimberries, you can use blueberries, raspberries or blackberries in this recipe instead. You can also replace half of the wimberries with apples, if you prefer.

You will need:

For the shortcrust pastry:
6oz plain flour, and extra for dusting
3oz butter, diced
2–3 tbsp cold water

For the filling:
2 tbsp honey
½ tsp cinnamon
1 tbsp lemon juice
3 tbsp demerara sugar
5oz wimberries

Method:

1. Preheat the oven to 200°C/180°C/gas mark 6.
2. Sieve the flour into a large bowl, then add the diced butter. Rub it in between your fingertips, until the mixture resembles breadcrumbs.
3. Add the water, and mix together until it forms a smooth dough.
4. Knead this on a floured surface, then divide the pastry in two.
5. Roll out the first section into a circle about 1cm thick, and wide enough to line a pie dish or pastry tin. Press lightly into the dish, and trim off the edges.
6. In a separate bowl, mix together the honey, cinnamon, lemon juice and 2 tbsp of demerara sugar, then carefully stir in the wimberries.
7. Pour this mixture into the pastry case.
8. Roll the second section of pastry out into another circle, and lay on top to form the lid.
9. Brush the edges with water, and press them down to meet the pastry case below. Trim off the edges, then cut a small hole in the centre of the lid.
10. Bake for 25–30 minutes until the pastry has lightly browned.
11. Remove from the oven and sprinkle with the remaining demerara sugar.
12. Enjoy!